Born and educated in Texas, Mark Gimenez attended law school at Notre Dame, Indiana and practised with a large Dallas law firm. He is married with two sons.

THE COMMON LAWYER

Mark Gimenez

SPHERE

First published in Great Britain in 2009 by Sphere
This paperback edition published in 2010 by Sphere

A CIP catalogue record for this book
is available from the British Library.

ISBN 978-0-7515-4130-4

Papers used by Sphere are natural, recyclable products made from
wood grown in sustainable forests and certified in accordance with
the rules of the Forest Stewardship Council.

Mixed Sources
Product group from well-managed
forests and other controlled sources
www.fsc.org Cert no. SGS-COC-004081
© 1996 Forest Stewardship Council
FSC

Typeset in Bembo by Hewer Text UK Ltd, Edinburgh
Printed and bound in Great Britain by Clays Ltd, St Ives plc

Sphere
An imprint of
Little, Brown Book Group
100 Victoria Embankment
London EC4Y 0DY

An Hachette UK Company
www.hachette.co.uk

www.littlebrown.co.uk

For Clay and Cole

Acknowledgements

My sincere thanks to:

In London: Everyone at Sphere/Little, Brown UK, including David Shelley, publisher, editor, and friend, Thalia Proctor for the copy-editing, Sean Garrehy for the brilliant cover, Nathalie Morse for everything she does so well, and Sarah Jones for the international publicity and the New Zealand/Australia tour.

In New Zealand: Kevin Chapman, Margaret Samuels, and Karen McMillan at Hachette Livre and Little, Brown for their hospitality and a wonderful book tour through their country.

In Australia: Bernadette Foley, Matt Hoy, Sean Cotcher, Cassy Nacard, Amy Hurrell, Jaki Arthur, and Nicola Pitt at Hachette Livre and Little, Brown for the Brisbane Writers Festival and the night out in Sydney.

In Austin: Noel Escobar, Jr, and Chuy Soberón at

Texas Custom Boots for the finest boots made by hand, Gail Chovan at Blackmail for talking with me about SoCo, Doug Gimenez for his insight into extreme athletes, and Guy Gimenez for rescuing us after a hot summer day in the Barton Creek Greenbelt.

In Houston: Joel Tarver at T Squared Designs for my website and email blasts to my readers.

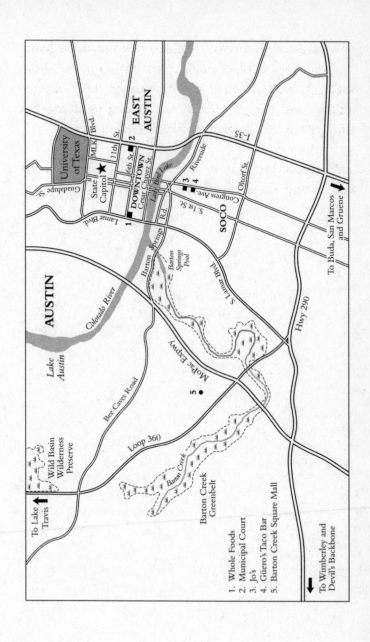

Client's privilege: Right of client to require attorney to keep secret communications made to him in the attorney–client relationship and to prevent disclosure on the witness stand.

Black's Law Dictionary, Fifth Ed.

Prologue

St Aloysius Children's Research Hospital
Ithaca, New York
2:55 A.M.

He stared down at her; his expression was stern and unyielding. He disapproved, as she knew he would.

'Don't look at me like that, Luigi. I'm *not* crazy.'

They stood alone in the vestibule just inside the front entrance where the warmth and disinfectant held their ground against the invading cold air and horde of germs. She brushed snow from her parka and removed her gloves, then reached up and caressed his cold cheek. He was just a boy.

'You're not being fair. Of all people, you should understand. God didn't mean for us to live forever.'

Over the last three months, they had developed a relationship of sorts. She had often come downstairs late at night and talked to him, Catholic to Catholic, about life and about death, and about life after death, all subjects he knew well. She would look into his eyes

1

and wait for answers that never came. His eyes had always seemed able to see into her soul, but tonight they revealed only his sadness, as if he knew what she was about to do.

'It's the only way.'

He did not respond – he never did – so she dropped her eyes like a repentant child from her father's glare. They fell onto the engraving at the base of the stone statue that told of his short life: Luigi Gonzaga had been born in 1568 in Italy, joined the Society of Jesus when he was seventeen, and studied to become a Jesuit; he had contracted the plague while working in a Catholic hospital in Rome. He had cared for the worst victims of the disease, those whom no one else would touch, and he had died at age twenty-three. The church awarded him sainthood because he had sacrificed his life to save others: St Aloysius, the patron saint of children.

'And I'm the Virgin Mary.'

Her eyes ran up the life-size figure of the boy saint for one final glance at his face – one final look into those haunting eyes. He could not understand. She turned away and continued into the hospital, past the reception desk and the elevators. She saw no one, and no one saw her. The hospital on the night shift was a lonely place; she had often paced the vacant corridors during those still hours, unable to sleep but unwilling to leave the child. The last few nights she had timed the exact route she was now taking: seven and a half minutes, in and out.

Bright murals stretched down the corridors and elaborate mobiles hung from the ceiling. Oversized stuffed cartoon characters sat in play areas waiting for the children. The patients' own colorful paintings adorned the walls like pieces of art in a museum. The nurses wore scrubs that were bright splashes of color. The colors, the art, the sunlit atrium, the healing gardens – the hospital tried desperately to present an upbeat mood, but the scent of death permeated the place. It was inescapable.

But they would escape that night.

Her rubber-soled shoes fell silent as she climbed the stairs to the third floor and turned left. Third Floor West. The research wing. Only a handful of nurses would be on duty during the night shift, and those who were took their meal break at 3:00 A.M. She slowed as she approached the nurses' station and listened for voices; she heard none, so she hurried past. She was about to turn a corner when the sound of footsteps came close; she ducked inside a storage closet. The footsteps passed, and she peeked out and saw the uniformed backside of Kelly Fitzgerald, the charge nurse. Kelly was an Irish girl, too, and at thirty only five years older; they had become fast friends. They had often shared late-night coffee and cigarettes on the back stairs.

She did not greet her friend that night.

She stepped out of the closet, shut the door quietly behind her, and continued around the corner and down the corridor. She stopped at Room 312, pushed the door open, and stuck her head inside.

3

The child was asleep.

She backed out and walked down to Room 320. On the bed, a sixteen-year-old boy lay sleeping in the dim light. Jimmy had been paralyzed from the neck down in a street racing accident in California when he had lost control and wrapped his car around a telephone pole. He had undergone experimental spinal cord treatment. He was a guinea pig. Everyone on Three West was a guinea pig.

Jimmy was her friend, too. They had talked often, and she had consoled him when he cried. He knew he would never walk again, never play ball again, never date again, never live a normal life again. One stupid teenage mistake and he was in a wheelchair for life. He said he wanted to die. She leaned over and kissed him on his forehead then unplugged his ventilator.

She exited the room and ran back down the corridor to Room 312. She stepped inside and closed the door just before the entire night-shift staff, led by Nurse Kelly, rounded the corner pulling a crash cart. The alarm had sounded back at the nurses' station. They were racing to save Jimmy, as she knew they would. She wasn't there to kill Jimmy.

She was there to save this child.

She quickly pulled a knit cap over the five-year-old girl's head and stuffed her curly red hair inside. It was cold out. She tucked the St Aloysius pendant and chain she had bought in the gift shop that first day inside the child's pajamas then wrapped her in the hospital blanket

4

and scooped her up. Her adrenaline was pumping hard; the child weighed nothing in her arms. She went to the door and peeked out. No one was in sight. She walked out of the room and hurried down the corridor past the vacant nurses' station.

She descended the two flights of stairs to the ground floor. Only the reception desk stood between them and the front door. She paused at the corner and again listened; she heard no one. Bert, the grandfather moonlighting as the night-shift security guard, would be grabbing a soda and gabbing with the nurses in the break room. She took a deep breath and darted around the corner, past the desk, and over to St Aloysius. But she did not stop and look into his eyes this time; she could not bear to see his disappointment. She only said, 'Goodbye, Luigi,' then carried the child out the front doors and through the thick snow to the Jeep 4x4 in the parking lot. She opened the back door and laid her on the seat. The child stirred.

'Mommy?'

She stroked the child's face.

'Shhh. Everything's going to be okay now, honey. No more tests.'

The child smiled in her sleep.

She secured her daughter with a seat belt, then climbed into the driver's seat. She started the engine, shifted into gear, and drove off into the dark night.

They were free.

5

THREE YEARS LATER

Chapter 1

Andy Prescott told his mother he went to church every Sunday morning. He lied. He never went to church on any morning. And that Sunday morning he was sure as hell not in church, at least not the Baptist or Catholic version of church. He was in the Austin version of church: the out of doors. Austinites worship nature.

'You're insane, Andy!'

True. But then, a certain degree of insanity was part of the job description for a hammerhead. Point of fact, you had to be freaking nuts to ride a mountain bike at these speeds over a single-track hacked out of the wilderness and teeter on the edge of a steep ravine with nothing but a foam-padded plastic crash helmet standing between you and organ donor status. Nobody in his right mind would do such a thing.

But Andy loved to go fast.

He glanced back at Tres. Arthur Thorndike III – a family name, the poor bastard, so upon his arrival in Austin ten years before he had quickly acquired the nickname Tres, as in 'uno, dos, tres' – lagged Andy by a dozen bike lengths and only that much because Andy was taking it easy on him . . . and because Tres never tempted fate. Tres Thorndike had a) a trust fund, b) a gorgeous girlfriend, and c) a Beemer with personalized license plates that read TRES; consequently, he didn't want to die at twenty-nine. Andy had d) none of the above, so death before thirty was of no concern.

They were biking the back trails in the Barton Creek Greenbelt, a wilderness preserve on the western outskirts of Austin. The trails tracked Barton Creek from where the crystal-clear spring water bubbled out of the Edwards Aquifer at the base of the Balcones Escarpment east for eight miles through Sculpture Falls, Twin Falls, Three Falls, Airman's Cave, and Campbell's Hole. But while the creek coursed along on a gentle path deep down in the canyons, the back trails climbed precarious ledges high on the limestone face of the escarpment and cut through dense woods along treacherous paths that featured blind curves and sudden drops and dangerous obstacles and countless other opportunities to kill yourself.

'Andy, you're gonna kill yourself!'

Possibly. But at least he'd die knowing he had already made it to heaven.

Austin, Texas, was known for its natural beauty, and compared to Dallas or Houston, it was the Garden of Eden; but twenty-five years of unrestrained development had devoured almost all that was nature in the city. All but the greenbelt. The eight hundred acres offered an escape from the crowds and concrete, the noise and exhaust of a million automobiles, and the stifling August heat. Here there were grass and trees, water and waterfalls, clean air and a cool breeze. Only the sounds of the wind whistling through the trees and the water rippling over rocks below broke the silence.

In the greenbelt, the city seemed distant.

But it wasn't. The city was near, pressing in on all sides. The greenbelt now sat squeezed between residential developments and shopping malls and bounded and bisected by busy freeways. And developers wanted it, too. They wanted it all. The greenbelt was the Alamo of Austin, the final stand for nature; and the tree-huggers, hippies, hikers, bikers, swimmers, and runners would fight to the death to save it.

'In case you don't know it, Andy, suicide's against the law!'

Andy stood five-ten and weighed one-fifty-five; he hadn't been big enough for football or good enough for the skilled sports. But the first time he had saddled up on a mountain bike and careened down a hill completely out of control, he knew he had found his calling, a sport he was actually good at. Andy Prescott could stay on a bike. And he wasn't afraid to fall off.

Andy was that new breed of athlete: an extreme athlete. The kind of individual crazy enough to snowboard down a mountain poised for an avalanche or surf the big waves of a hurricane coming ashore or ride a bike down a treacherous trail at breakneck speed – all for the adrenaline rush. And that was the payoff for

11

adrenaline junkies, young men and women taking sports to the limits where there were no rules. Where there's just you and what's inside you.

Inside Andy at that moment was an intense accumulation of lactic acid in his thighs and quadriceps; his pistons were burning like butane torches. They had just come off a full-power granny-gear grunt up a two-hundred-foot vertical on the Hill of Life and were now running Mach 2 back down the hill, flying off low limestone ledges and skidding over crushed rock and swerving east onto the steepest back trail at full throttle, although Andy could hear Tres' brakes squealing like wild pigs and no doubt he was in full panic skid, digging his heels deep into the dirt as he tried to slow his descent. Tres piloted a top-of-the-line full-suspension Cannondale Prophet, but he was a bit of an Aunt Bee. Andy was anything but; he was bombing the descent on a secondhand Schwinn hardtail. No brakes. Pure gonzo.

'Yee-hah!'

His pre-ride rocket fuel – two cans of Red Bull – had given him one heck of a caffeine high. He was buzzed and in the zone, shredding the trail and carving the corners like a downhill skier in the Olympics; the knobby Kevlar tires bit into Mother Earth like a pit bull's teeth into soft human flesh. He veered around blackened trunks of burned-out oak trees then flew through a tunnel of thick brush and pruned a few low-hanging limbs, all just a blur in his peripheral vision.

12

He hit a monster bump and caught air for ten feet; he bounced hard on reentry but maintained his position in the cockpit. One slip and he would tumble down the ravine to a certain death – the thought of which triggered the rush. Adrenaline surged through his being like a narcotic, supercharging his mind and body.

Andy Prescott had never felt more alive.

He was wearing cargo shorts, Converse sneakers, and a T-shirt he had sweated through in the heat and humidity of late August in Texas. His only accessories were a pair of cheap sunglasses, the CamelBak strapped to his back that packed his personal effects and one hundred ounces of Endurox R4 – the sports drink of choice for extreme athletes – and the crash helmet. Andy Prescott was crazy but not stupid.

'Slow down, Andy!'

They always came out early on Sunday morning because they didn't have anchors holding them at home – although Tres was living on borrowed time; his girlfriend was already planning marriage and offspring – and because weekend walkers, hikers, joggers, and your less adventuresome bikers wisely stayed on the family-friendly double-track down by the creek a hundred feet below them. Which meant they could hammer the back trails without fear of pedestrian injury.

'Andy, you're gonna biff!'

Andy Prescott . . . wipeout? Not a chance: he was stoked. He glanced back at Tres.

'No way, dude!'

'Andy, look out!'

He turned back, and his heart almost stopped.

Uh-oh.

Just ahead, three white-haired women stood huddled together right in the middle of the trail.

For Christ's sake, not a tea party on a back trail!

Andy was going too fast to stop in time and there wasn't enough room on the narrow trail to go around them: to his left was the sheer rock wall of the escarpment; to his right the abyss of the ravine. If he plowed into the senior citizens at that speed, he'd kill them for sure. But if he veered off the trail, he'd fly down the ravine and kill himself.

The women saw him. He tried to wave them off the trail – but they stood frozen in place, like deer caught in headlights, terrified by the bike and rider hurtling at them at high speed. One screamed. She looked like his mother.

Andy said, 'Aw, shit,' cut the handlebars hard to the right just a split second before impact, and rode straight off the trail – and the Earth. He caught big air. He was now flying through the blue sky and enjoying an incredible panoramic view from high above the greenbelt, suddenly free of all worldly constraints, and he experienced an awesome nirvanic sensation . . . until gravity clicked in.

He dropped fast.

He looked down and saw the Earth rushing toward him. He pushed down on the pedals and pulled up on the bars as if doing a wheelie so the bike's rear tire

14

would hit the ground first; he had a momentary vision of actually riding the bike down the ravine. But that vision proved fleeting when the back tire caught a gnarly stump immediately upon reentry, which yanked the front tire down abruptly, which threw him forward over the handlebars, which sent him endo; he executed several flawless albeit involuntary three-sixties before crashing through tree limbs and landing on his Camel-Bak. But the ride wasn't over. He bounced hard, and his momentum took him tumbling like a rag doll down the ravine and through thick juniper bushes and across the lower trail. He heard Tres' voice from above – 'Andy!' – just before he hit the water of Sculpture Falls.

The next thing he knew, Tres was pulling him out of the water and slapping him across the face.

'Andy! Andy, are you okay?'

He then heard a different voice. A smaller voice.

'Is he dead?'

Damn. He hoped he wasn't dead.

Andy opened his eyes onto a dark, blurry world. He saw two figures standing there. A big Tres and a little Tres. No, Tres and a kid . . . holding a rope?

'Is he dead?' the kid said again.

Andy had gone into the falls right where kids played Tarzan on a rope hanging from a tree. Tres frowned at the kid then put his cell phone to his ear. Andy heard Tres' distant voice.

'Hello? Hello? Damn. Can't ever get a signal down here in the canyons.'

15

Tres resumed slapping Andy across the face.

'Andy! Andy!'

Andy tried to fend off Tres' blows before he suffered irreparable brain damage, but his arms were spaghetti.

'Dude, quit hitting me!'

'I'll run up and call nine-one-one.'

'I don't need an ambulance, man. I need a beer.'

'You sure?'

'Yeah, I'm sure I need a beer.'

'No. That you're okay?'

'Yeah, except I can't see. Tres – everything's dark!'

'Dude, you still got your sunglasses on.'

'Oh.'

Andy removed the glasses. Tres studied him from close range for a long moment then broke into a big grin.

'Man, that was a spectacular stack! The most awesome face plant I've ever witnessed!'

Andy extended a closed hand to Tres; they tapped knuckles. A fist-punch.

'Glad you enjoyed it. Did get the adrenaline pumping, I'll give it that.'

The kid turned away and yelled to someone, 'He ain't dead!' Then he swung out on the rope and somersaulted into the water. Tres chucked Andy on the shoulder.

'The Samson theory held true – at least this time.'

Andy tried to shake his head clear, but it just made him dizzy.

'How's the bike?'

'The *bike*? Who gives a shit about your bike? Look at yourself.'

Andy looked at himself. He wasn't one of those weekend warriors who wore protective armor like the pros, so his body had absorbed the full brunt of the fall. Blood striped his arms and legs where tree branches had whipped him on reentry, and his knees and elbows sported strawberry-red road rash, which meant he would have to endure a week of painful bacon. His clothes were soaking wet and ripped to shreds, which wasn't much of a financial hit since he had acquired his entire wardrobe at the St Vincent de Paul Thrift Shop – well, except his underwear. He drew the line at used underwear.

No jagged bones jutted through his skin, and all limbs seemed in working order, although any movement of his right shoulder or left knee produced extreme pain – hence the term, 'extreme sports.' His brain bucket had stayed in place and he wasn't bleeding from his ears, so he had apparently suffered no closed-head injuries. But he was bleeding. He spit blood and wiped blood from his face, but it couldn't be that bad because Tres was still looking at him. Tres had gone to law school instead of med school as his parents had wanted because he couldn't stand the sight of blood.

'I'm good.'

His bike was not.

His sweet ride was now a yard sale. The wheels,

frame, seat, and tire pump lay scattered over the white rock that was Sculpture Falls, limestone carved into crevices and furrows by the running water over millions of years. The Schwinn had slammed into the rock and disintegrated upon impact. That was bad luck. He still owed five months' payments on it.

'Finally got the bike dialed in, then I run into a tea party.'

'Andy, if you'd hit those rocks instead of the water, you'd be in worse shape than your bike. Why didn't you bail?'

'Bike would've nailed the old ladies.'

'Oh. A boy scout.'

Andy stood. Either he or Tres was swaying side to side, he wasn't sure whom, until Tres grabbed his shoulders.

'Steady there, partner.'

When the world finally stood still, Andy said, 'My bike.'

'I'll get what's left of it,' Tres said.

Andy waited while Tres retrieved the remains of the bike. The wheels looked like potato chips and the frame like a pretzel, the tire pump would never pump again, and the seat was now floating in the water. Andy shook his head like John Wayne when the bad guys had killed his favorite horse.

'My trusty steed.'

They climbed back up the ravine to the trail where they found Tres' bike and the three women waiting;

18

they were wearing big wraparound sunglasses, visors that matched their color-coordinated outfits, and waist packs. The most dangerous obstacles on a single-track were not rocks, roots, or ruts, but white-haired walkers.

Andy sat on a boulder, removed his helmet, and ran his fingers through his thick wet hair that hung almost to his shoulders. He wore his hair long on the Samson theory: long hair made him indestructible on the bike. He dug out a few small rocks embedded in the raw hamburger meat that was his left knee, which made him grimace. One of the old ladies leaned over and yelled as if he were deaf: 'Are you okay, sonny?'

He recoiled. 'Yes, ma'am.'

The second one put on her reading glasses and examined his face from a foot away. Her breath smelled like mints.

'I was a nurse. You may need stitches.'

'Yes, ma'am.'

'At least put Neosporin on those cuts,' she said, 'so you don't get an infection.'

'Yes, ma'am.'

'The water's down there?' the third lady asked.

'Yes, ma'am.'

She turned to the others. 'I told you.'

'We got lost,' the first lady said. 'Took the wrong trail.'

'Yes, ma'am.'

'We were checking the map. I guess we shouldn't have stopped in the middle of the trail.'

19

'No, ma'am.'

She shrugged. 'Our bad.'

She unzipped her waist pack and pulled out a can of Ensure. She held it out to him like a peace offering.

'Homemade Vanilla.'

Tres turned away and choked back laughter.

'Thank you, ma'am,' Andy said, 'but I've got Endurox in my CamelBak.'

He reached around and found the rubber tube hanging from the hydration pack. He put the mouthpiece between his teeth and bit down on the bite valve. Nothing came out. The CamelBak must have punctured on the fall – but the three liters of liquid cushion had probably saved him from a serious spinal cord injury.

'Or I did.'

'Endurox?' the Ensure lady said. 'Does that relieve constipation?'

Tres couldn't hold back now; he buried his face in his hands and howled.

'Constipation?' Andy said. 'Well, no, ma'am, it doesn't. At least I don't think so.'

'The key to life is fiber. I mix Metamucil with my Ensure every morning. I can set my clock by my morning bowel—'

'Yes, ma'am.' He pointed west. 'Go back that way, hang a left on the white rock trail, then another left on the dirt path down by the creek. That'll take you to the falls.'

'Can we swim naked there?'

20

'Uh, no, ma'am. Only out at Hippie Hollow on the lake.'

The Austin chapter of AARP waved and walked off, chatting like sorority sisters. Tres fell to the ground laughing and started rolling around like a kid practicing a 'stop, drop, and roll' fire drill. He said, '"Does it relieve constipation?"' then howled again.

Andy shook his head.

'Get up. And help me up.'

High noon and Tres was still reliving the moment.

'"Does it relieve constipation?" You should've said, "No, ma'am, but taking a header down that ravine sure as hell did – I crapped in my pants."'

'Dang near the truth.'

The throbbing bass of 'La Grange', ZZ Top's hit song from the seventies, blared out from a boom box and reverberated off the limestone walls of the pool. Coming to Barton Springs was a trip back in time to the way Austin used to be. The music, the people, the pool. Old-timers swam laps in the icy water the Indians thought healed them and felt young again. Young people like Andy recreated their parents' fondest memories from the seventies and eighties – and every middle-aged parent in Austin had a fond memory of Barton Springs. And kids made new memories, floating on inner tubes, diving off the board, and playing in the turquoise water. For as long as anyone could remember, everyone in Austin – except developers – had desperately wanted the springs to stay frozen in time, at least for one more perfect summer.

Like that summer.

Andy stretched out on the south ledge of the pool and admired the lifeguard in her red Speedo sitting up in the tower. Barton Springs Pool was a thousand-foot-long natural swimming hole situated in Zilker Park, south of downtown Austin. Four million gallons of spring water filled the three-acre limestone cavity and maintained a constant year-round temperature of sixty-eight degrees Fahrenheit. And every hour, another million gallons gushed forth from the three springs the original owner, Uncle Billy Barton, had named after his daughters: Eliza, Zenobia, and Parthenia.

Poor girls.

It was a hundred degrees out, but the cold water had temporarily relieved the heat, just as the marijuana smoke riding the breeze from the college kids on the grassy bank south of the pool had temporarily relieved Andy's aches and pains.

'Hey, medicinal marijuana really works. My knee doesn't hurt anymore.'

Andy didn't do dope – his high came from adrenaline – but he inhaled the sweet smoke again just to make sure he had completed the full course of treatment.

'There's no place like Austin,' Tres said. 'Biking the greenbelt, swimming the springs . . . the live music. This is as good as it gets. I only wish I'd been around to hear Springsteen rock the Armadillo.'

The Armadillo World Headquarters, a cavernous National Guard armory converted into a concert hall, had put Austin on the live music map. The famous and not so famous had played the Armadillo back in the seventies, including Andy's father. To hear him tell it, those were the best years in Austin. He said the Armadillo was the soul of Austin – until it was razed for an office building in 1981. That was a dark day in Austin's history – the day of the coup. The day the developers seized power.

Austin had changed that day and hadn't stopped changing. Austin seemed more like LA every day, although Andy had never been to LA. More people, more traffic, more trendy lofts and lounges downtown. Less laid-back. Fewer hippies. No Armadillo. In ten years it would be just like – and this singular fear gripped all who loved Austin the way it used to be – Dallas.

But one place had not changed: Barton Springs.

Andy had broken a full-body sweat again, so he rolled off the ledge and into the water. He dove down fourteen feet below the diving board and put his sore back close to the Parthenia spring. The rhythmic pulse of the spring, the dim light, and the water wrapped around his body made sitting on the bottom of the pool a womb-like experience. But this was not your chlorinated backyard pool; he stirred the gravelly bottom and tiny red-gilled salamanders floated up. Unlike the salamanders, Andy needed oxygen so he pushed himself to the top. He climbed out of the pool and again stretched out on the warm ledge.

Andy's standard routine was to lie on the ledge ogling the female lifeguards in their towers and the college coeds tanning on the grassy bank until he had worked up a good sweat; then he would simply roll into the pool. After a few minutes in the cold water, he would climb out and repeat the routine. With enough experience, you got into a nice rhythm. Andy and Tres were in a nice rhythm.

'Arthur,' Natalie said, 'it says here we could hire an Indian surrogate.'

Natalie Riggs was Tres' gorgeous girlfriend; she insisted on addressing him by his given name. Against Andy's advice, Tres had dutifully reported in to her after their morning ride, apparently a condition of their engagement. She had decided to meet them at the pool, the only upside of which was the fact that she looked stunning lying there on a towel in a tiny string bikini with her smooth skin shimmering in sweat and suntan oil. *Jesus*. She was thirty-one and a sexy brunette; she wanted to marry Tres and have a baby – Tres said her biological clock was ticking so loudly it kept him awake at night – but she also wanted to retain her fabulous figure, a requirement both for her job as a local TV lifestyle reporter and her hopes of jumping to the networks. 'Have you ever seen a fat pregnant woman on the network morning shows?' she often asked Tres. So they had decided to have a baby by gestational surrogacy: Tres' sperm, Natalie's egg, a stranger's womb, and a binding contract.

'Which tribe?' Tres said.

Natalie eyed her fiancé over the magazine she was reading.

'Which tribe what?'

'Which Indian tribe? Apache, Comanche, Sioux . . . ?'

'Not those Indians. India Indians. You know, the ones with the little black mark on their foreheads.'

'They're having babies for Americans?'

'That's what this article says. You just send them the fertilized egg and nine months later they send you back the baby. And they're a lot cheaper than American surrogates.'

'Outsourcing babies to India?' Andy said.

'Every time my computer crashes and I call tech support,' Tres said, 'I'm talking to some Indian guy named Bob. Can't understand a word he says.'

'And the clinics have pre-qualified surrogates,' Natalie said, 'tested and ready to go.'

'Tested?' Andy said.

Natalie sipped her Pellegrino sparkling water then said, 'The surrogate's got to pass a criminal background check, a psychiatric test, and an STD test. Do you know how hard it is to find a surrogate in the US who can pass all three tests? That's why they're so expensive here.'

'Supply and demand,' Tres said.

'You gotta worry the woman who's carrying your

baby is a criminal, a nut, or diseased?' Andy said. 'Jeez, Natalie, seems a lot safer to birth that baby yourself.'

'And lose these abs?'

She had awesome abs.

'Why not outsource your baby to a nice Swedish girl?' Andy said. 'I'll implant the egg myself.'

'Commercial surrogacy is illegal in Europe,' Tres said. 'And it's only legal in twelve states over here.'

'Is Texas one of them?'

'Yeah, but you've got to get court approval, so we may do it in Illinois. You don't have to go to court up there. But, the doctor's got to sign an affidavit saying it's a medical necessity.'

'And saving Natalie's awesome abs might not qualify?'

'Exactly.' Tres reached over and patted her lean belly. 'Still, babe, I think we should use an American surrogate and support the troops.'

'Support the troops how?' Andy said.

'A lot of American surrogates are military wives,' Tres said, 'having other women's babies to make ends meet while their husbands are in Iraq. I figure we could do our share for the war effort.' To Natalie: 'I vote American.'

'I vote for her,' Andy said.

He nodded at a coed walking towards them. She was blonde and spilling out of her bikini in a good way. She jiggled past them and over to her spot on the bank where she sat and removed her bikini top. Topless sunbathing was legal at Barton Springs. For full nudity, you had to go out to Hippie Hollow on Lake Travis, a bit of a drive, so most coeds opted for topless at the springs.

'Only problem with her,' Tres said, 'is I'd have to manually fertilize the egg.'

Any perceived threat to Tres' trust fund got Natalie's immediate attention. She lowered her sunglasses and gave the blonde one of those brief but thorough head-to-foot once-overs that competitive females mastered by ninth grade. Natalie Riggs could now describe in detail every flaw on the blonde's body.

'*Puh-leeze.* You or my baby inside her? I don't think so.'

'Maybe I should conduct a pre-surrogacy exam first,' Andy said, 'check out her reproductive system personally.'

'In your dreams,' Tres said.

'Like there's anywhere else?'

'The standard surrogacy contract,' Natalie said, 'requires the surrogate to stop having sex for the entire gestation period. I doubt she could stop for an afternoon.'

'That's what gives me hope.'

'Andy,' Natalie said, 'her hair is bleached, she could stand to lose some weight, and in case you didn't notice, those are implants.'

'What's your point?'

'My God, Andy, she's drinking a supersized soda. That's three hundred forty calories. She'll be a size ten in two years.'

'Two *years*? Natalie, my relationships usually last about two hours.'

Natalie sighed in resignation.

'Then go over and ask her out.'

Andy sat up. He considered doing just that. But she wasn't alone. Rejection would be a painful public humiliation. A train whistle sounded in the distance; the park's miniature train was about to leave the station. Andy lay back down.

'And get shot down in public? I have my reputation to consider.'

Tres laughed. 'What reputation?'

'Andy,' Natalie said, 'you've got to date to have sex . . . well, maybe not with her, but with classy girls you do, like the kind you meet at Pangaea.'

'That's the place with the safari theme? Girls dressed like Tarzan's mate dancing on the tables? Natalie, I can't get past the velvet rope at places like that.'

The beautiful people of Austin now frequented the trendy new lounges springing up in the warehouse district a few blocks west of downtown. Andy was not and so did not.

'A guy from New York opened Pangaea,' she said. 'They've got tribal spears and shields on the walls, and the ceiling is draped like a tent. It's fabulous.'

'It's expensive,' Tres said.

Natalie rolled lusciously toward Tres and gave him a little kiss.

'But I'm worth it.'

Andy tried not to admire her body in motion, but he couldn't resist. But then, she and Tres weren't married yet, so it wasn't like Andy was committing a Ninth Commandment violation.

She rolled back and said, 'So when was your last date?'

'Last year.'

Natalie sat up, squirted a line of suntan oil onto her right thigh, and rubbed it in with long smooth strokes.

'When last year?'

'April.'

'April of last year? Andy, it's August of this year.'

'I'm working on it.'

'Anyone answer your ad?' Tres said.

Natalie now rubbed oil on her left thigh.

'What ad?'

'Andy put an ad in Lovers Lane.'

Lovers Lane was the online dating venue of the *Austin Chronicle*, the weekly alternative newspaper in town.

'Any responses?'

'Nope. Every "woman seeking man" wants a guy who's smart, rich, and looks like Matthew McConaughey. They don't want regular guys.'

McConaughey was Austin's resident movie star.

'Which is why they're alone and putting personal ads in the *Chronicle*,' Tres said.

'Which is why they're not going to answer my ad – I'm not smart or rich and I don't look like McConaughey.'

'Andy,' Natalie said, 'don't sell yourself short. You're sort of smart.'

That amused Tres almost as much as the old lady's 'Does it relieve constipation?'

'I'm a regular Joe looking for a regular Joan.'

'So lie,' Tres said. 'Everyone in those ads lies.'

'But that defeats the whole purpose of personal ads: you can be honest.'

'Andy, no one's honest. I know. I work for the IRS.'

Tres had hired on with the Internal Revenue Service after law school at the University of Texas; he had been a B student, so the best he could do was a government job. But he hoped to parlay his inside knowledge into a big firm job in a few years. He didn't need the money – there was the trust fund – but he needed a station in life.

Andy said, 'I'm honest.'

Tres: 'And poor.'

Natalie: 'With no girlfriend.'

Andy: 'Which requires money.'

Tres shook his head. 'It's a vicious cycle.'

Natalie gave Andy her 'wise mother' look, which told him she was about to offer more unsolicited personal advice. The fact that she was two years older than Andy apparently gave her standing.

'Andy, classy girls don't want slackers.'

She graciously omitted the implied 'like you.'

'They want guys with ambition,' she said. 'Like Arthur.'

'He has a trust fund.'

'Or that. They want someone who can give them the life – the house on the lake, the cars, the country club, the nightlife, the wardrobe, the accessories. Someone with money, or at least the ambition to make money.'

She squirted oil onto her upper chest and smoothed it over the exposed portion of her beautiful breasts.

'Andy, if you want a girlfriend, you need ambition.'

Andy turned away from Natalie's oily body and said, 'I need a beer.'

Chapter 2

La cerveza más fina.

Andy drained the Corona longneck and waved the bottle in the air until he caught their waitress' attention on the far end of the porch. Ronda was working the sidewalk tables fronting Congress Avenue that Sunday night. She was twenty-five, sweet, and a lesbian; her black hair sported purple and green streaks, and colorful tattoos covered every square inch of her visible skin surface, most of which was visible since she was wearing only a blue jean miniskirt and a red halter top. From that distance, the tattoos blended together and made her look like a walking Jackson Pollock painting. She held up four fingers and raised her pierced eyebrows as if asking, Another round for the table? Andy nodded and pointed at Tres behind his back. Tres didn't know it, but he was buying.

Andy Prescott couldn't afford to buy a round for the table.

At twenty-nine, his financial condition should be a major life concern. By now, he should be contributing

to a 401(k) plan, saving for a down payment on a mortgage, and planning for a secure future. Why wasn't he?
Why didn't he have a burning ambition to make a lot
of money, like Natalie said? Was it just a stubborn
refusal to grow up? Was it genetic, an inherited trait
like his brown hair and eyes? Or was it a character
flaw? Why didn't he care more about such mature
matters instead of—

'Jesus, Tres, check her out.'

A gorgeous girl glided past their table and into the
restaurant, but not before giving Tres a sly glance.

Andy yelled to her: 'He's taken! I'm not!'

Natalie had given Tres the night off – she was at
home researching the 'rent a womb' business in India
– so they were drinking Mexican beer with Dave and
Curtis, two buddies from their UT days, who were in
deep conversation on the other side of the table.

'She got back to the condo,' Tres said, 'jumped on
the computer, hasn't budged since. That magazine article
at the pool today really got her hormones pumping.'

'You really thinking about doing that? Outsourcing
your baby to India?'

'Not until Natalie compared the costs. With an
American surrogate, you're looking at a hundred thousand total out of pocket. In India, it's only five grand.'

'You paid more than that for your trail bike.'

'Yeah, but that's a fortune in India. Natalie said a
third of the population lives on a dollar a day. An
American surrogate makes fifty thousand, an Indian

33

twenty-five hundred – but that's like seven years' pay over there.'

Andy scooped salsa onto a tortilla chip and stuck the whole thing in his mouth, an act he immediately regretted: the salsa was seriously spicy. He turned his beer bottle up and tried to shake a few cold drops out onto his hot tongue. No luck. So he grunted and pointed at a cute coed behind Dave and Curtis; when they swiveled their heads around to check her out, Andy grabbed Curtis' beer and drank from it, then replaced it without Curtis being the wiser. He wiped his mouth on his sleeve.

'Nine months at twenty-five hundred dollars? That's what, three hundred a month?'

'Two seventy-seven,' Tres said.

'She's renting her womb for nine bucks a day?'

'Yeah, and they've got better quality control. The clinic boards its surrogates for the entire nine months, makes sure they get proper pre-natal care and nutrition – they eat better than they have their whole lives.'

'The women live together?'

Tres nodded. 'To prevent conjugal visits. They'll have twenty surrogates in one house.'

'Baby factories.'

'And you don't have to worry she'll abort like over here. We paid for it, it's ours, and she signed a contract. She's got to deliver.'

Tres drank from his beer.

'Only downside is, Indian women die in childbirth at ten times the rate of American women.'

'So the surrogate has a good chance of dying while birthing your baby?'

'Yeah . . . but Natalie's willing to take that risk. Besides, if she dies, we get a full refund.'

'I'm sure that'll make the surrogate feel better.'

'And Natalie gets to keep her figure.'

'Hers is a figure worth keeping, Tres, no question about it, but the whole thing seems kind of like "ugly American" stuff – you know, exploiting poor people in Third World countries.'

'You sound like your mother. Andy, it's no different than American companies manufacturing their products offshore for the cheap labor.'

'Exactly.'

Andy looked for Ronda with their beers, then turned back to Tres.

'So you're going to manufacture little Cuatro in India after having sex with a test tube?'

Tres shrugged. 'I get to look at a *Playboy*.'

'That's romantic.'

Dave broke away from his conversation with Curtis and said, 'It always is for me.' Back to Curtis: 'They figured you couldn't afford their drinks.'

Curtis scratched his scalp deep in the dark jungle that was his hair then examined his fingers as if he'd found something.

'So?'

'So you'd just be taking up valuable space. Rent in the warehouse district is out of sight.'

Curtis pushed his glasses up on his nose.

'The doormen at Qua, they laughed at me – and I'll have my PhD in nine months.'

'Advanced degrees won't get you in that door, Curtis.'

'Qua,' Andy said. 'That's the lounge with the aquarium in the floor?'

'Shark tank,' Curtis said.

'Curtis,' Tres said, 'those places have strict dress codes. What were you wearing?'

Curtis gestured at his attire.

'Same clothes I teach in.'

He was wearing black-framed glasses, a white T-shirt with 'got root?' across the front, baggy cargo shorts, and burnt-orange Crocs. He was scrawny, twenty-eight, and a grad student working on his PhD in mathematics; he was a TA at UT. One of hundreds of teaching assistants employed by the University of Texas at Austin, Curtis Baxter taught math to undergrads so the tenured professors had time to write political op-eds.

'Curtis,' Tres said, 'you wouldn't get past the security guard at my condo wearing those clothes. This is the only place you can dress like that.'

This place was Güero's Taco Bar, formerly the Central Feed & Seed. Güero's still looked like a feed store, but it was now an Austin institution – everyone came to Güero's for Mexican food and beer and margaritas and mariachis: UT students and faculty, politicians and lawyers, trust-funders and slackers. The dress code was 'come as you are,' and so they came.

Andy was wearing shorts, a Willie Nelson 'Don't Mess With Texas' T-shirt, and flip-flops. Dave wore a red-and-black cowboy shirt over shorts and sandals, although he had recently tried to upgrade his appearance for his burgeoning business career; he now wore white socks. He swept his black hair back like a young Elvis, meticulously and often, like now.

'You missed a spot,' Andy said.

'Where?'

Dave checked his hair in a spoon; Andy shook his head. What a crew. Tres Thorndike appeared sophisticated and worldly with his stylish clothes and professionally cut hair; he was from Connecticut. After flunking out of the Ivy League, Tres enrolled at UT for the frat parties – UT consistently ranks as the number one party school in America – and ended up president of the most exclusive fraternity on campus. Dave Garner had gotten into a lesser fraternity on a legacy. Curtis Baxter had been denied admission to every fraternity at UT. Andy Prescott had never wanted to join a fraternity.

The story of their lives.

Ronda returned with four cold Coronas. Tres told her to put them on his tab; he was good about having a trust fund. Andy leaned back in his chair and took a long drink of the cold beer. It was another great night at Güero's. The sun was setting behind them, the heat of the day had broken, and they were sitting at their regular sidewalk table, a prime location to enjoy the live music of Tex Thomas & His Danglin' Wranglers playing in the adjacent Oak Garden and to check out every female entering or exiting the establishment. *God, the girls of Austin.* Between the twenty-five thousand UT coeds and the thousands of young women who moved to Austin every year for the nightlife, there were beautiful girls everywhere you turned in Austin.

Except, of course, at their table.

It wasn't that they were homely individuals. Tres, in fact, was rather handsome, and he exuded that confident aura of a trust-fund beneficiary, for which girls seemed to have a sixth sense, like dogs could smell fear; consequently, he attracted frequent glances from passing females. Curtis, Dave, and Andy did not. They were just regular guys, not something you put on your curriculum vitae in Austin. Sure, Curtis was a math genius, but that meant absolutely nothing outside the math department at UT. And, worst of all, they were broke.

Tres' phone pinged.

'She's texting me again.'

'Natalie?'

He nodded and checked the message.

'Says she found an Indian clinic that'll do it for four thousand.'

'You sure you want to hire out your baby to the lowest bidder?'

'Hell, Andy, I'm not sure I even want a baby . . . or to get married.'

Tres drank his beer then leaned toward Andy and lowered his voice.

'You know a PI?'

'A private investigator? No. But I know someone who does.'

'Can you get me his number?'

'Sure. What's up?'

'I think Natalie's cheating on me.'

'*What?* Why?'

'To have sex.'

'No. Why would she cheat on you? Dude, she wants to have your baby.'

'She wants an Indian woman to have my baby. And maybe she wants to have one last fling before marriage and motherhood.'

'She wouldn't leave you.'

'She wouldn't leave the trust fund. Me, I'm not so sure.'

He drank from his beer.

'See, you guys complain about being broke, but being rich isn't all it's cracked up to be either. If you guys ever do get a girl, at least you'll know she's not after your money.'

'It'd be nice to have a girl after me for something.'

Andy smiled but Tres didn't. This was serious.

'What's got you worried?'

'She's acting different.'

'How?'

'She stopped wearing underwear.'

That got Dave's attention. 'No shit?'

'Look, guys,' Tres said, 'this is confidential, okay?'

39

'Oh, absolutely,' Dave said. 'Sure thing. Now tell us about the underwear.'

'Well, you know, she's always worn thongs—'

'What kind?'

Tres shrugged. 'I don't know. Just thongs.'

'Lacy ones?'

'Curtis,' Andy said, 'douse him with your beer.'

'Anyway,' Tres said, 'all of a sudden she just stopped wearing anything.'

'God, that's hot,' Dave said.

'Not if she stopped for some other guy.'

'Oh, yeah, that wouldn't be so hot.'

'Did you ask her why?' Andy said.

'She said that was the fashionable thing now.'

'You don't believe her?'

Tres took no notice of a girl checking him out.

'I think she's having an affair with the weekend sports anchor at the station. Bruce, he's an ex-UT jock, lives out at the lake.'

'You want a PI to follow her?'

Tres' expression turned grim. 'I need to know. Besides, it's nothing compared to what my father will do before we get married.'

'Track her cell phone,' Curtis said. 'It's GPS-enabled, isn't it?'

'It was expensive.'

'Then it is.'

'GPS, like with a satellite?' Andy said.

'Like with three satellites,' Curtis said. He pointed

40

up. 'The Air Force has twenty-seven global positioning satellites orbiting the Earth. GPS tracking requires three to plot a location – it's a mathematical equation called trilateration. The GPS chip in your cell phone receives signals from three satellites, determines the distance to each, and plots a sphere around each satellite—'

Curtis was now teaching a class. He pulled out a mechanical pencil and on a napkin drew the Earth, three satellites orbiting the Earth, a stick figure holding a phone on Earth, and circles around each satellite.

'—and those three spheres intersect at only two locations, one in space and one on Earth. Your phone is located at the intersection on Earth.'

Andy handed his cell phone to Curtis, who served as their personal tech support staff.

'Does mine have that GPS chip?'

Curtis dug in his pants pocket and pulled out a little utility tool. He opened the tiny screwdriver and then the back of Andy's cell phone. He shook his head.

'Nope. Let me guess: you got it free with your cell contract?'

Andy shrugged. 'Yeah.'

'Dude, you can get a GPS phone for a few hundred bucks.'

'Exactly. That's why I chose free.'

'Well, they can still track your phone.'

'How?'

'Triangulation. See, when you make a call' – Curtis flipped the napkin over and drew again – 'the phone sends signals to the nearest cell masts – the towers. As you move from cell to cell – the area covered by each mast – the masts monitor the strength of the signals. When the signal is stronger at the next mast, that mast takes over the call. By calculating and comparing the time it takes the signal to travel to each mast – a mathematical equation called TDOA, time difference of arrival – and the AOA, angle of arrival – the computer determines the distance and angle from each mast to the phone, triangulates the signals, and plots out the location.' He shrugged. 'It's simple math.'

'Must be why I don't understand it,' Andy said.

'Triangulation isn't as precise as GPS. In the city they can track a phone to within thirty feet of its location. Out in the country, with fewer masts, it's maybe a thousand feet.'

'I never knew they could do that.'

Curtis pushed his glasses up. 'Cell phones are just tracking devices that make voice calls. Government mandated tracking capability for nine-one-one emergency calls, now the Feds use them to track terrorists and drug dealers.'

'Man, that's kind of scary, the government being able to track us with our cell phones.'

'It's not just the Feds. LBS providers do it, too.'

'What's an LBS?'

'Location Based Services. They've got deals with the carriers to capture the tracking data and they'll ping a phone for a fee. They say they require the permission of the person being tracked. They're mostly used by employers to track their employees, like truck drivers.'

'Natalie was reading about these chaperone services,' Tres said. 'You put a GPS-enabled phone in your kid's backpack and if they leave their school, you're automatically notified. In case they're kidnapped.'

'With their backpack.'

'So I can track Natalie the same way? See if she goes out to the lake to meet Bruce?'

'Sure,' Curtis said. 'Give me her phone number and when you want her tracked. I've got a friend at an LBS. Geeks rule.'

'Except at Qua,' Dave said.

Andy turned to Tres. 'You gonna ask Natalie's permission?'

Tres frowned. 'What if I don't? Would that be illegal? Maybe a violation of her privacy or stalking?'

'Don't ask me, dude,' Curtis said. 'You're the lawyer. I'm a mathematician.'

Tres sat back in his chair, obviously considering the ramifications of committing an illegal act versus his need to know if Natalie were cheating on him. Andy shook his head: how many men throughout history had been driven to crime by a woman? There was Adam, of course, and Clyde Barrow of Bonnie and Clyde, and . . .

'*Ooh!*'

They all turned to the street. A car had almost nailed a pedestrian. Sitting on the porch, they had front row

43

seats at a sporting event: watching jaywalkers trying to make it across the five lanes of Congress Avenue alive. The spectators *ooh*ed and *aah*ed with each near miss.

'That would've left a mark,' Dave said.

'Guys, listen to this girl's personal statement.'

Curtis had returned to the stack of personal ads from Lovers Lane online. He always printed out the promising ones and read them at their Sunday night beer bash at Güero's.

'She says, "I'm everything your mommy wants for you. I'm cute and cuddly and love to cook. I hate shopping. My favorite season is football season. Hook 'em Horns! Barbecue is my favorite food, beer my favorite drink. I like black lacy undergarments. I love to take long walks at night, especially through the cemetery . . ."'

'Whoa!' Dave said. 'The cemetery? Damn, she was sounding good.'

'Says she's looking for an LTR.'

'A long-term relationship? With who, Dracula? Next.'

Curtis flipped to the next ad. Tres leaned over to Andy.

'I break the law, I lose my law license. Better get me the PI's number.'

Andy nodded. 'I'll get it tomorrow.'

'This one's looking for "friends with benefits."'

'Means sex,' Dave said.

'Here's her profile: "Age . . . twenty-two. Body type . . . full figured, HWP." Height-weight proportionate.

"Occupation . . . hair stylist. Want children? . . . I want children to stay away from me. Drinking? . . . I'm drunk right now. Drugs? . . . Let's burn one." She says she spends her free time working out and having sex.'

Dave was shaking his head; he was about to vent.

'Every girl in those ads says she spends her free time working out and having sex. If they're having so much sex, why'd they put an ad in the personals for "woman seeking man"? Answer me that.'

'I can't,' Andy said.

'There you go. They're lying. They haven't been laid since high school prom night.'

'Neither have you.'

'And when was your last serious relationship, Romeo?'

'With a female?'

'*Homo sapiens*.'

'Fourth grade. Mary Margaret McDermott at St Ignatius. My first kiss.'

It had happened during recess behind the slide. Andy let her go up the ladder first, hoping to look up her uniform skirt only to discover that she wore privacy shorts underneath; she had abruptly turned and kissed him right on the lips. He could still feel that kiss. Andy realized that Dave was staring at him.

'What'd you do this time?' Dave said.

Between the pool and Güero's, Andy had doctored his cuts and abrasions and taken two Ibuprofen, but his

45

entire body still hurt like he'd fallen a hundred feet down a ravine. Oh, he had. Of course, the four Coronas were acting as a nice anesthetic.

'He took a header for some senior citizens,' Tres said. 'The ravine above Sculpture Falls.'

'Ouch. You see a doctor?'

Andy tapped the Corona. 'I self-medicate. And I need my prescription refilled.'

He held up his beer bottle for Ronda again. He wasn't worried about driving home drunk because a) he didn't own a car, and b) he lived only a few blocks from Güero's. He had often biked home drunk, which wasn't a crime, at least not in Austin.

'You were bombing the Hill of Life again,' Dave said.

Andy shrugged.

'Hill of Death is more like it. Andy, are you afraid of anything?'

'Women.'

'Amen, brother,' Curtis said.

They fist-punched in the air above the table.

'You're gonna die on that bike one day,' Dave said.

'Not *that* bike. And there are worse ways to go.'

The guys fell silent and dropped their eyes. Tres put an arm around Andy's shoulder.

'How's he doing?'

'Still waiting for the call.'

After an awkward moment of silence, Tres said, 'Curtis, read us another one.'

'Okay.' He turned a page. 'This girl wants a guy who's kind and considerate and loving and intelligent with a sense of humor and a pleasing personality . . . and, oh yeah, he's got to have the mind of Einstein and the body of Matthew McConaughey.'

'That's what they all want,' Dave said, 'the perfect male.'

Dave pulled out his comb and swept his hair back again. He smiled at a passing girl; she smiled at Tres. Dave shrugged it off then slapped Curtis on the shoulder.

'Well, we've got half of perfect right here – the Einstein brain.'

'And the other half with Andy,' Tres said.

'Please. McConaughey's pumped. I'm . . . wiry.'

'Natalie says you've got a great body. Hell, I'd be worried she was cheating with you if you had any money.'

'Thanks.'

'McConaughey probably thinks pi is something you eat,' Curtis said.

'It's not?' Dave said.

'I'll bet he couldn't solve a quadratic equation to save his life.'

'What's that?'

Curtis twisted around to reveal the back side of his T-shirt, on which a long mathematical equation was printed.

'This. Simple algebra.'

Tres laughed. 'Curtis, movie stars like McConaughey, they've got people to do their algebra for them.'

'I saw him in here a while back,' Dave said. 'The girls were falling all over themselves to get near him. Even Ronda.'

'She's a lesbian,' Andy said.

Dave turned his palms up. 'The allure of celebrity.'

'We'll never get a date if they want McConaughey,' Curtis said.

'I know how we can get dates,' Dave said. 'Answer the ads from women over forty. There's a lot of older women out there rebounding from divorces – they're lonely and desperate.'

'But are they desperate enough to date us?' Curtis said.

'You're desperate – how high are your standards?'

'Excellent point.'

'Still, a forty-year-old woman,' Andy said, 'that'd be kind of creepy, like dating your mother.'

'My mother's dating a thirty-five-year-old guy she found in the personals,' Dave said. 'Says he can be the older brother I never had.'

'No kidding?'

Dave nodded. 'And my dad's dating a twenty-six-year-old girl. He says she can be the sister I never had. But what does it mean if I want to have sex with my new sister? And if he marries her, then I'll want to have sex with my stepmother.'

'See, that is creepy.'

'You haven't seen her.'

Ronda dropped off four Coronas and took their orders. Beef tacos, chips and *queso*, and more beer. All the essential food groups.

'I revised my ad,' Dave said.

'No hits?'

'*Nada*. So now I'm six-two, a Democrat, and a vegan.'

'You're five-nine, a Republican, and you eat meat like a freakin' T-Rex.'

Curtis: 'This girl's ad says "absolutely no Christians or Republicans."'

'See?' Dave said. 'Easier to find a virgin than a Republican in Austin. You tell a girl you voted for Bush, you're history.'

'But you're lying.'

'Everyone lies in those ads, Andy. It's like a resumé, a way to get your foot in the door. Doesn't have to be true.'

Dave was in real estate.

Curtis said, 'This one says, "I'm cute, smart, funny and all that other shit I tell myself as part of my daily self-affirmation routine."'

'She's in therapy,' Dave said. 'Next.'

'"I'm romantic and at times emotional. I get teary-eyed from sad commercials — those animal shelter commercials are soooo sad." She has a frown-face emoticon.'

'Needy. Next.'

49

'This girl says the four people in history she'd invite to dinner are Jesus, Gandhi, the Dalai Lama, and Paris Hilton.'

'Dumb and dumber. Next.'

'Okay, listen to this one. She's twenty-six, a kindergarten teacher, and lives in SoCo. She's five-five, one-ten, athletic build, drug and disease free, drama free, and maintenance free. Reads the *Chronicle*, shops at Whole Foods, works out at the Y, and gets her coffee at Jo's. Says her idea of a perfect date is shrimp *fajitas* at Güero's and Mexican Vanilla ice cream at Amy's. She drinks socially but doesn't smoke. Her favorite activity is – get this, Andy – biking the greenbelt followed by swimming at the Barton Springs Pool.'

Andy sat up. 'Wow, she's perfect.'

'Except there's one catch.'

'What's that?'

'She's seeking a "man *or woman*" for dating.'

'She's bi?'

'Apparently.'

'Now there's a girl you could take home to your mother,' Dave said. 'Or to your sister.'

'I wish I had a sister,' Curtis said.

'Maybe I can take her home to my new sister.'

Andy Prescott leaned back and turned up his beer. He was twenty-nine years old and the last girl he had taken home to meet his mother was Mary Margaret McDermott. He was on a twenty-year losing streak with women. He considered that sad record a moment, then sighed and waved his empty Corona bottle in the air until Ronda spotted him.

'*Uno más, señorita.*'

He had read that beer was not only a natural anesthetic, but also an herbal remedy for depression.

Chapter 3

At exactly seven-thirty the next morning, loud rock music woke Andy Prescott from his coma-like state of sleep with all the subtlety of a SWAT raid. He reached over and smacked the radio across the room, but it was just a symbolic gesture. He was awake. He tried to sit up, but the movement sent a sharp pain ricocheting around his skull like a pinball.

A dozen Coronas sure packed a wallop.

His head ached from the beers and his body from the fall down the ravine, and he was as stiff as a two-by-four from sleeping in one position all night. His right arm was numb. He must have slept on it – or he had suffered permanent nerve damage in the fall.

Heck of a start to a new week.

He rolled out of bed and realized he was still wearing the same clothes from the night before. There was a sizable salsa stain splashed across the front of his T-shirt; Willie looked as if he had been blasted in the face with a double-barreled shotgun. Andy tried to recall the last hours of the evening, but all his mind could retrieve was a vague image of falling over a table . . . and not his table.

He dropped his clothes on the floor and limped to the bathroom. The anesthetic properties of the Coronas had worn off; his left knee burned with each step. He turned on the hot water in the shower then relieved himself of the beer and brushed his teeth. He stared at his reflection in the mirror.

He looked every bit as bad as he felt.

He walked into the living room and found Max stretched out on the couch. The Keeshond bolted to the front door; he needed to relieve himself, too. Andy opened the door and recoiled from another bright, sunny day. His front porch looked out onto the Texas School for the Deaf campus across the street, which made for a quiet neighborhood. His neighbor was walking her little white Lhasa Apso past the house; while the dogs sniffed each other's butts, Liz called over to him.

'Nice look you've got going there, Andy.'

He had forgotten he was naked.

He waved lamely to Liz and returned to the bathroom. The hot shower brought most of his brain cells back to life, but there would be no quick fix for his body. The red scratch marks across his face made him look like Geronimo with his war paint on. Nasty scabs had already begun to form on his elbows and knees. His left knee was swollen. The feeling had returned to his right arm, but he couldn't raise that arm above his shoulder. He would hurt for a week, but all in all, it wasn't that bad. If you can't take the pain, don't go extreme. Stay at home and play pretend bowling on your Wii.

His home was a one-bedroom, one-bath rent house on Newton Street just across the river from downtown in the part of Austin known as 'SoCo' because it straddled South Congress Avenue. Newton paralleled Congress two blocks west. The other houses on the street had been renovated by urban frontiersmen and women like Liz and her husband, young professionals who had braved the neighborhood back when SoCo's leading citizens were hookers and addicts.

Now SoCo was a hip and happening place to be, a highly desired and highly priced in-town location. The houses on either side, nothing more than cottages, were valued on the tax rolls at over $300,000, and the one a few doors down was on the market for $600,000; his place was still awaiting renovation and so was valued at only $87,500. Andy's landlord had been transferred to California six years ago by his high-tech employer; he hoped to return to Austin one day. Andy hoped he wouldn't because he was charging only $600 in monthly rent, way below market for SoCo.

Andy dug through clothes piled on furniture until he found a pair of jeans and a clean shirt with a collar. He tried to shake the wrinkles out of the shirt – he didn't own an iron – then got dressed, grabbed his electric razor, and went outside. The remains of his trail

54

bike lay on the front porch like the aftermath of a tornado. Andy Prescott felt like a man without a reason to live: he had no mountain bike.

He was a gutter bunny – he commuted to work by bike – but he had always commuted on a mountain bike. His only mode of transportation that day was an old Huffy BMX that Tres had lent him until he could replace the Schwinn – but who knew when that would happen. He sat on the Huffy and sank; it had a flat tire.

Figured.

He went back inside and found a pump. He inflated the tire then climbed aboard again. He strapped on the helmet, inserted his sunglasses, and rode down the porch steps and the front sidewalk to the street. He stopped and looked both ways. He could turn south and take James Street, which was more direct, or he could turn north and take Nellie Street, which held the promise of an early morning adrenaline rush.

He turned north.

No doubt he looked like a dork riding a boy's candy-apple-red twenty-inch Huffy, but it was that or walk to work. He clicked the razor on and ran the rotating blades over his face. He whistled to Max, who bounded after him. Two houses down, he saw Liz out front tending her Xeriscape landscaping; he gave her a sheepish 'Sorry about that.' She just smiled. Of course, it wasn't the first time she had seen him naked.

He rode on and gazed upon the downtown skyline.

Austin sat at the edge of the Texas Hill Country where the flat prairie land first began to rise and wrinkle up like Andy's shirt, so the town's topography was full of ups and downs and twists and turns; the roadways followed the lay of the land. Newton Street was a narrow residential lane that ran north–south on one of the 'ups.' From that vantage point, Andy could see the skyscrapers of downtown rising in sharp relief against the blue sky and the construction cranes towering over new condos and hotels going up, all of which now blocked the view of the state capitol unless you were standing in the middle of Congress Avenue – a crime committed by developers and sanctioned by the city. Austin was a hot market, and there was money to be made, so city hall and developers, once lethal adversaries in Austin, had joined forces to pillage the place for profit.

His mother often said, 'Money makes good men do bad things.'

Newton followed the perimeter fence line of the School for the Deaf then made a sharp turn to the east – which turn Andy now made – and became Nellie Street. Nellie abruptly pitched downward at a sharp angle on its short journey to Congress Avenue, which ran north–south in one of the 'downs.'

Andy picked up speed.

By the time you hit Congress, you could build up a pretty good head of steam flying down Nellie. Andy had once hit Congress at full speed only to have his brakes fail; he flew right through the intersection and crashed into the patio at Doc's Motorworks Bar & Grill. He tapped the Huffy's coaster brakes; they were in working order.

He pushed the razor into his pants pocket. He sat up, adjusted his helmet and sunglasses, and watched the traffic light at the bottom of the hill. The white pedestrian WALK signal to cross Congress changed to a flashing red DON'T WALK; he had exactly twenty-four seconds.

Congress was a broad five-lane avenue that served as a major north–south commuting route. It was morning rush hour, and traffic was backed up at the light. Impatient drivers revved their SUV's big engines, in no mood to wait for pedestrians to cross Congress or share the crowded lanes with cyclists. Austin was officially a bicycle-friendly town, but the memo had never gotten to motorists; you get in their way and they'll run you down like a vindictive mother-in-law. Add in the fact that they were probably hung over and late for work, and a cyclist cutting in front of them made for a volatile mix on a Monday morning. Consequently, any gutter bunny foolish enough to challenge automobile traffic on Congress Avenue during rush hour was well-advised to have his last will and testament up to date.

On the other hand, if Andy timed it perfectly, he could hit the intersection just as the north–south light changed from red to green and beat the cars heading south on Congress; he'd be leading the pack instead of merging into the pack. Of course, less-than-perfect timing and he'd broadside a southbound car, be ejected from the bike, and hurtle through the air until his body collided with a northbound car, resulting in death or serious bodily injury.

He hadn't had a shot of caffeine yet, so it seemed like a reasonable risk. Max, though, wasn't so sure; he was keeping pace from a safe distance on the sidewalk.

Andy steered to the far left of the road. He picked up speed fast now; he tapped the brakes to time the light.

Forty yards from the intersection, he had ten seconds.

Thirty yards and seven seconds.

Twenty yards and five seconds.

Ten yards and three seconds . . . two . . . one . . .

He hit Congress just as the north–south light turned green, leaned hard to the right, and swerved into the southbound lanes in a wide arc. Angry horns honked behind him, but Andy was a block out front before the SUVs cleared the intersection. He straightened his course, sat up, and tried to raise both arms into the air like Lance Armstrong crossing the finish line at the Tour de France – but he winced with pain. His right arm still wouldn't go past half-mast, so he settled for one raised fist.

'Yee-hah!'

He had won that morning, for what it was worth. He glided past the 1200 block of funky SoCo shops and the Austin Motel, a favorite stop of Julia Roberts, then skidded to a stop at Jo's Hot Coffee. He leaned the Huffy against the newspaper racks lined up along the curb and removed his helmet. He passed on the Texas papers and the *New York Times* and grabbed a free *Austin Chronicle*, the bible of SoCo. Just then one of the SUVers drove past, yelled 'Asshole!' and gave Andy the finger.

'Drink decaf!' Andy yelled back.

Okay, that was lame, but it was the best retort he could come up with before his morning coffee. Max barked to show his solidarity – or he wanted a muffin. Smart dog that he was, Max had stayed on the sidewalk all the way to Jo's.

'You want a muffin, big boy?'

Max bounced up and down and barked a *Yes! Yes, I do!*

A Great Dane the size of a small horse stood at the sidewalk tables next to its guardian – in dog-friendly Austin, you were not a 'dog owner'; you were a 'dog guardian.' The Dane gave Max a guttural growl. Max ducked behind Andy's legs.

They stepped to the back of the line that looped down the sidewalk. There was no walk-in lobby or drive-through lane at Jo's. It was a walk-up place, a small green structure stationed curbside on Congress in the parking lot of the hip Hotel San José. Jo's catered to those Austinites who loved good coffee but hated corporate conglomerates and so could not in good liberal conscience drink Starbucks. Jo's cost just as much, but Andy preferred the place because a) it was locally owned, b) the coffee was stronger than Starbucks, and c) you didn't have to say 'venti.' You could just say large.

Andy said, 'Large.'

'Like I don't know, three thousand straight days I've made your coffee.'

Guillermo Garza. Every morning since Andy had first moved into SoCo ten years before, he had stopped at Jo's and bought a large coffee and a muffin, two since his dad had transferred guardianship of Max to him.

'Banana nut muffin for me and a . . .'

Max was fixated on the muffins behind the low glass display; the intoxicating smell of the freshly baked muffins had him salivating only slightly more than Andy.

'Max, you want a banana nut or a blueberry?' Max barked. 'Blueberry?' Another bark. Back to Guillermo: 'Max is going for a blueberry this morning.'

Guillermo bagged the muffins and nodded at the Huffy.

'You steal a kid's bike?'

'Crashed the Schwinn.'

'You land on your face?'

'Several times.'

Guillermo pointed down the street.

'I saw that stunt you just pulled coming off Nellie. One of those SUVs hits you, dude, you're a piece of history . . . and Congress Avenue.'

Andy shrugged. 'Nothing like a little adrenaline rush to get your day going.'

'First step to recovery, Andy, is to admit you're a junkie.'

'Never denied it.'

'Brother, you got more guts than brains.' Guillermo Garza knew of what he spoke; he had an MA in political science. 'Any progress on the Slammer?'

Andy threw a thumb at the Huffy.

'You're looking at it.'

They fist-punched through the open window.

'Keep the faith, bro.'

Andy paid, grabbed the coffee and muffins, and walked over to the tree-shaded patio. Max slinked by the Great Dane as inconspicuously as possible. Andy sat at a table and placed Max's blueberry muffin and the coffee lid on the ground; he poured coffee into the lid. Max tasted the coffee and barked.

'It is good.'

Andy leaned back, took a long sip, and felt his body come alive when the caffeine hit his system; Jo's brew was double-strong. He bit into the muffin and glanced around at the other regulars.

'Keep Austin Weird' was the official slogan of the City of Austin. North of the river in downtown, it was just a marketing tool; but south of the river in SoCo it was a daily reality – and weird you would find at Jo's.

Young men and 'womyn' – you spell it 'women' in SoCo and they'll castrate you like a stray dog – were savoring a morning java at Jo's: Ray, tapping on his

61

laptop, a PhD in anthropology who was writing the Great American Novel when he wasn't driving a cab . . . Darla, Masters in psychology, with her tattoos and wild rainbow hair and Pippi Longstocking leggings and red high-topped retro sneakers; she dished out ice cream at Amy's across the street . . . Oscar, BA in art, grabbing a large Jo's before he started his shift at Güero's two blocks away . . . George, strumming his guitar and enjoying a latte before commencing his twelve-hour work day playing for tips on the curb . . . Dwight, typing his blog on his laptop, recording every thought that crossed his mind for all the world to enjoy; he averaged two hits per day . . . and an assortment of other tattooed-and-pierced oddballs.

SoCo was like a can of mixed nuts. Fortunately, the cashew of the neighborhood, Queen Leslie, wasn't present that morning. The sight of a middle-aged man in high heels, a black bra, and a pink thong first thing in the morning always made Andy nauseous. The Queen was a harmless homeless transvestite and a SoCo fixture. He was also a serial mayoral candidate; he once got three thousand votes despite campaigning in women's lingerie. His mere presence assured that SoCo would retain its perfect ten rating on the Weird-Shit-O-Meter-of-Life.

But weird was normal in the thirteen-block stretch of South Congress that constituted SoCo. The people, the shops, the music, the tattoos. Especially the tattoos. Getting a tattoo inked into your skin was a tribal ritual in SoCo, like Mayan Indians who scarred their bodies to declare their tribal identity. No tattoo and you were marked as an outlander in SoCo, a tourist, a pale-skinned spectator in this multicolored extravaganza called life. Andy Prescott was a member of the tribe. The tattoo on his upper arm was a steel-gray horse head, the American IronHorse motorcycle emblem. He had gotten stupid drunk one night and let Ramon ink it in.

And SoCo was about slacking off. Austin had always been a city of slackers; difference was, SoCo's slackers were credentialed, boasting BAs and MAs and JDs and PhDs from the University of Texas. But UT graduated ten thousand students every year, and none of them wanted to leave Austin. Consequently, the Austin job market was tighter than Queen Leslie's thong. So they drove cabs and waited tables and served coffee and wrote novels that would never be published.

And they all hung out at Jo's.

Andy stood, grabbed the *Chronicle*, and walked over to the pickup window. He paid again, and Guillermo handed him a small paper bag.

'Later, dude.'

He saddled up, folded the *Chronicle* lengthwise and tucked it inside his back waistband, put the helmet on, and whistled to Max. He steered and held the bag with his left hand and the coffee with his right hand. He rode up a gentle slope for two blocks past the San José with the tall agave plants lining the sidewalk and Güero's where Ronda was sweeping the front porch. He crossed over Elizabeth Street and pedaled down the sidewalk past Lucy in Disguise with Diamonds with its façade of faces from Jesus to the Beatles and Uncommon Objects with a metal sculpture of a cowboy riding a jackrabbit above the marquee.

Andy braked to a stop in front of a storefront at 1514 South Congress with BODY ART BY RAMON in neon script across the plate-glass window. The door was locked; Ramon didn't open until noon. Intoxication was a prerequisite to obtaining a tattoo; consequently, most of his clientele stumbled in between the hours of 10:00 P.M. and 2:00 A.M., closing time. Hence, Ramon Cabrera did not work mornings, except by appointment. Floyd T. was manning the stoop and writing in his Big Chief notebook.

'Morning, Floyd T.'

Andy got off the bike and removed the *Chronicle* from his waistband.

'Hello, Andy. How's the world treating you today?'

'A few too many Coronas last night.'

'I feel your pain.'

'You doing okay?'

Floyd T. shrugged. 'For a homeless person.'

Floyd T. was the 1500 block's resident homeless person. The business owners had adopted him. They watched out for him, they paid for his heart medicine, and once a week someone drove him over to the down-town homeless shelter for a shower. Andy hoped today would be that day because the August heat had ripened Floyd T. His hair was wild, his beard thick, and his eyes blue. He looked up at Andy over the red reading glasses he had recovered from a dumpster.

'You need a haircut, soldier.'

'You need a bath.'

Floyd T. frowned then sniffed himself.

'Has it been a week already?'

Andy handed him the paper bag. Floyd T. shut his notebook and tossed it into his grocery cart stationed next to him. He opened the bag and removed the coffee and muffin.

'Banana nut. My favorite. Thanks, Andy.'

Floyd T. – no one knew what the T stood for – was one of five thousand people who called the streets of Austin home. He was sixty-two years old and a Vietnam vet, like Andy's father. But while his father had come home intact, Floyd T. had come home without his left leg below the knee and addicted to heroin. He had been clean and sober for several years now, but his world did not extend beyond those few blocks of South Congress Avenue. He still wore his green Army jacket, ratty after forty years, and his Army boots.

Through a mouthful of muffin, Floyd T. said, 'You crashed again?'

'Yep.'

'You see a medic?'

'Just flesh wounds.'

Floyd T. pointed the muffin at the *Chronicle* in Andy's hand.

'Still looking for your one true love in the personals?'

'Or one night's love.'

'I had many of those nights, Andy, over in Nam. But I never had a woman lay with me for love. A man needs that. Love.' Floyd T. paused as if pondering his own words, then said, 'I gotta pee. If Ramon doesn't get here soon, I'll have to walk around back. Hand me my leg, will you?'

Andy reached into the grocery cart and grabbed Floyd T.'s artificial leg and foot encased in an old Army boot. He handed it to Floyd T., who secured it to his left knee.

'A whole man again.'

Andy put a $5 bill inside the cigar box in Floyd T.'s grocery cart, where he kept his Purple Heart and photos of his parents.

'Have a good day, Floyd T.'

Floyd T. gave him a little salute.

'You too, Andy.'

The next door over had a small window that was marked 1514½ South Congress. Painted in black script at the top of the window was 1514½-A VIOLIN STUDIO and painted in red script at the bottom was 1514½-B TRAFFIC TICKETS. Andy removed the helmet, unlocked the door, and entered. He did not teach the violin.

He was a lawyer.

Andy Prescott did not practice in state trial or appellate courts and certainly not in federal court. He did not represent major corporations making deals or rich people getting divorced or even personal injury plaintiffs suing over automobile accidents. He practiced in the municipal court of Austin, Texas. He represented irate drivers fighting traffic tickets issued by the Austin Police Department.

He oversaw his legal empire from a tiny office above the tattoo parlor. He sublet half of the upstairs from Ramon; the other half was sublet by the violin teacher. Fortunately, most of her students were advanced.

He leaned the bike against the wall just inside the door. Max bounded up the stairs. Andy followed and entered his office, which measured only ten feet by ten feet but had a nice view overlooking Congress Avenue. And he had a good landlord: Ramon charged him only $200 a month including utilities and allowed him use of the tattoo parlor's restroom and computer.

He propped open the window; the place had no air conditioning, but Andy enjoyed the sounds of SoCo. He sat in a swivel chair behind the folding card table that served as his desk. He had graduated four years before from UT law school with straight Cs, the same grades he had earned in college at UT. He had been admitted to the law school only because he was a faculty kid. But faculty kid status could not guarantee a job. Upon graduation, his classmates had gotten six-figure jobs with big law firms in Houston and Dallas or five-figure jobs with the state and federal government in Austin.

He had gotten a diploma.

Which was hanging on his wall. The University of Texas School of Law. Andrew Paul Prescott. Juris Doctor. Lawyer. He had somehow passed the bar on his third try; as his father always said, 'Even a blind squirrel finds an acorn now and then.'

So far this year, Andy had earned just over $13,000. George the guitar man was in a higher tax bracket than Andy. His clients paid him in cash, but Andy reported every penny of his income and paid his taxes, which was only the 15.9 percent social security tax. But this was a major bite out of his disposable income, especially since he didn't expect to live long enough to collect social security; not with his trail biking practices.

He drank his coffee then opened the *Chronicle* and turned to the personals. Women seeking men. Men seeking women. Women seeking women. Men seeking men. A million people in Austin, all hoping to love and to be loved; one half-million looking for the other half-million. Young people, old people, lonely people. People without someone to wake up to, go home to, or belong to.

Like Andy.

Sure, he had had a few dates along the way, but nothing that would qualify as a relationship under any definition of the word. Floyd T. was right: men needed love. But Natalie was also right: women wanted men with ambition. Someone who could give them the life they dreamed of. Andy could not. He couldn't even give Max the life he dreamed of. But he had good buddies and a good dog. He had both his parents, at least for now. He had his trail biking, if not a trail bike. And he had his work.

Such as it was.

But traffic court supported his passion and his dream: trail biking and a Slammer. He looked up at the American IronHorse motorcycle poster tacked to the wall. He could feel the massive engine pulsating beneath him and the wind on his face as he took that monster ride out west on 290 and opened the throttle and let the big dog run, leaning into the lazy curves as he climbed the escarpment, the machine just eating up the highway. Now that would be the mother of all adrenaline rushes, that would be the life . . .

'An-dy, you're gonna be late.'

Floyd T.'s voice from outside. Andy checked his watch: 8:56. Traffic court convened at nine sharp. Damn, daydreaming again. He jumped up, stuffed that day's tickets into his backpack, then grabbed the old blue sports coat hanging on a nail and put it on. He strapped on the helmet, inserted the sunglasses, and exited the office. He hurried down the stairs, grabbed the bike, and went outside. Max followed.

'Judge won't like you being late,' Floyd T. said.

Max ran alongside Andy as he rode back down the sidewalk. When they approached Güero's, Max bolted ahead and bounded up onto the front porch where Oscar was smoking a cigarette.

'Oh, what? You'd rather eat a burrito than come to court with me?'

Max barked back.

'Some loyalty. What about man's best friend?'

'I'll watch him,' Oscar said. He pointed his cigarette at the Huffy. 'You steal a kid's bike?'

'Long story. When you get tired of Max, send him down to Ramon. And no bean burritos, they give him gas.'

Andy pedaled fast toward downtown.

Chapter 4

Andy was late for traffic court. So he pedaled like a maniac north on Congress Avenue, raced through a red light at the Riverside intersection, and stood on the pedals to power up the incline leading to the bridge across the Colorado River.

Sailboats and kayaks and the UT women's rowing team on shells glided across the surface of the green water that flowed west to east through Austin. In town, the river was called Lady Bird Lake; it had been renamed in honor of Lady Bird Johnson after she died, an honor bestowed by the same people who had protested the Vietnam War back in the sixties when they were students at UT and taunted her husband, President Lyndon Baines Johnson, with chants of 'Hey, hey, LBJ, how many kids did you kill today?' whenever he had dared show his face in Austin. Andy's mother had been one of the protestors.

Today, the river divided Austin as distinctly as the war had America back then.

Andy crossed César Chávez Street that ran along the

northern boundary of the river and entered the darkness that was downtown Austin: not a figurative darkness of rich developers and shady politicians and their crafty lawyers making backroom deals that lined their pockets and screwed the citizens – well, it was all that, too – but downtown was literally a dark place. The skyscrapers, hotels, and condo towers that lined Congress Avenue created a canyon at street level and blocked out the sun as effectively as a solar eclipse; except for the one hour each day when the sun was directly overhead, downtown Austin was plunged into shadows. Only the pink granite state capitol that stood on a low rise ten blocks due north where Congress dead-ended at Eleventh Street was free of shadows; basking in the morning sun, the capitol dome looked like the light at the end of a tunnel.

For some reason, that sight always gave Andy hope.

A construction site had traffic backed up at Second Street, so Andy bunny-hopped the curb and rode on the sidewalk. He weaved around office workers wearing suits and dresses, poor people waiting for buses, vagrants packing their possessions on their backs, and drunks sleeping it off on benches. He dodged a pedicab and an eastbound bus and ran the red light.

Once across Second, he bounced back down to the street to avoid a group of slow-moving tourists on the sidewalk. He stood on the pedals again and swerved in and out of northbound traffic. Angry drivers honked their horns; they were inching forward in their luxury automobiles while he blew past them on the little red bike. The exhaust fumes were so thick he could taste the global warming. A siren wailed somewhere. He came upon another traffic jam at Fourth Street. He again hopped the curb and hammered the sidewalk – 'Coming through! Coming through!' – past the Frost Bank Tower that looked like something out of Spielberg's *Minority Report*. He carved the corner at the Mexic-Arte Museum and turned east on Fifth.

He checked his watch: 9:12.

His left knee burned with pain, but he stood on the pedals again and blew through the intersections at Brazos, San Jacinto, and Trinity – the north–south streets on either side of Congress were named after Texas rivers – then veered north on Neches past Lovejoys on the left and Coyote Ugly on the corner of Sixth. He swung east on Seventh and rode through a gauntlet of homeless people sitting on the curb near the shelter waiting for breakfast and around a green Dillo bus depositing passengers. He crossed Red River and Sabine then cut across the street and skidded to a stop at the entrance to the Municipal Court Building sitting in the shadow of the elevated southbound lanes of the interstate.

Andy locked the Huffy to a bike stand; he didn't want to return only to find some homeless dude joyriding around downtown on Tres' bike. It would be a long walk back. He hurried inside, digging around in the backpack until he found the red tie; he clipped it onto his shirt collar. He stuffed the helmet into the backpack then ran his fingers through his long hair.

He was ready for court.

Judge Judith 'Don't Call Me Judge Judy' Jackson gave Andy a stern look over her reading glasses as soon as he stepped inside Municipal Courtroom 3.

He was sweating. He had run into the building, emptied his pockets for Arturo at the security checkpoint – 'Judge ain't gonna be happy, Andy' – evaded the violators in the lobby waiting to pay their fines – 'Now serving number two-fifty-four' – and jumped into an open elevator. He had gotten off on the third floor and checked that day's docket posted on the wall outside the courtroom only to learn that two of his cases had been set for nine.

Andy slid into a pew.

A few cops in blue uniforms and two dozen citizens dressed like they were at a pro wrestling match occupied the spectator section. The courtroom was a small space, not like the district courtrooms in which felonies were tried over at the Travis County Courthouse. Here there were no grand staircases with polished wood rails, no fancy wainscoting lining the corridors, no portraits of revered old judges on the walls. There was a clock that read 9:24. This was cheap, no-frills justice dispensed in a courtroom built by the lowest bidder.

This was Muny Court.

It was a few minutes before his breathing returned to normal and Andy noticed the bare legs next to him; tanned and muscular, they emerged from a denim miniskirt hiked up high. Andy snuck a peek at their owner; she was young, blonde, and beautiful. He knew he was staring, so he broke away, but he couldn't resist going back for a second look. This time he ran his eyes up her legs and over the miniskirt, which ended below her navel, exposing a good six inches of tight torso before a black tank top took over. It was skin-tight and low cut, revealing a significant amount of soft cleavage.

Andy inhaled sharply.

Her perfume was more intoxicating than a Corona six-pack. Her lips and long fingernails were painted a shimmering red that made them look wet and inviting, like the springs on a hot summer day. He wanted desperately to dive into her lips, to immerse himself in their wetness, to feel their softness against his, to . . . he noticed her fingers kneading a traffic ticket like she was making dough – which snapped Andy's mind back to the fact that he was a traffic ticket lawyer who needed dough.

Dude, you zoned out.

Andy dug into his backpack and found a business card. He held it out to the young woman. She took the card and stared at it; then she stared at him – the old coat, the clip-on tie, the wrinkled shirt, the jeans, the sneakers – and said, 'You're a lawyer?'

'Yep.'

'My dad's lawyer doesn't wear jeans and sneakers.'

'Dallas or Houston?'

'Dallas.'

'This is Austin.'

'What happened to your face?'

'Trail biking accident.'

'My dad's lawyer—'

'Doesn't ride a trail bike.'

'He drives a Mercedes.'

'Figures.'

'You do traffic tickets?'

'My specialty.' He stuck out his right hand. 'Andy Prescott.'

She took his hand and said, 'Britney Banks.'

Her hand was soft; she gently pulled it away.

'UT?'

She nodded. 'Sophomore.'

'Speeding ticket?'

Another nod. 'In a school zone.'

'Ouch.'

'My fifth ticket. My dad'll go apeshit 'cause they'll raise my insurance premiums . . . again. He said one more ticket, and he'd take the car back. It's a Z.'

'Coupe?'

'Roadster. Graduation present.'

'You're only a sophomore.'

'High school graduation.'

Her proud parents had given her a $40,000 Nissan

Z Roadster convertible for getting through high school; she wanted desperately to keep her fine ride. Which presented Andy with an ethical dilemma: he could represent Britney Banks *pro bono*, get her ticket dismissed, and possibly snag a date with her; or, he could charge his standard fee – $100 – and be that much closer to a replacement trail bike. On the one hand, she would be the most beautiful girl he had ever dated, hands down; on the other hand, he could not bear the thought of being on the trail-biking sideline for long – by Sunday, he'd be suffering withdrawal. He pondered the possibilities for a moment. What were the odds that she would actually go out with him, considering that a) she drove a Z, and he rode a Huffy; b) she was probably a regular at the trendy lounges downtown, and he wasn't allowed past the red velvet ropes; and c) she had a rich daddy, and he would be a poor date? He sighed then doubled his fee. Her daddy could afford it.

'For two hundred cash, I'll get your ticket dismissed.'

She turned that stunning face his way.

'You can do that?'

'Yep.'

'And what if you don't?'

'No charge.'

She smiled. 'Okay.'

'When did you get the ticket?'

'Spring semester. I couldn't let my dad find out, so I called the number on the ticket and asked if they could postpone the hearing until this semester. The cop had gone on maternity leave, so they said okay.'

'Would you recognize the cop who gave you the ticket?'

'Sure.'

'You see him here?'

'Her . . . maternity leave. And no. So what do I do now?'

Andy held out his right hand again. She took it with her left hand, and smiled at him as if they were sweethearts holding hands. Okay, Britney probably wasn't on the Dean's List.

'No. Pay me the two hundred.'

'Oh.'

She removed her hand and pulled her wallet out of her purse; it was thick with green bills. She gave him two brand new $100 bills sharp enough to slice a brisket. He stuffed the bills into his jeans. He was now two hundred dollars closer to a replacement trail bike.

But her legs were incredible.

Britney Banks had stumbled onto the secret behind a successful traffic ticket defense in much the same way Andy Prescott had: by necessity. Back during his first year of law school, he had gotten a speeding ticket driving Tres' Beemer. Much like Britney's father, Tres also would have gone apeshit if he had found out, and Andy had had no money to pay the fine. So he had studied the Rules of the Municipal Court of the City of Austin. Then he had requested a trial and was informed that there would be a minimum one-year delay due to the heavy backlog of cases; a trial by jury would be a two-year delay. He immediately requested a jury trial. When his case finally came to trial in his third year of law school, Andy went to court prepared to lose; but the cop didn't show. Without the cop's testimony to prove up the ticket, the prosecution failed. His ticket was dismissed.

And his career was born.

Now, for $100 cash, Andy guaranteed his clients a dismissal of their tickets; if he failed, he would pay the fines. In every case, he requested a trial by jury; he asked for continuances; he delayed the trial date for as long as possible. Two years later, when the trial date arrived, the cop always failed to show, for any number of reasons: he had died, retired, or quit the force; he was ill that day; he was working overtime on real crime; or he had just forgotten. No cop, no testimony, no conviction, no fine, no ticket on his client's record, no increased insurance premium. Case dismissed. Andy had handled over six hundred traffic tickets. Not once had the cop shown up. Not once had he paid a client's fine. All for $100. It wasn't much money, but it was easy money.

'City of Austin versus Doris Sullivan.'

Andy's first case. He leaned toward Britney.

'Wait here till your case is called.'

He stood and walked up to the bench. He winked at the municipal prosecutor, Denise L. (for luscious)

Manning; she was two years out of UT law school, pretty, and held the promise of passionate love-making. She ignored Andy. The judge did not.

'Mr Prescott, you're late again.'

'I must say, Your Honor, you're looking quite lovely this morning.'

'Save the flattery, Mr Prescott. It doesn't work with me.'

But her lips formed a slight smile, as if she just couldn't help herself. Judge Judith was mid-fifties, black, and tough as nails. But she had a soft spot for the losers of the world who appeared before her daily, including Andy. She put her hand over the microphone in front of her.

'Trail biking again, Andy?'

'Yes, ma'am.'

'Are you okay?'

'Concussion and possible brain damage, but nothing serious.'

A bigger smile.

'Anytime you're ready, Judge, I'll show you the trails.'

'Not in this life, Andy.' Back to the microphone. 'Mr Prescott, is your client present?'

Andy looked out on the sea of faces as if his client would stand and come forward. Of course, she wouldn't. She wasn't there. None of his clients were there. He never asked his clients to attend their trials or even told them the trial date. It was a waste of time. If the cop didn't show, the city could not make its case and the ticket would be dismissed; the defendant's testimony would not be required. If the cop did show, Andy would have to make good on his guarantee.

'Judge, perhaps Ms Manning should go forward with her prosecution.'

The judge turned to the city prosecutor.

'Ms Manning?'

Ms Manning shrugged her narrow little shoulders.

'My witness isn't here.'

'Case dismissed.'

They followed the same script for Andy's first four cases. His fifth case was called – 'City of Austin versus Donna Faulkner' – and someone changed the script without notifying him.

'Your Honor,' the prosecutor said, 'the issuing officer is present.'

Andy faced Ms Manning. 'The cop showed?'

She was grinning. 'Can you believe it?'

No, he couldn't believe it. Andy turned to the spectator section. A bald paunchy guy in a blue Austin PD uniform stood and walked up to them.

Andy said, 'You showed up?'

The cop gave Andy a warm police officer smile.

'I always show up. I just sit here and read all day.' He held up a book: *Harry Potter and the Order of the Phoenix*. 'Easy money.'

Easy money. Andy wanted to say, 'I'll show you easy money,' and whack the cop upside the head with the book, but given it was a Harry Potter, the sheer weight of the thing would probably kill him.

The judge administered the oath to Officer Bobby Joe Jack, then Ms Manning elicited his testimony that he had issued a ticket to Donna Faulkner two years before for driving sixty through a residential zone with a maximum allowed speed of thirty miles per hour and for running a stop sign. The applicable fine was $501.

Andy was sweating bullets now and not just because he had never before cross-examined a witness. He was sweating because his net cash assets totaled $27, two hundred dollars more if he won Britney's case. He did not have $501. He could not fulfill his guarantee to Donna Faulkner. He could not lose her case.

'Your witness, Mr Prescott.'

Judge Judith gave Andy a sympathetic expression. She was feeling his pain. But Andy Prescott wasn't going to pay out money he didn't have without a fight.

'Officer Bobby Joe Jack . . . you do realize you have three first names?'

'What?'

'Do you remember issuing this ticket?'

'I sure do.'

'How many tickets have you issued in the last two years?'

'Hundreds.'

'Two years and hundreds of tickets later, but you specifically recall issuing this ticket to Ms Faulkner?'

'Yes, I do.'

'And why is that?'

'Because of certain unique identifying characteristics.'

'Which were?'

'Her headlights.'

'Her *headlights*? Why would you remember her headlights?'

'Because they were really special.'

'Special headlights? Were they Bi-Xenon?'

'What?'

'Officer Jack, I don't understand your testimony. You were driving behind Ms Faulkner when you pulled her over, correct?'

'Yes.'

'Then you got out of your cruiser and walked to the driver's side window, correct?'

'Yes.'

'So when did you see her headlights?'

'When she rolled her window down.'

'But how could you see her headlights from that vantage point?'

'I was looking right down at them.'

'You were looking right down at them . . . ?'

Officer Bobby Joe Jack grinned. Andy shook his head.

'I see,' Andy said. 'And by headlights, you're referring to Ms Faulkner's breasts, is that correct?'

'She was wearing a very low-cut shirt.'

'Did you look at her face?'

'Sure.'

'How old was she?'

Officer Jack consulted his citation.

'License said twenty-two.'

'What color was her hair?'

'License said brown.'

'What do you say?'

'Must've been brown.'

'Officer Jack, how often are driver's licenses in Texas re-issued?'

'Every six years.'

'Are you married?'

'Yes.'

'Does your wife color her hair?'

'All the time.'

'More often than once every six years?'

'Seems like every other week.'

'So Ms Faulkner might have had brown hair when you issued the ticket but blonde hair today?'

Officer Jack shrugged. 'Sure.'

Andy addressed the judge. 'Your Honor, may my client come forward now?'

Judge Judith nodded. Andy turned to the spectator pews and motioned to Britney Banks, the UT student, to come forward. She glanced around as if he had meant someone else, then stood and walked forward. She was frowning.

'Please stand in front of the witness,' Andy said. To

84

the witness he said, 'Officer Jack, this is my client.' Which wasn't a lie; she was his client, just not his client on this ticket. 'Do you remember issuing that ticket to this woman?'

Officer Bobby Joe Jack's eyes locked onto Britney Banks' breasts like a hungry infant.

'Yep, that's them. No question about it.'

'Officer Jack, you're making a positive identification that you gave this ticket to my client based upon her headli— . . . her breasts?'

'Can I do that?'

'Officer Jack, you're sure this is the woman you gave the ticket to?'

He again addressed her breasts.

'Absolutely positive.'

Andy turned to Judge Judith. 'Your Honor, this woman is my client, but not on this ticket. Her name is Britney Banks, not Donna Faulkner.' To Officer Jack: 'Sorry, but you've identified the wrong set of headlights.'

'You sure?'

Judge Judith had had enough. 'Case dismissed.'

Officer Jack stared at Britney's breasts as he walked past her. She gave him a dirty look. Fortunately, Officer Bobby Joe Jack wasn't in SoCo; stare at a womyn's breasts in SoCo and she'll drive her knee into your nuts so hard you'll be able to hit higher notes than Celine Dion.

Since Britney was already standing there, Judge Judith called her case next. Her cop didn't show. The judge dismissed her ticket. She put her hand over the microphone.

'See you next Monday, Andy. Try to be on time. And get a haircut, okay?'

Cut his hair and risk death or serious bodily injury on the trails? Not a chance.

'Yes, ma'am.'

Britney said thanks, took a handful of his business cards for her sorority sisters, and bopped out of the courtroom. Her Z was safe for now. Andy passed out cards to the waiting defendants on his way out of the courtroom. It wasn't exactly mergers and acquisitions, but it paid the bills. Almost.

Five clients would be very happy when Andy told them their tickets had been dismissed. He pulled out his cell phone and dialed the number for Doris Sullivan.

Ten blocks due north, in the offices of the Russell and Kathryn Reeves Foundation on the top floor of the Reeves Research Institute located on the University of Texas campus, Doris Sullivan was sitting behind her desk when her cell phone rang. She pulled her purse from a lower drawer and fished the phone out.

'Hello.'

The voice on the phone: 'Is this Doris Sullivan?'

'Yes.'

'Ms Sullivan, this is Andy Prescott.'

'Who?'

'Andy Prescott, your lawyer.'

'My *lawyer*?'

'The traffic ticket on South Congress? Two years ago?'

'Oh, yes, I remember now.'

Two years before, an Austin cop had stopped Doris for speeding down the 1500 block of South Congress Avenue; she had pulled into one of the angled parking spaces along Congress. The cop gave her a ticket for driving fifty in a thirty-five zone, a $240 fine. She had unwisely asked why he was wasting his time on speeders instead of dealing with the real criminals in Austin; he had added a reckless driving citation, an additional $200 fine. If she had told the cop who she worked for, he would have torn up the ticket and apologized. But her boss wouldn't have approved of her using his name to pull strings. So she had sat silent while the cop wrote the ticket.

When the cop drove away, she had stewed in her car; her insurance premiums would double. When her anger had subsided, she noticed the sign on the door directly in front of her: TRAFFIC TICKETS. She climbed the stairs to the little office and hired Andy Prescott, Attorney-at-Law. She paid him $100 cash, and he gave her a guarantee: her ticket would be dismissed or he would pay the fine.

'The ticket was dismissed this morning.'

'So it won't be on my record?'

'No, ma'am.'

'My premiums won't go up?'

87

'Not from this ticket.'

'Well, thank you, Andy.'

'You're welcome.'

She hung up, dropped the phone into her purse, and shut the drawer. She was smiling when she turned and saw Russell Reeves standing there with another armload of medical journals.

'Your lawyer? Is something wrong, Doris?'

'Oh, no, Mr Reeves. Just a traffic ticket.'

She tried not to laugh as she recounted the story, including SoCo's version of Clarence Darrow.

'He was wearing jeans and sneakers and a clip-on tie, said he was headed to traffic court – on a bicycle. His office, it's no bigger than a closet and it's above a tattoo parlor – tattoos and tickets. His desk was a card table. He had a motorcycle poster on the wall next to his diploma. I'm pretty sure he didn't graduate at the top of his class.' She shook her head. 'But he got the ticket dismissed.'

Mr Reeves now had an odd expression on his face, as if he had just experienced another epiphany.

'A traffic ticket lawyer in SoCo?'

'Yes, sir.'

'He offices above a tattoo parlor?'

'Yes, sir.'

'His name is Andy Prescott?'

'Yes, sir.'

Mr Reeves' eyes drifted off her, and he said, 'He's perfect.'

He walked toward his office but abruptly turned back.

'Call Darrell. Tell him to have the car out front in ten minutes.'

Doris Sullivan picked up the phone but thought, Perfect for *what*?

Chapter 5

Andy was in no hurry to get back to the office. He never had appointments; his clients just dropped in (usually right after having been ticketed) or left their tickets and $100 bills with Ramon. And Britney's $200 was burning a hole in his pocket. So he had decided to eat lunch at Whole Foods, check out the bikes at REI, and then pay a visit to his mother.

He turned the Huffy west on Sixth Street at the Texas Lottery Headquarters – gambling was illegal in Texas unless the profits went to the state – and gave a wide berth to a mentally ill man wandering aimlessly and obviously talking to God because no one else was listening. A block down, he waved at a pretty young woman in a blue dress pedaling a bike. The breeze blew her dress up to her thighs; she had nice thighs.

Live-music clubs, shot bars, pubs, and lounges lined both sides of Sixth Street from the interstate to Congress Avenue – places like Bourbon Rocks, Blind Pig, Agave, Pure, and Peckerheads – and had earned Austin top ranking as the hardest drinking city in America. The street sat silent and seedy-looking that morning, but nights had become notoriously raucous with punks, panhandlers, and binge-drinking college kids puking on the sidewalks. *God, those were the days.* Sixth Street had seemed sane back when Andy was one of those UT students; at twenty-nine, it seemed insane. At his age, he just wanted to drink Coronas at Güero's.

He was getting old.

He rode past the five-star Driskill Hotel and stood on the pedals across Congress Avenue, hoping not to get nailed by a speeder running a red light. Once on the other side, Andy breathed a sigh of relief. Sixth Street sloped down from there, so he coasted through the intersections at Colorado, Lavaca, Guadalupe, San Antonio, Nueces, and Rio Grande – more Texas rivers. Beads of sweat were rolling down his body by the time he turned into the parking lot at the Whole Foods eighty-thousand-square-foot flagship store and corporate headquarters, which occupied an entire city block at Lamar Boulevard.

Whole Foods gave the slackers of Austin hope: if a twenty-five-year-old college dropout and his twenty-one-year-old girlfriend could open a small organic grocery store in 1978 and build it into an international organic food conglomerate with three hundred stores and $7 billion in revenues in thirty years, couldn't Andy Prescott be successful enough one day to rent a decent place in SoCo and own a top-of-the-line trail bike? Okay, just the bike then.

Was that asking too much from life?

Andy parked the Huffy at the Bicycle Pit-Stop, stuffed his coat and tie into the backpack, and hung the pack on the handlebars. He entered the food court through sliding glass doors and proceeded directly to the breakfast taco counter. He ordered his usual from Team Member Brad (a fifteen-year member sporting a white chef's coat, a green Whole Foods cap, clear sterile gloves, and a $500,000 net worth from his stock options): scrambled eggs, bacon, cheese, and refried beans on wheat tortillas with enough salsa to clear out his sinuses.

'*Dos.*'

'You need one for Max?'

'He's lunching at Güero's today.'

And by now napping on Güero's front porch. Andy took the tacos from Team Member Brad, stepped past the Gelato counter to the day2day juice bar, and ordered a Jumping Grasshopper smoothie from Team Member Charlene: wheatgrass, lemon, lime, apple juice, pine-apple, banana, and fat-free plain yogurt, his personal added ingredient. Breakfast tacos and a smoothie: his version of a power lunch for under $10. He returned to the Gelato bar and sat on a stool with his back to the counter.

Whole Foods had been created as an alternative to the corporate grocery stores of America; the original name was 'Safer Way' and back then the little store had catered to the hippies of Austin, like Andy's mother, who wanted whole, organic, non-corporate food. Fast forward thirty years and Whole Foods was now much more than an alternative grocery store for hippies. It was an alternative lifestyle. A way of life.

And its customers lived the life.

They were young and fit, hip and organic, green and liberal, educated and employed. But mostly fit. Men and women, but Andy didn't come for the men. He came for the women. Young, incredibly fit women. Lean and toned, muscular and tanned, the hard female bodies of Austin worked out at gyms and hung out at Whole Foods, their awesome anatomies tightly encased in segmented polyurethane, a magnificent long-chain synthetic polymer fiber known around the world as Spandex or Elastane. Tube tops, tank tops, short-shorts, leggings – *God, the Spandex*. These girls did not put personal ads in the *Chronicle*. They came to Whole Foods.

Whole Foods girls were the finest and fittest females in Austin, Texas.

Looking at the girls now, Andy Prescott was moved again to offer a silent thanks to Joseph C. Shivers, the DuPont scientist who had invented Spandex in 1959. He had dedicated an entire decade of his life for the betterment of mankind. Or at least man.

Andy finished off one taco, sucked down half the smoothie, and then dove into the second taco. He loved to sit right there in the food court and girl watch, but there was one distinct downside: spotting a law school classmate who had done better. Which is to say, any law school classmate. Like Richard Olson. Rich. Which he was. Pale-skinned and soft-bodied, he looked like the tax lawyer he was. Rich was talking to two girls, who were hanging on his every word and sidling close like cats rubbing against his leg – *two* Whole Foods girls flirting with Rich Olson, the bastard. Andy shook his head.

What does he have that I don't?

But Andy knew the answer to his own question: an income. Rich had graduated at the top of their class. Four years with the biggest firm in Austin and the guy's making $250,000, driving a Porsche, living in a downtown loft, and dating beautiful girls.

Andy sucked hard on the smoothie straw and felt the heat of jealousy building inside him when a lovely vision passed a few feet in front of him. She was blonde, lean, and fit. She was wearing Spandex, but not much. She was twenty-five years old. She was Suzie.

'Hi, Suzie.'

She stopped, spun around, and assumed a perfect pose . . . until she saw it was just him. The pose evaporated like spit on the hot sidewalk.

'Oh. Hi, Andy.'

Suzie was the kind of girl whose engine was always idling, just waiting to be shifted into gear by a stud. Which is to say, not by Andy. He had never come close to touching her gearbox, but he never quit reaching for the stick shift. He said, 'I'm free tonight.'

'I'm not. Free. I'm a very expensive date.'

'Jeez, Suzie, you sound like a Dallas girl.'

'Andy, Austin girls are no less superficial than Dallas girls. We're just in better shape.'

Suzie was in extremely good shape. She was awesome. She looked like an airbrushed model in a magazine, but without the flaws. She was a top-of-the-line Whole Foods girl. She was digging in her waist pack. She was pulling out a familiar-looking piece of paper. She was holding it out to Andy.

'Andy, I got a speeding ticket. Fourth one this year. Can you take care of this for me?'

'Sure . . . for a hundred bucks. I'm not free either.'

Suzie snatched the ticket out of his hand and stormed off. He still had his pride. Well, sort of.

Andy rode the Huffy north across Sixth Street to a large L-shaped building on the corner that housed Anthropologie, a women's clothing store, BookPeople, an independent bookstore that had achieved cult status in Austin, and Recreational Equipment Inc. He wasn't there for the blouses or the books; he was there for the bikes. He parked and went inside REI.

He stopped just inside the door and gazed around like a kid in a candy store. REI housed all of Andy's dreams, except Suzie. And the Slammer. Every manner of extreme sports gear stood on the floor or sat on the shelves or hung from the ceiling or on the walls – for running, hiking, climbing, skiing, snowboarding, canoeing, kayaking, and biking. REI didn't sell sporting goods. It enabled outdoor adventure.

Andy was admiring the new mountain bikes hanging from the ceiling just out of his reach when he heard a familiar voice.

'Dude, you get the number?'

Wayne. In his green REI employee vest.

'What number?'

'The number of the train that hit you.'

Wayne laughed. He was funny like that.

'Seeing your face and that Huffy you rode up on – you steal that from a kid? – I'm gonna take a wild guess and say you crashed another bike.'

'Yep.'

'Three months, that's gotta be some kind of record. What happened this time?'

Andy gave Wayne a brief recap of the old ladies and his ride down the ravine. By the time he had finished, Wayne was shaking his head.

'Dude, you're pushing that Samson theory.'

Wayne was the bike man at REI. He repaired bikes in the bike shop and sold bikes on the floor. He had sold Andy every one of his bikes; this one would make six. Or was it seven?

'Don't ever cut that hair.' Wayne slapped Andy on the shoulder. 'Come on, let's see what trade-ins I've got.'

They walked under the new bikes that Andy coveted even more than Suzie – the Novara Method 2.0 . . .

the Marin Rift Zone XC Quad . . . the Cannondale Prophet . . . the Stumpjumper – top-of-the-line trail bikes that he had about as much chance of riding as he did Suzie.

'Andy,' Wayne said, 'I wish you were rich. You buy more bikes each year than my Dellionaires!' 'Dellionaires' were employees of Dell Computer – founded in Austin by Michael Dell, a college drop-out – who had become millionaires off their company stock. Their spending habits were legendary in Austin. 'Difference is, you buy cheap bikes. Speaking of which, check this one out. She's another Schwinn hardtail, but your butt's used to that. I was gonna upgrade some of the components, sell it for four-fifty, but I'll let you have it for four.'

'With the upgrades?'

Andy had already saddled up. Damn, this seat was a little hard on the boys.

'Sure. You get her dialed in, she'll be a sweet enough ride, at least for the few months till you crash her. I'll add it to what you owe. That'll be six-fifty.'

'Fifty a month like now?'

'Can you pay a hundred?'

'How about seventy-five and . . .'

Andy dug out the two $100 bills and held them out.

'Two hundred down.'

'What, you hit the lottery?'

'I got lucky all right, but at traffic court.'

Wayne took the bills but said, 'You still gonna be able to eat?'

97

'I'd rather ride than eat.'

'You got that right, brother.'

They fist-punched.

'You can pick up the bike tomorrow.' Wayne pointed a thumb at the front door. 'But park that Huffy over at BookPeople.'

In 1839, the Republic of Texas authorized the creation of a state university in Austin and endowed it with 231,400 acres of barren, worthless land in West Texas. Thirty-seven years passed − statehood, the Mexican–American War, secession, the Civil War − and still the university did not exist.

In 1876, the State of Texas ratified a new constitution which mandated the establishment of a 'university of the first class' and added another million acres of barren, worthless West Texas land to the endowment.

In 1883, the University of Texas opened with eight professors teaching 221 students in one building on forty acres north of downtown known as College Hill. Texas politicians were so darn proud of their new school that they added another million acres of West Texas land to the endowment for a total of 2,231,400 acres − all barren and worthless. That land generated total income of less than two cents per acre in 1900.

The University of Texas was poor.

And so it might be today had two wildcatters named Frank Pickrell and Carl Cromwell not drilled an oil well on that West Texas land in 1923, which they named the Santa Rita No. 1. They hit pay dirt: the great Permian Basin oil field lay directly under the university's land. Billions of barrels of black gold. That barren land was no longer worthless.

The University of Texas was rich.

Today, the original Santa Rita No. 1 pump jack sits on the UT campus as a monument to the oil that built the school, oil revenues have generated a $15 billion endowment, and 2,700 professors teach 50,000 students in 130 buildings sprawled across 350 acres of land located north of the state capitol.

The University of Texas is filthy rich.

Andy had ridden the Huffy north on the Drag, the stretch of Guadalupe Street that bordered the campus on the west and that had once been a cool strip with the Nighthawk Diner and the Varsity Theater and subversive bookstores and protesters railing against the government on street corners. Today, the Drag was just another string of expensive stores catering to rich students.

Andy entered the campus at the West Mall, the free speech zone where student activists pushed their political agendas between classes. He rode past long-legged girls in short-shorts (wow), oversized athletes acting as if they owned the place (they did), and tenured leftist professors (who made the Harvard faculty look like a Republican caucus) strolling with the confidence of knowing they could never be fired by the school's conservative alumni. He looked up at the three-hundred-foot-tall UT clock tower rising in front of him; in 1966 a deranged shooter had gone up to the observation deck with a high-powered rifle and killed thirteen people below.

Andy's mother had been on campus that day.

New buildings were going up everywhere, as if the goal were to pave over every square inch of green space on campus; of course, the only green that mattered at UT was the kind printed by the US Treasury. Hence, the construction of more naming rights. For say, a $50 million donation, the university would name a building after you – 'naming rights' in the vernacular; and rich Texans were lining up to buy theirs. UT buildings were named after corporations and CEOs, doctors and lawyers, athletes and coaches, politicians and presidents. The crown jewel was the Lyndon B. Johnson School of Public Affairs, which Andy's mother always said made about as much sense as a Joseph Stalin School of Humanities.

Andy emerged onto San Jacinto Street in front of the Reeves Research Institute and rode past the massive Darrell K. Royal-Texas Memorial Stadium where 96,000 fans watch the Texas Longhorns play football, listen to the public announcers on the $9 million sound system, and view instant replays on the 'Godzillatron,' the $8 million high-definition video screen that measured 55 feet in height by 134 feet in width, the biggest HDTV screen in America.

How's that for bragging rights?

One hundred thirty-two years later, some might debate whether the State of Texas had fulfilled the constitutional mandate for a university of the first class, but anyone who dared argue that the university's football team was not first class would be met with a simple, irrefutable rebuttal: the Longhorns had won four national football championships.

Andy parked the bike outside the Fine Arts Building then went inside and found his mother's classroom; the door was propped open. He leaned against the wall outside and listened to his mother teach art history. All that he knew about art had been learned by listening in on her classes, a practice begun at birth. She had taken him to class with her every day until he had entered kindergarten; she said he had listened intently to her lectures. He liked to listen to her still and to watch her in moments like this, when she wasn't being his mother; when she was a human being engaged in her life's pursuit: Dr Jean Prescott, artist, PhD in art history, and tenured professor.

She was sixty-one and slim, pretty and passionate. Her hair was black with gray streaks. She wore a colorful skirt, a red shirt, sandals, and a smile. She was pretty even with her minimalist makeup, but back in her day she had been a beautiful flower child. She was passionate about art and about life, politics and education, immigration and global warming, war and football. She had protested every American war from Vietnam to Iraq and the presidents who had waged them; to this day, she remained proud of her extensive arrest record. Andy wished that he had known her back then – and that he possessed more of her passion for life. His passion was reserved for the bike. That was when he felt alive. The rest of the time, he felt as if he were just sleepwalking through life.

He waited for her class to end and the students to file out, then he stepped into the room.

'Andy.'

She came to him and embraced him as if she hadn't seen him in years instead of just a few days. Then she pulled back and examined his battered face as if checking for skin cancer.

'The bike?'

He nodded. 'I'm good.'

His mother had never once asked him to stop riding. She understood passion. She brushed his hair back.

'I like your hair long.'

She gathered her books and notes into her arms.

'Walk with me to my office.'

'I'll carry your stuff.'

She passed the load off to him, and they went upstairs. Students greeted her with a cheery 'Hi, Professor Prescott' along the way. Tenure had earned her a ten-by-twenty-foot office with a prime view of the football stadium, which at UT was along the lines of a prime view of Central Park. She could have swapped offices for a view of the tower, but the stadium stoked her fire each morning. Until Iraq, she hadn't had a war to protest for thirty years, so she had taken on football – which is to say, she had taken on not just the University of Texas, but the State of Texas. She held out a newspaper to him.

'Read that.'

Andy took the paper but didn't read it; he knew his mother would summarize the story for him. She did.

'Says that Texas universities spent over a billion dollars the last five years to build football stadiums.'

She pointed at the UT stadium looming large in the window. The new north end zone was under construction; the workers looked like ants scurrying about the two-hundred-foot-tall structure.

'That's another hundred and eighty million dollars for football, and the regents just authorized another thirty million. How much have they spent on our Taj Mahal? Five, six hundred million? For a dozen football games a year? That's obscene.'

'That's Texas, Mom.'

'And the governor wonders why Texas' brightest math and science students go to the Ivy League or California for college. It's simple: Texans invest in football, not math and science.'

'Mom, you ever meet a math major who could play strong safety?'

'What's a strong safety?'

'A football player.' His mother had a confused expression. 'I'm just pulling your chain, Mom.'

He had pulled her chain, but he hadn't slowed her down.

'A fifteen-billion-dollar endowment and we make middle-class kids pay twenty thousand dollars to attend a public university. But the athletic department has a hundred-and-twenty-five-million-dollar budget for five hundred athletes and the football coach makes three million a year.' She shook her head. 'The University of Texas isn't a university – it's a football team.'

His mother had protested war and fought football – she said the government was controlled by the military-industrial complex and the university by the athletic-alumni complex – since she had first arrived on campus as a freshman in 1966. She had never left the campus or quit the fight.

Andy had seen photos of her from 1970 when professors and students had chained themselves to thirty oak trees along Waller Creek to block their being bulldozed for the football stadium expansion. Frank Erwin, Jr, an LBJ crony and chairman of the Board of Regents at the time who had loved Longhorn football, driven a school colors orange-and-white Cadillac, and been dubbed the 'Emperor of UT' by *Time* magazine, called in the cops and had everyone arrested, including Jean Prescott. Then he bulldozed the trees and expanded the stadium. His mother had lost that fight and every fight since. But she had never tired of the fight, and she wasn't tiring now. So Andy changed the subject.

'How's Dad?'

She took a deep breath.

'He won't leave home. Won't even sing in church. At least he still tends his garden. You need to come out, Andy, he'd like the company. How about this weekend? I'll pick you up on the way home Friday, bring you back in Monday.'

Her face showed her hope that he'd say yes.

'I'll ride out Saturday morning.'

The bike would be faster than the twenty-year-old Volvo his mother drove.

'It's forty miles.'

'Piece of cake.'

'And ice cream.'

'I mean, the ride out and back.'

'I mean cake and ice cream. It's my birthday.'

'*Your birthday?* Mom, I'm sorry. I forgot.'

'But no presents, Andy, okay?'

She said the same thing every year.

'Saturday, then?'

'I'll be there.'

'Promise?'

He went over and kissed her on the cheek.

'Cross my heart.'

'Bring Max. Your father misses that dog.' She hugged him then said, 'Oh, tickets.'

She handed him two tickets; a $100 bill was clipped to each. The left-wing UT professors drove hybrids, but they drove them fast. They knew that Professor Prescott's kid could take care of their tickets; and

Professor Prescott acted as if she were not the least bit ashamed that her only son was a traffic ticket lawyer. What kind of woman was she?

'Do you need more money?'

'I'm good.'

He was very good. Four hundred bucks in one day – his all-time career record. He considered how he would spend that $200. He could a) pay next month's office rent, b) ask Suzie out, although a date with Suzie would run $500 minimum, or c) upgrade the replacement bike with a RockShox suspension and a gel saddle, which sounded particularly good. But Andy was just kidding himself. He knew all along that he would spend the $200 on d) a birthday present for his mother.

Chapter 6

Andy Prescott always had a thing for redheads.

He was staring at one now. She had long legs and a sensuous smile. Her lips were red and her skirt was short. Her red hair was a wig, but she was still incredibly sexy. For a mannequin.

'Need a date for the prom, Andy?'

Andy hadn't noticed Reggie standing there. They were at the display window out front of Lucy in Disguise with Diamonds. Reggie chuckled and entered the store. He was a real funny guy for a white dude wearing dreadlocks and black eyeliner.

Andy had arrived back in SoCo on the little Huffy, checked for Max at Güero's only to learn that Oscar had sent him down to Ramon's, and found Floyd T. pushing his grocery cart from dumpster to dumpster searching for treasures in other people's trash. His responsibilities satisfied, he had then begun his quest for the perfect birthday present for his mother.

He had first tried Tesoro's Trading Company and then Maya Star and was walking the bike past Lucy in

Disguise with Diamonds when the mannequin had caught his eye. He took one last look at her then continued down the sidewalk to Yard Dog. And there in the front window he spotted the perfect present for Jean Prescott: a white owl hand-carved from a small log. Yard art for her native Texas garden. She'd love it. He checked the price tag: $1,000.

He sighed and shook his head. He couldn't even afford a nice birthday present for his mother. Natalie was right: he needed ambition.

Andy walked down the street to Uncommon Objects. He searched the booths for a secondhand gift he could afford but found nothing special except an armadillo purse for $125 – a real armadillo made into a purse. It was cool but creepy. Jean Prescott was a different sort of woman all right, but maybe not that different.

He gave up and went into the tattoo parlor to collect Max and his mail. His email. He couldn't afford a computer or Internet service either, so Ramon let Andy use his computer and maintain an email address on his Yahoo account.

The parlor reeked of antiseptic. Fortunately for his clients – hepatitis C was a constant concern in a tattoo shop – Ramon Cabrera was a clean freak; he wiped the entire place down a dozen times a day. It was as clean as a hospital and had the same look: bottles of alcohol and green germicidal soap, sterile gloves and gauze, the autoclave, a hazardous waste disposal box for used needles, vials of colored ink . . . well, maybe not the ink.

Andy walked around the front counter and found Max snoozing in the corner so he headed over to Ramon's computer on the back desk – but he stopped dead in his tracks. Lying face down on Ramon's padded table was a blonde girl clothed only in a black T-shirt and thong; her shorts lay on a chair. Her bare bottom was smooth, round, and glowing in the light of the bright fluorescent bulbs overhead. No doubt she was a UT coed getting a tattoo to assert her independence from her parents – at least until she needed more money.

'Tickets on the counter,' Ramon said without looking up.

Ramon was sitting next to the girl and leaning over and peering through his little reading glasses only a few inches away from her smooth skin. *Jesus*. First Britney at traffic court, then Suzie at Whole Foods, and now a bare butt at Ramon's. The pressure of daily life in Austin was almost unbearable.

Andy grabbed the two tickets – each with a $100 bill attached – then stepped over for a closer look, careful not to breach Ramon's sterile field. Ramon wore a white muscle T-shirt and white latex gloves; he was inking in a 'Yellow Rose of Texas' tattoo on her left buttock, one of a matched set. The buttock, not the tattoo.

'Not polite to stare, dude,' Ramon said.

But he smiled when he said it. Ramon Cabrera was only six years older than Andy, but the hard life he had lived and the tattoos on his body had aged him.

Ramon had practiced what he preached: his entire upper body was a mobile mural commemorating Austin and Mexico, Latino culture and the Catholic religion, the Aztec sun god and the Tejano goddess Serena. It was beautiful and weird at the same time.

Ramon Cabrera was an artist with a tattoo needle.

The thing sounded like a dentist's drill, which made Andy's skin crawl. With his left hand Ramon stretched the skin on the girl's bottom tight and with his right hand he moved the needle from spot to spot on the stenciled outline of the yellow rose in rhythm with the Latino music playing in the background. The tattoo machine drove the needle into her skin – actually through the epidermis and into the dermis, the second layer of skin – puncturing her bottom hundreds of times per minute and depositing a drop of insoluble ink upon each insertion.

It hurt like hell.

But the girl had iPod buds stuck in her ears and her eyes closed, oblivious to the pain and the world around her . . . including Andy admiring her butt. After a long, wonderful moment, he broke eye contact and sat in front of Ramon's computer. He logged onto his email account and checked his messages. He shook his head.

'All I get is spam promising to make my penis longer.'

'Don't waste your money,' Ramon said. 'None of that stuff works.'

Andy logged onto the *Chronicle*'s website and clicked 'Classifieds' then 'Personals' and then 'Lovers Lane.'

He checked for responses to his ad. There were none. So he looked for new ads from 'women seeking men.' All were from women over forty hoping to find their Prince Charming (since the first two hadn't worked out) and live happily ever after. He wondered if it ever really worked. His mother said she had fallen in love with his father when she was a grad student at UT and saw him on stage at the Broken Spoke. It was love at first sight. They had married three months later and were still married thirty-five years later. Those kind of relationships weren't found in the personal ads. But Andy still looked.

'Man, you ain't gonna find a woman in those ads,' Ramon said. 'You gotta find a woman the old-fashioned way – in a bar.'

'Like that worked for you.'

Ramon had met his wife in a bar two years ago. She left him a year later for another man she had met in a bar. Which reminded Andy: he had promised Tres the phone number of a private investigator.

'Ramon, who's that PI you hired to tail your wife?'

'My *ex*-wife.'

'She was your wife when you hired the PI.'

'She was a cheating, no-good, two-peso . . .'

Andy was never sure what bothered Ramon more, that she was cheating on him with another man or that she was cheating on him with another tattoo artist. She had allowed her lover/artist to finish the mural that Ramon had begun on her body. Once he got started,

Ramon could go on about his ex-wife like Andy's mother could about football.

'The PI's name?'

'Lorenzo Escobar, down Congress a few blocks.'

Andy logged off, took one final glance at the coed's bottom, and headed to the door.

'Wake up, Max.'

But he stopped short when Ramon said, 'Oh, dude was here looking for you. In a limo.'

Andy turned back.

'A limo? Down here? Looking for *me*?'

'What'd I say?'

'Who?'

'White dude. In a suit. Checked out my flash' – his standard tattoo designs displayed on a flip rack like art stores used for prints – 'then asked did I know where you were at. I said, "I look like a secretary?"'

'These tickets his?'

'Didn't leave a ticket.'

'Who was he?'

Ramon wiped blood from the girl's butt then pointed the needle end of the tattoo machine at a newspaper on the counter.

'Him.'

Andy picked up the paper. On the front page was a photograph of three middle-aged white men wearing suits and a younger white woman: the mayor of Austin, the governor of Texas, a famous billionaire, and his beautiful blonde wife, all faces well known in Austin.

'The mayor was here?'

Ramon laughed. 'What the hell would the mayor want with you?'

'The governor?'

A bigger laugh. 'What've you been smoking?'

That left only one, the least likely of all.

'Russell Reeves was here?'

Ramon nodded without looking up from the girl's butt.

'When?'

'Couple hours ago.'

'What'd he want?'

'You.'

'Why?'

'Didn't say. I didn't ask. I mind my own business.'

'Since when?'

Ramon gave him a look over his glasses and a half-smile.

'Okay if I borrow the paper?'

A nod. 'Later, bro.'

Andy and Max climbed the stairs to his office. Max turned around three times and curled up on his pad in the corner. Andy sat and read the newspaper article. Russell Reeves had just donated $100 million to a scholarship fund so low-income students could attend college. He was being hailed as a visionary philanthropist by the governor and the mayor, the latest in a long line of politicians to honor Russell Reeves.

Russell Reeves was an Austin legend, like Michael

Dell. When Reeves was only twenty-two, he invented a computer gizmo that had revolutionized the Internet; he sold it for billions in stock during the high-tech boom years on Wall Street. He then invested in other high-tech companies and made billions more as the NASDAQ climbed to 5000. But he saw the technology boom about to bust, so he sold everything right before the stock market crash of 2000. He walked away from the nineties with over $20 billion in cash. Everything he touched had turned to gold.

Then he gave the gold away.

He gave money to liberal politicians and poor people, environmental causes and alternate energy research, the arts and AIDS; he gave money to build low-income housing and health clinics in East Austin and to buy computers for the public schools and parkland for the people; he gave money to fight global warming and defeat Republicans. Russell Reeves was a devout do-gooder with a heart of gold and a bank account to match. To date, the Russell and Kathryn Reeves Foundation had donated over $2 billion to make Austin a better place.

Reeves was forty now and married to a former Miss UT. Seeing him standing there next to his beauty queen wife in the photo while the governor called him a Texas hero and the mayor said he was Austin's favorite son, and knowing he was worth $15 billion according to the latest *Forbes* ranking, you'd probably think Russell Reeves was the luckiest man on the face of the Earth . . . unless you knew about his son.

His seven-year-old son was dying.

Zachary Reeves had a rare, incurable form of cancer. All known medical therapies – chemo, radiation, bone marrow transplant – had failed. So his father had established the Reeves Research Institute on the UT campus, a state-of-the-art cancer research laboratory dedicated to finding a cure for his disease. Russell Reeves had hired renowned scientists from around the world and brought them to Austin. He had spent money and spared no expense. But five years and $5 billion later, there was still no cure. The doctors gave the boy a year.

Consequently, while Russell Reeves was beloved and admired by everyone, he was envied by no one. He was viewed as a tragic figure in Austin. And he was standing in Andy's doorway.

'May I come in?'

Andy dropped the newspaper and stood. Max sensed something was up, so he stood, too.

'Mr Reeves. Yes, sir. Please come in.'

Reeves glanced over at Max. 'Does it bite?'

'Only Jo's muffins. Name's Max.' Andy stuck his hand out. 'I'm Andy Prescott.'

Andy had never before shaken the hand of a billionaire. Or even a millionaire, except for Tres.

'Andy, I'm Russell Reeves.'

Russell Reeves' net worth made him seem bigger than life, but he was actually no bigger than Andy. His suit was tailored and expensive and draped like silk over his shoulders. He had once worn thick glasses, but Andy had read that he had gotten laser eye surgery. His black hair, once famously thick and curly, was now thinner and shorter and gray on the sides. None of the girls at Whole Foods would call him handsome, but they'd be all over him like bees on honey. Especially Suzie. Fifteen billion dollars in the bank improved a man's looks.

Russell Reeves was frowning.

'You get mugged?'

'Trail biking. Took a header on the greenbelt yesterday.'

Reeves nodded then surveyed the small office.

'No wasted space. I like that.'

'You do?'

Reeves smiled. 'When I first started out, I lived at work, an old building in the warehouse district. Couldn't afford an apartment, so I showered at the Y.' He gestured at the open window. 'No air-conditioning, like this place.'

Violin music drifted in from next door. The student was advanced. Reeves cocked his head to listen.

'Nice.'

'Comes with the rent.'

'Mind if I sit down, Andy?'

'Oh, yeah, sure, Mr Reeves.'

They sat across the card table from each other. Russell Reeves studied Andy for a long, uncomfortable moment; the last time Andy had felt this uneasy was when he had met with the dean of the law school to learn whether he had been admitted.

'Andy, I need a lawyer.'

'You've got hundreds of lawyers.'

'This is special.'

'You got stopped speeding through a school zone?'

Reeves smiled. 'A little more special than a speeding ticket, Andy. I want to fix SoCo.'

'What's wrong with it?'

'Nothing a billion dollars can't fix.'

'I don't represent developers.'

'Ah, a man of principle.'

'Uh, no. I've just never been asked.'

'Oh. Well, Andy, I want to purchase those eyesores – old abandoned grocery stores, strip centers, slum apartments – and build quality low-income housing so regular people can afford to live in SoCo. Town homes with pools and playscapes for kids.'

'We've been trying to get the city to build low-income housing down here for years.'

'Governments are bureaucracies, Andy. I have the money and power to cut through the bureaucracy and get things done. The same people said it couldn't be done in East Austin, but we did it. And I want to do it here. Austin should be for all people regardless of wealth and I want you to help me make it that way. Andy, I want you to be my lawyer in SoCo.'

'Why me?'

'Like I said, Andy, I've got the money and power to make this happen at city hall. What I don't have is the trust of the people down here. They'll say I'm trying to take over SoCo. Change it. Make it like North Austin.'

'People down here don't trust anyone north of the river.'

'Which is why I need a lawyer who's trusted south of the river.'

'I do traffic tickets.'

'You're a lawyer, aren't you?'

Andy glanced up at his diploma hanging on the wall next to the American IronHorse poster.

'Yeah, I guess so.'

'And you know everyone down here and everyone knows you?'

Andy shrugged.

'And everyone down here trusts you?'

Another shrug.

'And you office above a tattoo parlor, so I'm betting you've got a tattoo?'

Andy nodded. Russell Reeves held his hands out.

'You're perfect.'

'I am?'

'Andy, I send my downtown lawyers into SoCo wearing Armani and acting like assholes, the locals will shut us down before we get started. It'd be a disaster.'

He was right.

'Mr Reeves, how'd you get my name?'

'My secretary, Doris Sullivan. You handled her traffic ticket.'

'I called her this morning.'

'I overheard. I've been thinking how to handle this, so when she mentioned you, I checked you out and liked what I learned.'

'You did?'

'Look, Andy, you didn't graduate at the top of your class, we both know that. And I wouldn't hire you to handle an IPO, but you're the right man for this job. How much do you charge?'

'Well, uh . . .'

Andy hadn't had an hourly fee client in his entire career.

'. . . how about for—'

'Four hundred? My downtown lawyers charge twice that.' Reeves waved a hand in the air. 'But then, you don't have their overhead. All right, four hundred dollars an hour it is.'

Four hundred dollars an hour? Andy was going to say forty. His pulse ratcheted up while his mind raced through the financial implications of billing four hundred dollars an hour: one billable hour would cover his office rent for two months, two billable hours his house rent and utilities, and another his entire month's living expenses. And twenty billable hours – My God, that would buy a Stumpjumper!

'So, Andy, do you want to be my lawyer or not?'

Andy's mind was playing a video of himself hammering the Hill of Life on a Stumpjumper, shredding the trails, carving the corners, bombing the descent . . .

'Andy?'

Andy blinked hard and returned to the moment. He focused on the billionaire sitting across from him – on the answer to all his dreams.

'Yes, sir, Mr Reeves. I do want to be your lawyer.'

'Excellent. First purchase is the old grocery store site this side of Oltorf.'

'They've been asking five million. We've stopped two office buildings from going in there.'

'They're taking four, and we're going to build two hundred low-income town homes. The purchase is contingent upon the residents approving the redevelopment plan. That's your job. You get them on board and the deal closed. My downtown lawyers will provide the contracts and handle all the title matters. We've identified a dozen more properties. You'll be a busy lawyer, Andy. I hope you've got a lot of free time.'

'I'll juggle my schedule.'

'Good.'

Russell Reeves stood and held out a business card.

'My numbers. Call me on my cell phone anytime.'

Reeves' business card was fancy with embossed lettering. Andy's was not. He had made his cards on Ramon's computer. He handed one to Reeves.

'That's my cell phone.'

As if he had another phone.

'Welcome aboard, Andy.'

They shook hands again, then Reeves reached into his inside coat pocket and pulled out an envelope. He handed it to Andy.

'This should cover the first week.'

Russell Reeves walked to the door then turned back.

'But get a haircut, okay?'

'Yes, sir, Mr Reeves.'

He disappeared down the stairs. Andy stepped to the window and saw Russell Reeves emerge on the sidewalk below and walk over to a waiting limousine, which was double-parked. A cop had stopped and was standing next to a big bald white dude in a black suit and sunglasses; the cop was writing a ticket. He looked up when Reeves arrived. The cop's body language suddenly changed; he now appeared to be apologizing. He shut his ticket book. He smiled and shook Reeves' hand. Then he left the scene.

The big dude opened the back door for Reeves, then got into the driver's seat. The limo drove off. Andy sat down, opened the envelope, and removed a cashier's check made payable to 'Andrew Paul Prescott.' For $10,000.

Ten thousand dollars.

Andy was suddenly overwhelmed with excitement . . . and a foul smell that could only mean one thing. He glanced down at Max, who was looking sheepish.

'You had a bean burrito at Güero's, didn't you?'

The limo was barely out of sight before Andy had raced downstairs, dropped Max off with Ramon (after conducting only a cursory examination of Ramon's work on the coed's bottom), and jumped on the little

Huffy. He hammered the pavement to the bank and deposited the check, his heart beating like a teenager about to cop his first feel. When the teller said, 'Funds are available,' Andy wanted to throw his arms around her and give her a big kiss. Instead, he said, 'Thanks,' as if it were a normal occurrence.

Then he rode directly over to REI.

He wished he had had a camera to capture Wayne's expression when he told him what he wanted. Of course, Wayne had called the bank to confirm funds before he accepted Andy's check. 'Nothing personal,' he had said. Two hours later, Andy Prescott was riding a Specialized S-Works Stumpjumper mountain bike on the Hike-and-Bike Trail around Lady Bird Lake. Max was trotting alongside.

Trail rules required he keep his speed under ten miles per hour, and the trail was crowded with the after-work crowd anyway, so Andy was just getting a feel for the bike – and enjoying envious glances from other bikers. And who could blame them – the carbon-steel full-suspension frame, the hydraulic disk brakes, the Shimano derailleur, the carbon trigger shifters, the race rims and tires. All top of the line. The way the guys stared with such open envy, Andy felt as if he were riding down the trail with Suzie perched on the handle-bars in her Spandex short-shorts and tube top.

The ten-mile-long crushed granite trail ran right along the shoreline. Runners and riders crowded the trail every weekday after five and all day on weekends;

some were serious, some were social, but most were fit and showing it off. Running or riding around the lake had become a central part of the Austin social scene, another place to see and be seen. To be active and fit. To worship nature. To wear Spandex.

He felt good.

Like a real man. A real lawyer. With a rich client. Not that he hadn't considered the strangeness of the situation: what were the odds that Russell Reeves, a billionaire, would just walk into his office and hire Andy Prescott, a traffic ticket lawyer, for a multimillion-dollar real-estate deal? Astronomical. A lightning strike. And it made him nervous. Like his father always said, 'If something is too good to be true, it probably isn't.'

On the other hand – and Andy found himself desperately seeking the other hand – Reeves was right about the SoCo locals: they would oppose him every step of the way. They were activists and they would get active, raise hell at city hall, stop him in his tracks. They didn't trust anyone north of the river, so he needed a lawyer south of the river whom they did trust. Someone like Andy Prescott.

He *was* perfect.

A noise caught his attention. Andy was riding the section of the trail that ran right along César Chávez Street. Directly across the street a group of protestors stood in front of the construction site for the Seaholm project – the biggest single development in the history of downtown Austin being built by a Dallas developer

– chanting 'City hall sold us out! Vote 'em out!' and holding signs that read THEY WANT TO MAKE AUSTIN LOOK LIKE DALLAS and THE DEVIL IS IN THE DEVELOPER and, more to the point, DEVELOPERS SUCK. As far as native Austinites were concerned, no more despicable creatures roamed the Earth than real-estate developers; heck, the little whack job running North Korea these days ranked higher in local opinion polls than developers. And now Andy Prescott was lawyering for one.

Or was he?

Andy averted his eyes from the protestors and considered his new client's intentions. Russell Reeves didn't want to *develop* SoCo; he wanted to *renovate* SoCo. Andy wasn't representing a *developer*; he was representing a *renovator*. He wasn't the devil's defender; he was an angel's advocate. A billionaire angel who wanted to renovate rundown properties into uplifting low-income housing, for Christ's sake. Who does that today? Not the city. Not a developer wanting to make a quick buck. Only an angel would do that. Only Russell Reeves. The residents were being pushed out of SoCo by high rents, high home prices, and high taxes. They needed what Reeves was offering. By convincing the residents to go along with his plans, Andy would be helping them. And helping them helped him.

Four hundred dollars an hour!

He had been overjoyed because he had made four hundred dollars in one day – but in one hour? If he billed forty hours a month, that would be *sixteen thousand dollars*. He didn't make that much money in a year of traffic tickets. Was he supposed to just walk away from that? Was he supposed to return this stupendous Stumpjumper to Wayne and go back to riding a Schwinn? Was he supposed to return the log owl to Yard Dog and show up for his mother's sixty-second birthday without the perfect present? Is that what the residents of SoCo would want?

I don't think so.

His father also said, 'Never look a gift horse in the mouth.'

Fifteen hundred miles to the north, Alvin Adams bit down on a huge hamburger. He was sitting in a booth in a bar in Queens drinking a beer and eating the hamburger and French fries. It had been another long dull day at the shop; and he now had another headache that would require two or three beers to relieve. In other words, it had been just another day in Alvin Adams' exceedingly boring life: eight hours poring over text of articles in the medical journals his company printed, checking for errors, and calling the authors to confirm footnotes and spelling of the exotic diseases they researched. Hell, he could qualify for an MD or a PhD or some kind of advanced degree, what with all the research he had read over the last decade.

He hated his job.

But it paid the bills. Or at least it allowed him to

stay one step ahead of his bills, paying the minimum monthly payment on his ten maxed-out credit cards. Thirty percent interest, the bastards. There used to be laws against usury, but the credit card companies bought themselves a federal law preempting all state usury laws. What a deal. Just as he again bit into the hamburger, a middle-aged man wearing a suit and wielding a briefcase slid into the seat across from him. He looked like a lawyer. Alvin swallowed and said, 'Can I help you?'

'We can help each other, Alvin,' the man said.

'How's that?'

The man opened his briefcase and removed an envelope. He pushed it across the table. Alvin put the hamburger down and picked the envelope up. It was thick. He opened it. Inside were $100 bills. Lots of $100 bills. He shut the envelope and set it on the table.

'That's a lot of money.'

'Fifty thousand dollars.'

'Who are you?'

'Mr Smith.'

Alvin smiled. 'Okay, Mr Smith, what do you want?'

'A name.'

'Whose?'

Mr Smith again reached inside his briefcase and removed a document this time. He placed it on the table so Alvin could read the title: 'Patient X: The Savior?' Alvin recognized the document; it was a research article that had run in one of the journals his company printed. When was it – two, three years ago?

Alvin recalled the article because the author was 'Anonymous' and because the article was a—

'Crock of shit.'

'What?'

Alvin pointed a French fry at the article.

'That.'

'What, you're a research scientist?'

'Pretty much. I've read hundreds of those research articles. That one was a crock. No one in the field believes that crap. It's all just a big hoax.'

'Do you know who this is?'

'Patient X?'

'Anonymous.'

'Why do you want to know?'

'Need to know basis, Alvin, and you don't need to know. All you need to know is that that name is worth fifty thousand dollars. Tax free.'

Alvin knew who 'Anonymous' was because he had emailed the author several times to correct the copy of that article as well as two follow-up articles.

'You know that's confidential.'

'Are you a lawyer, Alvin?'

'No.'

'Then what do you have to lose?'

'My job.'

'How will anyone know?'

Alvin thought about that. How would anyone know?

'They wouldn't. But . . .'

The man reached across the table and put his hand on the envelope as if to take it away.

'Tony Falco.'

Alvin remembered the name because he had never had an 'Anonymous' author before.

'And who is Tony Falco?'

'A doctor.'

'Where?'

'Here. In New York. Or at least he was back then.'

Mr Smith stood and walked out of the bar. Alvin looked again at the cash in the envelope, then put the envelope in his inside coat pocket. He ordered another beer even though his headache was gone.

Two hours and four beers later, Alvin stumbled out the bar. It was now dark. Half a block down the sidewalk, he noticed a tall man leaning against the hood of a black sedan parked along the curb. He stood as Alvin neared. Then he stepped alongside Alvin and clamped a strong arm around his shoulders.

'Alvin, what did you tell the lawyer?'

'What lawyer?'

'The lawyer who gave you the cash.'

'What cash?'

The man tapped his finger on Alvin's coat over the inside coat pocket.

'That cash. Look, Alvin, I don't want the cash. I want the information.'

'Nothing.'

The man pulled his coat back to reveal a gun.

'Come on, Alvin, it's not worth dying for.'

He was right.

'Tony Falco.'

'And?'

'He's a doctor, here in New York.'

'Thanks, Alvin.'

The man released his grip on Alvin's shoulder. Alvin breathed a sigh of relief just before the man shoved him into an alley a block down from the bar. Alvin looked back just in time to see the man raise a gun with a long, thick barrel to his head. And Alvin Adams knew he would never suffer another headache.

The voice on the phone said, 'Jesus, Harmon, why'd you kill Adams?'

'To silence him.'

'Who was he going to talk to? They just bribed him, for Christ's sake. And he gave you the name.' A deep sigh. 'From now on, Harmon, let the lawyer do the work for you. No more unauthorized killing, you understand? Remember – there's only one person we want dead.'

Chapter 7

Andy Prescott turned to his back-seat passenger.

'Max, how about a swim in the creek after lunch?'

Max barked a *Yes! Yes, I'd like that very much!*

It was the following Saturday morning, and Andy was pedaling the Stumpjumper south on Ranch Road 12. He was packing the log owl in his backpack; it rose above his head like a lookout. Max rode behind him in a seat Andy had rigged up over the rear wheel. They both wore helmets.

Andy enjoyed biking the country roads outside Austin. The air was cleaner, the views of the Hill Country went on forever, and the odds of getting nailed by a speeding motorist were considerably lesser . . . except for—

Max barked.

He had heard it before Andy, and now Andy heard the roar of the massive engine. He looked back. The pickup truck rounded the last curve and barreled toward them at a high rate of speed. It was not your standard-size pickup. It was a black 4x4 with wide off-road tires and a grill guard and its suspension jacked up high. It looked like an Abrams battle tank hurtling down the narrow farm-to-market.

Andy steered onto the shoulder and braced himself for the blast of air current that buffeted them when the pickup blew past. The guy hammered his horn like a kid with a new toy. Andy dabbed so as not to fall over. He considered giving the guy the finger, but a new law allowed Texans to carry a weapon in their vehicles, purportedly to protect themselves against carjackers. No doubt that bubba was armed and stupid. So Andy just pedaled on down the road.

The quaint Village of Wimberley, Texas, population 3,946, sits at the intersection of Ranch Road 12 and Cypress Creek forty miles southwest of Austin, far enough off the beaten path to discourage commuters but close enough to attract Austin's creative types. Wimberley has long been an idyllic colony inhabited by artists, sculptors, singers, writers, craftsmen, glass blowers, and dope smokers.

Jean Prescott had inherited fifty acres just outside town back before Wimberley had been discovered by city folk sick of the city; but city folk had since moved to the country and driven up land prices. His mother's land would bring a million dollars or more, if she wanted to sell out to a developer. She didn't. Real-estate developers ranked just below football coaches on her list. But the property taxes had risen along with the land values. His grandparents had kept cattle for the agricultural exemption, which reduced the taxes to a few hundred dollars. But his mother had sworn off red meat, so she and his father raised a few dozen ostriches instead.

Andy opened the barbed-wire gate. A few of the big birds – ostriches stood eight feet tall and weighed almost four hundred pounds – had wandered over to greet him; he shooed them away, then rode in and closed the gate behind him. He pedaled up the gravel road to the house.

Tall oak trees shaded the old two-story farmhouse with the wraparound porch where Andy had played as a child. A rainwater collection system gathered nature's water for irrigation and solar panels gathered the sun's energy for electricity; his father enjoyed the summer months when he sold surplus electricity back to the grid. Drought-hardy native Texas plants grew in the garden that followed the porch around the house – the log owl would fit right in – and vegetables in the organic garden out back. A compost stood by the fence line. His folks had been green before green was fashionable.

There was no place like home.

Max was barking. Andy parked and lifted the dog down. Max ran off to chase after birds and squirrels and the ostriches; and the ostriches would chase him. The two-toed birds could hit speeds of forty miles per hour. So they enjoyed free rein on the land, from barbed-wire to barbed-wire; the fence kept them from wandering onto the farm-to-markets and ending up road kill. Even a four-hundred-pound bird had no chance against a three-ton pickup.

Andy unbuckled the backpack and removed the owl. He stepped up onto the porch and entered the house through the screen door. His folks avoided the air conditioner even in the summer; but the house had been built to catch the breeze up from the creek. From the front door, he knew his mother had been baking a cake in the back kitchen.

'Mom!'

No answer. He knew where he'd find her. He walked through the kitchen where a still-warm strawberry cake – his mother knew Max couldn't eat chocolate – sat cooling on the counter. He continued through the screened-in back porch and out the door. Wind chimes hung from the eaves and limbs of the oak trees and played a symphony in the soft breeze. Colorful yard art – metal birds and coyotes and wind catchers – stood in the open space like a sculpture garden. Thirty steps farther and he was at the barn. From all outward appearances, it was a working barn; but once through the open double doors, the classical music playing on the stereo system told otherwise.

This was his mother's private place, where she could lose herself in her art. It was the same for her in there as it was for him out on the trails: she was free of all worldly constraints. She was in the zone. Jean Prescott was a sculptor. And the barn was her studio.

133

Andy found her in the back corner where the natural light from the windows filled the space. The back doors were propped open and the cool breeze from the creek blew in like a whisper. She stood there in her natural element, all five feet five inches of her lithe body clad in jeans and a T-shirt, her stance almost athletic before the sculpture, like a lioness on the African savannah stalking her prey. Some humans belonged in a corner office thirty stories up; others in a coal mine three miles down. Jean Prescott belonged in an art studio. She was putting the final touches on the clay figure of an angel.

'Nice.'

She turned to him and smiled.

'Andy.'

But her smile turned into a frown.

'You cut your hair.'

He had. Her eyes now seemed so sad Andy almost apologized, but then she saw the owl under his arm and her eyes brightened.

'Andy, I told you, no presents.'

'I know. But this is pretty cool, don't you think? For your garden. Happy birthday, Mom.'

'It's beautiful. But you can't afford this.'

'I can now.'

'How?'

'I'll tell you later. Where's Dad?'

'In his office.' She wiped her hands and said, 'Go tell him it's time for lunch. Tofu burgers. I've got him on a feeding schedule like the birds.'

Andy stifled a groan. Not tofu burgers again.

Andy set the owl on a nearby table then walked out the open doors and past the vegetable garden; the tomatoes were fattening up. He continued down the sloping land to Cypress Creek, a lazy slice of shallow water that coursed gently over river rocks and around limestone boulders and under bald cypress trees whose trunks snaked into the creek like long straws. He came up behind his father sitting in a rocking chair on a shady rock outcropping at the water's edge – his office for the last thirty-five years. A fishing pole stood against a nearby tree in case he spotted a catfish worth catching in the clear creek. He was strumming his guitar and singing softly, as if performing for the half dozen ostriches that grazed nearby.

Paul Prescott was tall and lanky as a fencepost with a gray ponytail and a neat beard; he wore old jeans and older cowboy boots. He could pass for Kris Kristofferson, and he possessed the same gravelly voice and the same songwriting ability. But Paul Prescott had never hit it big. Never gotten his big break. Never gotten lucky. So for forty-five years he had sung his songs at local joints in and around Austin, just him and his guitar. And his constant companion, José Cuervo.

Saturday nights at the Broken Spoke or Cheatham Street Warehouse or Gruene Hall, sitting in the back listening to his father sing and falling asleep in his mother's lap – those were Andy Prescott's childhood memories. Other kids had grown up watching G-rated

135

Disney movies; Andy Prescott had grown up in honky-tonks with drunk cowboys and wild women.

It had been a great childhood.

Andy had met Willie and Waylon, Kris and Kinky, Ray Price and Merle Haggard – all the country greats in all the Texas bars. Paul Prescott had opened for all of them, but no one had ever opened for him; he had never been the headliner. When Andy was ten years old, he had been so proud of his father – a star singer up on the stage. By the time he was fourteen, he understood that his father wasn't a star. By eighteen, he knew his father would never be a star. Andy Prescott had always figured on following in his father's footsteps – not as a singer, but as a failure. He wondered if Russell Reeves would be his big break.

His father paused his singing, coughed hard, and spit blood.

Paul Prescott was dying. He was sixty-five, and he had outlived his liver, as he put it. In fact, he had killed his liver with tequila. 'Alcoholic cirrhosis,' the doctors called it. His scarred liver could no longer adequately absorb vitamins, produce proteins that enabled his blood to clot, or cleanse his body of toxins. He needed a new liver. Without a transplant, he would eventually develop a fatal case of bacterial peritonitis or suffer hepatic encephalopathy and slip into a coma, or the scarring in his liver would cause his blood to back up and he would bleed to death.

His father was one of seventeen thousand people on

the national waiting list for a 'cadaveric liver transplant' – a liver from a dead donor. He had been put on the list a year before, and the doctor said he would be on the list a year from now. Only six thousand people would get a liver in the next twelve months; his father would not be one of them. Alcoholic cirrhosis patients sat at the bottom of the waiting list.

Donated livers are allocated first to those transplant patients classified as 'Status 1,' which requires they be in the intensive care unit with a life expectancy of less than seven days. But by then it is often too late; only half of Status 1 patients survive a year after a transplant. Which seemed stupid: livers go to those patients who are least likely to be saved.

His father's only hope – and Paul Prescott struggled with the moral dilemma of hoping that someone else's life would not be saved so his would – was that a donated liver not match the blood type and body weight of the Status 1 patients in the Texas region; only after those patients were ruled out would the liver drop down the list, first to those patients in the region with a life expectancy of less than three months, then to those with longer life expectancies, and finally to the alcoholic cirrhosis patients. The odds were not good.

His father figured on dying.

But he had never complained; he said he had no one to blame but himself. And at least he had health insurance and could get on the waiting list; uninsured patients could not. Ability to pay was a qualifying factor:

a five-year-old child without insurance dies; a seventy-five-year-old man with insurance lives. Paul Prescott said, 'Life isn't fair. Sometimes that works for you and against someone else, sometimes that works for someone else and against you. But life is always unfair to someone.' Andy's father had long ago accepted the fact that life was not fair, even if his son had not.

Andy walked closer. His father's soft voice became clear:

'Honky-tonk heroes, we're a dying breed now,
The world's gone corporate and the music has too,
Honky-tonks are history and their heroes will soon be,
But their music lives on in the magic of CDs.'

'Sounds good.'

His father's fingers froze on the guitar strings; he turned and smiled.

'Andy, my boy. How're you doing, son?' He squinted into the light. 'You get in a bar fight?'

'The trails. I like that one.'

'Might work. Better write it down.'

His father jotted notes in the little notebook he carried with him these days. Forgetfulness was a symptom of liver disease.

'Used to sing thirty songs a night. Now I can't remember one all the way through.'

His father cut his own CDs at an Austin studio, then sold them in local stores and at his performances. He hadn't sung in public in two years. He wanted to cut one more CD before he died. He finished his notes and faced Andy again.

'You get a job?'

'No.'

'Why'd you cut your hair?'

'Oh. I got a client.'

'You cut your hair for a speeding driver?'

'I'll tell you later.'

Andy squatted next to his father; his skin glowed yellow in the shards of sunlight that cut through the cypress canopy above.

'How're you doing, Dad?'

'I'm still singing . . . to the birds anyway.'

Andy felt the tears come into his eyes. His father ran his hand over Andy's short hair.

'Son, don't cry for me. If it ends now, I've got no complaints. I've had a great life. I've lived life my way and I made music my way. I've had thirty-five years with the best woman I've ever known and twenty-nine years with the best son I could ever have hoped for. I only hope you get a woman as good as your mother and a son as good as you.'

'Dad, I'm a traffic ticket lawyer.'

'You're a good man, Andy. You've got a good heart.'

Andy wiped his face.

'Son, I'm not rich or famous either, but I didn't need to be. I needed to sing my songs, but I didn't need to be a star to be happy. You can't buy happiness in a store, Andy. You live it. I have. I did exactly what I wanted to do every day of my life. I've loved and been loved. That's as good as it gets in this life.'

Andy was close to blubbering uncontrollably, so he said, 'Mom says it's time for lunch. Tofu burgers.'

His father groaned.

'Damn, not tofu again. I need meat.'

'Not in that house.'

Paul Prescott pushed himself out of the chair; it took some effort. Andy would have helped, but that always annoyed his father. He had never required help.

'What do you say, Andy? Let's you and me sneak into town, get us a big ol' cheeseburger and French fries.'

His father swallowed a bite of his tofu burger.

'Mighty good, Jean.'

She gave him a 'Who do you think you're kidding?' look.

'Been reading about liver transplants in India, says I can get a liver sooner over there. And cheaper.'

They were on the back porch eating the tofu burgers and sweet potato fries and drinking iced tea. Andy never drank beer in his father's presence.

'Seems like everyone's going to India these days — for call centers, wombs, livers . . .'

His mother frowned. 'Wombs?'

'Natalie wants to hire an Indian surrogate to have their baby. It's a lot cheaper.'

'Global economy,' his father said. 'Americans shopping the world for cheap labor. Literally, in Natalie's case.'

'You really thinking about getting a liver in India?'

'Nah. Those poor folks don't need us coming over there to take advantage of their poverty, buying their body parts on the cheap like we buy auto parts from China.'

The Prescott men were hopeless liberals and lovable losers. They voted for McGovern, Humphrey, Mondale, Gore, Kerry, and Kinky. Their votes guaranteed the candidate would lose.

His father downed a handful of vitamins and chased them with iced tea then slowly pushed himself out of his chair.

'Hell, I gotta go again.'

He walked inside the house. Andy looked to his mother.

'The diuretics,' she said. 'They make his body produce more urine, to get rid of the fluid in his abdomen.'

'His skin and eyes, they're a lot more yellow than the last time I saw him.'

She nodded. 'The jaundice. Doctor said he'll look like a pumpkin before it's over.'

'I signed the organ donation authorization on the back of my driver's license.'

'Your face looks better.'

His father returned and said, 'Made a hundred bucks

this month, selling electricity back to those bastards.' He sat and pointed a fork at the log owl sitting by the back door. 'The hell is that thing, Andy?'

'It's yard art, Paul,' his mother said.

'You buy that in Austin?'

'Yep.'

'Couldn't have come cheap . . . or that fancy bike outside.'

'I got a new client this week.'

He waited until he had their full attention; he felt like a kid about to surprise his parents with a straight-A report card.

'Russell Reeves hired me.'

His parents stared at him as if he had said Dick Cheney would be joining them for dinner. When his mother could finally speak again, she said, 'Did you cut your hair for him?'

Only his mother would ask such a question. He answered with a lame nod.

'Russell Reeves hired you for a traffic ticket?' his father said.

'No. He wants to build low-income housing in SoCo.'

'Andy,' his mother said, 'you're representing a *developer*?'

'No, Mom. A *renovator*.'

'What's that got to do with you?' his father said.

'He needs a SoCo lawyer. He's paying me four hundred dollars an hour.'

'Why would he do that?'

'He built low-income housing in East—'

'No. Pay you four hundred bucks an hour?'

'He needs me.'

'Russell Reeves needs you?'

'I'm trusted in SoCo.'

'Is he?'

'Nope. That's why he needs me.'

'He's a billionaire ten times over.'

'Fifteen.'

'That's fifteen billion reasons not to trust him.'

His parents had fed their son a daily dose of populist politics right along with organic carrots and squash from the day he was born. And one article of that faith was to never trust 'The Man' – and The Man was always rich and powerful and politically connected . . . like Russell Reeves.

'Dad, Russell Reeves has done a lot of good for Austin. And, Mom, he didn't give his money to the UT football team. He built a research lab . . . and he has a sick kid.'

Now Andy was defending The Man.

His mother's expression softened. 'His son is dying, Paul.'

'But why Andy?' His father turned back. 'Nothing against you, son, but there's ten thousand lawyers in Austin who—'

'Did better than me in law school?'

'You're a traffic ticket lawyer, son. Now that's fine with me, but why is it fine with Russell Reeves?'

'Dad, he just wants to help regular people live in SoCo.'

'That's like politicians saying they want to help regular people when rich people put them in office.' He shook his head. 'Andy, when things don't seem right, they're usually not.'

'Dad . . .'

'A billionaire just walks into your office one day and hires you for a big real-estate deal? That make sense to you?'

'Don't worry, Dad. It's all good.'

His dad wasn't convinced. He chewed on that and the tofu, then said, 'How about staying the night, son? We'll go into town for dinner, get that cheeseburger, maybe check out the movie at the Corral—'

The Corral Theatre was an outdoor walk-in theatre that showed movies under the stars. You took your own chair.

'—maybe go to church tomorrow morning. I feel like eating meat Saturday night and singing gospel Sunday morning.'

Andy glanced from his father to his mother. She was trying to nod a yes out of him.

'Can we have cheeseburgers, Mom?'

'You and your father can.'

'Okay, Dad, I'll stay over.' He had promised Tres he'd ride the greenbelt with him the next morning, but he'd just have to break in the Stumpjumper another day. 'On one condition.'

'You want real French fries, too?'

'Well, yeah, I do, but that's not the condition.'

'A chocolate malt?'

'That, too, but you've got to let me buy you those boots, for your sixty-sixth birthday.'

His father had long yearned for cowboy boots hand-made by the same bootmaker who had made boots for Clint Eastwood and Kevin Costner when they had come to Austin to film *A Perfect World*, his father's favorite movie. The boots didn't come cheap; they started at $1,200. Just when his father had decided to bite the bullet and buy the boots, he had been diagnosed with liver disease; he had lost all desire for new boots.

'With my billionaire client, I can afford them. Any leather you want . . . except ostrich.'

Cowboy boots made of ostrich skin were highly coveted by Texans. But Andy had grown up with the big birds – the same ones outside had been his childhood pets; ostriches lived to be seventy – so he couldn't very well make them into boots.

'Maybe elk, Dad. That's soft leather, they'll fit like foot gloves.'

'Andy, those boots, they'll take six, seven months to make.'

'That means you've got to be here when they're ready.'

'Who says?'

'I do. And one other thing: I'm going to be real

busy for a while, working for Reeves – would you keep Max?'

His father's yellow eyes brightened.

'You sure?'

Andy nodded. His father looked down at the dog.

'Max, you want to stay with your grandpa a while?'

He leaned over and gave Max a bite of the tofu burger. Max gave it a chew, then spit it out. He liked meat, too. Jean Prescott leaned over and kissed Andy on the cheek then walked over to the counter where the strawberry cake sat.

'Max, are you ready for cake and ice cream?'

Max jumped up and barked a *Yes! Yes, I am!*

'You dating anyone?' his father said.

'Curtis and Dave. Tres is taken.'

'There's someone out there for you, Andy,' his mother said from across the kitchen. 'One day, you'll turn around and she'll be standing right there.'

'Sure, Mom.'

His mother was an artist. A hopeless romantic. Which was probably why she had ended up with two hopeless losers. Andy thought of his life with his father. Paul Prescott wasn't rich but it had never been about the money; for him, it had always been about the music. One day Andy's children – if he ever got married and had children – would listen to their grandpa's music, and they'd be proud. Andy fought the tears again.

He would give anything to save his father's life.

He had even tried to give his own liver to his father

– a 'live donor' transplant. The liver is the only human organ capable of regeneration; if Andy gave half his liver to his father, within two months each half would grow to a whole liver again, like something out of a sci-fi movie. But Andy had Type A blood; his father had Type B. His father's body would reject Andy's liver.

There was nothing more Andy Prescott could do to save his father's life.

Inside a $20-million Mediterranean-style mansion overlooking that portion of the Colorado River known as Lake Austin, Russell Reeves sat in a gaming chair facing a video screen that almost covered one wall; his seven-year-old son sat next to him. They were playing Guitar Hero III.

Zach was taking it easy on his father.

Zach's bedroom suite felt like a sauna – the boy was always cold. An orange-and-white Longhorns knit cap covered his bald head. Oxygen tubes wound over his ears and under his nose; the chemo shunt in his chest was concealed by his Dallas Cowboys jersey. He loved sports, but he had never played sports. He had never been just a kid. He had always been a sick kid.

Because of Russell Reeves.

He was a carrier of the mutated gene that had caused his son's rare cancer. The gene had not given the cancer to Russell, but he had given the gene to Zach – and the gene had given his son cancer. The man who loved this boy more than life itself had sentenced him to death.

Russell Reeves had killed his own son.

Zach had spent more of his life in the hospital than at home; he had been in and out of the children's cancer ward at Austin General Hospital so many times that Russell now kept the hospital's penthouse reserved year-round. When Zach stayed at the hospital, they stayed at the hospital.

And when Zach was at home, it was as if he were still at the hospital. His bed was a hospital bed; medical equipment lined the wall behind the bed; a nurse sat beside the bed, twenty-four/seven. And there was even the hospital smell: the inescapable scent of death.

The door opened and Kathryn walked in. She was only thirty-eight, but the last six years had aged her. She had been a beauty queen at UT and had looked the part when they had married fourteen years ago; now she looked like a woman about to lose her only child. But she never let on to Zach. Russell glanced away from the video screen just in time to catch her putting on her happy face.

'Zach!'

She came over and kissed her son.

'Are you winning, honey?'

Zach nodded without looking away from the screen. Kathryn checked his chart: pulse, blood pressure, temperature. Every thirty minutes. Zach's fingers were working the guitar-shaped controller expertly when he abruptly leaned over and vomited. He had had chemo that morning.

Russell grabbed a towel and wiped his son's mouth. He checked Zach's clothes; they were still clean. He lifted his frail son – he felt like skin and bones in Russell's arms – and carried Zach to the bathroom to rinse his mouth and brush his teeth. He then carried him over to the bed and gently set him down. Zach lay back on the bed. The nurse took his pulse, blood pressure, and temperature while Kathryn called the maids.

'You okay, son?'

'I'm just tired.'

'Okay, buddy, get some rest. We'll finish the game later.'

He kissed his son's forehead. Zach closed his eyes. He was so pale that when he closed his eyes, Russell knew he was looking at his son at the moment of death.

That moment was not far off.

The nurse returned to her chair, Russell dimmed the lights, and he and Kathryn walked out of their son's bedroom. Russell shut the door behind them. His wife faced him.

'He doesn't have a year, Russell.'

'I know.'

'We have fifteen billion dollars, but we can't save our own son.'

She began crying. Again. She cried constantly now. She paced the house all day and night. He often woke and found her gone. He would always find her in Zach's room, kneeling next to his bed while he slept, praying to God to spare her child. It scared him. Zach's doctor had recommended a psychiatrist. She had refused. He was losing them both.

'Kathryn, I've worked around the clock for six years now to save Zach. I've spent five billion dollars on the lab and the scientists and the research. I've—'

'Failed him.'

'No, Kathryn, I haven't failed him, and I won't fail him. I won't let him die. I promise you. I promise him.'

He took her by the shoulders; all he felt were bones. She had all but stopped eating. It was as if she were dying with Zach; as if the family were dying with him.

'I swear to God, Kathryn – I will save him.'

She wandered down the hallway; he walked to his office at the rear of the house. The back wall of the office was a bank of windows that offered a stunning view of the lake below and the hills beyond. White sails dotted the blue surface of Lake Austin. He could imagine the people on the sailboats looking up at this mansion and thinking that the people who lived there must have a perfect life. They would be wrong. Russell Reeves had everything money could buy, but his life wasn't perfect. Because his only child was dying. Would die.

Unless his father saved him.

He sat behind his desk and opened the newspaper

to the obituaries. It had become a daily ritual. Or an obsession. He read: 'Kenny Johnson, age seven, went to the Lord after a brave battle with cancer. Survived by his parents . . .'

How does a parent survive the death of his child? Her child? Their child? He looked at the young faces, and he read of their short lives. After the children's obituaries, he turned to the obits for adults that read: 'Preceded in death by his son, Henry . . .' or 'by her daughter, Janice . . .' And he always wondered how they had gone on with their lives after the death of their children. Or had they?

And he saw his son's obituary as clearly as if printed in the paper: 'Zachary Reeves, age seven, is survived by his parents, Russell and Kathryn Reeves . . .'

Would he survive the death of his son? Would Kathryn?

He had maintained a steadfast public persona, the billionaire philanthropist helping others while his son inched closer and closer to death. But his public life belied his private torture. His personal hell. His life that was now consumed by a single objective: finding a cure for his son. He had devoted the last six years of his life to saving his son; he would spend every dollar of his fortune and devote every day of the rest of his life to save his son . . . or the rest of his son's life, whichever came first.

He had read every article ever written, talked to every scientist who had ever studied, and learned everything there was to learn about his son's rare form of cancer: Philadelphia Chromosome-Positive Acute Lymphoblastic Leukemia. Fewer than one percent of all children's cancer was Ph-positive ALL, as it was referenced in the medical journals. It's almost always fatal.

Immediately upon diagnosis, Zach had started chemotherapy. But remissions were always short-lived. The only hope for a cure was a hematopoietic stem cell transplantation from a 'matched related' donor – from a blood-related brother or sister. Which Zach did not have and would never have. And even if he had a sibling, there was only a twenty-five percent chance of a match. But they couldn't have a second child whose stem cells could save their first child; Russell might pass the cancer gene to that child, too. He couldn't take that chance. He couldn't sentence two children to death. So Russell had established the Reeves Research Institute. He built the facility, hired scientists, and spent $5 billion searching for a cure for his son.

But without success.

He then dispatched his scientists around the world searching for a matched unrelated donor, even though the prognosis for such an unrelated stem cell transplant was not good. No cost was spared, but no match was found.

Until now.

Perhaps. Possibly. Maybe. There might be hope. A chance. A prayer. But there were issues to be handled.

Problems to be solved. Decisions to be made. Difficulties to be overcome. Things to be done.

Things that had to be done to save his son's life.

Russell stood at the window and gazed out at the world. What if the world found out what he was about to do? What if what he did in here became known out there? What if he were exposed for what he really was – a man desperate enough to commit a crime to save his son? What would he say to the reporters and television cameras who turned on their favorite son? And they would most certainly turn on him.

Russell Reeves would stand before the world just as he now stood and say as he now said to the world beyond the window:

'What would you do if your child were dying of a rare, incurable disease?

'If you're a normal person with limited financial resources, you would hand your child over to the doctors and you would pray. You would go back to work because you need your job to keep your health insurance to pay for your child's care. That's all you could do. That's all normal people can do.

'But what if you weren't normal?

'What if you had unlimited financial resources?

'What if you were worth fifteen billion dollars?

'What would you do then?

'What if you had already spent five billion searching for a cure, but to no avail?

'What if you had chased down every possible hope,

every chance of a cure – no matter how far-fetched – but without success?

'What if you had searched the world for a matched donor, but had come home empty-handed?

'What if, just when all seemed lost, you learned that there was hope – a chance – of a cure for your child? Of life for your child? Instead of certain death?

'What would you do then?

'Would you stand by and watch your child suffer and die? Or would you save your child?

'I chose to save my son.

'And I would make the same choice again.

'And you would have made the same choice, too – if you had fifteen billion dollars.'

That's what he would say. And that's what he would do.

Russell Reeves would do whatever it took to save his son.

Chapter 8

Tony Falco believed in God. But he also believed in science. He did not hold to the view that those beliefs were mutually exclusive, that to believe in God meant one must deny science or to believe in science one must deny God.

He was a faithful scientist. He had always followed the science wherever it led him, without moral, ethical, religious, or political restraints, because those restraints, he believed, were man-made, not God-made. But he had grown weary of American politics that restrained science. Too many Americans believed faith trumped science, as if God had given us our inquiring minds but demanded that we ignore the world around us – the very world God had created, directly or indirectly. He had tired of people who used politics to enforce their moral and religious restraints on science.

Stem cell treatment might well be the medical breakthrough of the century, but the religious right possessed the political power to take stem cells out of play in America – simply because scientists termed the process 'embryonic stem cells.' The anti-abortionists latched onto the word 'embryo' like a Doberman Pinscher's teeth into a T-bone steak and dragged an entire field of scientific research into the abortion debate – notwithstanding the fact that no human life is aborted.

Scientists create embryonic stem cells by taking the sick patient's skin cells and extracting the nucleus. They then insert the nucleus into an unfertilized human egg. The egg – or embryo – grows and divides until a blastocyst – a single layer of cells shaped like a sphere – forms, at which time they remove the stem cells. Those stem cells are injected into the sick patient, and by some – miraculous? – process, they morph into other kinds of cells – blood, brain, heart, nerve – and repair the patient's sick body. They save the patient's life.

So wherein lies the political issue? Without the stem cells, the egg dies. Not a distinct human life, but cloned cells of a human patient. But those two words – embryo and cloning – were red meat in politics today. And when it was discovered that most of the existing stem cell lines in the US had been contaminated and were useless for medical treatment, replacement was all but impossible. And so embryonic stem cell research in the US ground to a halt.

But Tony Falco had devoted his life to saving lives; and allowing the cloned cells – call it an egg, an embryo, whatever – to die in a Petri dish in order to save a child dying from cancer was an easy moral decision for him to make. It was a no-brainer, for him and the child's parents. And Tony Falco did not want to die of old age conducting trials on rats while waiting for the US government to approve treatment for dying patients; he wanted to save patients now. He wanted to give them longer lives through science.

So he had moved to China.

There were no such political constraints in China. Embryonic stem cell research was encouraged, promoted, and funded. The facilities were world-class and the researchers Western-educated, and stem cell research and treatment flourished without government control. Chinese stem cell research now led the world. Science, not faith, ruled in China. Americans could bring their faith to China with them, but Tony Falco would treat them with science.

And Americans desperately wanted the science. They flocked to Chinese institutes for experimental stem cell treatment that was illegal back home. They paid up to $50,000 per treatment. Yes, they were guinea pigs, but when you're looking death in the eye, money and risk mean nothing, because you have nothing to lose. Human beings, Falco had learned, want to live.

His colleagues back in the US publicly mocked his treatments in Western medical journals as unethical and exploitive – they called it 'stem cell tourism' – but privately wished they enjoyed his freedom to follow the science without political interference. And they knew that if stem cells were effective in treating blood cancers like leukemia, they might well be effective in treating a wide range of diseases. They, however, were willing to wait twenty years to find out.

Tony Falco was not.

So he had injected embryonic stem cells into the spinal cords of patients with Lou Gehrig's disease, multiple sclerosis, spinal cord and brain injuries, epilepsy, cerebral palsy, ataxia, Batten disease, optic nerve hypoplasia, and many other debilitating afflictions. He had conducted experimental trials in the US before the contamination of the stem cell lines was discovered, but he could not have performed such treatments outside of trials because the Food and Drug Administration had not approved the procedures for human medical treatment. Results had ranged from disappointing to remarkable. Which brought more Americans to China every day.

Falco had assumed the American sitting across from him had come to Beijing for stem cell treatment. He had assumed wrong.

'Mr Smith, you want to donate fifty million dollars to my research lab?'

'Yes.'

'No strings attached?'

'Only one.'

'And what is that string, Mr Smith?'

'A name.'

'Whose name?'

'Patient X.'

Falco leaned back in his chair and folded his arms.

'Patient X is a myth.'

Mr Smith reached down and opened his briefcase; he retrieved several documents and tossed them onto the desk. Falco recognized the top article: 'Patient X: The Savior?'

'Mr Smith, I've read the journal articles.'

'You wrote the journal articles.'

'The author was anonymous.'

'The author was you, Dr Falco. We traced these articles to you through the printing company. Alvin Adams.'

Falco remembered emailing Alvin several times on each article.

'We just need the woman's name,' Mr Smith said.

'The woman's name?'

'Yes, the woman's name.' Mr Smith read from the introduction to the article: '"Patient X is a white female, age twenty-five to thirty-five . . ."'

'Ah, yes, the woman. And why do you want her name?'

'She has something we want.'

'Yes, I suppose she does. Something everyone wants. Something I wanted. But she did not want to share her gift with the world.'

Patient X had been Tony Falco's greatest professional disappointment. Three years later, he was still not over it.

'I'm sorry, Mr Smith, I can't help you.'

'A hundred million.'

'Are you the donor?'

'My client is.'

'You're a lawyer?'

'Yes.'

'And who is your client?'

'Confidential. I've been sworn to secrecy. The attorney–client privilege.'

'So was I.'

'An attorney?'

'Sworn to secrecy.'

'The law doesn't recognize a doctor–patient privilege.'

'I do.'

'Two hundred million. Just give me the woman's name.'

'Mr Smith, I take it you work for the pharmaceuticals?'

Smith said nothing.

'Patient X wouldn't be good for business, would she? Well, neither am I. Sorry, Mr Smith, but I'm trying to put your clients out of business. Goodbye.'

Harmon Payne sat across the desk from Tony Falco. The doctor was gaunt, probably a runner, and middle-aged. His hair was gray and thinning, and he wore wire-rimmed glasses. He looked smart. Harmon wasn't in China to kill Dr Falco, just to bribe him or threaten him into revealing a name. Which, in his experience, seldom worked. Killing was a much more effective tool. But he was just a hired hand, so he had to keep his employer happy. Those corporate suits were so conservative.

'What can I do for you, Mr Payne?' Falco said.

'It's what I can do for you, Doctor.'

'And what's that?'

'Money.'

The doctor smiled. 'Two Americans in two days offering me money. Just a coincidence, Mr Payne?'

'What did you tell Mr Smith?'

'Not that it's any of your business, but nothing. I don't help the pharmaceuticals.'

'Smith was working for the drug companies?'

'I assumed he was.'

'Which one?'

'He didn't say.'

'What did he want?'

'Again, Mr Payne, that's none of your business.'

'Patient X?'

'Mr Payne, I told Mr Smith nothing and I'm telling you nothing.'

'You don't want money?'

'Not your money.'

'I have other methods.'

Dr Falco clicked a button on the intercom. 'Ling Su, please call security.' He turned back to Harmon. 'Mr Payne, security will be here in under two minutes. You can leave now or be arrested and spend the rest of your life in a Chinese prison. They do things differently here.'

Harmon stood.

'We'll meet again, Dr Falco, when you come home.'

Chapter 9

Cactus chandeliers, metal tables and chairs, a neon Budweiser sign, and Mexican movie posters constituted the decor of Güero's back room. Andy Prescott scanned the crowd. The room was noisy with conversation and the clinking of beer bottles and silverware against white porcelain plates piled high with enchiladas and tacos, flautas and fajitas, refried beans and Spanish rice. All of SoCo had packed into the back room that evening: residents and homeless, shop owners and tattoo artists, students and professors, male and female, straight and gay, white, brown, black, and Asian; and their tattoos. A room full of wackos and weirdos—at least that's what the people north of the river would call them.

Andy called them his friends.

It was two weeks later, and they had all come to see Russell Reeves' plans for their neighborhood and to hear Andy Prescott explain why those plans were good for SoCo – Reeves was *renovating*, not *developing* – and to drink Coronas and margaritas and eat Mexican food for free. Russell's secretary had sent over a blank check to cover the night's expenses.

The artist's rendition of the town house project was displayed on one easel and the architectural plans on another. The locals were studying the plans and arguing over the future of SoCo. But on their faces was the knowledge that they no longer controlled SoCo's future.

The money did.

Andy rapped a fork against a beer bottle and whistled loudly to quiet the room. When the noise subsided, he said, 'So, guys, what do you think?'

Rodney (PhD in English, adjunct faculty member at UT, worked at a bookstore) said, 'Andy, what's to prevent Reeves from changing his mind and putting up an office building instead of low-income housing?'

'Zoning. It'll be changed from commercial to multi-family residential with a special use permit that allows only low-income housing.'

LuAnn (nose ring, tattoos, MA in sociology): 'How are you going to choose who gets in?'

'I'm not. We are. It'll be a co-op with rules to keep the place nice. There'll be a lottery among current SoCo residents who apply. There'll be criminal back-ground checks – not drug use, but dealing and violent crimes. We all want this to be a safe place for the residents.'

Zelda (struggling artist, part-time masseuse): 'How much will the rent cost?'

'Three hundred to a thousand, depending on your income.'

Gustavo (dreadlocks, tattoo of Our Lady of Guadalupe across his back, limo driver): 'Noticed you got a new bike sitting out front there. Russell Reeves' money buy that?'

'Gus, I wouldn't sell out SoCo for a trail bike.'

'What about an IronHorse? Would you sell us out for a Slammer?'

'I'd sell my soul for a Slammer.' Everyone laughed. 'But I wouldn't sell out SoCo. This is my home, too.'

'You sold out your hair, Samson.'

'Gus, my hair, it's not as important to me as your dreads, okay?'

'Point is, Andy, his money's changing you. And his money's gonna change SoCo.'

'Yes, it is, Gus. For the better.'

'A developer's gonna make SoCo better? Man, I can't believe you're lawyering for a developer.'

'He's not a *developer*. He's a *renovator*.'

Ray (taking a break from the Great American Novel): 'Andy, it's hard for us to trust someone north of the river who says he wants to make SoCo a better place. Every time they come down here, they just want to make money.'

'That's why I've fought those developments with you, Ray. With all of you. But Russell's doing this through his foundation. It's a charitable organization. Not all rich guys are bad, Ray.'

'Not when they're paying you.'

'Yes, Ray, I'm getting paid.'

'By a developer.'

'By a renovator.'

'By a rich guy north of the river.'

'Yes, he lives north of the river. But look what he did in East Austin. Look what he's done for all of Austin. He's in the business of giving his money away. And now he's trying to give it away down here in SoCo, and you want us to say no? We've been trying to get the city to do this for years. Now Russell Reeves wants to do it and you're balking? Would you rather have that vacant grocery store? Guys, I wouldn't tell you we should do this if I didn't believe it. There's no ulterior motive here.'

Helping them helped him.

LuAnn: 'Andy's right.'

'Guys, we've been through this before. Apartment rents in SoCo run fifteen hundred for a one-bedroom, two thousand for a two-bedroom. With regular developments, the city tries to get ten percent of the units designated as affordable housing, and that's at eighty percent of median family income, but the developers always balk and the city always backs down. This project is one hundred percent affordable housing at fifty percent median income. Who else would do this kind of deal except a billionaire who doesn't need to make money?'

A grudging murmur of acknowledgment from the crowd.

'Russell Reeves is going to give us affordable housing – that's what we've always wanted. Are you going to turn it down because he lives north of the river? Because he's rich? Guys, he hates Republicans! And he's thinking about getting a tattoo! He's one of us!'

Gus: 'Only difference is, he's got billions. We don't.'

Ramon Cabrera banged a beer bottle against a tin chip bowl.

'Yo, people! This ain't rocket science. It's an easy decision: Do you trust Andy? I do. I vote in favor of Russell Reeves' development.'

'Renovation,' Andy said.

'Whatever.'

Floyd T. said, 'And tell him thanks for the food.'

An hour later, the crowd voted unanimously in favor of Russell Reeves' plans for SoCo.

'Dude, these are good. You want one?'

The downtown lawyer sitting across the table from him lifted his eyes and gave Andy Prescott a 'God bless the children' smile, then shook his head and returned to the stack of documents in front of him. Andy shrugged and thought, More for me.

He was getting down on the fresh chocolate-chip cookies the title company had set out in a little bowl in the center of the conference room table. They were free. His only regret was that he didn't have a glass of milk to dip them in.

A week to the day after the neighborhood meeting

at Güero's, Andy Prescott was sitting in a cushy leather chair in front of a long wood table in the fancy offices of a title company in downtown Austin; the place smelled like a new luxury car, leathery and rich. He was eating cookies and about to close the first real-estate transaction of his legal career.

Russell Reeves' downtown lawyers had drafted the documents, reviewed title and survey, and obtained city approval for the low-income housing. His in-house accountant had wired $4 million to Andy's new trust account; he had never had a trust account before because he had never received a retainer in excess of $100. Russell's lawyers had done all the legal work, but Andy was the front man. The face of SoCo. He was Russell Reeves' lawyer south of the river.

Even though he was now sitting north of the river.

The seller's lawyer sat across the table from Andy. He was a partner in a downtown firm; he was wearing a slick suit and a confident expression as he flipped through the documents. Andy was wearing his traffic court outfit: blue sports coat, jeans, wrinkled shirt, clip-on tie, and Converse sneakers.

Reeves and the seller had already signed; the closing was about the lawyers dotting i's and crossing t's and swapping legal documents for legal tender. Andy felt like he should be doing something, so he started flipping through his stack of documents, too. The documents looked professional with indemnities and representations and warranties. Andy had taken a real-estate course in law school, but he had never even drafted a deed.

Damn. Some of the chocolate on his fingers had rubbed off on the bright white paper of the top document. Andy glanced around for a napkin, but he didn't see one. So he licked his finger and tried to rub the chocolate off, but only succeeded in smearing it across the page. Just as he was going back down with a rewetted finger, the title agent said, 'Andy, are you okay with the form of the Affidavit as to Debts, Liens and Possession?'

Andy vaguely remembered seeing a document with that title.

'Uh, yeah, sure.'

He had no idea what he had just agreed to. He knew it, and she knew it. But neither of them cared. She cared about the $22,777 title insurance premium her agency would pocket; he cared about the $800 he would pocket for this two-hour closing spent eating cookies. *Ka-ching!* God, is this how it worked for downtown lawyers? It was a freaking cash register, this billable-hour scheme. Only a lawyer could have dreamed it up.

He could get used to this, the life of a big-time lawyer.

An hour later, when he walked out of the title company with a half dozen cookies in his coat pocket for Floyd T. and Ramon, Andy stood a moment on the sidewalk and basked in the warmth of the September sun. He had wired the $4 million from his trust account to the title company's bank account; he had taken the deed to the land; he had closed his first major legal transaction.

For the first time in his life, Andy Prescott felt like a success.

Chapter 10

Kelly Fitzgerald ducked out the back door of the hospital to grab a quick smoke. She always felt a bit stupid, a nurse smoking on the job. She had tried to quit, but she could not beat her addiction. Still, she was down to two cigarettes per shift. And she never allowed her craving to interfere with her patient care. It was 3:00 A.M. and all the patients on Three West were asleep. Five minutes off the floor wouldn't harm anyone. She had almost finished the cigarette when the door behind her opened, and a man in a suit walked outside.

'Ms Fitzgerald?'

'Yes.'

The man flashed a badge. 'I'm Agent Smith, FBI.'

She laughed. 'And I'm the president.'

'What?'

'Take your store-bought badge and your game somewhere else.'

'Pardon me?'

'Try another line.'

'What are you talking about?'

171

'What I'm talking about is, I'm an Irish girl married to a cop, my two brothers are New York City cops, and my father was a cop. You're not a cop. You're a lawyer.'

The man seemed disappointed.

'How'd you know?'

'Cops don't say "pardon me."'

'I knew that wasn't good as soon as I said it.' The man sighed. 'Okay. I'm a lawyer.'

'And use a better name – I mean, *Smith*?'

'That is my real name.'

'Oh. Well, Lawyer Smith, what do you want?'

'You were the night-shift charge nurse on Third Floor West three years ago?'

'Yes.'

'You attended Dr Falco's patients?'

'Why are you asking?'

'We're looking for one of his patients.'

'Who?'

'Patient X.'

Kelly took a slow drag on the cigarette and exhaled. The smoke hung like a gray cloud in the cool night air.

'I guess you would be looking for her. Kind of surprised it took this long.'

'She's in hiding.'

'She would be.'

'So she just walked out of here three years ago? What kind of security do you have here?'

'You got in easy enough.'

'And she's never been seen since?'

Kelly had been on duty that night. Falco had not been pleased to find his prized patient missing the next morning.

'No.'

'We don't want to harm her.'

'You want to use her, like Falco.'

'All I need is the woman's name.'

Kelly turned to the lawyer. 'The woman's name?'

'Yes.'

Kelly's mind raced. She bought time with another long drag on the cigarette. She exhaled again.

'I never knew her real name. Falco was paranoid.'

'Ms Fitzgerald, she won't be harmed in any way. We just need to find her and talk to her. We will pay her well. And we will pay you well for her name. One million dollars, Ms Fitzgerald. For her name.'

'I don't know her name.'

'Two million.'

'Goodbye.'

Kelly dashed the cigarette on the iron railing, flicked the butt into the garden, and walked back inside; but she thought, *What is his game?*

The next morning, Dennis Lott sat behind his desk. He would soon be fired as administrator of the hospital. He was sure of that. He had been hired two years ago, just six months before Tony Falco had jumped ship for that Chinese research institute. It was like getting the last berth on the *Titanic*.

Falco had left and the research grants had followed. Dennis was now the administrator of a research hospital without funds to conduct research. The money followed the name scientists like groupies followed rock stars. Falco was a star.

Dennis Lott was not.

He had been completely unsuccessful in attracting new scientists and funding to the hospital. So the board of trustees would soon find another administrator who might prove more successful. Dennis figured he had two months, at the longest. This was his fifth hospital. There would not be a sixth.

Ellen, his secretary, knocked lightly on the door and entered. She shut the door behind her.

'Mr Lott, there's a gentleman here to see you. A Mr Smith.'

'What does he want?'

'He says he wants to give money to the hospital.'

'Give him a brochure and tell him who to write the check to.'

'He wants to give us fifty million dollars.'

Dennis sat up.

'Fifty million?'

Ellen nodded. Dennis stood up.

'Show Mr Smith in.'

Dennis came around his desk while Ellen opened the door and said, 'Mr Smith, please come in.'

A middle-aged man in a suit entered. Dennis had met enough lawyers in his time to recognize another one. He extended his hand, and they shook.

'Mr Smith . . . Dennis Lott. Please sit down.'

Smith took a seat in front of the desk; Dennis sat behind it.

'So you want to donate fifty million to our hospital?'

'That's correct, Mr Lott.'

'Dennis. Well, that's wonderful, Mr Smith. May I ask why we're the lucky beneficiary of your generosity?'

'Because you have something I need, Dennis.'

'And what is that?'

'A name.'

'Whose name?'

Mr Smith dug papers out of his briefcase and put them on Lott's desk. Dennis looked at the top page and laughed.

'What, you work for a drug company?' Mr Smith didn't answer. 'You think Patient X is real?'

'Don't you?'

'No. I think it was all a hoax perpetrated by Falco to hype his research and attract more funding. Researchers do that, you know. Hell, it worked. The Chinese paid him millions to move his research over there.'

'I talked to Falco.'

'You went to China?'

'Yes. I need that name.'

'Falco wouldn't reveal it?'

'No.'

'Did you offer him a donation?'

'Yes.'

'That's Tony. Well, Mr Smith, I'd take your money and give you the name, but unfortunately for both of us, I don't have the names of Falco's research patients.'

'They're not in the hospital records?'

'No. Falco insisted on absolute privacy for his patients. Only he knew their names.'

'But it's your hospital.'

Dennis snorted. 'That's not how things work, Mr Smith. Falco brought in hundreds of millions in research grants. Three West was his kingdom.'

'Well, Dennis, I have fifty million dollars to offer you, if you can give me that woman's name.'

'What woman's name?'

'Patient X.'

Dennis sat back and thought about what Mr Smith knew and what he did not know. Which made him smile. Because what Mr Smith did not know had just saved Dennis Lott's career.

'Mr Smith, I have something much more valuable than a woman's name. But it will cost your client one hundred million dollars.'

Larry Smith was sweating profusely. How could he end up here, kneeling on the concrete floor of an abandoned warehouse in Ithaca, New York, with two thugs standing over him and a gun pointed at his head? He had graduated *summa cum laude* from Yale Law School and had been recruited by prestigious law firms from New York to LA. Ten years later, he was a partner making $800,000 a year. Sure, that required he handle somewhat sleazy assignments from time to time, but even sleazy clients were entitled to a lawyer, right? Well, if they had enough money.

'What did the nurse tell you?'

'Nothing. I swear.'

'What about Lott? Did he give you her name?'

'I can't tell you that. My God, that's attorney–client privileged information!'

The man named Harmon touched the barrel of the gun to Larry's head.

'This is a Glock 9. It doesn't recognize the attorney–client privilege, Mr Smith.'

To hell with the privilege.

'In my briefcase.'

'Open it.'

Larry opened the briefcase. 'There.'

The man removed the papers Lott had given Larry and thumbed through them.

'Very good. Is this all he gave you?'

'Yes.'

That was a lie.

'Who else knows this?'

'I can't say.'

'Give me a name.'

Larry tried to think. He had already sent the items

177

he had purchased from Lott to his client by overnight delivery. So he had completed his assignment. If he revealed his client's identity to this creep, and if that got his client killed, his career would be over because his richest client would be dead; on the other hand, if he revealed his client's name and his client survived, his career would still be over – he would have violated the attorney–client privilege and could be disbarred. He would certainly be fired. Either way, it was so long $800,000 salary. So there seemed to be no upside to revealing his client's identity. But his only chance of survival was to give the man a name. So he gave him the name of someone whose life he would readily trade for his own.

'Andy Prescott.'

'Who's Andy Prescott?'

'A lawyer in Austin.' Larry looked up at the man named Harmon. 'Please don't kill me.'

'Motion denied, Mr Smith.'

Chapter 11

A rich client changes a lawyer's life.

Six weeks to the day after Russell Reeves had walked into his little office above Ramon's tattoo parlor in SoCo, Andy Prescott woke with a mane of blonde hair across his face and a slender arm across his chest – and not his hair or his arm. He smiled, as he often found himself doing these days.

He had closed three deals, billed one hundred fifty hours, and collected $60,000 in legal fees from Russell Reeves. Consequently, he was not waking up that Monday morning in the cheap $600-a-month rent house on Newton Street. (Although he was still renting the house; he wasn't sure why.) He was waking up in a king-sized bed on the top floor of a $3,000-per-month tri-level loft on Fifth Street in downtown Austin. With a girl. A beautiful girl. One of those superficial but incredibly fit Whole Foods girls, like Suzie.

In fact, Suzie.

He propped himself up on his elbow and admired

her; she was awesome. Perfect face, perfect body, perfect smell. She didn't snore. She was like a dream, lying there in his bed. He gently touched her bare bottom; she was real. The touch of his skin against hers, especially that particular patch of her skin, felt even better than that day when he had first run his hands over the new Stumpjumper. Suzie stirred and opened those blue eyes.

'I had a great time last night, Andy.'

They had gone to Qua, the trendy lounge with a shark tank in the floor.

'You were right,' Andy said.

'About what?'

'About being an expensive date.'

An $800 date. Only two billable hours.

'But I'm worth it.'

He rolled over on top of her.

'Oh, yeah.'

Andy Prescott was the happiest man on the planet.

The bedroom on the third level had a fabulous view of Lady Bird Lake. The bathroom had granite counter-tops, a Jacuzzi tub, a two-person, four-jet, walk-in steam shower, and a bidet. The kitchen and living room were on the second level, and the first level was a one-car garage half-sunk into the ground. The place had come fully furnished. All for only seven and a half billable hours per month. The owner was a friend of Tres; he had been temporarily relocated. Andy was renting month-to-month, but who knows – if the owner didn't come back, he might be able to buy the place. Living in a downtown loft was indeed sweet.

An hour later, Suzie was gone and Andy was dressed in a stylish sports coat, a wrinkle-free button-down shirt, a tie that didn't clip on, slacks, and leather shoes and riding the Stumpjumper the two blocks to Whole Foods. He couldn't bring himself to buy a car because of the pollution and high gas prices, but he was wearing new clothes, riding a new trail bike, living in a new place, and dating a new girl. Andy Prescott was a new man. The man he had always dreamed of being.

Thanks to Russell Reeves.

He parked and locked the bike outside Whole Foods and went in for his breakfast tacos — but his journey to the taco bar was interrupted.

'Hi, Andy.'

Bobbi. A senior brunette majoring in nightlife ('journalism' in the curriculum catalog). Another top-of-the-line fit-and-Spandexed Whole Foods girl.

'Oh, hi, Bobbi. You're looking especially delicious this morning.'

She smiled and inched closer. Andy could feel movement south of the border.

'Where's Suzie?'

'Who? Oh, Suzie . . . yeah, she's, uh, somewhere.'

'I saw y'all at Qua last night. I'll be there tonight. If you come alone, maybe we could hang out . . . or whatever.'

Whatever sounded good. But there was Suzie. She

would call him later about his plans for that night. He could just not answer his phone, but then she might unexpectedly stop by the loft. (Funny how territorial women were, which was a new and fascinating experience for Andy.) Or he could . . . Bobbi stepped closer to allow a woman pushing a cart past; her breast – covered only by a thin layer of Spandex – rubbed against Andy's chest and wiped his mind clean of all thoughts of Suzie as effectively as an eraser on a chalkboard.

'I'll see you tonight, Bobbi.'

She squeezed his arm.

'Tonight.'

She walked away. Andy stared after her. Bobbi had a bodacious body.

You couldn't slap the smile off Andy Prescott's face.

Andy was a new man, but he still got his coffee at Jo's.

'Mr GQ dude himself,' Guillermo Garza said when Andy stepped up to his window for his coffee. 'Looking sharp, bro. Large coffee and a muffin?'

'Just the coffee. I ate at Whole Foods. But give me Floyd T.'s.'

Guillermo nodded at the trail bike.

'That's an awesome ride, dude.'

'Stumpjumper.'

'What'd that set you back?'

'Sixty-five hundred.'

'Living large now.'

'I'm still the same guy.'

Guillermo laughed. 'If Russell Reeves hired me, I sure wouldn't be the same guy.' He pointed past Andy. 'You forget something?'

'What?'

'The *Chronicle*.'

'Nah.'

'Oh, don't need to look for love in the personals anymore, huh, Andy?'

Andy smiled. 'I found a better place.'

Now Guillermo smiled. 'Whole Foods.'

'Amen, brother.'

They fist-punched.

'Keep the faith, bro.'

Andy paid then pedaled to his office. He found Floyd T. on Ramon's stoop and gave him his breakfast; he put a $20 bill in Floyd T.'s cigar box. Floyd T. whistled.

'A high-roller. Thanks, Andy.'

Andy Prescott was still the same guy, albeit better dressed and with better transportation. He still worked in the little office above Ramon's tattoo parlor, he still mooched off Ramon's Yahoo account, and he still went to traffic court.

He was trapped by his own traffic ticket scheme.

He had requested a jury trial on every ticket for every client; consequently, he had cases set for trial every Monday of every week for the next two years. If he didn't show up to contest, the city would win by default; and he would have to make good on his guarantees to his clients. At $500 a pop, the fines would add up fast. He had five cases set for that Monday morning, so he was looking at upwards of $2,500 out of pocket. His pocket. Out of which he had just paid $15,000 to the IRS for quarterly income taxes, social security taxes, and Medicaid taxes – an outrageous sum! Six weeks' hard work, and he had netted only $45,000 after taxes. Now he understood why rich people complained about the government taking their money.

He could not afford to pay his clients' fines.

So just before nine, Andy Prescott walked into the Municipal Court Building. Arturo waved him through the security checkpoint without making him empty his pockets. Andy rode the elevator to the third floor and entered the courtroom. Judge Judith immediately motioned him forward. When he arrived at the bench, she smiled at him like a mother whose prodigal son had returned home – with a job. She put her hand over the microphone.

'Andy, you're looking quite professional today. And your hair – very nice.'

'Thank you, Judge. You're looking as beautiful as ever.'

'I know you're busy with Mr Reeves, so we'll call your cases first.'

'Why, thank you, Judge.'

Fifteen minutes later, his five cases were dismissed and Andy was walking out the door. Ms Manning stopped him and handed him her business card. She leaned close and whispered.

'Come by my office, Andy. We'll lock the door and bang out a plea bargain.'

She gave him a wicked wink. Ms Prosecutor had a wild streak beneath that buttoned-up suit.

Andy was smiling when he walked out the courtroom door.

And he was still smiling when he arrived back at his office where he found Floyd T. sitting on the sidewalk with his back to the building writing in his notebook and a limo parked out front with an action figure named Darrell leaning against the back door. Russell Reeves' driver/bodyguard jutted his jaw toward Ramon's.

'He's in the tattoo shop.'

Andy went inside and found Russell Reeves in deep conversation with Ramon Cabrera.

'Does it hurt?'

Ramon laughed. 'Of course, it hurts, Russell. Pain is part of the experience.'

'I don't know, Ramon. I really like the idea of my son's face tattooed on my back, but I'm not big on physical pain.'

'Russell, my man, excruciating physical pain is the threshold a man must cross to get to the other side of life.'

'And what's on the other side?'

'Enlightenment.'

'Have you been to the other side, Ramon?'

Ramon pulled his sweatshirt over his head to reveal his painted upper body. He spread his arms and turned slowly.

'Russell . . . I *am* the other side.'

Russell Reeves regarded the living mural that was Ramon Cabrera.

'My God, you're a work of art.'

'I am an artist and I am art.'

After a moment, Russell said, 'I'll think about it.'

'You do that.'

'Later, Ramon.'

Ramon stuck his fist out; Russell gave him a fist-punch like he had done it before then turned and walked outside.

'Tickets,' Ramon said to Andy.

'What are you doing in so early?'

'Appointment.' He checked his watch. 'She's late.'

Andy grabbed the two tickets off the counter, then followed Russell outside where he found Darrell jabbing Floyd T. with his shoe.

'Get out of my way, you stinkin' bum.'

Andy vaulted past Russell and pushed Darrell in the chest as hard as he could; the ape barely budged.

'Leave him alone, you big jerk!'

The big jerk grabbed Andy by the shoulders and squeezed; the pressure of Darrell's stubby fingers pressing deep into his bones made Andy's knees buckle. He thought he would faint when he heard Russell's calm voice.

186

'Let him go, Darrell.'

Darrell's dark eyes moved off Andy and onto his billionaire boss.

'Now.'

Darrell released his grip. Andy almost fell to the pavement.

'Apologize.'

Darrell sighed and turned to Andy.

'Sorry for grabbing you and—'

'Not him. Floyd T.'

'*What?*'

'Apologize to Floyd T.'

Darrell pointed down at Floyd T. 'To a homeless bum?'

'To a war hero.'

'A war hero?'

'Yes. Floyd T. is a decorated war hero, Darrell. He gave his leg for his country. You should respect that.'

Darrell's face softened; he looked down at Floyd T.

'Hey, man, I'm sorry. For calling you a bum.'

Floyd T. turned an expressionless face up to Darrell and said, 'Asshole.'

Russell laughed. 'Touché, Darrell.'

Darrell shook his head and returned to his position by the limo. Russell handed a $100 bill to Floyd T.

'Sorry, Floyd T.'

Floyd T. took the bill.

'Thanks, Russell. But you shouldn't employ assholes. You can't trust them.'

'You're probably right.'

Andy and his client climbed the stairs to the little office. Andy propped open the window and checked to make sure that Darrell wasn't bullying Floyd T. again.

'That was nice, what you did for Floyd T.'

'Just a hundred bucks.'

'No, making Darrell apologize.'

'Floyd T. earned it.'

'I didn't know you two had met.'

'First time I stopped by, when you weren't here. We visited a while. He's a human being, Andy. And an interesting one.'

'Darrell's lucky Floyd T. was sitting down. If he was standing, he might've taken his leg off and beaten the hell out of Darrell with it.'

Russell sighed. 'Darrell is . . . Darrell.'

'Why do you have a guy like him working for you?'

'Because it's hard to find a compassionate bodyguard, Andy.' He shook his head. 'It's the world we live in. I'm worth fifteen billion dollars, so I'm vulnerable to kidnapping. So is my wife. So I need a bodyguard. Being wealthy has its benefits, but there are burdens, too.'

They sat across the card table from each other.

'I just drove by the development sites.'

'*Renovation* sites.'

'Construction is progressing well. I knew you were the right lawyer for that job, Andy.'

'Thanks.'

'And I think you're the right lawyer for this job.'

'What job?'

Russell leaned back.

'Andy, I want to make amends.'

'For what?'

'The past. I've reexamined my life and found it wanting.'

'Wanting for what? You're a billionaire.'

'For what money can't buy. Peace. I'm not proud of everything I've done, Andy. I deeply regret certain of my actions.'

He sounded like that senator who had gotten caught with his pants down in an airport bathroom. Andy nodded.

'I know what you mean, Russell. Fortunately, my mind has blocked out the memories.'

'Because of the psychic pain?'

'Because of the Coronas.'

'Oh. Well, what I've done is a bit more serious than getting drunk and making a fool of myself.'

He didn't know about making a fool of himself.

'Andy, I—'

Andy had tried to lighten the moment, but Russell was having none of it. He remained deadly serious. Andy was sure his client was about to confess to murder.

'—I didn't treat the women in my life well.'

Andy realized he had been holding his breath; he exhaled. *That's it?* But then he thought, Maybe he had abused them, although any womyn in SoCo could kick

Russell Reeves' ass into next week. He didn't have the body mass to abuse women.

'Your wife?'

'My girlfriends.'

'What happened?'

The billionaire across the card table sighed.

'I loved them and left them.'

'You mean, you broke up with your girlfriends?'

Russell nodded.

'But you didn't hurt them . . . physically?'

'Oh, no. I just left them without concern for their emotional pain. I thought only about myself.'

'So you're feeling guilty about your ex-girlfriends, from what, fifteen, twenty years ago?'

Russell nodded again.

'How many are we talking – one, two?'

'Seventeen.'

'*Seventeen*. You had seventeen girlfriends? Before you were rich?'

He shrugged. 'I had a great personality.'

'You must also have the biggest . . .' Andy shook his head. 'Seventeen. Wow. That's impressive, Russell.'

'Andy, haven't you thought about your old girlfriends? Wondered where they're at, how they're doing?'

'I've only had one girlfriend, back in fourth grade. Mary Margaret McDermott. She's married to a doctor, got four kids.'

'You're twenty-nine and your last girlfriend was in fourth grade?'

'Until now. Thanks to you.'

'Me?'

'You pay me well.'

Russell Reeves smiled. 'Yes, I suppose a Whole Foods girl doesn't come cheap.'

'You know about Suzie?'

Or Bobbi.

'I stopped in one day for a smoothie and saw you talking to a young woman. A blonde.'

Suzie.

'I assumed she was your girlfriend. She's quite lovely.'

'She is sweet.'

Andy's thoughts drifted back to that morning in bed . . . Suzie's awesome naked body . . . and they—

'Andy?'

'What? Oh, yeah, your ex-girlfriends.'

'I want to make it up to them.'

'How?'

'The only way I can – money.'

'You want to give your old girlfriends money because you broke up with them a long time ago?'

'Because I used them as sexual objects for my own pleasure.'

'Russell, that's what men do. Women, too. Down here in SoCo, we just ask that they do it inside.' He shook his head. 'Was it consensual?'

'Of course.'

'Then what's the problem?'

'Guilt.'

191

'Are you Catholic, too?'

'No.'

Andy grunted. 'So what's the job?'

'Find them. Give them money. Make their lives better.'

'You want me to find your old girlfriends and give them money? As simple as that?'

'As simple as that.'

'I just hand each woman a check and say, "Russell Reeves says hi"?'

'No. I want to do this anonymously.'

'Why?'

'Seventeen women, one might go to the press. Can you imagine that in the tabloids? They'd have a field day.'

'I guess that would make the papers.'

'Andy, I want you to find my old girlfriends. If they're in debt, I'm going to pay off their debts. If they're sick, I'm going to pay for their medical care. If they're homeless, I'm going to buy them a home. I'm going to make things right by making their lives better. But this assignment must remain absolutely secret. You must not reveal this to anyone – not even Suzie.'

'Why don't you just hire a PI?'

'PIs talk. They sell information. And they can testify. You can't.'

Andy leaned back in his chair.

'The privilege.'

Russell Reeves nodded.

'The attorney–client privilege,' Andy said. 'I can't disclose anything to anyone. I can't even be compelled to testify about this in a court of law.'

'Exactly. And if you did tell your girlfriend and it ended up in the papers?'

'I'd be disbarred.'

His billionaire client nodded again.

'Absolute secrecy, Andy.'

Russell handed a document to Andy across the desk. It was two pages of names and addresses.

'That's all you have?'

'Their names and last-known addresses.'

'Russell, I don't even know where to start.'

Russell gestured at the document.

'Bottom of the last page, there's a name. Hollis McCloskey. He's a private investigator downtown, ex-FBI. Upper-echelon type. My lawyers have used him on corporate investigations. He doesn't usually hunt people down, but he will for the right price.'

'I thought you didn't want to hire a PI?'

'I don't. I want you to hire him. Give him the list, nothing more. Don't mention my name. Tell him to find them, learn everything about them – their assets, debts, husbands, children – and compile a dossier on each. But his job ends there. He is not to make contact with the women. That's your job. Figure out what they need and how I can help them. Then bring it to me.'

'How will I know if I've got the right women?'

'Take photos. I'll know.'

'I don't have a camera.'

'Buy one. My tab.'

'This big-time PI, he's not going to be cheap, Russell.'

'I wired fifty thousand to your trust account this morning, while you were in traffic court. Pay him whatever it takes.'

'Russell, why me for this job? I mean, I understand the SoCo deals, but your downtown lawyers can do this. They can hire this McCloskey dude.'

'I don't want my regular lawyers to know anything about this.'

'Why not?'

'Because I know Hollis and he knows me. And he knows my lawyers. If my lawyers hire Hollis, he'll know I'm the client. And if he knows, then his employees will know . . . and their wives and husbands and girlfriends and boyfriends will know. Everyone will know. I can't have that, Andy. No one can know.'

Andy shrugged. 'You're the boss.'

'Good. These are the ground rules. We only discuss this matter in person, not over the phone. No emails. Nothing in writing. When you have something, call me on my cell phone and I'll come down here.'

Andy scanned down the list. 'These addresses, they're in Houston, Chicago, New Orleans, Miami, LA, Denver . . . Were they students at UT back then?'

'No. I met them on my business travels.'

'You'd go to Chicago or Miami and meet a girl and she'd have sex with you? For free?'

Russell just raised his eyebrows, as if to say, I don't want to brag, but . . .

'You want me to fly all over the country to find these women?'

'First class.'

'I can fly first class?'

'Of course.'

Andy had never flown first class.

'And luxury rental cars. You do know how to drive something other than that bike?'

'Sure.'

'Five-star hotels, room service, whatever you want.'

'Can I watch those pay-per-view movies in my room?'

'Sure. But not porn.'

'Oh.'

He tried not to sound disappointed.

'And I'll pay you five hundred an hour. Because you'll be traveling a lot . . . and because you'll have to defer sweet Suzie until this job is done. Think you can do that?'

'Sure.'

He didn't say anything about bodacious Bobbi.

'Russell, what about the other SoCo deals?'

'Put them on the back burner. Work this job twenty-four seven. I want these women found ASAP.'

'You're the boss.'

Andy's rich boss. He sat back. Okay, this was all a bit weird – Andy gave it a seven on the Weird-Shit-

O-Meter-of-Life – but then, his mother always said, 'Rich people are different than you and me.' And Dave said he had read about a black rapper who takes a bubble bath every day and an Irish movie star who coats himself in honey then takes a steam bath – and female stars who do regular body cleanses to stay skinny. Heck, compared to that, Russell Reeves wanting to find a few old girlfriends seemed almost normal. Almost.

Andy realized his boss was staring at him.

'Something bothering you, Andy?'

Something was.

'Russell, can I ask you something?'

'Sure, Andy. What?'

'Is there more to this than you're telling me?'

Russell considered him a moment, then stood and walked to the window. He looked out a while before speaking.

'Andy, do you read the obituaries?'

'No. Do you?'

'Every day.'

'Why?'

'Because of my son. You know about him?'

'Just what I've read in the paper.'

'He's a great kid. And brave. He's dying, but he faces each day with a smile.' He paused. 'I killed my own son, Andy.'

'Killed your son? How?'

'I'm a carrier.'

'Of what?'

196

'A mutated gene – a cancer gene. I gave it to Zach.'

'Russell, it's not your fault. You didn't know you had the gene – did you?'

'No. But that doesn't change the fact that Zach is dying because of me. That I sentenced him to death.'

'Your scientists . . . they can't save him?'

'No, Andy, they can't. My only son is going to die.'

Jesus. Andy felt like an absolute jerk. In the six weeks since Russell Reeves had hired him, he had not once thought about his client's personal pain – his only son was dying. Andy had never thought of his client beyond the fees he had paid and the fees he would pay. Russell Reeves had given his lawyer Suzie and the Stumpjumper, the loft and lounges, standing in Muny Court and at Whole Foods. Andy had not given his client a second thought. He had looked upon Russell Reeves solely as a source of income. Andy Prescott had become a bona fide lawyer.

'I'm sorry, Russell.'

He thought his client might cry, but Russell caught himself.

'I'm sorry for you, too, Andy. For your father.'

'You know about him?'

Russell nodded. 'I listen to his CDs in the limo. He's good. Should've been a big star.'

Now Andy thought he might cry.

'He never got his big break.'

Attorney and client regarded each other. They shared a common fate. Russell blew out a breath.

'So I read about dead people. About their lives. What they did, who they loved, who loved them. It's made me think about my own life . . . what I've done, who I've loved, who loved me. How I've treated other people in my life. I want to make things right . . . with my son, with these women, with my life . . . before I . . .'

His client looked as if all the strength had left him. He turned to his lawyer.

'Andy, will you help me?'

'Yes, Russell. I'll help you.'

'Thanks.'

Russell Reeves walked to the door, but turned back.

'Andy, my secrets are safe with you, right?'

Andy nodded. 'I'm your lawyer.'

Chapter 12

Lawyers keep secrets. Their clients' secrets. It's called the attorney–client privilege. You learn about the privilege in your first year of law school. By your third year, without ever making a conscious decision, you have accepted the argument as truth: that everything a lawyer learns about a client must remain secret. It is your legal duty.

Andy Prescott was Russell Reeves' lawyer.

He read the first name on the list: Sue Todd. Her last known address was in Houston. Andy pulled out his cell phone and called long-distance information in the Houston area code. He asked for Sue Todd's number and gave the operator her address; the operator said no Sue Todd was listed at that address. He hung up.

How do you find someone?

Hollis McCloskey's private investigation firm maintained offices in the Frost Bank Tower at Fourth and Congress in downtown. When McCloskey strode into the reception area that same afternoon, Andy felt as if he should assume the position – lean into the wall, hands above his head, feet back and spread – so McCloskey could frisk him.

The guy was intimidating.

He looked every bit the ex-FBI agent: mid-fifties, broad-shouldered, square-jawed, sharp suit, and shiny shoes. His hair was blow-dried perfection with streaks of gray on the sides. He even smelled like a cop; Brut aftershave, Andy figured. McCloskey stuck a big hand out and they shook.

'Hollis McCloskey. What can I do for you?'

'I'm Andy Prescott. I need to find seventeen people.'

'We don't find people, Andy,' McCloskey said. 'We ferret out corporate malfeasance.'

Malfeasance? Andy vaguely recalled that word from law school.

'Mr McCloskey, what's your standard rate?'

'Two hundred an hour.'

'I'll pay you four hundred.'

McCloskey sized up Andy, then said, 'Let's talk in my office.'

Andy followed Agent McCloskey down a corridor to an expansive corner office with a grand view of the capitol and the UT Tower. Diplomas and FBI certificates covered the walls, along with photographs of McCloskey with politicians Andy recognized and even a president. Handguns sat encased in glass boxes on shelves. Mounted on the wall was a Tommy gun like FBI Special Agent Elliot Ness carried in that movie, *The Untouchables*.

'Sit down.'

It sounded like an order; Andy obeyed.

'So you're a lawyer?'

'Yes. You were highly recommended by one of your clients.'

'Who?'

'Confidential.'

McCloskey folded his arms across his broad chest.

'Your client wants to locate seventeen people?'

'Women. ASAP.'

'That would require overtime.'

'I'll pay five hundred an hour, twenty-four-seven.'

Andy felt like a politician, spending other people's money freely and without concern.

'Why do you want to find these women?'

'I don't. My client does.'

'Who's your client?'

'That's also confidential.'

'And why does your client want to find these women?'

'Sorry. Confidential.'

'Andy, I don't like all this mystery.'

Andy reached into his shirt pocket and pulled out a cashier's check drawn on his trust account for $25,000 made payable to Hollis McCloskey. He pushed it across the desk. The G-man glanced at the check then back at Andy.

'Call me Hollis.'

'Hollis, there's more where that came from. But this

assignment must have your full attention. I need a complete dossier on each woman – personal, employment, and criminal history, financial condition, family problems . . . everything.'

'Andy, so we're clear, I go by the book. I do not wander off the reservation, understood?'

The reservation?

Andy shrugged. 'Sure, whatever. When you complete a dossier, bring it to me. Fifteen-fourteen and a half B South Congress.'

'You office in SoCo? I'll send a courier.'

'If I'm not there, tell him to leave it at the tattoo parlor downstairs.'

'There's a nude yoga class on Thursday,' Dave said. 'You guys want to go?'

'You in the lotus position, naked,' Andy said. 'That's not an image I want in my head.'

'Listen to this girl's statement,' Curtis said. He was reading personal ads again. 'She says, "I'm working on a PhD in cosmology and consciousness, looking specifically at the continuum between time and time-lessness from the perspective of physics and subjective experience. I'm trying to live a less abstract version of reality these days."'

Dave stared blank-faced at Curtis.

'So does she want sex or not?'

'Guys,' Andy said, 'you're not going to find true love in the personals.'

They both now stared at him. Dave shook his head.

'How quickly you forget those of us still stranded in the sexual desert.'

Tres laughed. 'The sexual desert? I like that, Dave.'

'Thanks. But I've got a plan to escape that desert.'

'What's that?' Andy said.

Dave pulled out his comb and swept his hair back.

'I'm gonna get a tattoo. A big one.'

'Why?'

'Girls love tattoos.'

'But they hurt.'

'Girls?'

'Well, yeah, them too. And you hate pain.'

'I'm gonna get a general anesthetic first.'

'It's called alcohol. Dave, you think a tattooed real-estate broker is going to get a lot of clients?'

'Doesn't matter. I've got to find another job anyway – the market's tanked. I've got one listing – a subprime foreclosure over by the greenbelt – one-point-five-million-dollar mortgage. The borrowers just walked away.'

'You sell it for a million, a six percent commission is sixty grand.'

'Split with the buyer's broker.'

'Thirty grand.'

'Split with my office.'

'Fifteen grand. That'd keep you in beer for a while.'

'True, but chances of selling that place are nil. No one's even looked at it.'

Ronda delivered their Coronas. Andy told her to put it on his tab. It was that night, and they were at their regular table on the front porch of Güero's. Erin Jaimes and Her Bad Habits were playing in the Oak Garden. The beer was cold, the music good, and the early October weather perfect.

And so was she.

Conversations stopped. Heads turned. Men stared. Girls frowned. A TV truck had pulled up, and Natalie Riggs, local TV personality, had stepped out. She walked up the sidewalk, stunning in a yellow sundress. The setting sun outlined her body beneath the dress. No underwear was evident. They stared at her like prison inmates.

Her teeth were movie-star white. Her figure was incredible. Her diamond engagement ring could choke a horse. She came to Tres, leaned over, and gave him a kiss. She whispered to him then stood tall and addressed them.

'Hello, boys.'

Not *Hidi, y'all*. Born and raised in Odessa, Natalie Riggs had worked diligently to erase 'hidi' and 'y'all' and every other trace of Texas talk from her speech. 'The networks don't find twang-talking Texans cute anymore,' she had said. 'Not after Bush.'

Tres walked her back to the truck. He waved at the driver, then dug in his pocket and handed a few bills to Natalie. She kissed him again then jumped into the truck and drove off. Tres returned to the table through a gauntlet of envious eyes. He sat down.

'See – no underwear.'

They drank their beers. The crowd noise picked up again and things soon returned to normal on the front porch of Güero's. Andy hoped that Dave had the good sense not to comment. He didn't.

'Tres,' Dave said. 'You think Natalie would cheat with me? I mean, I love you like a brother, but . . . *damn*. She is hot.'

Andy was giving even odds whether Tres would smile or reach across the table and smack Dave. After a moment, he smiled.

'She is, isn't she?'

Tres Thorndike was good about having a gorgeous girlfriend who didn't wear undergarments.

A loud *aah* went up from the front porch. They looked out to the street; a jaywalker had narrowly dodged death by bus.

'I answered this ad,' Curtis said.

'What ad?'

Curtis held out an ad. Andy took it and looked at the girl's photo. Poor thing.

'Well, Curtis, she's, uh . . . well, she's . . . cute.'

'Read her interests.'

'Let's see. Her interests range from DNA research to quantum physics. Okay, I see why you answered her ad.'

'Read on.'

'She likes Amy's and Whole Foods . . . she's pagan and liberal . . . she recycles . . . she . . . Curtis, she's *forty*.'

'I went older, like Dave said.'

'I was joking,' Dave said.

'I was alone.'

'So what's she like?'

'I don't know. She turned me down.'

'How long has her ad been active?'

'Two years.'

'That's way low, bro.'

'Girls do hurt,' Curtis said.

'Tell me something I don't know,' Dave said.

Andy almost felt guilty for having Suzie and Bobbi while they had no one. Almost. He didn't because he knew he was just a surfer riding a monster wave, always knowing it would end but wondering when it would end. And how. He read the rest of the forty-year-old woman's ad and immediately spotted the problem.

'Curtis, she wants a man with Christian Bale's body.'

'Forty years old, you'd think she'd lower her standards.'

'She wants Christian Bale, she'll still be waiting when she's fifty.'

Curtis shook his head and huddled with Dave over the personals. Andy drank from his beer then turned to Tres.

'How many girlfriends you figure you've had?'

'Since when?'

'Since you started having girlfriends.'

Tres thought a moment. 'Ten. Not counting relationships that lasted a night, you know, at frat parties.'

'And you've been rich all that time?'

Tres shrugged. 'Yeah.'

'How many girlfriends you figure a guy like Russell Reeves would have had in his life?'

'Before or after he was a billionaire?'

'Before.'

'Zero. Without the money, he's got less to offer a girl than Curtis.'

'Those ten girlfriends . . . you ever wonder how they're doing now?'

'Sure. I hope the two that dumped me are miserable and alone. The others, I hope they're doing great.'

'Seriously.'

'Seriously? No, I don't think about them.'

'You ever feel guilty?'

'About what?'

'Having sex with them then leaving.'

'Why should I feel guilty?'

'You shouldn't, but do you?'

'No.'

'Would you give them money?'

'For what?'

'To make yourself feel better about leaving them.'

'I feel fine about that.'

Andy drank from his beer.

'Lorenzo,' Tres said, 'the PI? He followed Bruce.'

'Bruce who?'

'The weekend sports anchor.'

'Thought you wanted him to follow Natalie?'

'I did, and he did. For a month. Then he followed Bruce . . . to Oilcan Harry's.'

'He's gay?' Andy said.

'Apparently.'

Oilcan Harry's was a popular gay bar in downtown Austin.

'Wasn't he a UT linebacker, All-American?'

'I guess being in locker rooms with naked guys all those years got to him.'

'So Natalie's not cheating with him?'

'Nope.'

'Then who's she cheating with?'

'No one.'

'Maybe you should trust her, Tres, underwear or no underwear, if you're going to marry her.'

'Maybe I will. Trust her.'

'So what's the latest on your Indian surrogate?'

'Name's Prisha. Eighteen years old, never been married, no drug use, no criminal record, no diseases . . . she's a virgin.'

'That'll be a rude awakening, birthing your baby.'

'She'll probably never have sex after that. Speaking of which, you going to Qua later?'

'Might as well.'

'Suzie?'

'Bobbi.'

'Bobbi's nice.'

'Very nice.'

Tres chucked Andy on the shoulder.

'Being Russell Reeves' lawyer changed things for you. Before, you were looking for love in the personals, couldn't get into Pangaea or Qua . . . or Suzie or Bobbi. Now look at you.'

'I'm still the same guy.'

Tres drained his beer.

'No, Andy, you'll never be the same guy. Once you get a taste of money, what it can do for you, how it changes the way people look at you . . . value you . . . you can never go back. You won't want to go back. You'll do whatever you have to do so you don't go back. And you'll never be the same.'

Chapter 13

The next morning, Andy Prescott arrived at his office to find a young man with a Marine haircut, military tattoos, and a package in his lap sitting on Ramon's stoop next to Floyd T., who was hefting his left leg like a log. War stories. The man looked up at Andy.

'Mr McCloskey said to leave this package in the tattoo parlor if you weren't here, but the place isn't open yet.'

'Ramon works late so he sleeps late.'

'I told him,' Floyd T. said.

Andy handed Floyd T. his breakfast then signed for the package and went upstairs. He sat down and removed a binder detailing the life of Sue Todd. Tabs divided the dossier into personal history, work history, and criminal history.

She had no criminal history. Her work history was short. Her personal history was sad. Sue Todd was thirty-six years old, unmarried, and unemployed. She lived in a rent house in Pasadena, a working-class suburb of Houston. She drove a twelve-year-old Honda and had a twelve-year-old son named Ricky.

Andy checked the time: 9:15. He put the camera with the zoom lens he had bought the day before inside his backpack, then called a cab.

Andy flew Southwest to Hobby Airport on the south side of Houston; it was only a forty-five-minute flight. Southwest's Austin-to-Houston flights departed every other hour, as convenient as taking the bus and almost as glamorous.

He arrived in Houston at eleven-thirty and rented a Cadillac CTS with a navigation system – which was useless without Curtis there to operate it. So he navigated by the Houston area map he found in the glove compartment. It wasn't hard. The City of Pasadena lies just a few miles due east of the airport across Interstate 45; its northern boundary butts up against the Houston Ship Channel, which serves the Port of Houston.

The Port of Houston is the second busiest port in the US, no minor feat given that Houston is situated fifty-two miles from the nearest navigable deep-water body, Galveston Bay. But after the Great Hurricane of 1900, which leveled Galveston, killed seven thousand residents, and destroyed the thriving Port of Galveston, Houston's civic boosters saw a golden opportunity. They went to Washington and convinced the Feds that the country needed a more secure inland port, at say, Houston. So they dredged Buffalo Bayou from just east of downtown Houston all the way to Galveston Bay to create the Houston Ship Channel.

During World War Two, oil refineries and petro-chemical plants set up shop along the banks of the channel to provide fuel and supplies to fight the war. Pollution was of no concern; there was a war to win. Sixty years later, pollution was still of no concern. Today, the ship channel has the single largest concentration of refineries and petrochemical plants in North America, the water is contaminated with dioxins and polychlorinated biphenyls, and the air is so thick with pollutants you don't breathe it as much as swallow it.

Andy entered the City of Pasadena.

Blue-collar workers had followed the refineries and plants for the jobs; neighborhoods had grown up along the banks of the ship channel. Cities like Deer Park and Galena Park and Pasadena flourished. But today, only poor people live along the ship channel and breathe the contaminated air. The middle class have moved away. And the upper class have always lived on the other side of Houston.

Andy arrived at Sue Todd's home just after noon.

She still lived at her last-known address on Russell's list; the phone was still listed under the name of a boyfriend who had split. Her small home sat in the shadows of the smokestacks that towered overhead just beyond the neighborhood and spewed steam and smoke into the air. The old Honda was parked in the front driveway, so Andy stopped down the street where he had a clear view. Maybe Russell would buy Sue Todd a new car and a nicer house in a better part of town.

212

Andy left the Caddy idling and the air conditioner on high. He had settled in and begun reading the dossier when a woman wearing jeans and a T-shirt walked out of the house. Andy snapped a few close-up photos with the zoom lens before she got into the Honda. He followed her to a school where she pulled into the carpool lane. A boy soon walked out of the school and got into the car. He was wearing a knit cap. Andy trailed them to a medical clinic. They parked and got out. The boy had removed the cap. He was bald.

Andy had a bad feeling about this.

He took a few more photos then followed them inside and onto an elevator. The woman gave him a grim smile. He followed them off the elevator and down a corridor. They entered an office with a sign that read ONCOLOGIST.

Ricky Todd had cancer.

Damn. When he had taken this job, Andy had figured he'd jet around the country in first-class cabins, stay in five-star hotels, and eat fancy food. He'd live large on his rich client's expense account. For a lawyer, it didn't get any better than that. He'd meet Russell Reeves' old girlfriends and give them money to pay off debts or buy a new house or maybe take a dream vacation. Pay college tuition. Braces for the kids. A wedding.

He never figured on a sick kid.

Andy stood in the hallway. He hated doctors' offices. Bad smells, bad thoughts, bad endings. But he bucked himself up and entered the oncologist's office. The

213

reception area was vacant except for the woman and the boy. Andy sat down across from them. She stared at him; her grim smile was now a look of confusion. He started to explain, but a glass window in one wall slid open and a voice called out, 'Sue Todd.' She stood, walked over, and talked to the window. Andy could hear the conversation.

The voice: 'Still no health insurance?'

'No.'

'Credit card?'

'Try this one.'

Sue Todd handed a credit card through the open window. A minute later, a hand returned the card.

'Do you have another one?'

'Not one they'll approve charges on.'

'Ms Todd, we need payment.'

The hand again emerged through the open window and pointed at a sign posted there: IF INSURANCE COVERAGE IS NOT VERIFIED, PAYMENT IN FULL IS REQUIRED AT TIME SERVICES ARE RENDERED.

'Please, I'll get it to you, somehow. He needs the chemo.'

'I'll check with the business manager.'

The glass window slid shut. Sue Todd leaned her head against the wall and closed her eyes. She shook her head and said, as if she didn't know whether to laugh or cry, 'The business manager decides whether he gets chemo.'

Andy glanced at Ricky. Their eyes met for a brief

moment, then the boy looked down and stared at his hands. The glass window slid open again. The voice: 'He said this time only, Ms Todd. You must make arrangements to pay your bill in full prior to his next treatment.'

'Thank you.'

The window slid shut. A side door opened, and a nurse appeared.

'Ricky.'

'I'll be right back, honey,' Sue Todd said.

The boy stood and walked through the door like he'd walked through it many times before. The nurse shut the door behind them. Sue slumped into a chair and breathed out as if it were her last breath.

'I try not to cry in front of him.'

She cried.

'They give him chemo, but it won't stay in remission . . . the lymphoma. He had experimental stem cell treatment a few years back, in a clinical trial, but it didn't work. Nothing works.'

'How long?'

'Four years.'

'No health insurance?'

She shook her head. 'I lost my job a year ago. No one will hire me now because his cancer will increase their health insurance rates.'

She wiped her face.

'Where's his father?'

'Gone. I picked the wrong man.'

'How are you handling things?'

215

'Credit cards. I owe a hundred thousand now. They send me nasty letters.' She gestured at the glass window. 'I don't know how I'll pay the doctor.'

She ran her sleeve across her face.

'I'm spilling my guts to a complete stranger. That's what it does to you, cancer. It kills you every way possible. Your finances, your pride, your life. It beats you into the dirt.'

'What are his chances, your boy?'

'Not good. It's because of all those refineries and chemical plants.'

'His cancer?'

She nodded. 'Kids in the neighborhood, they cough all the time, get nosebleeds. You live by the ship channel, your kids got a fifty percent better chance of getting cancer, because of the toxic chemicals those plants put out – carcinogens. Twenty times higher level than anywhere else in the country. It was in the paper. The stuff is killing kids, but the government won't stop it.'

'Why don't you leave?'

'If we leave here, we live in the car.'

Sue Todd appeared twenty years older than her age. Life had beaten her down, stolen her middle age, robbed her of her best years. She must have gone straight from a young woman to an old woman. She wasn't one of those thirty-something 'women seeking men' in Lovers Lane; she was just hoping to survive the day. And save her son.

★   ★   ★

Three hours later, Andy was sitting in his office across the card table from a billionaire whose son was also dying of leukemia. Cancer was an equal-opportunity killer.

Andy had flown back to Austin and taken a cab to SoCo and the digital camera to a photo shop. The photographs he had taken of Sue Todd and her son were now spread across the card table.

'You recognize her?' Andy said.

Russell Reeves was examining the photos. He shook his head.

'She looks so much older. The boy has cancer?'

Andy nodded. 'I trailed them to a cancer clinic, talked to Sue. She doesn't have insurance, so she maxed out her credit cards, owes a hundred grand. The clinic didn't want to give the boy his chemo treatment because she couldn't pay. She begged.'

Russell rubbed his temples as if he had a headache.

'I'll wire five hundred thousand to your trust account. Take her a cashier's check.' He paused. 'No, I'll wire a million. And I'll make a call. Send her over to the children's cancer ward at M.D. Anderson. They'll be expecting her. Her son will have the best care available. For free.'

'Have you been there?'

'Yes, Andy, I've been there. And so has my son.'

Russell got up and walked out without another word. Andy could swear he had tears in his eyes.

★   ★   ★

The next morning, Andy flew back to Houston. He didn't drink a beer or flirt with the flight attendant. Instead, he thought of Sue and Ricky Todd and the cashier's check he had in his pocket.

Would the money save the boy's life?

He drove straight to Sue Todd's house. The Honda was in the driveway. He was thinking exactly what he would say to her when the front door opened and she appeared. She walked to the mailbox at the curb and pulled out a stack of thick envelopes. Credit card statements, no doubt. She sat on a bench on the front porch and opened the envelopes; with each one she seemed to become smaller. After the final envelope, she put her face in her hands. Andy got out of the car and walked up to her.

'Sue.'

She wiped her face.

'We met yesterday, at the clinic. May I sit?'

She nodded. Andy sat next to her.

'I'm Andy Prescott. I'm a lawyer.'

'I can't pay.'

'I'm not here to collect your debts, Sue. I'm here to pay them off.'

He pulled the envelope out of his pocket and removed the cashier's check for $1 million payable to Sue Todd. His hand was trembling when he handed it to her. She wiped her face again and stared at the check.

'What's this?'

'A cashier's check.'

218

'A million dollars? What's it for?'

'For you. And Ricky.'

'Why?'

'To make amends.'

'For what?'

'The past.'

'Who's it from?'

'I can't reveal that, Sue. But my client has made arrangements for Ricky to be treated at M.D. Anderson.'

Andy handed her his business card with a doctor's name and number written on the back.

'They're expecting you. His care will be free.'

'Can he go today?'

'Yes. But deposit the check first.'

She turned the check over, as if to make sure it was real.

'This isn't a joke?'

'No, Sue, it's not a joke.'

Tears rolled down her face, but she smiled and suddenly looked younger. He stood, and she stood.

'Thank you, Andy. And thank your client.'

'And Sue . . . move away from here.'

She hugged him and buried her face in his shoulder and sobbed until his shirt was wet. When Andy walked away, he was crying, too.

Chapter 14

Flying first class to Chicago two days later, Andy Prescott hoped the search for the second woman would involve only eating a thick steak at Morton's that Friday night, finding a rich woman with healthy kids on Saturday, and then catching a Chicago Bears game on Sunday.

He rented a Lexus, stayed at the Ritz, ate that steak, and found Amanda Pearce the next morning. She was thirty-seven and appeared healthy when she walked out of her house to get the morning paper. He took photos. She lived in a nice suburban neighborhood; a late-model Buick sat in the driveway. They weren't rich, but they weren't poor. A few minutes later, a middle-aged man came out the front door followed by a cute teenage girl in a cheerleader uniform; they both appeared healthy. Andy took more photos. The dossier said Amanda also had a fourteen-year-old boy.

Andy was feeling good about the Pearce family . . . until the garage door opened. A van backed out and stopped in the driveway. It wasn't a family minivan or a cargo van or a tricked-out travel van. It was a specially equipped van. Amanda got out and walked back inside the garage. When she returned, she was pushing a boy in a wheelchair.

Damn.

The van had a wheelchair lift. Amanda got the boy and the chair into the van, then backed out and drove off. Andy followed them a few blocks to a junior high school football stadium. Amanda parked the van in a handicapped space. Andy trailed them into the stadium. Amanda stationed the boy and wheelchair at the low chain link fence that surrounded the field. Andy leaned on the fence a few feet away and watched the game. After a few minutes, he smiled at Amanda and the boy.

'Good game,' he said. 'You have a son playing?'

'Our daughter's a cheerleader.' She pointed to the far sideline. 'The one on the right. Becky. And this is our son, Carl.'

'Hi, Carl.'

The boy suffered tremors. He tried to say 'hello,' but he couldn't get the whole word out. Amanda leaned toward Andy.

'CP. Cerebral palsy. He can't walk on his own anymore. Bilateral spastic paraparesis.' She was quiet for a moment, then said, 'I look at all those strong healthy boys running out there on the field, and I can't help but wonder, Why Carl?'

Andy returned to Austin the next morning and met with Russell Reeves that afternoon. Russell read the dossier and studied the photos of Amanda Pearce and her son. Andy sat quietly until his client spoke.

'Why's he in a wheelchair?'

'Cerebral palsy. Bilateral spastic parapa . . . para-para . . .'

'Paraparesis. Partial paralysis.'

Russell Reeves rested his elbows on the card table and sat with his head in his hands for the longest time. Andy said nothing, but his client hadn't seemed surprised to learn that Amanda Pearce also had a sick child.

'They're a normal middle-class family,' Andy said. 'They've got health insurance, but his care is still a big financial burden. When I asked Amanda about that, she just smiled and said, "He's worth it."'

'A mother's love.'

The next morning, Andy flew back to Chicago and drove to Amanda Pearce's house. He knocked on the front door and handed her a cashier's check for $1 million and sent Carl to Children's Memorial Hospital for treatment, all expenses paid. She cried.

The day after that, Andy flew first class to New Orleans. He prayed he wouldn't find another sick child. He didn't.

He found something worse.

He rented a Corvette, stayed in the French Quarter, and ate at K-Paul's. He found Tameka Evans that same day. She was thirty-five, poor, and a single African-American mother raising three boys and a girl – or so the dossier said. She was an attractive woman who might have been beautiful fifteen years before. Andy took photos from the car then sat on the front porch of the small shotgun house that had survived Katrina but sustained damage that had gone unrepaired. He talked with Tameka Evans about her life and her children's lives. Then he sat in the Corvette for a long time before driving off.

He flew back to Austin and met with Russell the next day. His client read the dossier and studied the photos and asked the same questions about Tameka and her children.

'How old are her sons?'

'Seventeen, fifteen, and thirteen.'

'Anything wrong with them?'

As if he expected something to be wrong.

'No. They're healthy.'

'Her daughter?'

'She would've been ten.'

Russell looked up.

'Would have been?'

'She's dead.'

'Dead? The dossier says she's alive.'

'Hollis must've missed her death certificate. Maybe because of Katrina, all the lost records. She had sickle cell anemia. They tried experimental treatments a few years back, but she died a year ago. Stroke.'

Russell shook his head.

'Three women,' Andy said. 'And three sick kids. That's odd, don't you think?'

'That's bad luck.'

'Russell, is there something you're not telling me?'

'About what?'

'About these women.'

'Such as?'

'Such as, Tameka Evans is a poor black woman who didn't get past the ninth grade. You're a billionaire genius. I can't picture you two dating.'

They stared each other down a moment, then Russell's face sagged. He exhaled.

'We didn't date, Andy. I bought her for a night in New Orleans, okay? When I was young. I'm not proud of it.'

Andy hadn't figured on that.

'Look, Andy, all I know about these women is that years ago I had a brief connection with each of them. And today they need my help. So I'm going to help them. Now, do you want to help me help them or not?'

Andy thought of Tameka Evans on her front porch, crying over her dead daughter.

'Yeah, I want to help you.'

The next day Andy flew back to New Orleans and gave Tameka Evans a cashier's check for $1 million.

Every other day, Andy arrived at his office to find another dossier from Hollis McCloskey waiting for him. He flew to Seattle and found Beverly Greer; her last-known address had been in Denver, but she had since moved to Seattle. Andy took photos and returned to Austin and met with Russell.

'How old?'

'Thirty-five.'

'Her boy?'

'Nine.'

'What's wrong with him?'

An expectation now.

'Optic nerve hypoplasia. He's blind.'

Andy flew to Dallas and found Pam Ward, who had moved there from LA. He took photos and met with Russell.

'She's thirty-two.'

'The girl?'

'Eleven.'

'What's wrong with her?'

'Batten disease.'

Andy flew to Miami and found Sylvia Gutierrez. Then he met with Russell.

'She's thirty-eight and her son is fifteen.'

'What's wrong with him?'

'Seizures, from a head injury playing football.'

Andy flew first class, he rented luxury vehicles, he stayed in five-star hotels and ordered room service; he found more women with sick children; he delivered a cashier's check to each woman for $1 million. They cried; he cried. Andy Prescott was being paid well to do good. He felt like Robin Hood, except he wasn't having to steal from the rich. The rich guy was just giving it away.

But the expense-account lifestyle had grown less exciting with each passing day; Andy had come to dread meeting another desperate woman with another sick child. Six old girlfriends . . . six sick children. What were the odds? When his rich client had called that morning about the delay in finding the seventh woman, Andy had decided it was time to find out what the hell was going on. Russell Reeves had sent the limo.

Darrell did not say a word on the ride over. He did not jump out of the driver's seat and run around to open the back door for Andy. He just stopped under the porte-cochere at Russell Reeves' lakefront mansion and waited for Andy to get out. Then he drove off.

Jerk.

Andy walked to the door and rang the doorbell. A middle-aged Latino woman opened the door. It was just after noon.

'Mr Prescott?'

'Yes, ma'am.'

'Please come in.'

Andy stepped into a magnificent marble foyer.

'Mr Reeves, he is on a conference call. He said he will be with you shortly. Would you like a refreshment?'

'I'm good.'

'You here to see my dad?'

A skinny, bald-headed boy wearing a blue New York Yankees cap on backwards and a green Boston Celtics sweat suit had walked into the foyer. Another sick child.

'Uh, yeah. I'm Andy Prescott.'

'Zach.'

The boy stuck out a closed hand. They fist-punched.

'You play Guitar Hero?' Zach asked.

'Zach, I *am* the Guitar Hero.'

'Please. Don't embarrass yourself.'

Andy grinned.

'Bring it on, dude.'

'Dude, you're killing me.'

The kid was good. Real good. Too good for Andy.

'I give,' Andy said.

They leaned back in the gaming chairs. Zach's bedroom suite was bigger than the little cottage on Newton and housed every electronic gadget and game money could buy. The boy must have noticed Andy's envious eyes.

'I've spent most of my life in here. Thanks for playing, Andy. My dad's not very good.'

'Don't you play with your friends from school?'

'I've never been to school. My dad hires tutors. TAs at UT. Grad students teach me English, science, Spanish – *¿Le gustaría una revancha, por favor?*'

'You like that?'

'Spanish?'

'Tutors.'

'They're okay. But I'd rather go to school like normal kids.'

'So what do you want to be when you grow up, Zach, a professional Guitar Hero player?'

'You mean, *if* I grow up.'

'When.'

'Either centerfielder for the Yankees, point guard for the Celtics, or quarterback for the Cowboys.'

Andy looked at the boy. He was staring off, as if contemplating the odds of becoming a star athlete . . . or of growing up. After a moment, he turned to Andy.

'What about you, Andy? What do you want to be when you grow up?'

'I haven't decided yet.'

'Who are you?'

A stern female voice. Andy turned and recognized Kathryn Reeves standing there. He jumped up. She came and stood next to Zach, like a mother standing between her child and a strange dog.

'Hi, Mrs Reeves. I'm Andy Prescott. I work for Russell.'

'In what capacity?'

'Uh, legal.'

'Are you a courier at his law firm?'

Andy was wearing jeans, sneakers, and an 'Austin Sucks – Don't Move Here' T-shirt. It wasn't a travel or traffic court day.

'Uh, no, ma'am. I'm a lawyer. At my own firm.'

Okay, 'firm' was a serious stretch, but what was he

228

supposed to say, the truth? And no doubt Russell hadn't mentioned to his wife their search for his seventeen former girlfriends.

'I've never heard him mention your name. And what exactly do you do for Russell?'

'Special projects, Kathryn.'

Saved by Russell Reeves.

'Andy,' his client said with a big smile, 'is my secret weapon.' He gestured at the video screen and said to Zach: 'You win?'

'Of course.'

'I want a rematch, dude,' Andy said.

'*Revancha*. At my birthday party. Friday. Okay?'

'Yeah, sure, I'll be there. Here. Wherever.'

Zach gave Andy a grin and another fist-punch.

'Let's go back to my office, Andy,' Russell said.

'Later, dude.' To Kathryn Reeves, he said, 'Very nice to meet you, Mrs Reeves.'

'Nice to meet you, Andy.'

She didn't sound convinced.

Andy followed his client out of Zach's room. Once in the hallway, the smile dropped off Russell's face.

'Kathryn doesn't know what you're doing for me.'

'I figured.'

They walked down the hallway in awkward silence.

'Zach's a neat kid,' Andy finally said.

'The chemo knocks the cancer down, so once he recovers from the treatments, he has a good period. But the remissions are shorter each time.'

'He said he wants to go to school, be a normal kid.'

'I wish he could. He's always been too sick to go to school. So I hire tutors. Matter of fact, I need a new math tutor. You think your buddy Curtis would want the job?'

Was there anything Russell Reeves didn't know about Andy Prescott?

'Russell, Curtis Baxter is like a math genius. He'll have his PhD in seven months. Don't you think he's overkill for a seven-year-old kid?'

'Zach's IQ is one-sixty-five.'

'I'll give you Curtis' number.'

They entered an expansive office, exactly the kind of office Andy would have expected of a billionaire. He went over to the back wall of windows that offered an incredible view of Lake Austin.

'Nice view.'

Russell sat behind a desk and slumped in the chair. Three weeks and he had given six million dollars to six different women. Russell Reeves was making amends big time. But it wasn't making him happy.

'They're not exactly living happily ever after,' Andy said. 'Your old girlfriends.'

'No.'

'What's going on, Russell?'

'With what?'

'These women. You have a sick kid, they have sick kids. Why is that?'

'Like I said, Andy. Bad luck.'

'Six out of six . . . what are the odds?'

'One in a million. Those are the odds of Zach getting Ph-positive ALL, his type of leukemia. When it comes to disease, Andy, odds don't matter. And it's six out of seventeen women, not six out of six. We haven't found them all yet.'

That was true.

'Actually, it's six out of all their children – sixteen so far, maybe thirty or forty when we find all the women.'

That was also true.

'But still, Russell, why do I think there's something you're not telling me?'

'Why would I hide something from you? You're my lawyer. You have to keep my secrets.'

He paused.

'Look, Andy, I know this is a tough job, seeing those sick children. You're not around a sick kid every day like I am. But we're helping them, and that's what's important. Still, if this job is too tough for you, I'll find someone else.'

Andy stared out the window and thought of all those women and sick kids whose lives had been made better by Russell Reeves. No matter what his rich client wasn't telling him – and he was pretty sure his rich client wasn't telling him something – the bottom line was that they were helping those women and those kids. That was important. That was a good thing. Andy Prescott couldn't help his father, but he could help these kids.

'I'll do it.'

'Thanks, Andy. Who's next?'

'Hollis said he's having trouble with the seventh woman.'

'What kind of trouble?'

'Finding her.'

'He can't find her?'

'Apparently not.'

'Go see him. McCloskey. Pay him whatever it takes, Andy, but I want these women found.'

Russell walked Andy to the front door where Darrell was waiting in the limo. Andy got in and Darrell drove through the gates and toward town. Andy looked down the list at the seventh woman's name, the woman Hollis could not find.

'Where are you, Frankie Doyle?'

Karen James craved a cigarette, but she was determined to quit. She steered the old Toyota into the carpool lane at the elementary school and stopped. When the car ahead inched forward, she inched forward. Kids were emerging from the school, running down the walkway – their oversized backpacks made them look like little mountain climbers – and jumping into their parents' cars.

She didn't see Jessie.

Karen glanced around at the other drivers: mothers, grandmothers, a few fathers, and a handful of Mexican nannies, even in this small town. They were driving cars and SUVs and pickups; high-end, low-end, and barely running. The public school took all comers regardless of class, race, ethnicity, citizenship, or length of residency in the school district. Which was good; they had moved into town only two months ago, right before school had started.

Where was Jessie?

Karen had arrived at the pickup point, but her daughter had not yet appeared. The carpool traffic monitor – the PE teacher who looked like she could bench press the Toyota – stuck her head in the open passenger window and told her to pull around to the side parking lot. Karen steered out of the drive-through lane in front of the school and turned into the parking lot, but she had to wait for a black van with darkened windows to exit. She glanced at the driver, and he glanced at her. She felt a sudden chill.

Where was Jessie?

Her mind began conjuring up possibilities and dark images soon followed; she got out of the car. She watched the black van drive off, then she went into the school. Her pace increased without conscious thought as she walked down the corridor to Jessie's third-grade room. Ms Nash, her teacher, was marking papers at her desk. She was alone.

'Excuse me.'

Ms Nash looked up. 'Oh, hi, Karen.'

'Where's Jessie?'

'Why, she's gone.'

'She didn't come outside to carpool.'

'She didn't?'

'No.'

'Well, then—'

Karen was already hurrying down the hall and checking each room. Ms Nash caught up with her at the principal's office.

'Karen, I'm sure she's here somewhere.'

The principal walked out of her office.

'Is there a problem?'

'We can't find Jessie,' Ms Nash said.

'I'll call the police.'

'No!' Karen said.

'Jessie left with the other kids,' Ms Nash said. 'Karen says she didn't come out for carpool.'

'Let's check the rooms.'

They searched every room on the west corridor. No Jessie. They went down to the gym; kids were playing volleyball and basketball. But not Jessie. They walked into the locker rooms.

'Jessie! Jessie!'

Principal Stephens' expression showed her fear: a child lost on her watch.

'I'd better call the police.'

'Let's check the east corridor,' Karen said.

They hurried out of the gym and down the east corridor. Jessie wasn't in the science lab or the library or the art room. Karen's mind was on the verge of full-scale panic when she spotted a head of red hair in the music room.

'Jessie!'

Her eight-year-old daughter swiveled around on the bench in front of the piano. She smiled.

'Hi, Mom.'

Jessie's eyes moved to her teacher and the principal standing behind Karen; the smiled dropped off her face.

'Uh-oh. I didn't tell anyone where I'd be. I'm sorry.'

'We've been looking all over school for you.'

'I just wanted to practice a little.'

Karen took a deep breath and turned to the others. 'I'm sorry.'

They nodded and patted her shoulder. They were mothers, too. After they had left, Jessie said, 'Am I in trouble?'

'No, honey. Let's go home.'

God, she needed a cigarette.

Texas Custom Boots on South Lamar Boulevard in Austin shares a small space with a taxidermy shop; in one stop, you can get your custom boots fitted and your dead buck stuffed. Paul Prescott was standing in his white socks on a sheet of heavy paper while the bootmaker wrote down his exact desires – toe, heel, puller, collar bands, cross-stitch design, leather, and color – and then traced his feet and took meticulous measurements.

'Black elk,' Andy said. 'They'll be soft but sturdy.'

'Like your mother.'

Jean Prescott, PhD, smiled like a smitten teenager.

His father was good, Andy had to give him that. Paul Prescott had that twinkle in his blue eyes that appealed to women of all ages; perhaps that was why his wife and son had accompanied him to so many honky-tonks. One day eight or nine years back when they were down at the creek, Andy had joked about the groupies who had hung out at the bars; his father had said, 'Andy, you're old enough to know the truth about your old man. I'm a drunk, but I'm a faithful drunk. To José Cuervo and your mother. I never betrayed her love.'

And Jean Prescott had stood by her man.

She had driven him into town that afternoon for his monthly transplant evaluation. He met with doctors (hepatologist, hematologist, cardiologist, gastroenterologist, and psychiatrist), a social worker (to ensure a reliable post-transplant caregiver was still available), and the financial representative (to confirm he still had insurance and could pay for the surgery and the expensive post-transplant drug regimen), and underwent the regular battery of tests to continue his place on the waiting list. And the team verified that he remained stone sober; one drop of alcohol, and Paul Prescott would be kicked off the list and left to die like road kill.

The bootmaker finished his measurements, Andy paid half of the $1,500 price of the boots as a down payment pending delivery in seven or eight months, and they went outside. It was after six.

'How about dinner at Threadgill's?' Andy said. 'I'm buying.'

Andy expected his father to decline; he no longer liked to be seen in public because his skin was now a shade of orange. But his father surprised him.

'Hell, don't see how I can turn down a chicken-fried steak at Threadgill's. Only way I'm gonna get meat.'

Andy stowed the bike in the back of his mother's 1989 Volvo station wagon (she was terribly proud of the odometer that registered over 300,000 miles) and got into the back seat. They drove the short distance over to the restaurant on Riverside, located just down from where the Armadillo had stood.

'Breaks my heart,' his father said, 'every time I see that office building where the Armadillo used to be. Those were good times. Best times were opening for Willie.'

'How old is Willie now? Ninety?'

His father chuckled, a sound Andy enjoyed.

'He's damn sure lived ninety years, but he just turned seventy-five back in April.'

Willie Nelson was a poet, a singer, a songwriter, and a Texas icon who lived on a ranch just outside of Austin.

'He's still singing around town.'

'Willie will sing and write his songs till the day he dies. That's what he is. That's what we all are – Willie, Billy Joe, Jerry Jeff, Kris . . . we're singers and songwriters.' He paused and pulled out his little notebook and pen. 'Singers and songwriters. Might be able to use that.'

The Prescott men ordered the world-famous chicken-fried steak, Threadgill's specialty. Andy's mother ordered a salad.

'How's the loft?' she asked.

'Sweet.'

'And your girlfriend?'

'The blonde or the brunette?'

His father leaned back and laughed. 'Listen to him now. Two months ago he's dating Curtis and Dave, now he's got to beat the gals off with a stick.'

'The blonde.'

'Where'd you see us?'

'Whole Foods. She doesn't wear a lot of clothes.'

'Would you cover up that body?'

'Hell, son,' his father said, 'you'd better eat two of those steaks. You need the protein.' He drank his iced tea and said, 'Reeves, he changed your life.'

'For the better.'

'Andy . . .'

'Yeah?'

'Don't get too comfortable with that new life.'

'Are you still working on those SoCo developments?' his mother said.

'Renovations. I got three approved by the residents. Construction's already started on those. I've been traveling, so the others are on hold.'

'Whereabouts?' his father said.

'Houston, Dallas, New Orleans, Seattle, Miami, Chicago.'

'For Reeves?'

Andy nodded.

'Real-estate deals?'

'Not exactly.'

'What exactly?'

'Dad, I can't say. It's confidential. But it's all good.'

'If you say so.' He grunted. 'Damn, I'd love a cold beer with this steak.'

"'I'm looking for a friend. You cannot be a liar and must have a job.'"

Curtis looked up from the personal ad.

'That seems a little harsh.'

Andy paid Ronda for another round of Coronas for the table. His folks had dropped him off at Güero's on their way back to Wimberley, Natalie had paroled Tres for the night, Curtis was reading personal ads aloud, and Dave was standing by the front door of Güero's waiting for his date to arrive. He appeared as nervous as a lawyer taking a polygraph.

'I can't believe someone answered his ad,' Tres said.

'Gives me hope,' Curtis said.

'Curtis,' Tres said, 'you'd do better looking for a date on Mensa-dot-com.'

'Dave's wearing cowboy boots,' Andy said, 'to look taller. Still doesn't look six-two.'

'He'd have to stand on a chair to look six-two.'

Curtis turned to the next ad. 'This girl says "I strive to find justice and equality in life."'

'And she's seeking casual sex?'

'How'd you know?'

Tres turned to Andy. 'You've been gone a lot. Reeves?'

'Yeah.'

'Where?'

'All over the country.'

'What for?'

'Confidential. He swore me to secrecy.'

'You're not in over your head, are you, Andy?'

'Nothing like that. Actually, I'm playing Robin Hood.'

'She's here,' Curtis said.

They all turned to the front door. A very attractive blonde – she wasn't Suzie or Bobbi, but then Dave wasn't Russell Reeves' lawyer – had just walked up to Dave. They exchanged a few words, then she kissed him on the cheek.

'Wow,' Curtis said.

Curtis Baxter had never been kissed by a female unrelated by blood.

Dave and the blonde went inside and were seated at one of the tables in the first room where the bar was located. From their position on the front porch, they had a clear view of Dave and his date through the window. Ronda took their orders then returned with margaritas. They talked and laughed and ate Mexican food. Dave paid the mariachis to sing at their table.

'She's eating fajitas,' Curtis said. 'Beef.'

'So?'

'So he's got a chance. She's a carnivore, too.'

'She looks like she's having fun,' Tres said.

'Wow,' Curtis said again.

Dave and the girl had another round of margaritas, then Dave stood and walked through the double doors into the main dining room. She smiled and gave him a little finger wave.

'Restroom,' Curtis said. 'Margaritas go right through him.'

The restrooms were at the rear of the restaurant. As soon as Dave disappeared from sight, the smile disappeared from the blonde's face. She pulled out her cell phone. She said something into the phone, stood, downed her margarita then grabbed her purse and walked outside. Fast. She almost ran past them on the porch and down the sidewalk past the Oak Garden where Los Flames were playing. A car pulled up on Congress; she dove in and it drove off.

'Aw, man.'

They turned and looked back inside through the window. Dave had just returned to the table; he was glancing around with a confused expression. He looked over at them; Andy waved him out. Dave came over.

'Did she go to the restroom?'

Tres and Curtis averted their eyes from this train wreck. That left Andy to deliver the bad news.

'She bailed.'

'She left?'

241

Andy nodded. Dave's body deflated like a popped balloon. He fell into a chair.

'I thought we were having fun.'

Andy waved an empty beer bottle at Ronda. Another round for the table. Curtis gave Dave a buddy pat.

'Sucks, dude.'

Dave shook his head.

'Man, she smelled great.'

Chapter 15

'Why can't you find Frankie Doyle?'

'Because she doesn't want to be found.'

'You found the first six women.'

'They weren't hiding.'

At nine sharp the next morning, Andy was sitting across the desk from Hollis McCloskey. Hollis leaned back in his chair.

'See, Andy, America's a transient society. A hundred million people move every year, across the street or across the country, usually for a bigger home or a better job. But that means two hundred million people don't move. Sue Todd, Tameka Evans, Sylvia Gutierrez – they hadn't moved from their last known addresses. Amanda Pearce had, but to another house in Chicago. So those four were easy.'

'How'd you find Beverly Greer and Pam Ward?'

'Beverly moved from Denver to Seattle, so I called her old neighbors in Denver. I got their names from the tax records – properties are indexed by address – then I called information and got their phone numbers.

The first neighbor didn't live there when Beverly did, the second one did. She gave me Beverly's new address in Seattle.'

'What about Pam Ward?'

'She moved from LA to Dallas. I couldn't get hold of her neighbors, so I called the new owner of her LA condo.'

'How'd you get the phone number?'

'Criss-cross directory. You can search the physical address and get the phone number, if it's a land line. It was. Anyway, Pam had seller-financed the condo, so the new owner sent payments to her in Dallas. She gave me the address.'

'I never realized how easy it is to find someone.'

'It is, if you know what you're doing – and if they're not hiding. People who aren't hiding leave a paper trail – mortgages, leases, phone records, utility bills . . . but Frankie Doyle moved and didn't leave a paper trail. She's hiding.'

'From whom?'

'Her ex-husband.'

Hollis sat forward and opened a file on his desk.

'Frankie Doyle's last known address was in Boston three years ago. She was twenty-five, married to one Michael aka Mickey Doyle, with a five-year-old daughter named Abigail. Worked as a waitress in a bar at a high-dollar downtown hotel, the Boston Grand. Then she and Mickey got divorced, and she and the minor disappeared.'

'What makes you think she's hiding from him?'

'He hit her. Mickey – he's an ex-boxer, still lives at the same address in Boston – was convicted twice of assault, not on her, but everyone I talked to said he hit her. I figure she got fed up, divorced the bastard, and split with the kid.' He shrugged. 'Frankie Doyle doesn't exist anymore.'

'What do you mean, she doesn't exist?'

'I mean her paper trail ended with the divorce. I figure she changed her name so Mickey couldn't find her. Problem is, we can't find her either.'

'But she'd have to file a name change in the county court where she's living. Search those records.'

'I did, the ones that are online. Problem is, Andy, there are over three thousand counties in the US, each with their own records, and the smaller ones, probably half those counties, their records aren't online. If Frankie Doyle's smart, and I think she is, she moved to a small county in the middle of no-where, probably out west where there aren't many people, and changed her name there, where the records aren't online. Only way to find her is to do a manual records search in all those counties – fifteen hundred counties.'

'Needle in a haystack.'

'Exactly. And, even if your client was willing to foot the bill for me to hire PIs in every state to do a manual search in every county, that'd take months. By then, she'd probably have moved and changed her name again.

Then we'd have to search in every county again, under her new name.'

'So she just fell off the grid?'

'Living off the grid, that's harder than most people think. You can't have a cell phone in your name, or a credit card, you can't buy a car or a home, you can't live in a reputable apartment complex, you can't have a bank account or a driver's license. People talk about living off the grid, but it's just that. Talk.'

'So how are you going to find Frankie Doyle?'

'I'm probably not. Andy, I've run down every rabbit trail I could find. I searched all the online records – property taxes, voter and vehicle registrations, marriage and business licenses . . . she's not a lawyer, accountant, doctor, nurse, barber, PI, pest control technician, nothing that requires a license. She hasn't voted in any state, county, or local election, as least not as Frankie Doyle.'

'What about her driver's license? She's got to be driving a car.'

'I can't get driver's license records anymore. Federal law restricts access now, because of identity theft.'

'What else?'

'I searched all my proprietary databases, fee services for PIs. Nothing. Usually I have a good phone number, and I'm looking for a physical address. But I couldn't find any phones, land lines or cell.'

'But if she changed her name, it wouldn't be under Frankie Doyle anyway.'

'Exactly. I searched the federal PACER system – a national federal court search for civil, criminal, and bankruptcy cases. Nothing. I searched the state criminal records available online, but I need her DOB – date of birth – to do a thorough search. I ran a prison inmate search—'

'Prison?'

Hollis shrugged. 'You never know.'

'And?'

'She's not an inmate in the federal system or in most of the state systems – I can't search them all. Hell, I even called Mickey.' Hollis shook his head. 'Now he's a piece of work. Lives in his deceased parents' house, drives their car, works at his dad's garage. Probably wears his old man's underwear.'

'What'd he say?'

'Nothing. When I asked about Frankie, he hung up. So I called the bar she worked at, talked to the bartender, name's Benny. Said she worked there for seven years, didn't show up for her shift one night. Never saw or heard from her again. Didn't even collect her last paycheck.'

'Maybe she's dead?'

'I ran her name in the Social Security Death Master File – she didn't come up dead. But that doesn't mean she isn't. Anyway, Benny told me her mother lived a few doors down from her, so I called her. Number's listed. Colleen O'Hara. Nice lady, but she didn't know her own whereabouts, much less Frankie's. Alzheimer's.'

'How do you know?'

'I called the neighbors on either side of Mickey. They know Mrs O'Hara, watch out for her. Frankie's father, he's deceased. No siblings. But the neighbors didn't know Frankie's whereabouts. And they said Mickey hit her.' Hollis paused. 'He's not your secret client, is he?'

'Mickey? No.'

'Good. She was smart, to get away from him before she ends up on the news, another woman killed by a crazy ex-husband.'

'What about her credit report?'

'Two problems with credit reports. One, if I pull her report for an unlawful purpose, it's a federal crime – and finding an old girlfriend is not a lawful purpose, Andy. Beside, it's a moot point – she won't be using a credit card.'

'Why not?'

'Because she knows she can be tracked that way. Her credit report shows whenever a creditor – a lender, landlord, employer – makes an inquiry, so she won't have gotten a loan or a job or rented an apartment, at least not a nice one. Standard apps allow them to run a credit check.'

'What's the second problem?'

'Credit bureaus won't release their reports to PIs anymore. People sued them.'

'Dang. What about her social security number?'

'With a name only, my search pulled up thousands

of Frank or Frankie or F. Doyles. With name and DOB, I'd get hundreds. With name, DOB, and social security account number, I'd get one. I checked the divorce records, but her SSAN was deleted. Problem is, it's almost impossible these days to get someone's SSAN legitimately. No one wants to release it — invasion of privacy laws.'

'You were with the FBI, maybe your buddies could get it . . . or pull her tax return.'

Hollis shook his head. 'That's jail time, Andy. We've got privacy laws in the US, even if the government forgets sometimes. I told you, Andy, I go by the book.'

'The book needs another chapter.'

'Andy, some PIs have arrangements with data brokers who cross the line. I don't.'

'Why not?'

'I don't need the money.'

'I'll pay you a thousand an hour.'

'Andy, I spent twenty-five years putting people in jail. I'm not about to join them now, not for you or your undisclosed client. You want me to continue with the other women?'

Andy nodded. 'Give me what you've got on Frankie Doyle.'

That afternoon Andy flew first class to Boston.

He had called Russell Reeves to report back about his conversation with McCloskey.

'Go to Boston, Andy,' Russell had said. 'Find her.'

249

Andy read her file on the flight. Hollis had compiled Frankie Doyle's life history from birth until three years ago. Then her life went blank. Andy was betting she was dead.

He arrived late, rented a BMW, and booked a $500-a-night suite at the Boston Grand Hotel in downtown, the same hotel where Frankie had worked. After checking in, he went into the bar and ordered a beer. Benny was on duty. He was maybe forty, a bald guy, big but not menacing like Darrell. Andy introduced himself and told him he was trying to find Frankie Doyle.

'Got a call a few days ago, Irish PI in Austin named McCloskey, asking about Frankie.'

'He works for me. I'm a lawyer.'

'So why do you want to find Frankie?'

'To help her.'

'What's wrong with her?'

'To help her child, actually.'

'Abby? What's wrong with her?'

'I don't know yet.'

Benny gave him an odd look. 'Well, like I told your man McCloskey, I haven't seen or heard from Frankie in three years. She didn't show for her shift one night, after seven years.' He paused. 'You don't think she's dead?'

'I don't know. Maybe.'

That seemed to take the air out of Benny.

'She was a good Irish girl married to a lousy Irish mug.'

250

'Mickey?'

Benny nodded. 'He hit her.'

'So I've heard.'

'When she divorced him, I asked her to marry me.'

'Did y'all see each other?'

'Frankie Doyle cheat? No way. Catholic girl, lifetime of guilt, all that.' He shrugged. 'I still loved her. But she just wanted to get the hell away from Mickey.'

'Any idea where?'

He shook his head. 'She'd never been more than fifty miles from home, but she used to talk about moving to Montana or Texas, having horses. I told her she was a city girl, wouldn't know what to do in the country.'

Benny stepped away to serve a customer at the other end of the bar. Andy drank his beer and tried to imagine Frankie Doyle working there. It was a sports bar, but a classy place with an elegant wood bar and tables and leather chairs, a mirror behind the bar, and a flat-screen TV on the wall along with framed sports memorabilia – signed jerseys from the Patriots, Red Sox, Celtics, and Bruins – and sports-themed art. The only real art hung behind the bar, a black-and-white pencil drawing of Benny. Andy leaned over to read the artist's name: 'F. Doyle.'

'Frankie sketched that. One day, when we weren't busy.'

Benny had returned.

'She wanted to be an artist.'

'She was.'

Benny stared at his image.

'I hope she still is.'

Andy said goodnight and went up to his room. He ordered room service, drank three more beers, and watched a movie on pay-per-view.

The next morning, Andy found Frankie Doyle's last known address in a working-class neighborhood in South Boston. It was a brick row house situated among blocks of identical structures. He parked, went to the door, and knocked; no one answered.

'You looking for Mickey?'

The next-door neighbor, an old guy, was standing on the other side of a waist-high hedge.

'You know where I can find him?'

He pointed down the street.

'Doyle's Garage, two blocks down.'

'Thanks.' Andy stepped to the hedge. 'Did you know Frankie?'

'Sure. She's been gone three years now, since she divorced Mickey. He hit her. When he drank, which was every day. Guess she got tired of it. Took the girl and left the bastard.'

'Was the girl sick?'

'Abby? Not that I knew. She was a real tomboy, that one.'

Finally, a woman without a sick kid. Maybe it was just odds, like Russell said. But that was three years ago.

'Any idea where they went?'

The old man shook his head.

'Where does Frankie's mother live?'

The man nodded down the street.

'Three houses down.'

Andy said thanks and drove to Doyle's Garage. It was a small place, not much bigger than a two-car garage, with a dozen cars parked outside. Inside, Andy found the smell of oil and grease and a man ducked under the hood of a car.

'Mickey Doyle?'

From under the hood: 'Who's asking?'

'Andy Prescott. I'm a lawyer from Texas.'

The man came out now. He had closely cropped red hair; he looked to be a few years older than Andy. He was built like a boxer with a nose that had been broken more than once. His hands were black with grease. He didn't seem happy to see Andy.

'Go away.'

Andy pulled out his wallet and removed ten $100 bills. He placed the cash on the car.

'I need some information.'

The man eyed the cash, then Andy.

'What do you want to know?'

'You're Mickey Doyle?'

'Yeah.'

'I'm trying to find Frankie.'

'Did she come into money?'

'Not yet.'

'Well, I ain't seen or heard from Frankie since the day she divorced me. Three years ago.'

'Any idea where she's living?'

'Nope. Hand me that wrench.'

Mickey pointed at a tool stand.

Andy handed the wrench to Mickey. He now had grease on his hands. He searched for a rag.

'That's her real name, Frankie?'

'Yep. Sean O'Hara, her old man, he ran an Irish pub, good place, long gone now. Wanted a football player, got a girl instead. So he named her Frankie O'Hara. After Frank Gifford.'

Mickey went back to work. Andy didn't have a clue who Frank Gifford was.

'You and Frankie grew up together?'

'She's seven years younger than me. We married soon as she graduated high school.'

'And had a daughter. You don't see Abby?'

'Had to give up my rights, to stay out of prison. Three strikes.'

'Was she sick?'

'Frankie?'

'Abby.'

Mickey smiled. 'No, Abby wasn't sick.'

'You got any photos of her?'

'You want photos of Abby?'

'No. Frankie.'

'Oh. Burned 'em all. So I'd forget her.' He paused and stared at the engine. 'Didn't work.'

'She have any relatives still living here, other than her mother?'

'Frankie was an only child. Sean, he kept getting Colleen pregnant, but she kept miscarrying. Finally had to yank out her plumbing.'

'Is she at home?'

'Always.'

'She know where Frankie's living?'

'Colleen don't know where *she*'s living. She's got that Alzheimer's. She takes a walk, can't find her way back home. I gotta go looking for her two, three times a week.' He pointed again. 'Hand me that socket drive.'

Andy handed the tool to him.

'Mickey, you think Frankie's dead?'

'Nope.'

'Why not?'

''Cause she calls Colleen every day.'

'How do you know?'

'Colleen tells me, when I check on her.'

'You check on your ex-mother-in-law?'

'Every morning. Make sure she ain't hurt herself.'

'Mickey, you been trying to find Frankie?'

Mickey stopped working the socket drive. He rested his weight on the car frame. He didn't look at Andy.

'Why would I do that?'

'Because you want her back.'

'Look, I'd take Frankie back, but she don't want *me* back. Hell, she put a restraining order on me. I go near her or Abby, I go to prison.'

255

'Anyone else who might be looking for her?'

'You.' He faced Andy. 'Why are you looking for her?'

'I can't say. What's Frankie's birthday?'

'July seven. Nineteen eighty.'

'What's her social security number?'

'I can't say.'

'I'll double the cash.'

'I can't say 'cause I don't know. And even if I did, I wouldn't tell you. I don't know you from Adam. You come in here asking questions, I don't know what you're up to.' He gestured at the $100 bills. 'Can I have the cash now?'

Andy nodded, and Mickey grabbed the green. Andy handed his business card to him.

'That's my cell phone number. Call me if you think of anything, where she might be, okay? It's important.'

Mickey took the card and stared at it.

'Traffic tickets and finding people . . . must pay good.'

'Better than you'd think.'

Mickey stuck the card in his shirt pocket and ducked back under the hood.

Andy called Hollis McCloskey and gave him Frankie's date of birth. Then he drove downtown to the Suffolk County Courthouse. He found the clerk's office and asked for the divorce file for *Frankie Doyle vs. Michael Doyle* from three years before. The clerk checked her computer.

'That file's been sent to archives. You can put in an order, come back next week.'

'Do you show the attorney for Frankie Doyle?'

'Marty O'Connor.'

She gave him the lawyer's phone number. Andy stepped outside and called O'Connor on his cell phone. When he was put through, Andy identified himself and explained that he was trying to locate Frankie.

'For what purpose?' O'Connor said.

'That's confidential, Marty.'

'Well, so is what I know about Frankie.'

'Do you know where she's living?'

'No. But I wouldn't tell you if I did. Look, Andy, do her a favor, and leave her alone. She's been through enough.'

'With Mickey?'

O'Connor hesitated then said, 'Yeah, with Mickey.'

'My client wants to help her.'

'No, he doesn't. Just leave her alone, Andy.'

They hung up. Andy went to the tax office and checked the tax records; Frankie Doyle owned no real property in Suffolk County. He checked the Department of Motor Vehicles; no car in Massachusetts was registered to Frankie Doyle.

Andy drove back to Colleen O'Hara's residence and knocked on the door; an old woman answered.

'Mrs O'Hara?'

'Who?'

'Ma'am, are you Frankie's mother?'

'Where's Frankie?'

'I don't know, ma'am. I'm trying to find her.'

'I want to see my baby.'

'May I come in and talk?'

She smiled. 'Okay.'

Andy stepped through the door and into 1955. The carpet was shag, the upholstery brocade, and the room dimly lit by a few old lamps. He counted five cats lounging around. The television was on to the soaps. Mrs O'Hara sat in a thick chair directly in front of the TV. Andy looked around. A dozen framed black-and-white drawings by 'F. Doyle' hung on the walls. All were stark and desolate landscapes. They reminded Andy of West Texas and New Mexico.

'Frankie's an artist.'

'Yes, ma'am, she is. Mrs O'Hara, do you have a photo of Frankie?'

She reached over to the end table next to her chair and picked up a framed picture. She held it out to him. It was a photo of a pretty young woman and a cute girl in thick snow. They were wearing parkas with the hoods snug around their faces. They were happy. And alive.

Andy considered stealing the photo, but just the thought made him feel like a creep – stealing from an old lady with Alzheimer's. So he tried to memorize Frankie Doyle's image. Hers was not a hard face to look at. Her hair was tucked inside the hood of her parka, but he assumed a girl named O'Hara would have red hair – or perhaps it was wishful thinking, given his thing for redheads – and there was something about her that made him want to find her. To see her in real life.

Mrs O'Hara was focused on the soaps, so Andy walked into the adjacent kitchen. On the small table was a short stack of bills. He thumbed through them and saw a telephone bill.

'Mrs O'Hara, does Frankie call you?'

'Frankie's on the phone?'

'Uh, no, ma'am.'

Andy removed the telephone bill and scanned down the numbers listed for the calls that came daily. All were incoming but no location was noted; the numbers were all 888 prefixes. Hollis was right; Frankie was smart. She was using a prepaid phone card to call her mother. She could be calling from New York or LA; there was no way to know.

Andy couldn't think of anything else he might learn from Colleen O'Hara, so he went back into the front room and said goodbye then handed the framed photo back to her.

'Mrs O'Hara, where was this photo taken?'

She put on her reading glasses and looked at the photo.

'That's Frankie . . . and Abby.'

'Yes, ma'am. Where were they in this photo?'

'In the snow.'

'What state?'

She gazed off as if trying to find the answer written on the ceiling. Andy thought of his father, how his memory had deteriorated as a result of his liver disease. His forgetfulness frustrated the hell out of Paul Prescott; at least Mrs O'Hara didn't know to be frustrated.

'Thanks, Mrs O'Hara.' He gave her his business card. 'When Frankie calls, ask her to call me. It's important.'

She smiled.

'I'll let myself out.'

He was almost out the door when she said, 'Montana.'

Benny had said that Frankie Doyle had never traveled farther than fifty miles from Boston, so the Montana photo must have been taken after she had left Boston three years ago. Frankie Doyle had moved to Montana.

Where Andy Prescott now was.

Billings was in eastern Montana and the largest city in the state with a population of 100,000. Hollis McCloskey had said Frankie Doyle might have moved to a small county in a state out west to change her name. So Andy tried to think like Frankie Doyle. There was usually a statutory period to establish residency, typically six months, so Frankie would have to live in the county for at least that long before she could change her name. So she would find a small county near a bigger city. Billings wasn't Boston, but it would have some amenities. That's what he would do; maybe that's what she had done.

He had flown from Boston to Billings and rented a Lincoln Navigator. He had consulted a map and found the least populated counties near Billings: Golden Valley (population 1021), Petroleum (population 497), and Treasure (population 735). The latter county was located ninety-three miles east of Billings on Interstate 94. An easy drive.

Andy exited the interstate and drove into Hysham, population 330, the county seat of Treasure County. The Yellowstone River flowed through town; rolling land stretched in all directions as far as he could see. It was a stark and desolate landscape, and it was in one of Frankie Doyle's sketches at her mother's house.

He was in the right town.

Andy parked in front of the Treasure County Courthouse. He hurried inside – he wasn't dressed for thirty-eight degrees – and into the county clerk's office. He asked for name change filings from two to three years before for 'Doyle, Frankie.' The records were not online. The clerk had to search manually. But she found it.

Frankie Doyle had changed her name to Rachel Holcombe two years before.

Andy checked the tax records, but he could find no real estate or vehicles owned by a Rachel Holcombe. He found no Rachel Holcombe listed in the phone book for the greater Billings area. Andy bought a copy of the name change filing and went outside. He called Hollis McCloskey. When McCloskey came on the line, Andy said, 'Frankie Doyle is now Rachel Holcombe. H-o-l-c-o-m-b-e. Find her, Hollis.'

Chapter 16

The cell phone woke Andy at six-thirty on the last day of October.

'Hello.'

'Did you find Frankie Doyle?'

Russell Reeves.

'I found out she got divorced and moved to Montana three years ago. Changed her name.'

'Why?'

'She's running from her ex-husband. He hit her.'

'So you found her in Montana?'

'No. She moved again.'

'Where?'

'I don't know. Hollis searched under her new name, couldn't find her anywhere in Montana, so I flew home last night. I'm going to see him this morning.'

'Find her, Andy.'

Two hours later, Andy walked into Hollis McCloskey's office. The PI smiled.

'You didn't have to dress up, Andy.'

Andy was wearing jeans, sneakers, and a 'Don't Blame Me – I Voted Kinky' T-shirt. Hollis was being sarcastic. Again.

'Nothing else was clean.'

Hollis nodded. 'Best thing about having a wife, Andy. Clean clothes.'

Agent McCloskey was a romantic bastard.

'Tell me about Rachel Holcombe.'

'She ceased to exist a year ago. Same deal.'

'How can she do that?'

'Because she's smart. She knows what she's doing. Andy, this girl – she does not want to be found.'

'So she divorced Mickey, moved to Montana, changed her name, moved again, and changed her name again?'

Hollis nodded. 'She must really be afraid of him.'

'He didn't seem that interested in finding her.'

'Assholes like Mickey, they don't usually fess up.'

'But he's working at his garage every day.'

'Probably hired someone to find her. Like you did.'

'But you didn't. Find her.'

Hollis turned his palms up. 'Look at the bright side, Andy: neither will Mickey. Oh, I ran criminal background checks on Frankie Doyle, Frankie O'Hara, and Rachel Holcombe with that DOB. No arrests or convictions. She's clean.'

'Any luck on her social security number? That would follow her through her name changes.'

'It would, but she's using a fake number.'

'How do you know?'

'Because she hasn't gone to all this trouble only to be tracked down with her SSAN.'

'Hollis, isn't there anything you can do?'

'By the book, Andy.'

'Damnit, Hollis, we gotta find this woman!'

'Why? Why does your client want to find this woman?'

'I told you, that's confidential.'

'Look, Andy, I'm getting a bad feeling about this assignment – I smell a rat.'

'The woman?'

'Your client.'

'He's not a rat, Hollis.'

'Then why's he spending so much money to find these women?'

Andy and the ex–FBI agent stared at each other as if to see who would blink first. How much should he tell Hollis? How much information would allow Hollis to identify his client as Russell Reeves? He needed Hollis McCloskey to find Frankie Doyle.

'These women, they're my client's old girlfriends. He wants to find them and help them because he didn't treat them right. He wants to make amends.'

'How?'

'Money.'

'How much?'

'A million.'

'Each?'

Andy nodded.

'That sound reasonable to you?'

'Hollis, rich people are eccentric.'

'No, Andy, rich people are connivers, cheats, crooks, conmen, and criminals – at least all the rich people I met when I was with the FBI were.'

'Now you work for rich people.'

Hollis shrugged. 'I'm not with the FBI anymore.'

'My client's not that kind of rich guy. He's just . . .'

'What? Troubled, delusional, psychotic, sick?' Hollis sat back. 'Andy, this doesn't pass the smell test. I don't know what your client is up to, but I don't like it. I'm off the case.'

'You won't try to find her?'

'Not unless you tell me what this is really all about.'

Andy didn't think he should mention the sick kids. That might make the G-man suspicious; and he might connect the dots: sick kids . . . rich man in Austin with a sick kid . . . Russell Reeves.

'Hollis, it really is all about a rich guy finding his old girlfriends and giving them money. He wants to clear up his old debts, so he can have peace.'

Hollis shook his head. 'I don't buy it.'

'Why not?'

'Rich people don't give their money away for nothing. They always want something in return.'

'Hollis, I've personally handed cashier's checks to the first six women, for a million dollars each. He's never asked for anything in return. Will you at least look for the others?'

Hollis handed him a file. 'This is the dossier on the eighth woman.'

'So that's it?'

'I'm done.'

'Why?'

'Because I think I'm being used, Andy . . . and I think you are, too.'

Andy walked out of Hollis McCloskey's office and called Tres to ask a small favor: pull Michael and Frankie Doyle's income tax return from three years back then track her later returns. Get her social security number. Find her address. Tres laughed.

'Andy, did you get hit by a car and suffer a head injury?'

'No.'

'Well, you're asking me to commit a felony. Jail time, buddy. They can track our computer usage, every keystroke. I type in her name, Big Brother will know it . . . and want to know why I did it. Sorry, Andy, but no way.'

'Tres—'

'I told you, Andy.'

'Told me what?'

'That once you got a taste of money, you wouldn't want to go back to your old life. That you'd do whatever it took so you don't go back. I told you, Andy.'

* * *

Tres was wrong. Andy Prescott wasn't doing this for the money. He could walk away from Russell Reeves and his money any time he wanted to. He was doing this for Frankie Doyle . . . and for her sick kid. Okay, she might not have been sick three years ago, but she probably was now. And to find her and help her, he needed a more creative private investigator than some lame-ass by-the-book I-don't-wander-off-the-reservation ex-FBI agent.

So he rode the Stumpjumper straight from Hollis McCloskey's office in downtown Austin to Lorenzo Escobar's office in SoCo. PRIVATE INVESTIGATION and BAIL BONDS were painted in black letters on the plate-glass front window. Andy walked in and found a Spartan space and a handsome Latino man sitting at a big wood table and tapping on a laptop. Andy recognized Ramon's distinctive work on his forearms. He looked to be about forty and had jet black hair combed straight back, a neatly trimmed black goatee, and black reading glasses riding low on his nose. He was wearing a black T-shirt that was tight around his lean torso and muscular arms, black leather wrist bands, black jeans, black cowboy boots, and a black gun in a black holster clipped to his black belt. He was a good typist.

Without looking up at Andy, the man said, 'It's legal.'

'What?'

'The gun.'

The National Rifle Association's Austin chapter – also known as the Texas legislature – had recently passed numerous 'shoot first and ask questions later' laws giving Texans the right to a) kill any person unlawfully entering their homes, b) carry a weapon in their cars to protect themselves against carjackers, and c) carry a concealed weapon provided they take a firearms safety course. Twenty-four million people now lived in Texas; half were packing heat. The other half should be – to protect themselves against the first half.

'Lorenzo?'

Still tapping on the laptop: 'What can I do for you?'

'Ramon gave me your name. I'm Andy Prescott.'

'The traffic ticket lawyer.'

Some claim to fame.

'You sent me the rich boy.'

'Yeah, I gave Tres your number.'

Still typing away. 'Gorgeous little gal, that one. I enjoyed tailing her . . . tail. You know she don't wear underwear?' He whistled. 'That boy's got a lifetime of worrying whether she's cheating on him. 'Course, if it weren't for gals like her, I'd be out of business. Cheating wives, they account for seventy-five percent of my annual gross revenues. Easy money, or at least it used to be. Now with the new gun laws, job's gotten a little more dangerous – some wives can shoot. You know what I mean?'

Andy assumed that was a rhetorical question, so he didn't answer.

'So, Andy, wife cheating on you?'

'No wife.'

'Girlfriend?'

Suzie? Or Bobbi? Cheating on him? He had never even thought about it. Or cared.

'Nope.'

'I don't do boyfriends like that TV sports guy your buddy had me follow.'

'Not that either.'

'You need me to bond someone out of jail?'

Lorenzo smiled, revealing a set of bright white teeth.

'See, when I give a client the bad news about his cheating wife, he goes straight home and beats the hell out of her and gets arrested. So I bond him out. Then he finds the no-good bastard pumping his wife and beats the hell out of him and gets arrested again. So I bond him out again. My business is what they call "vertically integrated," like the oil companies.'

'No bond.'

Lorenzo finally stopped typing, removed his reading glasses, and looked directly at Andy.

'Then what services of mine do you require, Andy?'

Andy explained the efforts to find Frankie Doyle. After listening thoughtfully and stroking his goatee, Lorenzo said, 'McCloskey's a good man. Knows what he's doing.'

'He goes by the book.'

Lorenzo gave Andy a bemused expression. 'And you want something more than what's in the book from me, is that it?'

'I want you to find her and I don't care how you do it.'

'Woman don't want to be found, Andy – for that service, my fees are higher.'

'I'll pay whatever it takes.'

'Why do you want to find this woman so bad?'

'I don't. My client does.'

'Who's your client?'

'That's confidential.'

'Why does your client want to find this woman?'

'Also confidential.'

'Then my fee will be nine thousand nine hundred ninety-nine dollars. Cash.'

'Why?'

'Risk management, Andy.'

'No, why not ten thousand even?'

'Oh. You move ten grand in cash, you gotta fill out forms and answer questions at the bank, so the Feds can track your money. Which limits my tax-planning opportunities, if you know what I mean.'

Andy knew what he meant.

The money laundering law was purportedly to prevent criminals from using the banking system to launder their illegal profits – as if drug lords were stupid enough to move cash through their local savings and loan. Only politicians paying for high-priced call girls were that stupid, which is how the Feds nabbed the former New York governor.

'Okay. But you can't breathe a word of this, understand?'

Lorenzo laughed. 'Who am I gonna tell?'

'I guess you're right.'

'You know I'm right. Now, you said her last known address was Hysham, Treasure County, Montana, then she split. Any idea where she might've gone?'

Andy was about to say no, but he thought of the black-and-white drawings by F. Doyle at Colleen O'Hara's house. One had been of the Montana landscape. The others had reminded Andy of—

'New Mexico or West Texas.'

Lorenzo nodded. 'Gives me something to work with. Come back in a few hours, I'll have something for you. And bring the cash.'

Andy rode down to Cissi's Market and had a roast beef sandwich and a Brown Cow vanilla bean yogurt for lunch. Then he went to the bank and withdrew $9,999. Two hours later, he walked back into Lorenzo's storefront. He was waiting.

'Did you find her?'

'Did you bring the cash?'

Andy handed the bank envelope to Lorenzo. He thumbed the cash like a card shark thumbing a deck of cards. He smiled.

'I found her.'

'How? Did you get her social security number? Her credit report? How'd you do it?'

'Now, Andy, you're asking me to share my trade secrets, to reveal my proprietary information, to disclose my—'

'I don't want to know.'

'Correct answer. You don't want to know how, you just want results. And I got 'em right here.'

Lorenzo placed a piece of paper in front of Andy. Two years ago, Frankie Doyle had changed her name to Rachel Holcombe in Hysham, Treasure County, Montana. One year ago, she had changed her name to Irma Bustamante—

'Irma Bustamante?'

Lorenzo smiled. 'Irish girl got a sense of humor.'

—in Mosquero, Harding County, New Mexico. Four months ago, she had changed her name to Karen James in Mentone, Jeff Davis County, Texas.

'She likes small towns,' Lorenzo said. 'Only a hundred twenty folks live in Mosquero, fifteen in Mentone.'

'Why would she change her name so many times?'

'She doesn't want to leave a paper trail, but she doesn't want to live off the grid. She's not using credit cards, but she wants a bank account. She wants to be legit, live a normal life, but she doesn't want someone to find her.'

'Her ex-husband hit her.'

'Good enough reason.'

'But he said he wasn't trying to find her.'

'Asshole hits a woman, I'm not sure, Andy, could be he's a liar, too.'

'I guess you're right.'

'You know I'm right.'

Lorenzo now placed a printout of a Texas driver's license with a photo of Karen James in front of Andy.

He studied her image. It was the same face he had seen in the photo at Colleen O'Hara's house.

'That's her. That's Frankie Doyle.'

'Check out the address.'

Andy looked down the license then up at Lorenzo.

'Buda, Texas? All this and she's living fifteen miles down the road?'

'Rent house. But she's moving up: five thousand people live in Buda.'

'Why would she live in unpopulated places in Montana and New Mexico and West Texas, then move just fifteen miles from Austin?'

'She wants to hide in plain sight. Figures she's covered her tracks, now she can live near a city, put her kid in a good school, enjoy things. She's ready to start her life over now, as Karen James.'

Andy pedaled back to his office. He poked his head into the tattoo parlor and found Ramon at his computer.

'Ramon, can I borrow your car?'

Without turning from the screen, Ramon said, 'Hey, Andy, listen to this email I got: "Hello, I am pretty Russian girl, bored tonight. Would you like to chat and see my pics?" You think she's for real?'

'What's her name?'

'Candi. With an "i".'

'A Russian girl named Candi with an "i"? I don't think so, Ramon. Can I borrow your car?'

'I don't think so, Andy.'

★　　★　　★

274

Ramon Cabrera drove a metallic yellow 1978 Corvette convertible with mag wheels and wide white walls. It was in pristine condition with red leather seats, a stereo system with a subwoofer that shook the car with each beat, and a plastic Jesus magnetically attached to the dash. It was his prized possession – the Corvette, not the plastic Jesus – since his wife had left him. He would not allow Andy behind the wheel. But he wasn't inking anyone's body that afternoon, so he was now driving Andy down Interstate 35 to Buda, Texas. The top was down, the wind was whipping Andy's hair, and the volume on the Latino radio station was blaring. Sitting next to Ramon Cabrera in the low-slung hot rod, Andy felt like he was co-starring in a Cheech and Chong movie.

Buda, Texas, had long been a small farming town situated between Austin and San Antonio, nothing but cotton and cows and a cement plant. But over the last decade, developers had bought the farmland and subdivided the pastures and built homes for Austinites who could no longer afford the city. Buda – from the Spanish *viuda* – was now a bedroom community, home to five thousand residents who slept in Buda but worked in Austin. But tens of thousands of people regularly made the journey down I-35 to Buda these days, and not just for the 'World Famous Wiener Dog Races.' They came to shop at Cabela's, a 185,000-square-foot hunters' paradise, a place selling enough guns and ammo to satisfy any Rambo-wannabe. The chamber of commerce's slogan was 'Have a *Budaful* time in Buda.'

Or at least buy a gun.

Andy had printed out a map on Ramon's computer. The address on the driver's license was on Old Black Colony Road outside town where there was still some country left. A Toyota Corolla sat in the driveway. But they couldn't just park a yellow Corvette at the end of the driveway and take zoom photos. They would be easily spotted. So they parked down the road where they could see if she left.

Fifteen minutes after they had arrived, Frankie Doyle left.

Andy wrote down the Toyota's license plate number; no doubt the car was registered under her latest alias. They followed her to the Buda Elementary School where a cute girl with flaming red hair ran to the car and got in. She didn't appear sick. Andy took zoom photos of the girl, but couldn't get a clear shot of Frankie.

They followed Frankie and her daughter back to their house and again parked down the road. Ramon decided to take a nap. Andy leaned over to check the digital images on the camera in the dark under the dash and—

'Are you following me?'

Andy jumped and banged his head on the underside of the dash. He turned. Frankie Doyle was standing there. In real life.

'Jesus, you scared me.'

Ramon opened his eyes and lowered his sunglasses.

He gave Frankie a long admiring look. Her hands were now clamped on the window sill, and her face was no more than a foot from Andy's. She didn't have red hair. She had jet black hair, a smooth creamy complexion, and green glaring eyes whose dark pupils made him feel as if he were staring down the barrel of a loaded gun.

In his oily Latin accent, Ramon said, 'I am Ramon Cabrera. Your skin is magnificent. Have you considered body art?'

Her eyes moved to Ramon; she looked him over then said, 'No.' Back to Andy: 'Did you really think I wouldn't notice a yellow Corvette?'

No sense in lying.

'I had a heck of a time finding you.'

'I'm calling the cops.'

Andy held his cell phone out to her.

'You don't think I'll call?'

'Nope.'

'Why not?'

'Because I don't think you want the cops or anyone else to know who you really are . . . Frankie Doyle.'

She stared at him, but showed no emotion. Then she abruptly turned and walked fast toward the house.

'Nice looking lady,' Ramon said. 'I wonder what bar she goes to?'

Andy jumped out and ran to catch her. She was wearing a white long-sleeve T-shirt and blue jeans; from behind, she had a nice behind. Not like Suzie's, of course, but nice.

'Frankie, I know why you're running.'

She kept walking.

Over her shoulder: 'How'd you find me?'

'Your mother.'

She stopped and spun around. 'You saw my mother?'

'At her house.'

'Who are you?'

'Andy Prescott. I'm a lawyer in Austin.'

She looked him up and down – the sneakers, the jeans, and the Kinky T-shirt.

'You're a lawyer? Wearing that and' – she pointed at the yellow Corvette – 'riding in that?'

'Oh, that's Ramon's car. He's my landlord . . . and a tattoo artist.'

'Your landlord drives you around?'

'I don't own a car. I ride a bike.'

'You're a lawyer, you ride a bike, and you've got a tattoo artist for a chauffeur? Is this some kind of joke?'

'Uh, no.'

'You went to see my mother in Boston, trying to find me?'

'I went to Boston to see Mickey, trying to find you.'

'You met Mickey?'

'At his shop.'

'How is he?'

'Probably the same as when you were married to him.'

'God, I need a cigarette. See, you mention Mickey, and now I want to smoke again. How's my mother?'

'In and out.'

She nodded. 'It was hard to leave her.'

'She showed me the photo, in Montana.'

'How'd you find us here?'

'Benny said you wanted to get as far away as possible—'

'You saw Benny, too?'

'At the bar.'

'How is he?'

'He misses you.'

'I miss him.'

'Anyway, I knew the Montana photo was after you'd left, so I flew out there, figured you'd settle in the smallest county near Billings, until you could change your name. Then you went to New Mexico and West Texas. Changed your name each time.'

'How'd you know where to look?'

'Your sketches, at your mother's. I recognized the landscapes.'

'Montana and New Mexico, we liked it there. West Texas, that was hard. The wind was relentless, like Mickey's mother.'

'You're very good – at sketching and hiding.'

'Not good enough, apparently. So that's how you found me. Now why did you find me?'

'My client wants to help you.'

'How?'

'He wants to give you money.'

'How much?'

'A million dollars.'

'He wants to give a million dollars to a complete stranger?'

'He knows you.'

'What's his name?'

'I can't say.'

'Where would I meet a rich guy?'

'At the hotel bar.'

'What, I serve him a few drinks in the bar three years ago, now he wants to give me a million dollars?'

'Apparently.'

'Why?'

'Guilt. For not treating you well.'

'At the bar?'

'When y'all dated.'

She shook her head. 'Wrong girl, Andy. I never dated anyone I met in the bar. I was married to Mickey.' She sighed. 'One mistake can last a lifetime.'

'Mickey said y'all got married right out of high school.'

She nodded. 'To get away from my father, even if away was three doors down. So I married Mickey and found out I had married my dad. God, he was always so jealous, Mickey. Some guy on the street even looked at me, he'd want to beat him up.'

'I bet that happened a lot.'

A little smile; a crack in the ice.

'He hit you?'

She just stared off.

'Did he hit your girl?'

'He wouldn't be alive if he had.'

She seemed sincere.

'Frankie, I know you're running from him.'

She started walking toward the house again.

'Right now I'm running from you.'

'My client's just trying to help his old girlfriends.'

She stopped again.

'Your rich client is giving a million dollars to his old girlfriends?'

Andy nodded. 'Seventeen.'

'Your client had seventeen girlfriends? What, does he look like Robert Redford?'

'Redford? He's old.'

'Don't you watch old movies, like *The Way We Were*?'

'Is that an action thriller?'

'It's a love story.'

'Oh. Well, Frankie, you're number seven on my client's old love list.'

'It's a mistake. I don't belong on that list.'

They arrived at the front door. She turned to him.

'Andy, look, just tell your client you couldn't find me, okay?'

'I can't lie to my client.'

'You're a lawyer.'

'Frankie, he's given six million dollars to six former girlfriends. And he wants to give you a million, too.'

She held her hand out.

'Okay. Give it to me.'

281

He shook his head. 'It doesn't work that way. I get all the information and take photos first. Then I meet with him, show him the photos, and he gives me the money. Then I bring you a cashier's check for a million dollars.'

'What kind of information?'

'Your age.'

Like it was a joke: 'Twenty-eight.'

'Your daughter's age.'

'Eight.'

'Your debts.'

'None.'

'Your economic condition. You know, do you have any money?'

She waved her hand at the old rent house.

'Yes, this is my estate.'

'Do you have a job?'

'No.'

'How do you pay your bills?'

'I manage.'

'Any other problems in your life?'

'You.'

'Now, see, that wasn't hard. You're twenty-eight and broke, but otherwise all right, other than the fact that you're trying to quit smoking and you're hiding from your abusive ex-husband. You have an eight-year-old daughter who's . . . Oh, is she sick?'

Her expression changed. The joke was over.

'No.'

'She doesn't have a medical condition?'

A bit suspicious now.

'What kind of medical condition?'

'A disease.'

'No.'

'She's perfectly healthy?'

'Yes.'

Finally, a healthy child. The odds had turned.

'Well, that's good . . . and different.'

'From what?'

'The others.'

'The other girlfriends?'

Andy nodded.

'They have sick kids?'

'Yeah. Well, one of them died.'

'But all six of them had sick kids?'

'Yeah.'

'How sick?'

'Cancer, cerebral palsy, paralysis . . .'

'Does your client have a sick child?'

Andy nodded again. 'His son's dying. A rare form of leukemia.'

Her complexion was no longer creamy; it was pale. As if she were now sick, too. She stepped inside and shut the door in his face.

The elevator door opened on a clown.

Andy stepped out; the clown slapped a party hat on Andy's head and shoved a blowout in his mouth like a new father passing out cigars. A HAPPY BIRTHDAY, ZACH banner hung on the opposite wall, and colorful balloons and crêpe-paper streamers hung from the ceiling. Two hours after leaving Frankie Doyle in Buda, Andy walked into the cancer ward on the seventh floor of the Austin General Hospital.

More clowns passed out party favors, face painters made the kids look like lions and tigers and bears, and magicians and jugglers entertained. Balloon artists fashioned animals out of long balloons. Pretty nurses ate cake and ice cream with their patients. Bald boys and girls wore smiles bigger than their faces. They were sick kids yesterday and would be again tomorrow, but today they were just kids.

Andy heard cheers and spotted Zach Reeves perched atop a hospital bed being pushed down the corridor by a clown. He threw his arms into the air and screamed when his bed beat another kid's bed at the finish line.

Bed races.

Surveying it all was Andy's client. He walked over to Russell Reeves.

'Thanks for coming, Andy. Zach was looking for you.'

'Wouldn't miss it.'

'I told Zach he could have his birthday party anywhere he wanted it – Yankee stadium, Madison Square Garden, Disney World. Said he wanted it here, with his friends.'

'He's a good kid.'

And he was standing there. His face was painted like a zebra, and he was wearing a baseball cap on backwards.

'Andy, did you see the bed race? I won!'

'Awesome, dude.'

They fist-punched. Zach pulled the cap off his head. 'Look – my dad got it signed by the whole team.'

The whole New York Yankees team.

'That's way cool. Oh, here.'

Andy took his backpack off his shoulder and removed a small gift-wrapped box. The boy took it and ripped the paper off and opened the box. He pulled out Andy's gift: a black leather doo-rag.

'Aw, man, this is cool!'

'I didn't get anyone to sign it.'

Zach put on the doo-rag. Andy adjusted the fit.

'Happy birthday, Zach.'

'Thanks, Andy.'

The boy gave him a quick hug, then rejoined the party.

'He likes you, Andy.'

'I like him.'

'I try to be his big brother, too, but it's not the same.'

'He looks good today.'

Russell nodded. 'Today. Chemo tomorrow.'

They didn't speak for several minutes. Andy watched Zach playing with the other sick kids, then he watched Russell watching Zach. He knew exactly what was going through his client's mind.

'We found her,' Andy finally said. 'Frankie Doyle.'

'Let's go upstairs.'

They walked to the elevators. Russell used a special key to access the penthouse. The place looked like a fancy hotel suite. Russell led Andy into an office. They sat across a table from each other. Andy removed the dossier and photos of Frankie Doyle and her daughter from his backpack and spread them across the table.

'She wasn't easy to find, Russell.'

Russell studied the dossier and photos under a small fluorescent desk lamp.

'She moved from Boston to Montana to New Mexico to West Texas. Changed her name every time. She now lives in Buda.'

Russell looked up. 'You went to Boston and Montana and found her fifteen miles from here?'

'Yeah.'

Russell returned to the photos.

'So what's her story?'

'Frankie Doyle is twenty-eight, divorced, one daughter. She's eight.'

'Finances?'

'None to speak of. She drives an old Toyota and lives in a rent house. Unemployed.'

'Problems?'

'Cigarettes and her ex-husband up in Boston. He hit her. She's running from him.'

Russell shook his head slowly.

'These poor women. They all have a burden to bear.'

'I met hers. Ex-boxer, owns a garage. He's a jerk.'

'What's wrong with the girl?'

'Nothing.'

Russell's eyes came up again.

'Her child's not sick?'

'No.'

'You're sure?'

Andy shrugged. 'Frankie said she was in perfect health.'

'You saw her? The girl?'

'Yeah. Cute redhead. She seemed fine.'

'See, Andy. Just odds.'

Russell went back to the photos.

'And she's eight years old?'

Andy nodded. 'And Frankie is twenty-eight. Which means, Russell, she couldn't have been your girlfriend.'

Russell didn't react. He didn't even look up from the photos.

'Why do you say that, Andy?'

'I did the math. You've been married fourteen years, so she was fourteen when you got married. And she got married four years later.'

Russell slowly raised his eyes from the photos.

'I never said she was my girlfriend before I was married . . . or that she wasn't married.'

Now Andy tried not to react.

'You were married . . . and she was too . . . when you and her . . . ?'

'It's called an affair, Andy.'

287

'Russell, Kathryn is gorgeous.'

'Infidelity is a complicated thing.'

'I wouldn't know.'

'No one can know. The privilege, Andy.'

'That's why she denied it – she was a married woman having an affair.'

Russell again dropped his eyes to the photos of Frankie and her daughter. He examined them so intently that another thought crossed Andy's mind – a thought that made sense of a billionaire searching for seventeen former girlfriends.

'Is the girl yours?'

Russell Reeves looked up at Andy. His face was stern. Andy braced himself to get fired on the spot. Instead, his client sat back and blew out a resigned breath. As if it were finally time to come clean with his lawyer.

'Maybe.'

He stared into space, as if remembering.

'Frankie and I had an affair nine years ago when I taught a course at MIT one semester. Guest high-tech billionaire, that sort of thing. We met at the hotel bar. We were both married at the time.'

For some reason, Andy felt a little jealous at the thought of Russell Reeves having had an affair with Frankie Doyle.

'What bar?'

'I don't remember the name of the bar, Andy. It was in the Boston Grand Hotel.'

That was the hotel. It was mentioned in the dossier. Frankie had worked there nine years ago, when she was nineteen years old. A nine-month pregnancy and she'd have an eight-year-old child now. Which she had.

Frankie Doyle had lied to Andy.

'Her ex is a rough character. You're lucky he didn't find out back then.'

'No one can find out.' He sighed. 'Andy, I need to know if she's my daughter.'

'Why?'

'Because I passed a cancer gene on to Zach. I gave my son the cancer that's killing him. What if I passed the same gene on to this child?'

'But she's not sick.'

'Not yet. If she is mine, she might have the gene and she might become sick – next week or next month or next year. What if my scientists can prevent that from happening? They've made incredible advances in gene therapy, Andy. What if they can keep her from getting the same cancer as Zach?'

'But, Russell—'

'Andy, if she's mine, she might have a ticking time bomb inside her – what if we can prevent that bomb from detonating? What if we can save her from Zach's fate? What if we can save her life? Isn't that worth trying?'

'How?'

'DNA.'

'You want me to get her DNA?'

Russell nodded. 'We'll check her DNA against mine. Then we'll know the truth.'

'Russell, that's kind of creepy, sneaking over there and getting her DNA – assuming I can. Why don't you just talk to Frankie, tell her the situation, and ask to test the girl?'

'Because I haven't spoken to Frankie in nine years. She might be okay with that, she might not be. But what if she moved to Texas to extort money from me? She might want to go on TV and tell the world. Seems to me I should find out if the girl's mine first.'

'You're right. But it's still creepy.'

Russell stood and walked to the window. He stared out a long moment and then reached inside his coat.

'Oh, here, I brought these for you.'

Russell removed an envelope and held it out to Andy. He took the envelope and opened it. Andy couldn't believe what he was holding.

'Four tickets to the game tomorrow? UT versus Ohio State? On the fifty-yard line?'

'The school gave me season tickets when I built the lab on campus. I took Zach a few times when he was up to it, but I'm not a football fan.'

'Russell, Texas and Ohio State, they're both unde-feated. Whoever wins will be number one in the nation. This is the college football game of the year. You could sell these tickets for twenty thousand dollars.'

Russell shrugged. 'Take Suzie and have fun.'

'I'll take my buddies.'

He couldn't wait to see their faces.

'There'd be a bonus, Andy.'

'For the game?'

'For the DNA.'

Andy looked again at the tickets in his hand. The best seats in the stadium for the biggest game of the year.

'Ten thousand.'

Twenty thousand. Ten thousand. The guy tossed those figures around like they were Monopoly money. Russell faced Andy.

'When Kathryn and I conceived Zach, I didn't know I was sentencing him to death. I'd know about her. If she's mine, Andy, and if she were to get cancer because of my genes, I'd have sentenced two children to death. How am I supposed to live with that?'

'She has red hair, Russell. Frankie's ex-husband does, too. You don't.'

Russell gestured at the photos. 'Frankie's hair is black.'

'So?'

'So red hair is recessive.'

'Which means . . . ?'

'It means you must have two copies of the red hair gene to have red hair, one from your mother and one from your father. If only one parent has red hair, odds are their children won't have red hair. The other parent's hair color dominates.'

'So?'

'So the recessive gene skips generations. My mother did have red hair – Maureen O'Malley, that was her maiden name. Her red hair skipped my generation, but I'm a carrier and Frankie's Irish so she's a carrier. Put us together, and our child could have red hair. It's simple genetics, Andy.'

'Simple.'

'If she's mine. Get her DNA, Andy, and we'll know the truth.'

'So that's what you weren't telling me – that tracking down all these women was to find your child.'

'To find out if I had another child.'

'Were they really your girlfriends?'

'Yes . . . or at least I had a brief affair with them.'

'So you wanted to find out if they had children whose ages corresponded to the time of your affairs?'

'Yes.'

'The first six didn't?'

'No. Those children aren't mine, and neither are their siblings.'

'But this girl might be?'

'Yes.'

'And if she is your child?'

'I'll meet with Frankie, ask her to bring the girl in to the lab for testing. If she has the gene, we'll give her gene therapy. We'll save her life. What I can't do for Zach.'

Andy did not want Frankie Doyle's child to die.

'Okay, Russell, I'll get her DNA.'

'Thanks, Andy.'

'You want me to keep searching for the other women?'

'Yes. This girl might not be mine. One of theirs might be.'

They returned to the party. Andy got his Guitar Hero rematch with Zach; he lost again. But Andy's mind wasn't on the game; it was on Russell Reeves. And Frankie Doyle. And the girl.

What if she were Russell's child? And what if he had given her the cancer gene? And what if his scientists could save her from Zach's fate? Wouldn't Frankie want that? Wouldn't she beg Russell to save her daughter's life?

It all made perfect sense.

That Russell wanted to obtain the girl's DNA to confirm that she was in fact his child – and thus might have the cancer gene – before going to Frankie.

That Russell wanted to find this child and save her life.

That he did not want to be responsible for another child's death.

Perfect sense.

But it didn't explain why those six other children were sick.

Mickey Doyle stared at the traffic ticket lawyer's business card. His cell phone number was printed on it. Mickey had almost called the lawyer several times, to ask if he had found Frankie and Abby. Three years, he had tried to forget them, then this guy shows up and now he couldn't stop thinking about them.

He shoved the card back into his shirt pocket.

Jesus, Mary, and Joseph. His life was in the crapper. No wife, no kid, no future. Thirty-five years old, and he had hit the end of the line. He ordered another boilermaker.

He downed the whiskey shot and chased it with the beer. The warmth quickly followed by the cold. His body gave a little shudder. A few more and he would be able to sleep.

Of course, he had no one to blame but himself. His temper. His fists. He had slapped Frankie a few times, but that last time, he had actually hit her. And the way he hit, he could have killed her – the only woman he had ever loved.

He had loved her since she was ten years old. He watched her grow up three doors down. When she turned sixteen, he asked her out. They married two years later, when she graduated high school. She had been a virgin. And Catholic. And guilt-ridden. So sex had not exactly been adventurous. Mickey had strayed, early and often, like South Boston residents casting votes for a Kennedy. Back then, it had seemed like innocent fun; but on Sunday when they had gone to Mass, he had felt guilty. He no longer went to Mass, but he still felt the guilt.

And he missed them both.

He ordered another boilermaker. He had had only

two loves in his life: fighting and Frankie. Fighting had gotten him to semi-pro, weekend fights after a week at the garage. But his raw skills could take him only so far. So he had given up on the ring.

But he had never given up on Frankie. She would always be the love of his life. Sure, there had been other women in the last three years, but they were just distractions. When he was with them, he was thinking of her. His one true love, and he had screwed it up. He would give anything for a second chance. The judge had given him a second chance – and a third – but Frankie would not. Because of Abby.

He should have protected her.

He paid his tab and walked out the front door and down the sidewalk; it was three blocks to the house. One block down, a fist hammered him in the mouth and knocked him against a building. *Some asshole's mugging Mickey Doyle?* Hell, he fought best when he was staggering drunk, like now. He turned to a tall man leaning into him.

'Where's Frankie?' the man said.

'What?'

'Your ex-wife, Mickey, where is she?'

'You working for the lawyer?'

'What lawyer?'

'I told him – I don't know where she's at.'

'You don't tell me, Mickey, I'm gonna kill you. And then I'm gonna find Frankie and kill her, too.'

All the guilt Mickey had suffered over the last three

years, all the times he had cussed himself for hitting his wife, all the love he had felt for Frankie the last eighteen years, now seemed to build in his fists. He gave a little shoulder feint – the guy went for it – and popped him with a quick left jab to the nose. Then he came up with a right uppercut into his chin and a combo to his midsection. He heard the air come out of the man. A few more blows and Mickey had him on the ropes – or at least the side of an SUV.

'You ain't gonna hurt Frankie!'

Mickey pounded the guy's face and body – he felt ribs cracking under his fists – and he was determined to beat this guy to death to save Frankie, when he suddenly felt something else cracking: his skull. Mickey collapsed to the pavement and his mind went as black as the night sky. And Mickey Doyle's last thought before he died was, *I'm sorry, Frankie.*

Harmon Payne stood straight and spit blood.

'Thanks, Cecil.'

Cecil Durant, his driver, had clocked Mickey with the tire iron. Harmon rubbed his sore ribs. The boss said no unauthorized killing, now his ribs were going to hurt for a week. A bullet in Mickey Doyle's head would have been considerably less painful for both of them.

'Shit, this guy can punch.'

Harmon knelt and checked Mickey's pulse. He was dead.

'Or could.'

He then checked the body. In his shirt pocket, he found a business card: *Andy Prescott. Lawyer. Traffic Tickets. Austin, Texas.* With a cell phone number. Harmon stood.

'Cecil, we're going to Texas.'

Chapter 17

Andy paid Ramon $500 to get up early the next morning and another $500 to drive him to Frankie Doyle's house in Buda. Andy had to get the girl's DNA – although he had no idea how he would actually do that – get it to Russell, and get to the UT stadium in time for the 2:00 P.M. kickoff. And he wanted to see Frankie Doyle again. But when Ramon turned the yellow Corvette into the driveway of Frankie's house, he said, 'They're gone, bro.'

Andy knocked on the front door. There was no answer. He looked in the windows. The furniture was still in place, but Frankie and the girl had disappeared. The place was neat, as if it had just been cleaned. He went around back. Nothing. Ramon was right. They were gone. Andy walked around to the front of the house and got back in the car. He just sat there.

'Aw, man,' Ramon said.

Andy turned to him. 'What?'

'You wanted to see her.'

'So?'

'So you should never mix business with pleasure.'

'You do.'

'I never charged my ex-wife . . . until she cheated on me.'

'Why would they leave in the middle of the night?'

'Because you found her . . . and she don't want to be found.'

Ramon backed the car out of the driveway.

'Stop!'

Ramon hit the brakes. 'What?'

'That.'

A black rubber trash can stood by the road waiting for the next pickup. Andy got out and removed the top of the can. He pulled out a large plastic trash bag. He loosened the tie and opened the bag.

'Man, you going through her trash?' Ramon said. 'That's like Floyd T. dumpster diving.'

'She cleaned the place before they left.'

'So?'

'So there might be something in here.'

Andy didn't want to rummage through the trash with his bare hands, so he looked around and found a long stick. Then he dumped the contents of the trash bag onto the ground. He squatted and poked through the refuse with the stick – discarded food and food containers, dirty paper towels, banana peels, cigarette butts and an empty pack – she started smoking again – yogurt cartons, potato chip bags, feminine products, egg shells, Band-Aid . . . He froze. It was one of those big square

Band-Aids he often used when he got serious road rash. He flipped the Band-Aid over with the stick. It was stained with blood.

But with whose blood?

Andy had delivered the Band-Aid to Russell, and Russell had handed him a check for $10,000. Andy also had four football tickets worth $20,000 in his hands. He had considered scalping the tickets, but what's $20,000 compared to watching the college football game of the year on the fifty-yard line with your buddies? UT versus Ohio State. Longhorns versus Buckeyes. The number one and two teams in the nation playing a regular season game. And, of course, there were—

'Cheerleaders!'

Dave was pointing like a kid at the circus. The Longhorn cheerleaders dressed in their skimpy orange-and-white cowgirl outfits bounced past. They were cute and perky and fit. Andy, Tres, and Dave stood transfixed. They heard Curtis' voice.

'Man, these new RVs, they cost a million dollars, and they've got Wi-Fi, satellite dishes, GPS systems . . .'

'Curtis,' Dave said, 'you're looking at recreational vehicles instead of cheerleaders?'

Curtis' head shot around. 'Where?'

They were walking across the parking lot at the LBJ School of Public Affairs just a block east of the stadium. SUVs and RVs crowded the concrete and fans engaged in that all-American tradition: tailgating. A big party in a parking lot before a football game. Eating meat and drinking beer. Yelling fight songs. Acting obnoxious. The parking lot looked like a barbecue convention; smoke rose from grills on which beef simmered in thick molasses-based artery-clogging barbecue sauce. The cool breeze carried the smell like perfume. UT fans hollered 'Hook 'Em Horns!' to everyone who walked by. Anyone who failed to respond with a Hook 'Em Horns hand sign – pinkie and forefinger extended, thumb clasping the middle fingers down, so as to fashion horns – to show support for the Longhorn team was assumed to be an enemy combatant and empty beer cans were immediately launched their way.

Just good clean American fun.

They joined a wide stream of fans wearing burnt orange shirts and their favorite players' jerseys flowing west toward the double-decked stadium that rose in front of them like—

'The Coliseum,' Curtis said.

He had studied abroad in Rome.

'It's amazing,' he said, 'how American football parallels the gladiator combats of ancient Rome . . . except American football crowds are more bloodthirsty, of course.'

'I feel another Roman history lesson coming,' Tres said.

'Did you know that most gladiators were slaves or

poor men desperate for a way out of poverty – same as black football players from the inner cities today?'

UT had fielded the last all-white national championship team back in 1969. After that, the school had started recruiting black players from the wards of Houston and Dallas; the 2005 UT championship team had been mostly black.

'Gladiators were unusually large men fighting for the entertainment of wealthy spectators. Some became national celebrities. They wore tattoos, endorsed products, had groupies, just like football players today.'

'Jeez,' Dave said, 'even back then, girls loved athletes.'

'And the games were public spectacles held in specially built amphitheatres, just like cities today spend hundreds of millions to build stadiums to lure football teams to town. There were bands and mascots, fans placed bets and scalped tickets just like—'

'I could have done,' Andy said.

'The Coliseum seated fifty thousand and had separate entrances and reserved seating for VIPs, just like this stadium. And the arena was almost identical in size to a football field. It's really interesting how similar our society is to Roman society, when you think about it.'

'Didn't the Roman Empire fall?' Andy said.

'Curtis,' Tres said, 'you're a walking encyclopedia. Is there anything you don't know?'

'Women.'

'Amen, brother.'

Dave gave Curtis a fist-punch.

'Andy,' Curtis said, 'thanks for the gig with Reeves' kid.'

'You meet Zach?'

'Yesterday. His limo picked me up. His driver's a jerk, but it's a sweet ride. Reeves is paying me six hundred.'

'An hour? That's more than he's paying me.'

'Can you teach algebra?'

'I can't spell it.'

'Geeks rule.'

'Andy,' Dave said, 'can you get me a job with Reeves?'

'What can you teach?'

'I've got a PhD in beer-drinking.'

'Zach's a demon at Guitar Hero,' Curtis said. 'And smarter than most of the college kids I teach.'

'Curtis,' Andy said, 'what's the deal with red hair being recessive?'

'That's random. Okay, red hair is recessive, which means that both parents usually must have red hair in order for their offspring to have red hair because black, brown, and blond hair genes dominate over red hair genes. See, the red hair gene is M-C-One-R – melanocortin-one receptor. Everyone has that gene, but to have red hair you've got a mutated M-C-One-R gene . . . actually, two mutated genes, one from your mother and one from your father. If your parents both have red hair, you have a one hundred percent chance of having red hair.'

303

'What if a kid has red hair but only one of the parents does?'

'Then one of the kid's four grandparents will have red hair. Statistically, anyway. That's why only two to six percent of the US population has red hair.'

Russell Reeves hadn't lied. But why had Andy wondered if he had?

After walking through a metal detector, they entered the stadium. Ninety-six thousand screaming fans from Texas wearing burnt-orange shirts and Ohio wearing red shirts – the Buckeye fans had traveled a thousand miles for a football game – had packed the bowl of the stadium that surrounded the green playing field. They found their seats on the fifty-yard line just up from the governor of Texas. Tres pointed down at the UT bench.

'Look who's standing on the sideline – McConaughey.'

'Why does he get to be on the sideline?' Dave said. 'He never played football when he was a student here.'

Tres shrugged. 'The allure of celebrity.'

A blimp advertising an insurance company circled overhead like a vulture eyeing road kill. It would provide a bird's-eye view of the game which could be seen on the Godzillatron, the huge video screen in the south end zone. It was like looking at . . . well, at Godzilla's flat screen TV.

'Only bigger HDTV screen in the world is in Tokyo,' Curtis said.

Andy Prescott had attended most of the Longhorns' home games while he was a student at UT – he had never told his mother – but he hadn't come for the football. He had come for the girls. There was something about a football game on a Saturday afternoon – even on the first day of November – that made college coeds want to wear the most revealing outfits they owned. He always figured it was the TV cameras. Gorgeous UT coeds hoped to be discovered at a nationally televised football game. So they put their best breast forward.

Which alone was worth the price of admission.

For the next three hours, the Texas fans – rich white folks from the nice parts of Dallas and Houston – cheered the UT team – mostly poor black guys from the bad parts of Dallas and Houston, the guys watched the game, Andy watched the girls, Bevo, the Longhorn mascot, crapped in the end zone, the Ohio State quarterback was carried off the field on a stretcher with a head injury, the cheerleaders jumped and vaulted and somersaulted on the sideline as if auditioning for Matthew McConaughey, the lucky bastard, and, oh yeah, UT won.

Cecil Durant peered out the window of the airplane and said, 'Look, they're playing a football game, down in that stadium. Must be the Texas–Ohio State game.'

Harmon shook his head. Traveling with Cecil was like taking the kids on vacation. You'd think the guy had never been away from New Jersey in his life.

'My first time in Texas. Can we see the Alamo while we're here?'

'Cecil, the Alamo's in San Antonio.'

'Oh. How about J.R. Ewing's Southfork Ranch? I loved that show.'

'That's in Dallas, Cecil. Which is why they called the show *Dallas*.'

Cecil nodded. 'Makes sense. NASA?'

'Houston.'

'Well, what's in Austin?'

'Andy Prescott.'

Cecil Durant wasn't exactly a Mensa candidate, but he was a skilled driver and handy with a tire iron when the need arose. They had landed, rented a black Crown Vic, and driven out of the airport. When they hit Interstate 35, they turned south. Harmon's ribs hurt like hell.

'Can I buy some cowboy boots?' Cecil said.

'Let's buy some guns first.'

The only problem with flying commercial these days – well, other than crying kids, complaining passengers, lost luggage, late planes, and being strip-searched in the security line – was packing your weapons. There were forms to fill out and questions to be answered, and the silencer always raised the Feds' eyebrows when the luggage went through the X-ray machine. So while Harmon had flown to Texas, his weapons had stayed home in Jersey. Fortunately, buying an arsenal in Texas was considerably easier than getting an abortion.

Harmon had first checked the Austin paper for a gun

show; he could buy every imaginable firearm, silencer, ammo, assault weapon, and even a machine gun at a gun show for cash and with no questions asked or forms filled out or ID presented. Harmon had read that Mexican drug cartels were now buying their weapons at Texas gun shows and smuggling them across the border because Mexico's gun laws were stricter. But the nearest gun show that weekend was in Waco, ninety miles north of Austin. So he had checked the phone book at the airport and found the address of the nearest Cabela's. It was fifteen miles south of Austin in a town called Buda.

Cabela's is housed in a log structure roughly the size of an airplane hangar. Outside stands a life-size bronze of a cowboy on horseback. Inside stands a two-story faux-mountain stuffed animal display featuring deer, elk, moose, caribou, musk ox, Arctic wolves, and bears (grizzly, black, brown, and Polar). Stuffed animal heads line the walls. Stuffed birds hang from the ceiling. And Cabela's sells the guns to shoot all those creatures dead. The gun department offered weapons manufactured by Browning, Smith & Wesson, Winchester, Ruger, Glock, Savage Arms, Bushmaster, Remington, Colt, Sig Sauer, and Beretta. Middle-aged white men crowded the gun counter.

Americans were sure as hell exercising their Second Amendment rights that day in Buda, Texas.

Harmon was standing at the counter and hefting a short-frame Glock 21 semiautomatic handgun with a

307

thirteen-round magazine, on sale for $549.99. Cecil stood next to him making quick side-to-side movements with a .44 Magnum as if sighting in a target and growling through clenched teeth, 'Freeze, dirtbag!'

Harmon sighed.

'Put the gun down, Cecil. You're making me nervous. You're a driver, not a shooter.'

Harmon Payne was a shooter. And, notwithstanding his twenty years with the New Jersey mob and over two hundred shooting jobs, he had never been questioned, arrested, or convicted. Not once. He was that good. So the criminal background check called NICS – the Feds' National Instant Criminal Background Check System, enacted into law after that little wacko Hinckley tried to assassinate President Reagan – went through like a charm. Thirty seconds after feeding Harmon's name, address, place of birth, date of birth, social security number, height, weight, sex, race, and state of residence into the computerized Internet-based NICS E-Check System, the response came back: PROCEED WITH TRANSACTION. The clerk smiled at Harmon and said he had been cleared to purchase any weapon or weapons he desired.

He desired the Glock.

In Texas, there is no waiting period to purchase a firearm, no requirement for a license to own a firearm, and no required permit to carry a firearm in your vehicle. So fifteen minutes after entering the store and another fifteen spent searching for Cecil – he found his driver

in the ocean of camouflage that was the clothing department wearing a hunter's cap with the ear muffs down
and holding up a tiny camo bikini—

'Harmon, you think Harriet would like this?'

'Your wife in a camo bikini? I don't think so, Cecil.'

—Harmon Payne and Cecil Durant walked out with
two brand new Glocks (no silencer, but he'd have to
make do), two thirteen-round magazines, and enough
ammo to outgun the Texas national guard.

It was that easy.

Of course, it wasn't as if Harmon Payne was a
whacked-out college kid pissed off at his professor for
giving him a B on his term paper and heading directly
back to the campus to go on a shooting spree and kill
fifty or sixty students. Harmon Payne was a professional.
He was only going to kill one person.

'Let's go find Andy Prescott.'

Cecil turned the Crown Vic north on I-35.

'That's it,' Harmon said. 'Fifteen fourteen and a half
South Congress. Says "traffic tickets" on the door. Park
down the street.'

Cecil continued north on Congress until they were
in front of the Texas School for the Deaf, then he made
a U-turn and parked in front of a shop called Blackmail.
He chuckled.

'We're in the same line of business. Sort of.'

They got out. One quick look around told Harmon
they were overdressed in their sharkskin suits; they

always dressed as middle-management executives on business trips. So they removed the ties and unbuttoned the top buttons of their shirts. Harmon kept his coat on to conceal the Glock tucked into his back waist-band. Even so, they still looked like middle-aged accountants.

They had parked in the 1200 block; they would walk the three blocks back to Andy Prescott's office. They proceeded past stores called Pink Hair Salon & Gallery, Creatures Boutique, and Cocoon Massage & Body-works.

'We could catch a massage later,' Cecil said. 'Might make your ribs feel better.'

'If things go right, we could catch a plane home later.'

'If we stay the night, let's get some hookers.'

'What, you're the governor of New York now?'

They walked past a little motel, a coffee shop called Jo's, a bum playing a guitar, a Mexican food place called Güero's, and the weirdest looking people Harmon had seen outside a circus. 'Now we know what happened to all the hippies and Beatniks from the sixties.' He gestured at a young tattooed female loitering outside a store called Lucy in Disguise with Diamonds. 'That broad, she looks like a side-show freak, the tattooed lady.' Harmon shook his head in utter disgust at America's young people. 'Jesus.'

Cecil nodded. 'And the Beatles.'

'What?'

Cecil pointed up at the façade of painted faces. 'They got faces of Jesus, the Beatles, Marilyn Monroe . . . you think she really slept with Kennedy?'

'I don't think either one of them slept.'

They arrived at 1514½. Harmon tried the door, but it was locked. A bum was sitting on the steps of the tattoo parlor next door and writing in a notebook like Harmon's youngest daughter used.

'You know Andy Prescott?'

The bum didn't look up.

'Nope.'

They stepped away from the bum to get a breath of fresh air.

'He must not work on Saturday,' Harmon said.

'The bum?'

'Prescott.'

'Oh.' Cecil stretched and said, 'I'm hungry. Let's go back to that Mexican joint, get something to eat.'

'Yeah, okay. Then we'll find a hotel.'

'And hookers?'

'No hookers, Cecil.'

They walked back down the block to the place called Güero's. College kids crowded the porch fronting Congress Avenue. Harmon and Cecil could barely squeeze past the sidewalk tables. Three guys at one table were drinking Coronas – one wore a T-shirt that read 'Keep Honking – I'm Reloading'; Harmon liked that – and making fools of themselves with passing females.

311

'Dave, put your tongue back in your mouth, dude!'

Another guy carrying four beers joined them.

'McConaughey's inside. Ronda's trying to get his autograph, so I bought the beers at the bar. This round's on me.'

'You the man, Tres!'

They punched fists across the table like the Yankees players do after someone hits a home run. A scrawny little guy with black glasses and hair that looked like it had been cut with a weed-whacker said, 'What does McConaughey have on us?'

'Looks, money, fame . . .'

'Other than that?'

They all laughed like he was Letterman or something.

The scrawny guy said, 'Listen to this girl's ad: "I'm just a girl looking to share my heart with someone who doesn't mind my dog sharing the bed."'

The guy with Elvis hair said, 'Her dog? Man, that's too kinky even for me.'

The scrawny guy said, 'And the fleas.'

They laughed again.

Harmon shook his head. Spoiled college kids getting drunk on their daddies' hard-earned money. Harmon had not gone to college. His father had died when he was only ten, and he had a mother and two sisters to support. So he had gone to work for the mob right out of high school. He had wanted to be an engineer; he became an enforcer.

'Let's go inside. Maybe it'll be quieter.'

It wasn't. The Texas football team had beaten Ohio State, so the college kids were celebrating by getting drunk and being loud. Their waitress said a movie star was in the back room, which only added to the commotion. Harmon sighed; it wasn't going to be a nice quiet dinner.

Just inside the front door was the bar with a fountain in the wood floor and a stuffed wild turkey on the wall. Obviously a real classy joint. And the customers dressed to fit the decor. Their hostess – a cute little broad in a miniskirt and a Güero's T-shirt tight around her chest – led them into the main dining room and past the open kitchen and an attractive Mexican woman making tortillas on an open grill. Harmon caught her eye and winked at her; she responded with a demure smile. On a job in Cancún – staged to look like a drug buy gone bad – he had scored with a Mexican waitress at their hotel, his first bilingual experience.

The dining room's decor looked like something out of Cancún with Mexican calendars, curios, and art. They were seated in a booth along a brick wall covered with black-and-white prints of old Mexican bandits and graffiti like Harmon had written on the bathroom stalls at his school when he was a kid: JK♥RL. A mariachi wearing a bolo tie and playing a guitar strolled by, singing a Mexican ballad. He was good. The music and noise of the crowd reverberated off the concrete floor and brick walls and pounded into Harmon's head.

Maybe a beer would relieve his headache.

They ordered Mexican food and Dos Equis beer from a waitress tattooed and pierced from head to foot. She had to be a Democrat. The entire place was filled with Democrats.

'What a friggin' zoo,' Harmon said. 'Any normal people live in Austin?'

'Haven't seen any yet.'

But the beer was cold and the food was good. His spirits were starting to lift until he spotted a man with his family. Harmon's own wife and kids were at his son's soccer game at that moment. Two soccer games in a row he had missed. He was feeling like a lousy father. Cecil must have read his mind.

'Harmon, let's get some hookers. That'll improve your mood. And make your ribs feel better.'

Chapter 18

Harmon Payne found Andy Prescott's office door locked all day Sunday as well because Andy had flown first class that morning to San Diego to find the eighth woman on Russell Reeves' list. So while Harmon and Cecil spent the day in the hotel bar resting Harmon's ribs and watching the pro football games on the big-screen TV –

'Harmon, says here 1.5 million Mexican free-tailed bats nest under the Congress Avenue bridge and come out every day at dusk. Can we go watch? They say it's really neat.'

'No.'

'Can we go to the Lady Bird Johnson Wildflower Center?'

'No.'

'The capitol?'

'No.'

'But it's the biggest one in the country.'

'No.'

'We can take a tour of downtown on those Segways. That'd be fun.'

'No.'

'Can we at least get hookers?'

'No.'

– Andy spent the day following Sally Armstrong around La Jolla in a rented Audi.

Sally was thirty-eight, attractive, married, and wealthy; she lived in a large house with a view of the Pacific Ocean. She had two children, a fifteen-year-old daughter who was perfectly healthy and a nineteen-year-old son who was a quadriplegic. When he was sixteen, Jimmy Armstrong had lost control of his brand new Mustang and wrapped it around a telephone pole. He would be in a wheelchair for life. But he already had the best care money could buy.

He didn't need Russell Reeves' money.

Andy drove along the boardwalk and saw blonde California girls skating in bikinis – in November. He stayed overnight at the Del Coronado Hotel and ate crab enchiladas. He walked along the beach and watched the sun set into the Pacific Ocean. He thought about sick kids. Seven out of eight. It made no sense.

The next morning, Andy put on jeans and sneakers and took a cab to the airport. He called the Municipal Court back in Austin and told Judge Judith's clerk that he was out of town on business for Russell Reeves. The clerk readily agreed to postpone his cases set for that Monday. Then he boarded a flight to Austin.

★　　★　　★

While Andy Prescott's plane was over the Grand Canyon, Dr Glenn Hall, PhD, walked into Russell Reeves' office in the Reeves Research Institute.

'DNA matches,' he said. 'It's her.'

Andy's flight arrived at the Austin airport at three. He immediately called Russell Reeves; they agreed to meet at Andy's office. The black limo was already there when Andy arrived; but so was a crowd on the sidewalk in front of Ramon's shop. Andy paid the cabby and got out. He hurried over and pushed his way through the crowd and saw Floyd T. lying on the sidewalk.

'Floyd T.!'

Russell Reeves was kneeling next to him; Darrell was standing over him. Andy pushed Darrell.

'What'd you do to him?'

'Nothing. I swear. He was sitting right there, then he just fell over.'

'He had a heart attack, Andy,' Russell said.

'Is he breathing?'

Russell checked Floyd T.'s pulse.

'No.'

Ramon made the sign of the cross.

'Shit.' Andy turned in a fast circle. 'Anyone know CPR?'

'I do.'

Russell tilted Floyd T.'s chin back to straighten his airway, then pinched his nose. He put his mouth on Floyd T.'s. He blew slowly – once, twice –

'Mr Reeves,' Darrell said, 'you don't know where his mouth has been.'

– then he knelt up, put his hands together, and pushed on Floyd T.'s chest – 'one, two, three' – and again and again. Then he gave Floyd T. mouth-to-mouth again.

He came up and said, 'Darrell, let's get him in the limo.'

'But Mr Reeves, I just had it cleaned.'

'Pick him up!'

Darrell squatted, slid his arms under Floyd T., and lifted him off the ground as easily as if he were an infant. He carried Floyd T. over to the limo, where Russell was holding the back door open. Darrell hunched over and disappeared into the limo with Floyd T. in his arms. He lay Floyd T. down then backed out and ran around to the driver's seat. Andy yelled to Ramon, 'Put his grocery cart in your shop!' Then he followed Russell into the limo and shut the door.

Harmon and Cecil watched the scene from the front seat of the Crown Vic parked down the street.

'One less homeless person in the world,' Harmon said.

'I've never ridden in a limo,' Cecil said. 'Bet it's neat.'

'Not so much for the bum.'

They had staked out Andy Prescott's office most of the day, but so far no one had gone in or out of the door to 1514½.

318

Where was this guy?

'We don't even know what Prescott looks like,' Cecil said.

'Like a lawyer. You see anyone over there looks like a lawyer?'

'I haven't seen anyone in this whole town looks normal, except the rich guy in the limo. You think that's Prescott?'

'A traffic ticket lawyer with a limo and a bodyguard? I don't think so, Cecil.'

'Good point.'

Inside the limo, Russell told Darrell to drive to Austin General Hospital in downtown. Andy dug his cell phone out of his backpack and called ahead while Russell performed CPR all the way to the emergency entrance where a team of nurses and doctors had gathered outside. Andy opened the door and jumped out. He and Darrell lifted Floyd T. out and placed him on the waiting gurney. The doctors and nurses stood frozen, staring at Floyd T. like he was an illegal Mexican immigrant walking in the front door.

'Come on, get him inside!' Andy said.

'Is he homeless?' a nurse asked.

'Yeah. So?'

'So we're a private hospital. If he doesn't have insurance, you have to take him to the public hospital.'

'He's a war hero!'

'Then take him to the VA hospital,' a doctor said.

'Where's it at?'

'San Antonio.'

'That's eighty miles from here!'

Russell climbed out of the limo.

'He has insurance. Me.'

The nurses' and doctors' expressions changed.

'Mr Reeves,' the nurse said.

'Take care of this man.'

'Get him into the ER!' the doctor said. 'Stat!'

The entire medical team sprang into action. One jumped up onto the gurney and straddled Floyd T. and started CPR. The others pushed the gurney inside through the automatic doors. They disappeared around a corner.

Thirty minutes later, Andy had registered Floyd T., Russell Reeves had signed a financial responsibility form, and they were sitting in the waiting room. Waiting. And drinking a Jo's coffee. Russell had sent Darrell on a coffee run. Floyd T. was in emergency bypass surgery.

'Thanks, Russell.'

'Good coffee.'

'Not for the coffee. For Floyd T.'

'I know.' Russell shook his head. 'Hospitals. This is a private non-profit hospital – they pay no state or federal taxes in exchange for providing free care to indigents. But they don't. They send poor people to the public hospital. And when they do treat the uninsured, they charge them double what they charge insured patients.'

320

'Why?'

'Because they can. And because the insurance companies demand discounts normal people can't get.'

'Different prices for different people for the same treatment? That's not fair.'

'No, Andy, it's not. They should have their tax exemptions revoked. But the government doesn't enforce the law. Politics. I've been against national health care, but now I know it's the only fair way to go. Otherwise, it won't be long before only people like me will have health care. At least then we could operate the health care industry like a business instead of politics. The US government is the biggest single purchaser of drugs in the world – Medicaid, Medicare, the VA – but it doesn't negotiate discounts from the pharmaceuticals. It pays list price. How stupid is that? But the drug companies bribe politicians with campaign contributions, so Congress makes it illegal for a US citizen to go to Canada and buy the same drugs cheaper.'

Russell took a few moments to calm himself.

'So tell me about the eighth woman.'

Andy handed the dossier to his client. Russell thumbed through it while Andy gave him a full report on Sally and Jimmy Armstrong in San Diego. Russell was shaking his head.

'Paralyzed at sixteen . . . his whole life in a wheel-chair.'

'Seven out of eight kids, Russell.'

'He's not mine, Andy. And neither is his sister. I knew Sally twelve years ago.'

'Another married woman . . . while you were married.'

'She was divorced. She must have remarried.'

Andy recalled that Sally Armstrong's divorce and second marriage were mentioned in the dossier.

'All these sick kids.'

'You're overthinking this, Andy. Life is random. Cruelly random.'

'At least Jimmy's getting great care.'

'I'll still wire a million to your trust account. You can fly back out to San Diego and give it to her . . . after you find Frankie Doyle.'

'The DNA matched?'

Russell Reeves nodded. 'The girl's mine, Andy.'

'Natalie Riggs is pregnant?'

Tres' face was grim. 'Two months, the doctor said.'

Andy and Tres were sitting at their usual table at Güero's. Dave was at his nude yoga class, and Curtis was teaching an evening seminar.

'How's she handling it?'

'She's happy.' Tres shrugged. 'Hormones must've kicked in. She and her mother, they're at Neiman Marcus right now picking out maternity clothes.'

'She'll probably start wearing underwear now.'

'Yeah – big underwear.'

'There's just no pleasing you, Tres.'

'She took her cameraman with her.'

'To buy underwear?'

'For the news. Says she's going to do a series on pregnancy and motherhood from start to finish, in real time.' He drank from his beer. ''Course, that means we've got to get married now. You'll be my best man?'

'Do I get free beer?'

They drank Coronas and contemplated life for a few minutes, as if offering a moment of silence for Tres' bachelorhood.

'Man, she had a great body,' Tres said softly, as if speaking of a deceased dear friend.

'She'll get it back, Tres. Natalie's not the type to keep the baby fat.'

'That's what she says. But you should've seen her getting down on the double-chocolate cookie-dough ice cream last night.'

Another moment of silence, this time for Natalie's great body. Tres broke the silence again.

'How's Floyd T.?'

'Good. Double bypass surgery. They said he needed to sleep, so I left, came straight here. Doctor said he'll be in the hospital for a week.'

'Reeves took him over there in his limo? Paid for his care?'

'And gave him mouth-to-mouth.'

'Can't say I would've done the same. He really is a good guy, like they say.'

'Yeah, I guess so.'

Tres turned to him.

'You *guess*? Talk to me, buddy.'

Andy hesitated then said, 'Tres, you can't breathe a word of this to anyone, not even Natalie.'

'With what you could tell her about me?'

'I can't imagine what Russell Reeves would do to me if this got out. And Natalie's a reporter.'

'I can't imagine what Natalie would do to me if she found out I hired a PI to follow her. We're in a Mexican standoff, buddy.'

Andy drank beer for courage.

'I'm tracking down Russell Reeves' old girlfriends. Seventeen.'

'*Seventeen?* No way.'

'Way. All over the country.'

'That's why you've been traveling so much?'

Andy nodded. 'We found the first six women easy enough.'

'We who?'

'Downtown PI, ex-FBI. Russell gave me his name, only the PI doesn't know Russell's the client. Anyway, we found them, and Russell gave each woman a million bucks. Anonymously.'

'Why?'

'He doesn't want anyone to know—'

'No. Why'd he give them money?'

'To make amends, he said. Because he treated them badly and they're down on their luck.'

Tres nodded. 'He's suffering that rich-guilt complex.

324

Feels guilty for being filthy rich, so he relieves his guilt by giving his money away. It's a common affliction among the rich . . . not for me, but for some rich people.' Tres shrugged. 'Course, for him, a million is like us giving a bum a buck. Well, for you anyway.'

'Thanks.'

'So he's giving away a bunch of money. What's the problem?'

'We had a hard time finding the seventh woman – her name's Frankie Doyle. So I went to her last known address in Boston, talked to her ex-husband. Name's Mickey. He hit her, so she divorced him three years ago and took off with their five-year-old daughter. They moved to Montana then to New Mexico and West Texas and now to Buda.'

'As in Buda just down the road?'

'Yeah. And they changed their names every time.'

'She must really be afraid of Mickey.'

'Maybe. But we found her. Or Lorenzo did.'

'Why not the FBI guy?'

'He goes by the book.'

'You meet her?'

Andy nodded. 'Says she never dated anyone but Mickey.'

'She's lying.'

'Why would she lie about that?'

'Everyone lies.'

'Maybe.'

'Okay, so she's on the run from Mickey. And Reeves

325

wants to give her a million bucks. I still don't see the problem.'

'Russell says the girl is his.'

'*Whoa*. Hold on. How?'

'He says they had an affair while he was up in Boston, teaching at MIT. Nine years ago.'

'While he was married?'

'And while she was.'

'Now that's a problem, Russell Reeves with a love child. How does he know the girl is his?'

'DNA.'

'How'd he get her DNA?'

'He didn't.'

'You did?'

Andy nodded.

'How?'

'Band-Aid in the trash.'

Tres seemed impressed.

'Does she know Reeves is the father of her child?'

Andy shrugged. 'When I went back out to get the DNA, she and the girl, they had already bolted.'

'Why?'

'They're scared.'

'Of what? Or whom?'

'I don't know.'

'So Reeves had you tracking down his old girlfriends to find this girl?'

'Yeah . . . or to find out if he had another child. But here's the weird part.'

Tres laughed. 'Like none of that was weird?'

'Seven of the eight women have sick kids, like Russell.'

'How sick?'

'Cancer, paralysis, cerebral palsy . . . The only kid who's not sick is—'

'Reeves' love child.'

Andy nodded. 'But Russell's worried she might get sick. Says he might have given the girl the same cancer gene he gave his son.'

'Who's dying.'

'Exactly. Said if she has the gene, he wants his scientists to give her gene therapy. To save her life.'

'So she's running from Mickey . . . or someone . . . but doesn't know her daughter might have cancer . . . or might get cancer.'

Andy nodded again.

'And Russell wants you to find her again.'

'Yep.'

'Complicated.'

They sat quietly and finished their beers.

'Tres, can I ask you a rich-person question?'

'Municipal bonds.'

'Is Russell Reeves a complicated person because he's rich? Or is he rich because he's complicated?'

'He's rich because he's a genius. He lives a complicated life because when you're rich, the simple stuff of life is easy. You don't have to worry about paying the bills or buying medicine or affording college tuition.

So life can get boring unless you create complications to make it interesting.'

'Like having affairs while you're married to a Miss UT?'

Tres nodded. 'Like most rich people, he figures the rules don't apply to him. He can do whatever he wants. Of course, the past always comes back and bites you in the butt . . . like finding out you have a love child. Then life gets complicated.'

'Are you like that?'

'I probably will be by the time I'm forty.'

They watched a pedicab try to cross Congress and almost get nailed by a speeding SUV.

'That would've hurt,' Tres said. He turned to Andy. 'Be careful, buddy.'

Andy laughed at his friend's serious expression.

'Tres, this deal is definitely a ten on the Weird-Shit-O-Meter-of-Life all right, but I don't think I'm in danger or anything.' He pointed at the pedicab. 'Riding in one of those down Congress, now that's dangerous.'

'You read yesterday's paper?'

Andy shook his head. 'I was in San Diego.'

Tres reached to his back pocket and pulled out a folded-up page from a newspaper. He unfolded and smoothed the page on the table. It was a newspaper article about an Austin lawyer who had been shot and killed in Ithaca, New York, the apparent victim of a random robbery. He was only forty.

'What's he got to do with me?'

'Read the rest of the story.'

Andy read aloud: "'Laurence G. Smith had been a partner at Rankin Edwards & Phillips, a prominent Austin law firm whose clients include . . . Russell Reeves.'"

Chapter 19

First thing the next morning, Andy Prescott rode his bike down South Congress, parked outside his favorite PI's office, and walked inside. Lorenzo Escobar looked up from his laptop.

'Don't tell me you lost her?'

''Fraid so.'

Lorenzo seemed amused.

'Oh, I checked out that Maureen O'Malley Reeves.'

Andy had asked Lorenzo to run a search on Russell Reeves' mother. He wasn't sure why.

'She's legit. Lives out in California in a high-end retirement place on the ocean. Got a son lives here. Russell Reeves, the billionaire.'

Russell had told the truth.

'What color is her hair?'

'Blue.'

Lorenzo motioned Andy over to his laptop.

'My West Coast associate, he took this photo, emailed it over.' On the screen was a color photo of four old women. 'One on the right, that's her.'

'She does have blue hair. They all have blue hair.'

Lorenzo shrugged. 'Old ladies do that. Anglos, anyway.'

'I need you to find Frankie Doyle again.'

'She don't want to be found.'

'I've got to find her.'

'Same fee?'

Andy nodded. Lorenzo faced the laptop. Andy sat and read the local paper. Ten minutes later, he heard Lorenzo's voice.

'Gotcha.'

Lorenzo wrote a note and handed it to Andy.

'That's her new address.'

Andy turned to leave, but Lorenzo said, 'You forgetting something?'

'I'll get the money, bring it back later.'

Lorenzo grabbed his keys. 'I'll drive you.'

Lorenzo Escobar drove a black 2005 Cadillac Escalade with blacked-out windows and black leather seats. Selena, the Latina singing sensation who had been murdered when she was just twenty-three by the president of her fan club, sang softly on the CD player. Lorenzo had driven Andy first to the bank for his $9,999, and then to San Marcos, thirty miles south of Austin.

San Marcos is home to Texas State University and thirty thousand college students. If you're young and want to get lost in a crowd, it would be a good place.

Two days before, Frankie Doyle had rented an apartment in San Marcos under her real name. She had signed a rental application; the application authorized the landlord to run a credit check.

'Must not have read the fine print in her tenant app,' Lorenzo said. 'Smart girl, she'd know we could track her that way.'

Lorenzo had pulled her credit report and found the landlord's inquiry, which included the address of the apartment complex on Aquarena Springs Road, the main drag through town. It was the first activity on Frankie Doyle's credit file in three years. She was desperate.

They knew the apartment complex where she lived, but not the specific apartment. So Lorenzo stopped at the manager's office and went inside. When he returned, he said, 'Apartment 621. Upstairs.'

'How'd you get the manager to—'

Lorenzo gave him a look.

'Never mind.'

They drove through the parking lot until they found Apartment 621. Frankie's old Toyota was nowhere in sight. So they parked and waited. Frankie Doyle had lied; the DNA matched. Russell Reeves was the girl's father. And like any good father, he wanted to find his daughter, test her for the cancer gene, and save her life. What's wrong with that? Nothing. Nothing at all.

So why couldn't Andy sleep last night?

They ducked down in their seats when the Toyota pulled up and Frankie and the red-haired girl got out. Frankie was smoking a cigarette. Lorenzo reached over to the glove compartment and retrieved a pair of binoculars. He put them to his eyes and whistled softly.

'Good-looking lady. She wears underwear.'

'What, you got X-ray binoculars?'

'A trained eye. So your client really wants this woman?'

Andy nodded.

'She really doesn't want him.'

They watched Frankie and the girl climb the stairs and enter the apartment.

'Can we go home now?' Lorenzo said.

When they pulled out of the parking lot, Andy took one last glance back and saw Frankie standing in the window looking out.

'Harmon, can we go over to Sixth Street tonight? They've got live music.'

'Turn up the radio.'

They were sitting in the Crown Vic parked outside Andy Prescott's office. Harmon's cell phone rang. He checked the caller ID and answered.

'Yeah, boss?'

'Harmon, we got his home address. Prescott.'

'What took so long?'

'It's a rental.'

'Must be a real successful lawyer.'

Harmon wrote down the address then hung up.

'Let's go.'

Cecil started the engine and backed out.

Lorenzo waited for the two white dudes in the black Crown Vic to back out of the parking space in front of Andy's office; when they drove off, he pulled in.

'Thanks,' Andy said.

'What about your bike?'

'I'll pick it up later.'

Andy got out and went upstairs to his office. He had called Russell from San Marcos. A few minutes later, his client arrived. Russell Reeves didn't sit.

'You found her?'

Andy nodded. 'In San Marcos.'

'What's the address?'

Andy wrote Frankie Doyle's address on a notepad and tore the page out. Russell reached out for it. Andy hesitated a moment – he wasn't sure why – then handed it to his client.

'Good work, Andy. I'll take it from here. How's Floyd T.?'

'He's good. What are you going to do?'

'Pay his bills.'

'No. With Frankie?'

'Try to save my daughter's life.'

'If she has the gene?'

'Yes.'

'If the DNA was right?'

334

'DNA doesn't lie, Andy.'

Russell reached into his coat pocket and pulled out an envelope. He dropped it on the card table in front of Andy and walked out. Andy opened the envelope and removed a cashier's check for $25,000 made out to 'Andrew Paul Prescott.' As if he had just sold out Frankie Doyle.

He turned and looked out the window; Russell was getting into his limo. He glanced up at Andy and gave him a little wave. Andy watched the black limousine drive off. Then he ran downstairs to the tattoo parlor. Ramon was engrossed in something at his desk.

'Ramon, I need to borrow your car.'

Ramon held up a Big Chief notebook.

'Andy, you ever read Floyd T.'s stuff? He's good. This story's about Vietnam when he—'

'Ramon, your car.'

'No way, dude.'

'It's an emergency.'

Ramon stood. 'I'll drive.'

Four blocks north, Harmon knocked on the door of a little house on Newton Street. There was no answer.

'Are you looking for Andy?'

A cute little broad walking her mutt was standing on the sidewalk. Harmon gave her a smile.

'Yes, ma'am, we are.'

'He doesn't live here anymore.'

'Do you know his current address?'

335

She shook her head. 'Some loft downtown, but I don't know the address. Sorry.'

Harmon and Cecil walked toward the Crown Vic, but Harmon stopped short and looked down. He sighed.

'Cecil, what are you wearing?'

'Cowboy boots. You like them?'

'No.'

'I got them at the secondhand store down from Prescott's office. Good price.'

'Those boots belonged to someone else?'

'Yeah. They're already broken in.'

'Because some other guy's feet were in them.'

Cecil shrugged. 'So?'

'So they could have diseases.'

'The boots? Like what?'

'Athlete's foot, for one.'

'My feet do itch.'

'There you go.'

Thirty minutes later, Ramon parked the yellow Corvette in front of Apartment 621 in San Marcos. Andy didn't see the Toyota, so he got out and climbed the stairs. He knocked on the door, but there was no answer. He peeked in the windows, but saw no one. He went back to Ramon.

'Let's go to the manager's office.'

When Andy walked into the office, the manager was watching a game show on a small TV behind a waist-high partition.

336

'I'm looking for Frankie Doyle.'

'Popular girl. She left.'

'She moved out?'

'Paid a month's rent for two days.'

'Where'd she go?'

'Didn't leave a forwarding address.'

Cecil parked the Crown Vic directly in front of 1514½ South Congress Avenue. The bum was gone, the lights were off, and even the tattoo parlor was closed.

'People here work for a living?' Cecil said. 'And we wonder why our economy's in the crapper. No one wants to work anymore.'

'Except the Mexicans.'

'And us.'

'We're lucky, Cecil. Most men have to work at jobs they hate. My dad worked in that stinking factory till the day he died. But you and me, we're not stuck in a factory or an office. We get to be outside, do what we love to do. And make a hell of a nice living doing it. Not many men can say that.'

'You're right, Harmon. Sometimes we get so wrapped up in the moment that we don't step back and realize how blessed we are. Smell the roses and all that shit.'

'Amen to that, Cecil.' He paused a moment, then said, 'Now let's kill this target so we can get home to our families.'

★　　★　　★

Ramon dropped Andy off at Lorenzo's office. Andy got his bike and rode straight to the hospital in downtown where he found Floyd T. resting comfortably and watching the television that was perched high on the wall of his private room. His hair had been cut, and he was clean shaven. Floyd T. was a handsome man.

'You doing okay, Floyd T.?'

Floyd T. shrugged. 'For a homeless person just out of heart surgery.'

Andy pulled Floyd T.'s notebook out of his backpack and handed it to him.

'Thought you might want this.'

'Thanks, Andy. I need to catch up on my memoirs. Oh, did I tell you two men came looking for you Saturday?'

'No. What'd they want?'

'You. They weren't from here.'

'How do you know?'

'Shiny suits, and they talked funny, with accents.'

'Foreign?'

'Yeah. Maybe New York.' Floyd T. gestured at the TV. 'They just had a story about Reeves giving away money. He's quite a guy. Shame about his son.'

Andy nodded. 'He's a good kid.'

'You know, Andy, being homeless is like being invisible. People talk like I'm not even there.'

'And?'

'And I heard you and Russell talking, up in your

office. You leave your window open. Andy, I don't buy it.'

'What?'

'Seventeen girlfriends. Sending you all over the country to find them, give them a million bucks. Men don't work that way.'

'You heard all that?'

'I'm only sitting ten feet below your window.'

'So?'

'So Russell is a good man, Andy. But good men sometimes lose their way. I saw it during the war – buddies getting sniped every patrol, can't even find the enemy to shoot at, the pressure builds every day – the mind can snap. I saw it in soldiers' eyes, Andy, when they were about to snap. And when they did, good men did bad things.'

'Russell's not like that.'

'Every man's like that . . . under enough pressure. When we're desperate enough, we can all snap. On the TV, when he talked about his son, I saw it in his eyes.' He took a deep breath and exhaled slowly. 'I saw it in my own eyes, Andy, before I snapped.'

'Russell saved your life, Floyd T.'

Floyd T. nodded.

'And now I'm trying to save yours.'

Andy walked to the elevator and pushed the button. He was thinking about what Floyd T. had said when the doors opened on Russell Reeves.

339

'Russell.'

'Andy.'

'I was here visiting Floyd T. What are you . . . Zach?'

Russell nodded. 'He took a turn for the worse.'

'Can I see him?'

'Sure. Come on up.'

They went upstairs to the cancer ward and walked down the corridor. Andy followed Russell into a room. Zach Reeves was lying in the bed connected to oxygen and an IV and various monitors that beeped.

Shit.

The boy opened his eyes and smiled.

'Hi, Dad. Hey, Andy.'

His voice sounded weak.

'Hey, buddy,' Russell said then stepped over and checked his chart.

'Hi, dude,' Andy said.

Zach slowly extended his hand to Andy and closed his fist. Andy gave him a fist-punch.

'Dad?'

'Yeah, Zach?'

'Can Andy and I talk? Alone? Just for a minute.'

Russell glanced from his son to Andy and back.

'Sure, buddy.' He walked to the door but stopped. 'Andy, you want something to eat?'

'Thanks. I'm good.'

After Russell left, Andy said, 'Dude, what happened?'

'My blood counts went wacko again.'

'Man, you gotta get well soon so I can have another shot at you on Guitar Hero.'

Zach nodded.

'What's it like, Andy?'

'What's what like?'

'Kissing a girl.'

'Kissing a girl? Where'd that come from?'

Zach pointed a finger at the TV on the wall. It was tuned to a preteen show on the Disney channel.

'I don't think I'm ever going to kiss a girl,' Zach said.

'Dude, you'll have to beat 'em off with a stick.'

Zach shook his head.

'My parents won't talk to me about it.'

'Kissing girls?'

'Dying.'

Andy sat down next to the bed.

'I'm not stupid, Andy. I hear the doctors talking. I understand cancer. I need to talk about it with someone.'

'I'll talk with you about it.'

'Does it hurt?'

'No. The doctors don't let it hurt.'

'I heard my dad say your father is dying.'

Andy nodded. 'He needs a liver transplant.'

'I hope he gets it.'

'Me, too.'

'Do you think dead people hang around, you know, where they lived? So their family still feels them around?'

'I hope so.'

'Me, too.'

They talked about life and about death for a while longer. When Andy walked out of Zach's room, Russell Reeves was sitting in a plastic chair outside the door with his face in his hands. He looked up.

'Thanks, Andy.'

Andy wiped away a tear. Russell walked him to the elevator. He punched the down button. When the elevator car arrived, Andy stepped in. The doors began to shut, but Russell stuck his hand in. The doors opened.

'She's gone, Andy. Frankie Doyle.'

'I know.'

'Find her, Andy. So my daughter doesn't end up like my son.'

Chapter 20

Andy walked into his PI's storefront the next morning and found Lorenzo Escobar leaning back in his chair with his black cowboy boots propped up on his desk and his hands clasped behind his head. He was watching TV. He pointed at the screen.

'That's the most beautiful pregnant woman I've ever seen.'

Natalie Riggs was reporting live from the maternity ward at the public hospital. She stood outside the glass window of the nursery; behind her, dozens of little cribs were occupied by Latino babies wrapped like papooses. She wasn't showing yet; her abs still looked awesome in the tight knit dress. Lorenzo stood and pointed at the screen.

'See? No underwear.'

One last look and he clicked off the TV and turned to Andy.

'You lost her again?'

Andy nodded. 'I've got to find her.'

'For your client or yourself?'

'My client's paying.'

'Same fee?'

'Yeah, but you've got to drive me wherever she's at.'

'Deal.'

Lorenzo sat at his laptop and tapped on the keyboard.

'Now this time won't be as easy 'cause your girl, she's smart. She knows we tracked her with her credit report when she signed the tenant app, so she won't make that mistake again. She's gonna stay where she doesn't have to sign an app.'

'A hotel? Motel?'

'Maybe. But they usually require a credit card, and she knows we can track that, too. And she won't stay at some dive 'cause of her kid. So she's looking for a mom-and-pop place that'll take cash.'

'A bed and breakfast.'

'Bingo.'

'Lorenzo, there's hundreds of B&Bs around Austin, out in the Hill Country.'

'That is a problem.'

Lorenzo stroked his goatee, a sure sign he was thinking. After a moment he said, 'Didn't you say she calls her mama up in Boston?'

'Every day.'

'Cell phone?'

'Calling card.'

'Smart girl. But now we got something we can work with. Call information up in Boston and get her mama's phone number. It'll be listed.'

'Why?'

''Cause she's old.'

'No. Why do you want her number?'

'I've got an associate who works at the phone company.'

Frankie Doyle had called her mother in Boston at nine Texas time. At eleven Texas time, Lorenzo parked the Escalade in front of the Gruene Mansion Inn bed and breakfast in Gruene, Texas. Frankie had used a calling card on the house phone.

Gruene, Texas, is a faux town located just off Interstate 35 between Austin and San Antonio. It had once been a real town, but the Great Depression had rendered it a ghost town. Today, Gruene is a tourist destination on the Guadalupe River with B&Bs, restaurants, and shops selling antiques, pottery, and souvenirs. It gives off the impression of a movie set.

But one place in town is authentic: Gruene Hall, an old-time honky-tonk that had been built in the late 1800s, survived the Depression without closing, and hosted the likes of Bo Diddley, Jerry Lee Lewis, Kris Kristofferson, and Paul Prescott. Andy was recalling the nights he had fallen asleep with his head in his mother's lap while his father performed on stage, when Lorenzo nudged him.

'The woman.'

Frankie Doyle and her daughter had walked out the front door of the inn. Frankie stopped and lit a cigarette.

Andy stepped out of the Escalade and walked toward them. Frankie looked as if she had been crying. When she saw him, her shoulders sagged. He offered a smile.

'Those are bad for your health.'

'You're bad for my health. I had quit, until you showed up.'

'Oh. Sorry.'

She took a long drag on the cigarette, exhaled smoke, and said, 'What do you want from me?'

'Frankie, I need to talk to you – alone.'

She sighed then said to her daughter, 'Honey, go sit on that bench for a minute.'

The girl walked off.

'Frankie, you lied to me.'

'About what?'

'About not dating someone you met in the bar.'

'What are you talking about?'

Andy gestured at the girl. 'Her.'

'What about her?'

'She's his child.'

'Whose?'

'My client's.'

'I thought he wanted to give me a million dollars?'

'He was looking for his child.'

'He needs to be looking for a psychiatrist.'

'Frankie, she might have a cancer gene.'

'A cancer gene?'

'Yes. My client is a carrier. He passed a mutated gene to his son that gave him the rare cancer. He might

346

have passed it to her, too. Frankie, your daughter might be dying.'

Frankie Doyle didn't flinch at the news.

'She's not dying. She doesn't have a cancer gene.'

'She might.'

'She can't.'

'How do you know?'

'Because he's not her father.'

'Why'd you run again?'

Frankie stared at the dirt.

'You saw us in San Marcos?' Andy said.

She nodded.

'Frankie, is it Mickey? Are you running from him?'

'Andy . . . Mickey's dead.'

'*What?* How?'

'Someone cracked open his skull, outside a bar. I called my mother this morning, she told me. I thought it was just her mind playing tricks with her, so I went online and read the Boston newspaper. It's true.'

First the Austin lawyer and now Mickey Doyle. What did they have in common? Russell Reeves. And Hollis McCloskey quit because he thought he was being used . . . and that Andy was too.

'Frankie, you ever heard of Russell Reeves?'

'No.'

'He's a billionaire.'

'Is he your client?'

'Yes.'

'And he says he's her father?'

'The DNA confirmed it.'

'What DNA?'

'Hers.'

'How?'

'Band–Aid in your trash.'

She suddenly had the look of a cornered ostrich.

'Andy, now they'll come.'

'Who?'

'Your client. The people who killed Mickey.'

'Russell Reeves isn't a murderer. He's just rich.'

She looked at Andy like he was a moron. Maybe he was.

'You really don't have a clue, do you?'

'A clue about what?'

She flicked the cigarette away and turned to her daughter.

'Come on, Jessie, we're leaving.'

She grabbed the girl's hand and pulled her away. Andy ran after them.

'Where are you going?'

They kept walking fast.

'Somewhere we can hide from your client.'

'Why do you need to hide from him?'

'Because he's not her father.'

'Why would he lie about that? Why does he think she's his daughter if she's not?'

'Andy, I don't know Russell Reeves. I've never met him, I didn't have an affair with him. He's not her father, he didn't give her a cancer gene. She's not dying.'

'Then why does he want to help her?'

'He doesn't.' She stopped abruptly. 'Andy, the blood on that Band-Aid . . . it was mine.'

She pulled the girl up the path to the inn. Andy followed.

'Wait, Frankie!'

'You don't know what you've done.'

Andy ran to her and grabbed her arm.

'What, Frankie? What have I done?'

She said nothing.

'Frankie, I'll talk to Russell, straighten this out.'

'He's coming, Andy.'

'Frankie, let me help.'

'You've helped enough.'

Andy Prescott did not scare easily, but he was scared now – because she was scared. He saw it in her face.

'Frankie, I know a place you can stay, where you'll be safe.'

Paul Prescott was fixing lunch when he heard the big birds squawking to raise the roof. Someone was coming through the front gate. He walked to the screen door at the front of the house. A small car was coming up the drive. He didn't recognize it, so he grabbed the double-barreled shotgun and loaded two shells. Then he stepped out onto the porch.

It was just after noon.

Max bounded up to the car, barking like the place was being invaded. The car stopped, and Paul's son emerged. Andy squatted to greet the dog; a red–headed girl joined in. A young woman exited the vehicle. His son stood and walked over to the porch.

'Didn't recognize the car,' Paul said.

He unloaded the shotgun and dropped the shells into his shirt pocket and snapped the button.

'Dad, this is Frankie and her daughter, Jessie. They need a place to stay for a few days.'

'Welcome to stay here.'

'Thanks. Frankie, meet my dad, Paul Prescott.'

'Hi, Mr Prescott,' she said, but her eyes took in his orange skin.

'Just Paul. Jaundice. Got a bad liver.'

'He's waiting for a transplant,' Andy said.

'Y'all hungry? I was just rustlin' up some lunch. Your girl like grilled cheese sandwiches?'

The girl named Jessie ran over.

'I love grilled cheese.'

Paul held the screen door open for Jessie and her mother.

'Come on, Max, or you're gonna miss out on lunch.'

Max bolted up the porch steps and into the house. Andy was the last one in. Paul stopped his son.

'What's up, Andy?'

'You were right. Working for Reeves, it's not all good.'

'You in trouble?'

'Maybe.'

'The law?'

350

'Not yet.'

'What about them?'

'They're running, but not from the law.'

'Then from who?'

'Me, at first. Now Russell Reeves.'

'Your client?'

'Yep.'

'And now you're hiding them from him?'

'Yep.'

'Isn't that what you lawyers call a "conflict of interest"?'

'Yep.'

'That's not good.'

'Nope.'

Paul Prescott scratched his beard then said, 'Well, let's get them fed and fixed up in the spare bedroom. Pull her car into the barn, then we'll figure this deal out.'

'Thanks, Dad.'

Forty miles north, Harmon Payne and Cecil Durant were walking down South Congress Avenue asking the freaks they encountered if they knew Andy Prescott. Everyone said no, which annoyed Harmon because he knew they were lying. But his driver was whistling like a kid, a sure sign that he had—

'You got a hooker last night, didn't you?' Harmon said.

'Does it show?'

351

'It probably will in a couple of weeks.'

They stopped at the coffee joint called Jo's and ordered skinny lattes and deli sandwiches at the walk-up window.

'You know Andy Prescott?' Harmon asked the Mexican boy working the window.

'Andy Prescott? Nope. Never heard of him.'

The boy wasn't a convincing liar.

They got their food, but Harmon lost his appetite when he turned and found himself staring at a bare butt walking past. A man's bare butt. Right there on the sidewalk fronting Congress Avenue, before God and everyone. From behind them, the Mexican boy said, 'That's Queen Leslie. He's a local celebrity.' This Queen Leslie was older than Harmon, with gray frizzy hair pulled back in a ponytail and a gray goatee; he was wearing only a pink thong, a black bra, and running shoes.

Cecil grunted. 'You think he really jogs in that? Seems like it'd chafe your butt after a while.'

Harmon's cell phone rang. He checked the caller ID and answered. 'Hi, hon.'

Cecil walked a few steps away so as not to obviously eavesdrop on Harmon's conversation. But he still heard Harmon.

'Yeah, we're wrapping up a meeting now . . . a few more days . . . his playoff game's on Saturday? At noon? . . . I don't know, this deal's dragging on . . . Sure, put him on . . . Hey, little man, how're

352

you doing? . . . Three goals, that's super . . . I'm gonna do my best to be there, I promise . . . Okay, have fun at school . . . I love you, and tell your brother and sisters I love them too . . . Bye.'

Harmon tried to plan their trips around his kids' sports schedules. Four children, that wasn't an easy task, but Harmon seldom missed their games. Cecil hoped he was as good a father as Harmon, who hung up and turned to him.

'Cecil, we gotta find this guy fast. Between hanging around these freaks and missing my son's games, I'm liable to go postal.'

Andy carried Frankie's stuff up the stairs to the spare bedroom. He opened the windows to let the breeze in.

'It's nice at night, sleeping to the country sounds, the smell of the creek. Bathroom's across the hall. Towels, toothpaste, whatever you need.'

'Your dad's great.'

'I like him.'

'How soon does he need a liver transplant?'

'Soon.'

'I like your skin.'

Paul Prescott was showing the girl how to pet an ostrich.

'Aw, I look like a big ol' pumpkin.'

They started walking down to the creek. The girl

had told him about their travels and name changes. He had offered to show her the ostriches and the creek while her mother got settled into the spare bedroom.

'You're a lucky girl, Jessie. I've been stuck with the same name my whole life.'

'Esmeralda was my favorite name. Esmeralda Bustamante.'

'Why's that?'

'When I said it, it was like I was singing.'

Paul sang: 'Esmeralda, Esmeralda, my sweet Esmeralda . . . You're right, it is a song. You like to sing?'

'It's my dream. I want to be a country singer, like Carrie Underwood.'

'Well, now, that little gal can sing. Can you?'

Frankie said, 'It's nice out here.'

They had come outside looking for Andy's father and her daughter and so Frankie could smoke. He tossed a stick for Max to fetch. The dog shot off and returned with a stick – but not the same one.

'We haven't had a real home in three years. Before that we lived with Mickey, which didn't make for a great home life for either of us. It's nice to see a normal family.'

'Us? Normal? An alcoholic country-western singer waiting for a liver transplant, a leftist art history professor who's been arrested for protesting wars and football God knows how many times, and a traffic ticket lawyer who rides a trail bike? What's normal about that?'

'No one's getting drunk and hitting each other.'

'The Prescotts are a non-violent people. You want to see my mom's studio?'

'Sure.'

They walked into the barn and back to the studio. Frankie studied the clay angel sculpture.

'She's good.'

'So are you.'

'This was my dream – my own studio, a place to draw and paint and sculpt.' She was quiet. 'Just wasn't meant to be.'

'You're only twenty-eight, Frankie. Your life's not over.'

'I've got a billionaire chasing me. It might be.'

'I'm here.'

'Yes, you are. And so am I. And Jessie. We're all here, Andy.'

'I'm sorry, Frankie.'

They went outside and saw Jessie running toward them. She didn't look like a kid with a ticking time bomb inside her.

'Mom!'

His father followed behind.

'Paul's going to teach me to play the guitar.'

'That's great, honey.'

His father arrived and said, 'This little gal, she can sing.'

'That's her dream.'

Paul Prescott patted Jessie on the head. 'Let's go pick some tomatoes for dinner. My tomatoes are as red as your hair. Where'd you get that red from? Not your mama.'

'Red hair is recessive, Dad.'

He gave Andy a funny look. 'Okay.'

Jessie and his father headed over to the garden.

'I'd better help,' Frankie said.

She followed them. Andy watched after her a moment, then went back up to the house. He walked through the back door just as his mother entered through the front door with Earth-friendly canvas grocery bags in each arm. He took them from her, and they walked into the kitchen.

'I stopped at Whole Foods on the way home,' she said. 'Thought we'd have salmon. Where are they?'

'Picking tomatoes.'

She walked onto the back porch and looked out toward the garden.

'How old is the girl? Eight, nine?'

'Eight.'

'And her mother?'

'Twenty-eight.'

'Oh, I saw your girlfriend, the blonde. At Whole Foods. She was talking to a guy.'

'Who?'

'I didn't ask.'

'Did he look like a lawyer?'

'Now that you mention it, he did.'

'Richard Olson. He drives a Porsche.'

'What's going on, Andy? With them?'

★   ★   ★

Paul Prescott said, 'He gave you tickets to the biggest game of the year? Good Lord, don't tell your mother. What'd he want from you?'

'I already gave it to him. That's why they're here.'

Frankie and Jessie had gone upstairs to wash before dinner. Andy had parked the Toyota in the barn and was walking up to the house with his father. They found his mother in the kitchen, and Andy told them the rest of the story: his trips to Boston and Montana, Hollis McCloskey and Lorenzo Escobar, and the DNA from the Band-Aid.

'He thinks Jessie is his daughter.'

'Is she?'

'The DNA says yes.'

'What does Frankie say?'

'She says no.'

'I figure the mother would know.'

'He says she might have the same cancer gene he gave his son. Says he just wants to save her from Zach's fate. Why would he lie about that?'

Andy's cell phone rang; it was Russell Reeves. He went out onto the back porch and answered.

'Andy, have you found her?'

'Not yet.'

'Why's it taking so long?'

'She's smart, Russell. She knows we're looking for her. How's Zach?'

'Not good.'

'Tell him hi for me.'

'Come tell him yourself.'

'I will.'

There was silence on the line.

'Russell?'

'Andy, you're not lying to me, are you?'

'No. I'm gonna come see Zach.'

'About Frankie.'

'Russell, I'm your lawyer.'

'You didn't answer my question.'

'No. I'm not lying.'

He was lying about not lying. Tres was right. Everyone lies.

'Hurry, Andy.'

He hung up and went back inside.

'Reeves?' his father said.

Andy nodded. 'I can hold him off for a day or two, but he'll figure out I'm lying. Then he'll come for her. Frankie. We'll move on in a few days.'

'We?'

'I'm responsible for them now. I found them.'

'Well, he'll never find them here.'

'Dad, I've learned a few things about finding people. First thing they'll do is search the property tax records for "Prescott."'

'This land belongs to your mother, Andy. It's under her maiden name – Warren, not Prescott. They can stay here as long as they want. Be nice to have some company.'

★　★　★

358

Harmon and Cecil walked into the tattoo parlor at 1514 South Congress. BODY ART BY RAMON. A Mexican wearing a muscle T-shirt was sitting in front of a computer screen and tapping the keys.

'You Ramon?'

'Yep.'

'I'm looking for Andy Prescott. You know him?'

'Nope.'

'He offices right above you.'

'Oh, *that* Andy Prescott. The traffic ticket lawyer. He's never around.'

'What's he look like, this Prescott?'

'Six-four, black hair, fat.'

'What does he drive?'

'A Buick.'

Harmon walked out and snorted. 'You see that guy? Tattoos all over his body?'

Cecil nodded. 'He could play for the Knicks.'

Jean Prescott was tending to the salmon, Andy and Frankie were setting the table for dinner, and Paul was teaching Jessie a few chords on the guitar on the back porch. Andy could hear their voices in the kitchen.

'Sing this, honey.'

His father played a few notes, then her singing voice came through: 'Honky-tonk heroes, we're a dying breed now, the world's gone corporate and the music has too . . .'

Her voice was strong and full and good. Paul Prescott came into the kitchen carrying his guitar.

'Jean, you hear this girl sing? She's the real deal. We got us a country singer.'

Jessie followed.

'Paul, you're not teasing me, are you?'

'About what, honey?'

'About me being a country singer.'

'Honey, I never tease about dreams. Sing it again.'

He played and she sang.

'Honky-tonk heroes, we're a dying breed now . . .'

And his father joined in.

'The world's gone corporate and the music has too . . .'

They sang until dinner.

'We've had to move around,' Frankie said. 'Montana, New Mexico, West Texas. We hoped this would be our last move.'

'Well,' his father said, 'we've been here thirty-five years now. Jean inherited this land before we got married.' He winked at Frankie. 'I married her for her land.'

'I married him to feed the birds,' his mother said. 'Andy says you're an artist.'

'I want to be an artist.'

'I'd like to see your portfolio.'

'Really? It's upstairs.'

'After dinner, then.'

His father looked over at Jessie. 'You like that salmon? You'd better say yes, or Jean'll make you eat tofu tomorrow.'

'Is that Chinese food?'

'Should be.'

Two hours later, Andy found his mother on the back porch with a glass of wine. His father was already in bed; Frankie and Jessie were getting ready for bed. Andy sat next to her.

'I'm going to miss that man,' she said.

Andy felt the tears come again, so he didn't speak. They sat silently and listened to the night sounds and felt the soft breeze up from the creek.

'I remember sitting on this porch when I was a young girl, wondering what the man I would marry would be like. I never pictured Paul Prescott. But when I saw him that night at the Broken Spoke, those blue eyes, I fell hard for him. Thirty-five years later, I'm still falling.'

'Dave's folks are divorced, Tres' would be except for the trust fund – why'd it work for you and Dad?'

'Because we each have our own life, and a life we share. We never tried to change each other. And we both understand that a life without passion isn't much of a life. It's like a movie – a pretense of life. We've had a real life.'

Andy took her hand and squeezed it. She patted his.

'I knew it would happen.'

'What?'

'You'd bring a girl home to meet your mother. I was hoping Mary Margaret wouldn't be the last one.'

'Hey, she was hot – for a fourth-grader.'

'Frankie's a better fit for you.'

'Than Mary Margaret?'

'Than those Whole Foods girls.'

'It's not like that, Mom. Between us.'

'I saw the way you look at her . . . and the way she looks at you.'

'I think that's the urge to kill.'

She smiled. 'I don't think so.' She picked up Frankie's portfolio. 'No training and she can do this? She's a natural.'

'She hasn't had many breaks in life.'

'Her life isn't over.' She sipped her wine. 'It's good they're here. Your father was more alive today than he's been in a year. That twinkle was back in those blue eyes.'

Andy thought about life without Paul Prescott. His and hers.

'Mom, can I get a ride into town with you tomorrow? My bike's at the loft.'

She nodded. 'Come by the office. I've got tickets.'

In the penthouse at the Austin General Hospital, Kathryn Reeves grabbed her husband's shirt and screamed, 'Save him, Russell! Save him! Don't let him die!'

362

Zach had slipped into a coma.

And Russell's wife was slipping into a nervous break-down. He had found her crying in the bathroom and holding a pair of scissors. He had taken the scissors from her. She had slapped his face.

'You're a goddamn billionaire! Do something!'

'I'll save him, Kathryn. I'll find a way.'

Russell Reeves had never felt more desperate in his life.

Chapter 21

Harmon Payne's cell phone rang. It was the boss.

'Harmon, fifteen-fourteen-and-a-half South Congress, the lawyer's office – it's owned by Ramon Cabrera. He knows Andy Prescott. And Prescott was admitted to the ER at an Austin hospital a couple years back, some kind of biking accident. Records show he's five-ten, not six-four.'

'You got a photo?'

'Not yet.'

'Get one.'

Harmon hung up and sighed. He and Cecil were eating breakfast in the hotel restaurant.

'The Mexican – the tattoo guy – he lied to me.'

Cecil swallowed and said, 'Whoops.'

At that moment, Andy was riding the Stumpjumper south on Congress Avenue across Lady Bird Lake. His mother had dropped him off at the Fifth Street loft on her way in to UT. He had showered and changed clothes. He considered having breakfast at Whole Foods, but he didn't really want to see Suzie or Bobbi. Only Frankie and Jessie mattered now. He pulled over at Jo's and went up to the window.

'Still waiting for you to ride up on an IronHorse, Andy.'

Guillermo grabbed a banana nut muffin from the display and poured a large coffee. He nodded at the Stumpjumper.

'Can't believe you haven't crashed it yet.'

'Haven't had time to take it out.'

'Man, you must be suffering adrenaline withdrawal.'

'I do miss the rush.'

Guillermo stuck his fist out; Andy gave him a fist-punch.

'Keep the faith, bro.'

He sat down at a table and ate the muffin. The Jo's regulars were all present and accounted for, but Andy felt like a stranger in SoCo. His life had irrevocably changed the moment Russell Reeves walked into his office ten weeks before. He had been Andy Prescott, traffic ticket lawyer; now he was Andy Prescott, Russell Reeves' lawyer. He had been happy; now he had money. He had had a simple life; now he had a complicated life. None of this made sense. The DNA was Frankie's, not Jessie's. So why did Russell think she was his daughter? Andy felt a sense of impending doom, the same sensation he experienced when he was about to crash on the trails. Nothing psychic, just a feeling. A bad feeling.

He glanced around.

Ray, Darla, Oscar, George, Dwight . . . no one he didn't recognize. No one without a tattoo; only members of the tribe. He grabbed the coffee and saddled up on the Stumpjumper. He rode down the avenue to his office. It was only nine, but Ramon was already in.

'Andy!'

Andy went inside. 'What are you doing here so early?'

Ramon gestured at his table where the coed with the 'Yellow Rose of Texas' on her left buttock was lying face down, iPod buds in her ears, eyes closed, and bare butt exposed.

'Appointment. She's got an afternoon class. Wants a matching rose on her right butt.'

'Try not to enjoy yourself too much.'

'I think she's sleeping. Oh, he was here looking for you.'

'Reeves?'

'Not Russell. That ape that drives him.'

'Darrell? He was here without Russell?'

Ramon nodded. 'Said, "I'll be back," like that *Terminator* dude.'

Russell Reeves had left three messages for Andy that morning on his cell phone. Andy needed to call his client, but he wasn't a very good liar.

'Tickets on the counter,' Ramon said.

Four tickets with four $100 bills sat on the counter. Which reminded Andy: his mother had tickets for him, too.

'And two other guys were looking for you yesterday,' Ramon said. 'Not locals.'

'How do you know?'

'Shiny suits and accents. I lied, said I didn't know you.'

'Thanks.'

'You want me to tell the ape I seen you?'

'No. Or those other guys.'

Harmon and Cecil pulled into a parking spot in front of the tattoo parlor just as a kid wearing jeans, sneakers, and T-shirt came out the door, jumped on a bike, and rode off.

'He's about five-ten,' Cecil said.

'Cecil, you ever know a lawyer who rode a bike?'

'Good point.'

They got out and walked into the parlor. The Mexican named Ramon was hunched over a girl's bare butt with a tattoo needle in his right hand. Without looking up, he said, 'Help you?'

'Ramon,' Harmon said, 'you lied to me.'

The Mexican looked up at Harmon and Cecil standing in his doorway; his expression changed.

'You know Prescott. You're his landlord. And he's not six-four, he's five-ten.'

Harmon stepped closer.

The Mexican said, 'Hey, I'm working here! Stay out of my sterile field!'

'Where's Prescott?'

'Man, I look like a secretary?'

'You're gonna look like a dead Mexican, you don't tell me where he's at.'

The Mexican stood up and stared directly down the barrel of Harmon's brand new Glock.

'Hey, dude—'

'*Dude?* I look like a dude, Cecil?'

Lorenzo Escobar was cruising south on Congress, the windows down, sipping his Jo's coffee and enjoying the fine November morning, when he came to the tattoo parlor. He slowed. He saw a black Crown Vic parked outside Ramon's shop – the same Crown Vic he had seen there two days before – and two white dudes inside the shop. They didn't look like locals. Lorenzo got a bad feeling so he pulled the Escalade into a slot out front of Allen's Boots a couple of doors down.

Lorenzo cut the engine and got out. The street was quiet this early. He walked along the side of the building until he arrived at Ramon's door. He heard Ramon's nervous voice: 'Hey, dude, put the gun down.'

Lorenzo peeked inside and saw a tall white male pointing a gun at Ramon; the other man was standing to the side. Lorenzo pulled out his Beretta and chambered a round. He stepped inside with his gun extended.

'*Hombre* . . . put the gun down.'

The man holding the gun froze. He turned slowly toward Lorenzo and saw the gun pointed at his chest.

'Easy, bro,' Lorenzo said. 'On the counter.'

The white man set his gun on the counter. Lorenzo motioned both men against the wall. Without taking his eyes off them, he said, 'What's going on, Ramon?'

'They're looking for Andy.'

'That so? What do you want with Andy?'

The tall white man said, 'It's a personal matter.'

'Is it worth dying for?'

'Perhaps not.'

'Good.' Lorenzo stood away from the door. 'You may leave now. And don't come back.'

'Can I have my gun?'

'I don't think so.'

The men stepped to the door. The tall man said, 'Maybe we'll meet again, Pancho.'

Lorenzo smiled. 'Bring friends.'

The tall man chuckled. 'You hear that, Cecil? "Bring friends," he says. I like that.'

The men walked over to the Crown Vic, got in, and drove off. Lorenzo turned to Ramon, who was wiping sweat from his brow. The girl on the table hadn't budged. She had a nice ass.

Lorenzo said, 'Where the hell is Andy?'

Andy rode north on Congress until it dead-ended at Eleventh Street in front of the state capitol. Normally the seven-lane intersection would be crowded with cars and buses and pedestrians trying to cross without getting nailed by a road warrior talking on his cell phone while running a red light; but that day the wide stretch of asphalt was crowded with workers erecting big white circus-like tents for the Texas Book Festival.

The book festival was the biggest cultural event held in Austin each year. The streets had been blocked off in both directions and traffic was being re-routed down side streets. For the next three days, forty thousand people would pack the festival to enjoy musical performances, learn parenting skills, be entertained by magicians and puppeteers, attend cooking exhibitions, and listen to authors discuss their books. And, of course, Kinky Friedman would make his annual appearance, smoking long cigars and stumping for the governorship or promoting his latest book. Kinky alone was worth the price of admission, which was free.

Andy steered around the yellow barricades and cut through the capitol grounds. The wide checkerboard-patterned sidewalk – known as the 'Great Walk' – inclined steadily for five hundred feet to the south entrance of the capitol. He pedaled past grand monuments honoring the Confederate Dead, Terry's Texas Rangers and Hood's Texas Brigade (all of whom had fought for the Confederacy), two twenty-four-pound cannons (used by the Confederacy), and the Ten Commandments (which said nothing about slavery). He rode around the massive pink granite capitol and gazed up at the Goddess of Liberty hoisting a lone gold star atop the dome.

It always gave him hope.

Four blocks later, Andy entered the UT campus at

San Jacinto Street. He pedaled past the Santa Rita No. 1 pump jack and the football stadium. He turned east on Twenty-third Street then north on Trinity Street. He rode across a concrete footbridge leading to the second-floor entrance to the Fine Arts Building, a short-cut to his mother's office. He parked the bike, removed his helmet and went inside. He jogged down the hall to his mother's office. She was between classes. She stood and hugged him, then gave him the traffic tickets.

'Are you okay, Andy?'

'Not really.'

'You don't know whom to believe – your client or Frankie.'

'You're smart.'

'I have a PhD . . . and Jessie has red hair. Russell Reeves doesn't.'

'It's recessive.'

'What is?'

'Red hair. Russell says Jessie got it from his mother.'

'Why not from Frankie and her ex-husband?'

'Mickey had red hair but Frankie's hair is black. Both parents have to have red hair for their child to have red hair.'

'Did you ask her?'

'Ask who what?'

'Frankie – the color of her hair.'

'Mom, her hair is black. You saw her yourself.'

She smiled. 'Andy, we color our hair. Women.'

Andy walked out of his mother's office and pulled

out his cell phone. He called information for the Boston Grand Hotel. When he was connected, he asked for the bar. Benny the bartender answered.

'Benny, this is Andy Prescott, from Texas.'

'The lawyer. Did you find her? Frankie?'

'Yes, I did.'

'Is she okay?'

'For now. Benny, when she worked at the bar, what color was her hair?'

'Frankie's? Like I said, she was a good Irish girl. She has flaming red hair.'

Russell Reeves had lied.

Andy hung up and hurried down the hall. His phone rang. He stopped and answered. It was Lorenzo.

'Andy, two white dudes pulled a gun on Ramon in his shop, looking for you.'

'Jesus. Reeves has gone over the edge.'

'Russell Reeves? He's your secret client?'

'Yeah.'

'Andy, he's serious. Those two goons, they're professionals, if you know what I mean.'

Andy knew what he meant.

'Be careful, bro. I don't want to lose a paying client.'

Andy hung up. He put on the helmet and sunglasses and ran to the exit door and outside and right into a brick wall. Darrell's meaty hand clamped down on his arm like an iron vice.

'Mr Reeves wants to talk to you. In the limo.'

The long black limo sat at the curb on Trinity Street.

The back window lowered, and Russell's face appeared. Darrell yanked Andy across the footbridge and over to the limo. Then he released him but stood within arm's reach. Russell pushed the door open.

'Get in.'

Andy held his ground. His client looked as if he hadn't slept in a week.

'You didn't come to see Zach.'

'I was coming over there right now.'

Another lie. And about Zach.

'Andy . . . Zach's in a coma.'

Andy slumped against the limo.

'Shit. Is he gonna be okay?'

'I don't know. Where's Frankie?'

'Russell, your son's in a coma.'

'And my daughter might be next.'

'The girl's not yours, Russell. You lied.'

'Why would I lie to you?'

'That's what I don't know. But you lied – about the red hair. Frankie has red hair. She dyed it black. The girl got her red hair from her parents, not from your mother. And the blood on that Band-Aid wasn't the girl's – it was Frankie's.'

'*What?* No, that can't be. The DNA was a match.'

'You're after Frankie, Russell. Did you have Mickey killed to get to her?'

'Who's Mickey?'

'Mickey Doyle. Her ex-husband.'

'He's dead?'

'He was murdered in Boston.'

'And you think I'm involved?'

'Are you?'

'No.'

Andy pointed at Darrell. 'Is he?'

'No.'

'What about those two goons you sent to Ramon's?'

'What goons?'

'The ones looking for me.'

'I found you.'

'What about Laurence Smith? He's dead, too.'

'Yes, he is.'

'Was he trying to find Frankie?'

'Yes, but his death had nothing to do with her. Someone tried to rob him. Look, Andy, you're over-thinking again.' He pointed up Trinity Street at the law school sitting on a low rise. 'Remember, you were a C student over there.'

'I don't test well.'

Russell Reeves stared at Andy, and Andy saw in his client's eyes something he had not seen before: desperation.

'Tell me the truth, Russell.'

'Andy, the truth is, there's a million dollars in your trust account, for Sally Armstrong in San Diego. You can keep it. Just tell me where Frankie's at and you can go on with your life . . . but with a lot more money.'

Andy stared up at the UT clock tower, the white

sandstone highlighted against the blue November sky. It was a magnificent sight. At the base of the tower, carved into the south façade of the Main Building, were the words *Ye Shall Know The Truth and The Truth Shall Make You Free*. What was the truth? The legal truth was simple: Andy Prescott was a lawyer; Russell Reeves was his client. Andy owed a legal duty to Russell to tell him where Frankie was; he had paid for that information. The client was legally entitled to know what his lawyer knew.

What was Frankie entitled to?

Andy Prescott, Attorney-at-Law, owed no legal duty to Frankie Doyle. He wasn't her lawyer; she wasn't his client. She was simply the object of his client's desire, whatever that desire might be. And what a billionaire client desired, his lawyer obtained. That's how the legal system in America worked. For rich people. Who made their lawyers rich. All Andy had to do was tell Russell Reeves what he wanted to know, and he would have one million dollars. More money than he had ever dreamed of having. He would be rich. Suzie, Bobbi, the loft, the life. It would all be his. Everything he had ever wanted. All he had to do was tell his client what he knew.

Instead, he ran.

'Andy!'

He ran back across the footbridge, hopped on the bike, and stood on the pedals down the sidewalk along the west side of the building. Darrell gave chase, but he had no foot speed; halfway across the bridge, he turned back. Andy cut through the parking lot to Trinity Street and turned north. He powered up the hill and veered east past the law school; the street turned down, and he picked up speed. At the bottom of the hill, he swerved south on Robert Dedman Drive and sped past the LBJ School.

He heard tires squealing. He glanced back and saw the limo turning behind him. So he turned west on Twenty-third Street and hammered the pavement past the football stadium and across San Jacinto Street. He entered the campus at the East Mall fountain.

From there the land climbed steadily to the clock tower.

Construction on the sloping terrain required concrete retaining walls, which cut the campus into terraces. Andy carried the bike up two flights of concrete steps around the retaining wall on the east side of the fountain; once atop the first terrace, he looked back. The limo skidded to a stop down below. Darrell jumped out and gestured helplessly up at Andy.

They couldn't follow him up there.

He saddled up again but took it easy through the East Mall. He couldn't go fast anyway; fifty thousand students changing classes crowded the sidewalks. He tried to think. He couldn't go back to his office; Russell's goons would be waiting for him. He couldn't even go back to SoCo. But he could go to the loft. Russell didn't know he lived there and had no way of finding out.

Andy was about to turn south and head toward downtown when he heard screams and shouts from behind – 'Hey, watch out!' – and now high-pitched buzzing noises, like high-powered weed-whackers . . . like . . . motocross bikes. He looked back.

Shit.

Two riders dressed in black and wearing black helmets with dark visors on black dirt bikes were parting the crowd of students like Moses parting the Red Sea in that movie. Kids dove out of their way. They were coming for him. But Andy Prescott had grown up on this campus. He knew every path, walkway, alley, and road on the three hundred and fifty acres.

Andy stood on the pedals and cut between the ROTC indoor rifle range and the old Gregory Gymnasium, bounced hard down onto Speedway Drive, bunny-hopped the curb, whipped around the business school and across Campus Drive, and climbed concrete steps up two more terraces to College Hill. His pistons were burning by the time he arrived at the clock tower. He wiped sweat from his face and looked back.

He saw one dirt bike behind him.

The other rider would try to cut him off heading south toward downtown, so he turned north past the Will C. Hogg Building – Governor James Stephen Hogg had a son he named Will and a daughter he named Ima; is that cruel or what? – and raced around the tower to the West Mall. He heard screams and saw the riders coming at him from the South Mall. He cut between competing student protesters – a pro-abortion group versus an anti-abortion group – and pedaled hard. He planned to exit the campus on the west side and lose them on the Drag, but he arrived at the west exit only to find the limo parked at the curb and Darrell standing there with his thick arms crossed.

Not good.

He spun around and rode straight back at the dirt bikes speeding toward him. Just before they collided, he cut the handlebars to the right and caught air; he flew over a set of stairs leading down to a courtyard fronting Goldsmith Hall. He bounced hard on reentry then turned west down an alley that led back to College Hill. He swung south and careened down 'Confederate Hill' past statues of Jefferson Davis, President of the Confederate States, Albert Sidney Johnston, General of the Confederate Army, and Robert E. Lee, General in Chief of the Confederate Army. When he hit Martin Luther King Jr Boulevard, he left the campus and the two black riders behind.

He had lost them.

He sat up on the bike. He cruised down Guadalupe and caught his breath . . . until the dirt bikes cut him off at Sixteenth Street.

Shit.

He stood on the pedals again and swerved east on Sixteenth and then south on Lavaca against oncoming one-way traffic; the dirt bikes followed. He turned east on Fifteenth then south on Colorado, hopped the curb, rode on the sidewalk around the north side of the Supreme Court Building, and carved the corner at the Statue of Liberty replica. They followed.

The state capitol now loomed large in front of him.

They were right on his tail, so he pedaled past the gardens and around the chain traffic restraint and straight up the wheelchair ramp at the north entrance of the capitol – 'Hold the door!' – and through the tall door being held open by an old man.

'Thanks, dude.'

He looked back; the dirt bikes had not followed.

The interior of the Texas State Capitol boasted marble statues and terrazzo floors, fine hand-carved wood and delicate glass doors, massive staircases and well-armed state troopers. Andy wanted out. Straight through to the south entrance was the fastest route out, so Andy rode through the north foyer and into the rotunda where framed portraits of every Texas governor hung on the wall and two dozen blue-shirted school kids on a field trip stood on the Great Seal of Texas. The tour guide was saying, 'Our capitol is the biggest in the country . . .'

'Coming through!' Andy yelled.

The startled tour guide jumped out of the way.

'Hey! Call security!'

Someone already had. Two state troopers were running from the south foyer; they blocked his exit. So Andy turned right into the west wing then hung another right behind the wide staircase – even a

Stumpjumper couldn't climb those stairs – and circled back around to the north foyer. He'd leave the way he had come. But two more troopers were now blocking that exit, so he rode across the foyer and straight into an open elevator.

He punched the second floor button. The doors closed just as the troopers arrived. They weren't happy. Andy breathed a quick sigh of relief then realized he wasn't alone. A older couple was also on board. He looked at them and smiled.

'Shortcut.'

They backed into the far corner.

The elevator arrived at the second floor. The doors opened, and the old couple hustled out. Andy stayed in. Troopers coming up the west stairway had spotted him. He punched the third floor button. The doors closed again and opened on the third floor. He peeked out. The coast was clear, so he pedaled out and onto the circular balcony overlooking the rotunda. Down below, the students were pointing up and laughing. The troopers were not.

'He's gotta go down the elevators! Block every floor!'

That left the stairs.

Andy steered into the east wing and turned the bike down the staircase. He hung on for the two flights to the second floor, made the turn at the landing, and turned the bike down again. The Stumpjumper's suspension ate up the stairs.

The bike ripped!

He hit the first floor, turned west, and rode into the rotunda again. The troopers were now on the second and third levels pointing down. The students screamed with delight; no doubt this would rate as the best field trip of the year. Andy turned south and rode between life-size white marble statues of Sam Houston and Stephen F. Austin and through a gauntlet of white pillars and straight out the south entrance doors being held open by another old man.

'Thanks, dude.'

From there it was straight downhill to the Eleventh Street gates. He hit the Great Walk again and sped past the Confederate monuments and the trooper stationed in his cruiser at the exit—

Shit, the trooper was pointing his gun at Andy!

But he didn't shoot. Instead, he jumped into the cruiser and hit the lights and siren. Andy raced through the tall wrought-iron gates and right into the book festival. He swerved to avoid hitting a worker holding a tent pole – 'Sorry about that!' The worker fell down and the tent dropped on top of him.

Andy turned west on Congress then south on Colorado. He stood on the pedals past the once magnificent Governor's Mansion, now just a charred shell after some jerk torched the place. He didn't hear the motocross bikes. No doubt they had turned back at the sound of the siren. So he veered right at the US Courthouse on Eighth then crossed over Lavaca. He figured he'd go south on Rio Grande straight to the loft, but two black Mercedes-Benz sedans cut him off at Guadalupe.

Uh-oh.

He swerved south on Guadalupe. He picked up speed fast, no pedaling required; it was downhill to the lake. And that's where he was headed. The sedans couldn't follow him onto the Hike-and-Bike Trail. He ducked down to cut wind resistance. But there'd be no timing the lights; there'd only be luck.

He shot through red lights at Seventh and Sixth, barely avoiding collisions with motorists both times, and caught green lights at Fifth, Fourth, Third, and Second.

Dude, you're shredding Guadalupe Street!

His speed increased as he approached César Chávez Street, the four-lane east–west boulevard that bordered the north side of Lady Bird Lake. Cars were backed up in both directions. The Guadalupe light was still green, but the pedestrian signal showed a solid red DON'T WALK; the light was about to change. The green light turned yellow, and southbound cars on Guadalupe stopped; Andy didn't. He rode between the cars.

This is gonna be tight.

Andy hit César Chávez a split second after the east–west light turned green. Traffic surged forward in both directions; the gap between the eastbound and westbound cars closed fast. Andy flew through the inter-section just before the gap had closed completely. Horns honked, drivers cursed, cars missed.

Now that was an adrenaline rush!

He had made it across. Barely. But the sedans had not. The traffic had caught them. Andy hit the steep path leading down to the Hike-and-Bike Trail. Once on the trail, he turned west and rode under a bridge where two homeless guys were sitting on an abandoned car seat and fishing. The lake was calm and the breeze was cool. Canoes and kayaks and a guy on a surfboard fitted with a sail glided across the glassy green surface. The tourist paddleboat chugged upstream. Walkers, runners, and their dogs pounded the trail. Cyclists tried to avoid colliding with walkers, runners, and dogs.

Andy caught his breath.

Russell's mind had snapped, just like Floyd T. had said. But why did he think the girl was his? He had seemed genuinely surprised when Andy told him the DNA was from Frankie. None of this made any sense, and Andy didn't know what to think. But he did know one thing.

Frankie Doyle had more to tell.

He removed his sunglasses and put them in his pocket. Thick trees shaded the trail; the sunglasses made it too dark to see well. He passed the Pfluger Pedestrian Bridge; he'd exit the trail at Lamar Boulevard and cut over on Fifth to the loft.

He heard a distant scream.

He stopped pedaling and listened. He heard more shouts and a faint whining sound. He stood tall on the pedals and peered down the trail. He saw them. The black riders. The dirt bikes were heading directly toward him from the west.

Why don't you guys give it up?

Andy flipped the bike around and hammered the trail back east, weaving around walkers and joggers –

'On your left! On your left!'

– but the sound was gaining on him. He couldn't outrun them on the flat trail. So when he arrived back at the Pfluger Bridge, he stood on the pedals up the wide concrete spiral ramp that looped up to the foot-bridge over the lake. Once at the top, he stopped and looked down to make sure the dirt bikers were following him up. They were. When they flew off the up ramp, he turned the bike back down.

He knew where he'd lose them.

Once back down on the trail, he turned east and hit a narrow straightaway section; the lake was close on his right and an inlet of water close on his left. That stretch was sunny, but just ahead the trail plunged into shadows under a stand of trees.

They would catch him on the straightaway. But he wanted them to be running top speed when they did, so he hammered the trail like his life depended on it. He dodged pedestrians and slow-moving cyclists. He heard the noise behind him. He glanced back and saw the riders gaining ground fast.

They were soon on either side of him. He couldn't see their faces through the glare of the sun off their dark visors, but the visors would make it hard for them to see when the trail went into the shadows again.

At least Andy hoped so.

The rider on his right pulled a wheelie – *now that's just showing off* – then tried to kick him over, so he sped up. They gunned their bikes to catch up. He looked at them; they looked at him. They should've been looking at the trail.

Andy abruptly hit the brakes and skidded sideways to a stop right where the trail ducked back into the shadows – right before the trail made a sharp ninety-degree turn north along the water's edge. They didn't. They rode straight off the trail, hit a low rock wall, and vaulted over their bikes and somersaulted into the lake like synchronized divers. They hadn't seen the turn in the shadows through their dark visors.

Andy didn't hang around. He crossed over a little bridge then rode up the bank to César Chávez and rode north on San Antonio past Silicon Labs. He didn't see the black sedans so he cut over on Third and rode behind the Music Hall and turned north on Rio Grande. He rode directly to the loft, unlocked the front door, and rolled the Stumpjumper inside. He set the bike against the entry wall, went straight to the refrigerator, grabbed a cold Corona, and popped the top. He sat in the leather chair in front of the television.

He downed the beer in one long continuous drink.

He was safe in the loft. They couldn't find him there. Tres' friend had not required a tenant app, and nothing was in Andy's name – not the title, utilities, mail, newspaper, land line, or Internet account. Andy Prescott had left no paper trail leading to this loft.

The attorney was safe from his client.

Andy's brief tenure as Russell Reeves' lawyer was over, as well as everything that had come with it: the girls, the clothes, the lounges, the loft, the money. Except the complications; Andy's life remained complicated.

One complication was the money in his trust account. Russell had wired $50,000 for Hollis McCloskey and $1 million for Sally Armstrong in San Diego. Andy had paid $25,000 to Hollis and $9,999 three times to Lorenzo. That left $995,003.

Andy got a legal pad and pen and calculated his billable hours since his last bill to Russell: the Boston, Montana, and San Diego trips, tracking Frankie down, collecting her DNA, even the chase from UT. He came up with one hundred and twenty hours. Times $500 an hour, he was due $60,000 in fees. Plus $12,000 in expenses, including the $1,000 he paid to Mickey and the $1,000 to Ramon. Less the $25,000 Russell had already paid him (the $10,000 for the DNA was a bonus), and Andy was owed $47,000.

He would transfer that sum to his checking account. That would leave $948,003 in his trust account. He was legally obligated to return that money to his former client, Russell Reeves. It wasn't Andy's money. He pulled out his cell phone and called home. When his father answered, Andy asked for Frankie.

'Andy, are you okay?'

Her voice sounded good.

'Reeves' people just chased me all over town.'

'Why?'

'I wouldn't tell him where you're at.'

'I told you he'd come for me.'

'Frankie, you got a bank account?'

'In Buda.'

'How'd you get a bank account without using your social security number?'

'I used my mom's.'

'Are you her sole beneficiary?'

'Yeah, why?'

'Give me your account number.'

'Why?'

'Trust me.'

'But you're a lawyer.'

Notwithstanding that fact, she gave him her bank account number. He hung up. It was all his fault. If he had just taken no for an answer when McCloskey couldn't find Frankie Doyle, none of this would be happening. But he had wanted the money. He had wanted Suzie and Bobbi and everything else that came with the money. So he had gone to Lorenzo. He had found Frankie Doyle. He had brought Russell Reeves to her. Andy's mother was right: money makes good men do bad things. Now he would have to make things right.

He wondered if a C student was up to it.

Chapter 22

Andy woke early the next morning without the alarm. It was Friday, and he wanted to get to Wimberley. He needed to talk to Frankie. He showered and dressed in jeans, sneakers, and a T-shirt. He was starving, and there was no food or coffee in the loft. And coffee and a muffin at Jo's was out of the question. But he needed carbs.

He decided to pick up breakfast tacos and a coffee at Whole Foods, then hit the road. He grabbed his cell phone, the bike lock, and the Stumpjumper then stepped outside. He put on his helmet and saddled up. He looked around; no dirt bikes or black sedans were in sight.

The coast was clear.

He pedaled west on Fifth the two blocks to Whole Foods. He turned north on Bowie Street and entered the underground parking garage – just to be on the safe side. He parked and locked the bike outside the escalators. He went in through the automatic doors and stepped onto the up escalator.

The down escalator to Andy's left was crowded with shoppers heading to their cars in the garage with grocery carts piled high. The down escalator at Whole Foods was the kind that flattened out into one long ramp; the grocery carts didn't roll down the ramp because rings connected to the wheels locked the carts into the escalator grooves. So shoppers could take their carts down the escalator to the parking garage.

At store level, both sides of the escalator were protected by waist-high glass panels to prevent a customer from inadvertently falling down the escalator bay. As he rose into the store, Andy ducked slightly and peered through the glass panels for anyone who looked out of place. To his right was a dining area; to his left were the checkout lines. At the mouth of the escalator were the outdoor market and the floral department; beyond were shoppers gathered at the nut roaster. He saw tattoos and body piercings, unshaven legs and shaved heads, hippies and yuppies, and fit females in Spandex.

Just the normal Whole Foods crowd.

He got off the escalator and came around the checkout counters. He wanted to run straight down the gluten-free aisle and into 'Beer Alley' and hide out in the walk-in beer cooler for the day with a case of Coronas; instead he walked toward the food court with his head ducked down. He went past the Organic Clothes and Whole Body and Health & Beauty section selling environmentally friendly jewelry and was passing the juice bar when Team Member Charlene sang out, 'Hi, Andy!'

He cringed.

For Christ's sake, Charlene, why don't you just announce over the store's public address system that I'm here?

He stopped at the breakfast taco bar. Team Member Brad said, 'The regular?' Andy nodded then scanned the food court crowd. Nothing out of the ordinary.

'Hi, Andy.'

Except Suzie.

'Oh, uh, hi, Suzie.'

'You haven't called me.'

Still searching the crowd.

'I've been busy.'

'With Bobbi?'

'Work.'

'Do you like my new gym outfit?'

'What?'

Andy now turned his attention to Suzie and her gym outfit. She twirled around for him to see. *Sweet Jesus.* Now that was a gym outfit: a skin-tight white tube top that revealed much about her anatomy and white Spandex short-shorts that stretched the few inches from well below her navel to just below her cheeks. Body parts were snugly encased, ripped abs were exposed, and Andy's body was enthused. Spandex.

'That's a, uh, really nice outfit, Suzie.'

When Andy finally looked up at her face, his peripheral vision caught two black figures standing at the sliding glass entrance doors to the food court; two Darrell-wannabes had just entered from the outdoor patio. They wore black pants and black knit shirts stretched tight around their muscular bodies; they looked like they had cornered the steroids market. Andy had the urge to cut and run, but a) Suzie was standing between him and the men in black, so they didn't have a direct line of sight to him, and b) he was starving. He needed those carbs.

'Hi, Andy.'

Bobbi glided past Andy and Suzie and gave him a coy smile. Andy turned and stared at her Spandex. Wow.

'Andy!'

Back to Suzie.

'You're looking at Bobbi instead of me?'

Suzie was gorgeous, but Andy could never resist looking at other girls who walked by – why was that? Suzie put on her pouty face and stormed off. Andy turned his back to the front door, then ducked behind a tall display for Electrolyte Enhanced Water. He peeked around at the brutes in black.

Christ, they were talking to Suzie.

Figure her to find the two fittest men in Whole Foods. And they were fit. But not fit in the Austin way. They were fit in the military way. Their muscles weren't carefully constructed by a high-priced personal trainer for the express purpose of attracting the opposite sex at Whole Foods – although they were sure as hell attracting Suzie. Their muscles were made for fighting. He could read their lips: 'Have you seen Andy Prescott?'

Suzie turned and pointed at the breakfast taco bar.

Thanks a lot, Suzie.

'Andy, your tacos.'

Team Member Brad was holding out two hot delicious breakfast tacos wrapped in aluminum foil. Andy pulled a $10 bill from his pocket, stood with his back to the men, and handed the bill across the counter.

'Keep the change.'

Andy took the tacos from Brad, stuffed them in his pockets, and slowly turned. The men were ten feet away and closing. They had ear buds and were talking into their shirt collars. Andy walked the opposite way.

They followed.

Whole Foods employed an off-duty state trooper for store security. He was standing directly in front of Andy in his olive uniform, tan cowboy boots, and cream cowboy hat; he had a big gun in his leather holster and a bigger belly above it. He would be worthless in a foot chase. Andy walked up to the trooper and pointed back at the two men.

'Those guys are harassing the girls.'

The trooper stepped in front of the men, and Andy broke and ran down the main aisle past the checkout counters and toward the escalator. He was almost there when two more brutes in black emerged from the outdoor market; they were blocking his path to the down escalator.

Shit.

He glanced back and saw that the first two men had evaded the trooper and were now running toward him. Andy ran down the Whole Body System Support aisle, ducked around a display for Complete Body Cleanse (who would do that voluntarily?), and flattened his body against the shelves. When the thugs rounded the corner, Andy stuck his foot out; they tripped and went tumbling into a chlorine-free diaper display.

Andy ran back up the aisle to the checkout lines. He had to draw the other men away from the escalators, so he ran directly toward them until they spotted him and gave chase. Andy cut left at the nut roaster and ran down the bulk aisle lined with large dispensers holding nuts, beans, seeds, and granola. Without slowing, Andy stuck his hand out and slapped open several dispensers, flooding the concrete floor behind him with raw filberts, garbanzo beans, flax seeds, soy nuts, and yogurt maltballs the size of marbles. The first man stepped on the spilled bulk items and slipped and slid like a kid on roller skates then hit the floor hard; the second man stepped on his fallen comrade and vaulted over the organic debris.

He was gaining on Andy.

Andy turned right into produce, grabbed a yellow squash and a purple eggplant, and hurled them at the man; the vegetables did not slow him. Andy came to cantaloupes displayed like a tall teepee; he pulled one from the bottom. The teepee came tumbling down;

cantaloupes rolled across the floor in front of his pursuer. He fell.

Andy ran on past the raw foods counter to the rear of the store. He swung left through dairy and past fresh meat and poultry and skidded to avoid an elderly customer at the bread counter. He made a hard left at the chocolate fountain and ran past the olive bar. If he could make it out the food court exit he could run around the parking lot to the garage entrance.

But another thug was blocking the exit.

Damn.

That guy now ran toward him. Andy retreated and ran down the center aisle. He grabbed an empty shopping cart and rolled it at the guy, flung a few cans of organic refried beans at him – which he blocked with his arms as if they were sponges – then knocked over displays stacked high with cans of whey protein and energy drinks. Which slowed the dude down long enough for Andy to cut down the pet aisle offering socially conscious dog toys, through the wine cellar, and into Beer Alley.

Cases of beer were stacked high against the glass walls, so the view from outside the cooler was blocked. He hid behind a stack of Corona Extras. Dang, six-packs were on sale for only $7.99. He hated to pass up a sale, but there was no way he could get out of there carrying a six-pack. So he grabbed a cold bottle, placed the edge of the cap against the shelf, and slapped the top with the butt of his open hand. The cap popped off. He drained half the beer in one long drink.

He wiped his mouth on his sleeve and peeked out the glass enclosure; two of the men were arguing with the trooper over by the Bowie BBQ counter. Now was his chance. It was a straight shot up the chips and salsa aisle to the escalators. He stayed low to the ground until he got to the door of the beer cooler then – *damn* – one of the thugs spotted him.

Andy darted up frozen vegetables and ran full out to the checkout counters; the escalators were just beyond the counters. But the lines were packed with shoppers and grocery carts. So he dodged a cart, stepped on a stack of bottled waters, and leaped onto the moving belt at a checkout counter.

'Pardon me! Coming through!'

He jumped over the price scanner and then the recyclable brown paper shopping bags and hit the ground again; two big steps and he grabbed the metal railing, vaulted the glass panel and dropped onto the down escalator. He squeezed past customers and their carts and ran out the doors.

He was in the garage.

The bike was right outside the door, but he fumbled for the combination to the lock; he checked back for the men. He finally got the lock opened and hopped on the Stumpjumper just as the brutes blew out the door to the escalators. He stood on the pedals and raced around the garage; they ran around cars and climbed over cars and tried to cut him off. But he beat them to the Bowie Street exit, flew out onto the street, and turned south. He turned east on Fifth Street, cut through two alleys, and arrived at the loft. He opened the front door and pulled the bike inside.

He had made it.

He stood there a moment to catch his breath. Then he smiled. He had two breakfast tacos. And they were still warm. He went to the fridge, grabbed a Corona, and popped the top. He sat down and ate his breakfast. Protein, carbs, and beer – the breakfast of champions. He had just finished the second taco when he heard noises outside. He went to the window and peeked out.

The thugs were there.

The two black Mercedes-Benz sedans were there. How had they had found him in this loft? He watched them through the blinds. They were pointing at the other lofts; there were twenty in this building. They were splitting up and going door to door. Which meant . . . they knew he lived in one of these twenty lofts, but they didn't know which one. They had tracked him to this building, but not to this loft. How?

There was a knock on the door.

Andy finished off the Corona, grabbed his sunglasses, and went down a flight of stairs to the one-car garage that sat slightly below ground level. A short driveway ramped up to the street out front where the Mercedes-Benzes were parked.

He hit the light.

The garage was stark white and immaculate; there wasn't a broom, shovel, lawnmower, tool, or grease spot in sight. But parked in the center of the garage was a glossy black American IronHorse Slammer. Seven hundred forty-two pounds and one hundred ten horsepower of pure adrenaline rush. The biggest, baddest, ass-kicking motorcycle on the planet.

Andy saddled up and ran his hands over the dual gas tanks as if they were Suzie's smooth thighs. The front tire measured one hundred twenty millimeters in width, the back tire three hundred, the better to hold the road. The wheels were chrome Streetfighters and featured disc brakes front and rear. The S&S Sidewinder engine beneath him filled one hundred eleven cubic inches of space. The transmission was six-speed with overdrive. The price tag was $42,500.

He had ordered the Slammer a month before, right after Russell Reeves had hired him to find his old girlfriends at $500 an hour. He had taken delivery of the motorcycle only the day before, after Russell's men had chased him from UT to the Hike-and-Bike Trail. He had bought his dream with Russell Reeves' money – money Andy had earned finding Frankie Doyle.

Now he needed the Slammer to make things right.

Andy secured the black bowl-type crash helmet on his head and inserted the sunglasses. He took a deep breath then fired up the Slammer. He revved the engine just to hear the distinctive IronHorse roar. No other sound on Mother Earth could compare.

Adrenaline coursed through his body.

He stood the Slammer straight and kicked the stand back. The bike was pointed directly at the garage door. He hit the automatic opener clipped to the handlebars. The door rose. Andy shifted the Slammer into gear, but held the clutch in tight. When the door was high enough, he ducked down, popped the clutch, and gave it the gas. The Slammer shot under the door and up the driveway ramp past the startled thugs and between the Mercedes-Benz sedans and out onto Fifth Street. He leaned hard right and accelerated; he saw in the side mirrors the men scrambling into the sedans. He heard tires squealing.

He would lose them out on the big road where the IronHorse could do what it did best: go fast.

He turned south on Guadalupe Street and hit South First then accelerated across the bridge over Lady Bird Lake. He veered east onto Riverside past Threadgill's then south onto Congress Avenue. The sedans were six car lengths behind him. He accelerated up the hill past the School for the Deaf then slowed and yelled at Guillermo Garza hanging his head out the window at Jo's.

'Keep the faith, bro!'

Guillermo ran outside with his fists in the air.

'Andy, my man! You are the man!'

Andy gave Guillermo a fist-punch in the air then gave the Slammer the gas. He hit the center turn lane and blew past a line of slow-moving cars. He spotted Oscar sweeping the front porch at Güero's and shouted

'Dude!' as he drove past. In the side mirror he saw Oscar drop his broom . . . and the black sedans gaining on him.

He juiced the Slammer.

He passed his little office above Ramon's tattoo parlor and wondered if he'd ever contest another traffic ticket. When he had run from Russell Reeves yesterday, he had crossed the line. He had chosen Frankie over his client. Right over wrong. Morality over money. Love over law. All the wrong choices for a lawyer. He would be disbarred.

If he wasn't killed first.

He hit the brakes hard. Traffic was backed up at Oltorf Street.

He couldn't stop now.

So he veered across the northbound lanes, cut through a parking lot, turned back west on Oltorf, made it through the intersection and turned south on Congress before the light turned green. Fortunately, no Austin cop was around; the fines from those moving violations would top $1,000. But now he was ahead of the traffic and the sedans. He slowed when he came to the new low-income town homes his client was building for SoCo.

Russell Reeves was a complicated man.

Andy arrived at Highway 290 West. The road that climbed three hundred feet to the top of the Balcones Escarpment. A road that required a powerful engine. Like the Slammer's S&S Sidewinder.

Andy cut through a gas station to the access road then accelerated down onto the entrance ramp to 290. He poured on the power and had the Slammer doing seventy before he entered the highway. He had it running eighty through the split at the Capital of Texas Highway and past the MoPac Expressway located just south of the Barton Creek Greenbelt. He checked the side mirrors; the black sedans were nowhere in sight.

Which was a good thing because he was approaching Oak Hill, where the freeway portion of Highway 290 ended and stop lights interrupted the traffic flow. The road through Oak Hill was four tight lanes that squeezed past a fifty-foot-high limestone wall, one of the first terraces of the escarpment. There was no way around the traffic. The sedans would catch up in Oak Hill. Two red lights in they did; Andy was sitting between two massive pickups; he figured they couldn't see him from a dozen cars back.

He was heading due west at the Y where Highway 71 turned northwest and Highway 290 turned south-west. He could take 71, then turn back against traffic onto the 290 ramp; he might lose one of the sedans. The light turned green, and the traffic surged forward. Andy was in the left lane that stayed 290. Just before the road split, he gunned the Slammer and swerved into the right lane and took Highway 71. He accelerated as if making his move.

In the side mirror, he saw one black sedan follow. The sedan accelerated hard, so Andy slowed a bit. Just before the sedan was on him, he cut in front of the oncoming traffic and turned south onto the ramp leading back to 290. The sedan got caught by the traffic; horns honked. Those dudes were history.

But where was the other sedan?

Andy veered back onto 290 and headed west. He came around the first bend and spotted the other black sedan waiting at Convict Hill Road. He had open road until Dripping Springs fourteen miles away. The speed limit was sixty, but this was Texas; no one drove sixty. Andy blew past the sedan and took the bike through the gears. He weaved in and out of traffic. But he knew they were behind him.

He also knew Highway 290.

The highway inclined as the road began the long, winding climb up the escarpment. He would lose them on the climb.

He poured on the power and had the Slammer doing seventy-five past Rim Rock Trail on the left and the Polo Club on the right. He leaned into each curve and felt the wind on his face and the engine beneath him. Ten minutes later he crested a steep climb and checked the mirror; he could see back for miles and the road was empty.

That was easy.

He relaxed now and considered Frankie and Jessie. Could he make things right for them? Would they have to go back into hiding? Move to another state and change their names again? Was that their future? And would Frankie let him share that future with them? These questions were running through Andy's thoughts when he glanced in the side mirror and damn near fell off the Slammer: the black Mercedes-Benz sedan was coming up behind him – fast.

Goddamn German-made cars.

That German engine could power the sedan up the escarpment as well as the S&S Sidewinder engine could the Slammer. He wouldn't lose them with speed and power. So he had to test their stability on sharp curves. And if you wanted curves, there was only one road to ride.

He entered Dripping Springs and slowed to the prescribed forty-five. He turned south on Ranch Road 12 and accelerated to sixty. Passing was prohibited on the narrow two-lane road, so the sedan stayed two cars back. Fifteen minutes later, he glided down into the Wimberley valley and over Cypress Creek. He cruised through the town square and then accelerated across the Blanco River and up the hill on the south side of the valley. Four miles south of town he made a hard turn west onto Ranch Road 32.

The Devil's Backbone.

The backbone was a ridgeline that ran high and hard with nasty curves and sudden drops. If you're going to drive the backbone fast, you'd better know the road. Andy knew the road.

The first four miles were pure straightaway. The backbone set novices up for the kill with the easy drive and the beautiful vistas of distant hills and valleys. Andy had the Slammer running seventy.

The sedan stayed with him.

They passed Purgatory Road, and Andy accelerated to eighty. The sedan stayed on his tail. He ducked down low and pushed the Slammer to ninety. They flew past the Devil's Backbone Tavern, and they were suddenly in the curves – sharp swings right and left and right then climbing hard and curving left and right and left and then descending fast and curving right and left and right. Andy leaned into each curve, and the wide tires hugged the black asphalt like they were running down rails. He checked the rearview for the sedan; with each curve it veered farther out of his vision in the mirror – wider into the oncoming lane. The driver was overcompensating.

And suddenly the sedan was gone from his mirror.

Andy slowed and glanced back. They had gone off the road.

He turned north and circled back to town. As he entered the town square from the west, emergency vehicles headed south. He cut through town and turned into the Prescott homestead. He parked the Slammer out front of the house, cut the engine, and removed the helmet. His hair was soaked with sweat. He blew out a breath.

Hell of a morning.

'Sounded like a damn tornado.'

Andy's father unloaded the shotgun, stuck the shells

in his pocket, and leaned the gun against the porch rail. He stepped down off the porch.

'Damn thing's bigger than you are.'

'Russell's guys found me in Austin, chased me out 290. So I took them out on the Devil's Backbone. Good thing those big Mercedes have airbags all around.'

'Can't you find this guy?' Harmon said.

'We're working our contact,' the boss said.

'Well, work him harder!'

'You got a number?'

Harmon read the phone number and said, 'Now find Andy Prescott!'

Chapter 23

Andy stashed the Slammer in the barn then went into the house. His mother wouldn't be home for a few hours yet. They had lunch, then his father took Jessie down to the creek for a fishing lesson. Andy and Frankie followed, but Andy needed to talk to her alone; she needed a cigarette.

'You dyed your hair black.'

She took a drag on her cigarette and nodded.

'Your hair was red.'

Another nod.

'Red hair is recessive.'

'Which means?'

'It means Jessie isn't Russell Reeves' daughter. He lied to me.'

'I'm glad you finally believe me.'

'I don't. You're lying to me, too.'

'We'll leave.'

'No, Frankie, you don't need to leave. I'm just trying to figure out why you can't tell me the truth.'

She didn't tell him now. They walked down to the

405

creek and found his father and Jessie fishing from the rock outcropping. Jessie squealed at the sight of a small fish hooked on her cane pole.

'I always wanted Jessie to grow up in a place like this, maybe have some horses.'

'You can stay here as long as you want.'

'Or until Reeves finds me. And he will.'

Max was barking.

'I see them, boy,' Paul Prescott said.

They had followed Jean Prescott home. A black Mercedes-Benz sedan now sat just outside the front gate. A dozen ostriches had gathered at the gate like palace guards; at four hundred pounds each, they presented quite an obstacle. Andy's father was sitting in a rocker on the front porch with the shotgun in his lap, an even bigger obstacle for a trespasser.

'Paul, are they coming for us?' Jessie asked.

'Honey, they'll have to get through the birds first, then this double-ought buckshot.'

'Is that a no?'

His father smiled. 'That's a no. They're not coming through that gate.'

Not yet, anyway. But they might. So Andy called Russell Reeves.

'Hello, Andy.'

'Your men chased me all over town.'

'You ran.'

'Are they okay, your guys that crashed?'

'They're fine. German cars.'

'There's another German car parked outside our gate – what do you want, Russell?'

'I want to talk to Frankie.'

'No.'

'The DNA matched, Andy.'

'It matched Frankie.'

'Then tell her to get in the car. They'll bring her to me.'

'No.'

'I'll have you arrested for stealing my money.'

'I'll tell them you're trying to kidnap Frankie.'

'The privilege, Andy. My secrets are safe with you. You're my lawyer.'

'Not any more.'

'You go public, you'll lose your law license. Besides, no one will believe you. Your word against mine.'

'That's true, Russell, but you can't get your money back.'

'I can sue you. I can file a complaint with the bar association, have you disbarred for stealing trust funds.'

'No, you can't.'

'Why not?'

'Because there's an exception to the attorney–client privilege. If the client sues the attorney or files an ethics complaint, the client is deemed to have waived the privilege.'

'Which means?'

'Which means I can spill my guts, tell the world

everything I know about you. Your secrets won't be safe.'

'Who the hell made that up?'

'Lawyers. We make the rules to protect ourselves.'

A deep sigh on the phone.

'I hate lawyers.'

'Russell, I wired the money to Frankie's bank account.'

'I know. Nine hundred forty-eight thousand and three dollars.'

'You owe her that much.'

'I'll pay her more, if she'll come in.'

'Why?'

'Ask her, Andy. Ask her to tell you the truth.'

Andy disconnected and went over to Frankie at the window.

'We've got to leave, Andy. Before they start shooting.'

'They're not going to shoot. Russell wants you alive.'

'What'd he say?'

'He said you know the truth.'

'It doesn't involve you, Andy.'

Andy pointed at the sedan out front.

'It sure as hell does, Frankie. I've been chased all over Austin and the Hill Country by Russell's men because he wants you. Because of you, those men are parked outside my parents' home.'

'Because of you, those men found me.'

She was right.

'We can't get out the front gate,' he said, 'and your car won't make it through the pasture to the back gate.'

'Can your motorcycle ride the three of us?'

'You like camping out?'

They were in the barn loading the Slammer. Andy had packed a sleeping bag for Jessie. His mother gave Andy a hug and said, 'I'm sorry.'

'It's not your fault, Mom. They would've found her sooner or later.'

She then hugged Frankie and Jessie like they were her own children.

'Paul,' Jessie said, 'I want us to live here with you and Jean.'

His father squeezed her shoulders.

'Honey, this is your home anytime you want to come back.'

'We can't come back,' Frankie said.

His father's eyes watered up.

'Andy, I can still shoot.'

'Thanks, Dad, but it's best we leave.'

Andy strapped the pack to the front handlebars and fired up the Slammer. Frankie and Jessie climbed on behind him. Andy drove out of the barn and down the trail leading to the back gate. They were invisible to the men at the front gate.

'I know a campground. Nice place, with cabins and a shower.'

Andy circled back around town and headed west

into the sunset. Twenty minutes later, they rode into the Blanco town square. Four blocks south of the square was the Blanco State Park, straddling the Blanco River. Andy stopped at the park store and paid for a cabin down by the river. They bought food and supplies for the night, then drove down to the river and found their cabin. Andy unpacked their gear; Frankie and Jessie went to gather river rocks for the fire ring. When they returned fifteen minutes later, Jessie was giggling and Frankie was soaking wet and covered in mud.

'I fell in.'

She went inside the cabin and returned wearing only a towel; she had nice legs. She hung her wet clothes over the railing of the cabin porch and sat down by the campfire. Andy was roasting hot dogs on wire hangers. She took a hanger, laid her underwear over it, and held it over the fire.

'I don't like wet undies.'

They were black.

It was early November, and the park was vacant even though the temperature wouldn't drop below forty that night. Winter didn't come to Texas until January. They ate the dogs then Frankie stood.

'I need a shower.'

She grabbed her undies – 'All dry' – and the bar of soap and shampoo they had bought at the park store and walked over to the showers on the other side of the cabin. Andy watched her then turned to Jessie.

'You want another hot dog?'

410

'I'm stuffed.'

'Why'd you pick "Jessie James"?'

'Because we're outlaws on the run.'

Andy impaled a wiener on the wire hanger and dangled it over the fire.

'You like camping out?'

'This is my first time.'

'Really? I love sleeping outdoors.'

'I never have.'

'I got the cabin for you and your mom.'

'Can I sleep out here?'

'If your mom says it's okay. But it's damp, so pull your sleeping bag close to the fire, so you don't catch a cold.'

'I won't.'

'That a girl.'

'I heard you tell my mom I might have a cancer gene.'

'Oh, honey, look, I was just worried and—'

'Don't worry. I don't have cancer. I never get sick.'

'You're lucky.'

She pulled up the right leg of her jeans.

'I can't get sick.'

Andy nodded. 'Just like trail biking. It's a mental game. You gotta believe you can't crash or you will for sure.'

'No, I mean I *can't* get sick. Ever.'

'You've never been sick?'

'No.'

411

'You're eight?'

'Unh-huh. Ouch.'

Her leg had a nasty bit of road rash.

'I fell at recess last week, scraped my leg. It's scabbing up now.'

'So you've never been to a doctor?'

'Oh, I've been to lots of doctors.'

She was picking at the scab.

'If you pick at it, it'll bleed.'

'It is bleeding.'

'So you were sick?'

'No, I was at a hospital.'

She reached to her neck and held up a pendant on a silver chain. Andy's twelve years of Catholic school qualified him to identify it.

'Saint Aloysius, the patron saint of children.'

'That was the name of the hospital.'

'So you were really sick?'

'No, I wasn't sick.'

'Then what were you doing in a hospital?'

'They were experimenting on me.'

'Were those doctors called "psychiatrists"?'

'I'm not crazy, Andy.'

She was now digging in her mother's purse.

'But you weren't sick?'

'No.'

'So why'd they put you in a hospital?'

'To study me.'

'Why?'

412

'Because I can't get sick.'

'You mean, like research?'

'Unh-huh. It was a research hospital.'

She pulled something from the purse.

'And what did they find out?'

'I'm immune.'

'To what?'

She secured a big Band-Aid over her scab – the same kind of Band-Aid Andy had found in their trash – then she looked up at him.

'Everything.'

Andy yanked open the wood door to the shower. Frankie was wet and naked. She didn't flinch or try to cover up. She just stood there in the steam.

'That blood on the Band-Aid, it was hers. Russell's not after you. He's after her.'

She turned off the water.

'My towel.'

Andy tossed the towel to her.

'Why'd you lie, about the Band-Aid?'

'So you'd tell Reeves and he wouldn't take her.'

'Why does he want her?'

'To save his son.'

She dried off.

'How can she save his son?'

'Because she's immune to all known illnesses.'

'She can't die?'

'No, she can die. Of old age. Or a crime. Maybe a

413

car accident or if you kill us on your motorcycle. But she won't die of cancer or AIDS or the flu. She's Baby X . . . and I'm the Virgin Mary.'

'The Virgin Mary?'

'The mother of the savior.'

'The savior of what?'

'Mankind. They thought her stem cells would be the cure.'

'For what?'

'Everything. Every disease known to man. They wanted to clone her, make a guinea pig out of her. I wanted her to live a normal life . . . be a regular kid.'

'Russell thinks her stem cells can save Zach.'

She nodded and pointed.

'My undies.'

He tossed the black underwear at her, took one last look, and walked out.

'I was worried about her. I mean, she was five and had never been sick. Kids are supposed to get sick, right?'

Andy tossed another dry branch onto the fire. Jessie was sound asleep in the sleeping bag. Frankie was smoking a cigarette.

'One time, all her friends got strep throat, but not her. Then half her class went out with the flu, but not her. I started wondering if something was wrong with her.'

'She's never been sick?'

'Not even a cold. So I took her to the pediatrician.

He said he'd never had a five-year-old patient who'd never been sick, not an ear infection or pink eye or a runny nose. He asked if he could take blood samples, send them off to a friend, an immunologist at a research hospital in upstate New York. I said okay. I wish I hadn't.'

'So what happened?'

'A few months later, the doctor called and asked me to bring her in. His friend was there.'

'Mr Doyle, Mrs Doyle, this is Doctor Tony Falco.'

They shook hands and sat around a small table, like when they had gone to the lawyer's office to sign their wills. Doctor Falco smiled at them.

'I'd like to study your daughter.'

'Why?' Frankie said.

'Because she might be an anomaly.'

'You mean a freak of nature?'

Mickey Doyle laughed. 'Like Shaq, only smaller.'

'Mr Doyle, your daughter is far more special than any athlete. She could save the world.'

'What are you talking about?' Frankie said.

'I'm talking about a perfect immune system. I'm talking about stem cells that might cure every disease. I'm talking about changing the world.'

'You're talking about making her a guinea pig.'

'No, ma'am. We just need to study her. And both of you. Have you ever been sick, Mrs Doyle?'

'Yes.'

415

'Mr Doyle?'

'Hung over.' He chuckled. 'Yeah, I been sick.'

'And after you test us . . . her, then what?'

'If she's what I think she is, we would use her stem cells to create a new line—'

'You mean, clone her?'

'Yes.'

'No.'

'Mrs Doyle, the curative properties of her stem cells might be unlimited.'

'But you don't really know? It's all just an experiment?'

'So was going to the moon, until we did it. Mrs Doyle, imagine a world without disease. Without young children dying of leukemia and other childhood diseases. Without children in Africa dying of AIDS. Without pharmaceutical companies controlling who lives or dies. Your daughter can change all that.'

'Will there be enough stem cells for everyone?'

'No.'

'Who will decide who lives or dies? You?'

'Yes.'

'And what happens to her when all this becomes public?'

'It won't. It will all be anonymous. I guarantee it.'

Frankie shook her head.

'No one can keep that kind of secret. It'll get out. And when it does, the media will descend on her. She'll be turned into a freak show. She'll never live a normal life. She'll never go to college or get married or have children. She'll always be a freak.'

'Mrs Doyle, I'll be the only person at the hospital who knows her real name. I'll admit her as "Baby X". Her name will not be on any hospital record or in the computer. I can keep a secret.'

'And you won't want to tell the world? Write about your great discovery? Of course you will. You'll want to share it with the world. You'll want the credit. The glory.'

A faint smile. 'I've already thought about that. I'll write up the research as if you're the patient. Patient X, not Baby X. Twenty-five to thirty-five-year-old woman. No one will know the patient is really a child.'

'They'll know you're the author.'

'I'll write the research anonymously.'

'They'll find you. And when they find you, they find her.'

'We can pay.'

Frankie looked up from the fire.

'So we did it.'

'Why?'

'We owed thirty thousand to the IRS – Mickey played games with the shop's taxes. They were threatening to take our home and Mickey's shop.'

'How much did Falco pay you?'

'Fifty thousand. To start.'

'That's a lot of money.'

'Not with Mickey spending it. We paid off the taxes, Mickey gambled the rest away. Drinking, gambling, fighting – you marry the wrong man, it's like a bad dream you never wake up from.'

'So you took her to the hospital?'

She nodded. 'In Ithaca. She was so scared. I knew it was wrong. Mickey went back home, I stayed with her. They ran tests on her every day, confirmed that she was "the cure". That's what they called her. They wanted us to move, live there so they could study her the rest of her life. She'd be like an animal in a zoo. I said, what about school? They said, no, she can't go back to school. She's too important to take that risk. The world needed her. They'd have tutors for her at the hospital. Scientists from all over the world would come there to study her. Baby X.'

Andy looked over at Jessie.

'She cried every day, begged me to stop the tests. She wanted to go home. Mickey wanted the money.'

'What'd you do?'

'I knew it would never end as long as they were paying Mickey. They said there would be lots of money for us once we moved there – a house, cars, everything we needed or wanted. Of course, Mickey, he was all for it. Said it was like she had won *American Idol*. So I had to get Mickey out of her life. I went home and when Mickey got drunk, I taunted him until he hit me. He beat me up pretty good. I called the cops and pressed charges, filed for divorce. He'd been convicted twice before for assault, bar fights, so this time he would go to prison. Three strikes. To stay out of prison, he agreed to give up his parental rights. Then I took her from the hospital and we vanished.'

'Why couldn't you just check her out of the hospital? She's your kid.'

'We signed a contract. They paid us. They wouldn't just let her walk out the door. She was too important. They knew about her, and others would, too. I knew we had to escape and change our identities. That was the only way she'd be safe.'

'What've you been living on?'

'The second payment. Another fifty thousand. I kept it from Mickey.'

'Smart. How'd you learn to change your identity?'

'The Internet. At libraries.'

'So you've been running for three years but never knew if anyone was actually chasing you?'

'I knew it was just a matter of time.'

'Why?'

'Because she has what everyone wants.'

'Which is?'

'Immortality. Or as close as we can get to immortality. Think about it, Andy. With her stem cells, you wouldn't die of cancer. Guaranteed. Live to be a hundred, disease-free. What would you pay for that? What's Russell Reeves willing to pay for that?'

'For his son.'

'He wants to save his son. The next rich guy will want to save himself.'

She tossed another branch into the fire.

'What are we going to do, Andy?'

Russell Reeves sat in a chair next to his son's bed; he was holding Zach's hand. The girl was his only hope. The cell phone rang. Russell looked at the caller ID and answered.

'Andy, where are you?'

'Frankie told me the truth, Russell. I know it's the girl you want. And why. How'd you find out about her?'

'My scientists searched the world for a stem cell match for Zach. One of them said, If only they could get stem cells from Patient X, supposedly a woman. The others laughed because most scientists thought Patient X was just a hoax. I decided to find out if Patient X was real or a hoax.'

'How?'

'We found a source at the New York shop that printed the medical journals with the Patient X articles. He gave us Falco's name.'

'Is that what Laurence Smith was doing for you in New York?'

'Yes.'

'And now he's dead.'

'Random crime, Andy. It happens here, too.'

'And Mickey?'

'It happens in Boston, too.'

'And then what?'

'We found Falco in China, at a stem cell research facility. He refused to give us Patient X's name. So we went to the last US hospital he worked at – St Aloysius Children's Research Hospital in Ithaca. The administrator was agreeable to an arrangement.'

'A bribe?'

'A donation. He didn't have her name, but a hundred million got us three items: One, there was no "*Patient X*". There was "Baby X". Not a woman, but a child. Two, a list of the women whose children were in Falco's research program back then; he ran tests on the mothers, too. And three, Baby X's DNA sample.'

'That's why you needed her DNA.'

'Yes. To confirm it was really her. And it was her DNA, wasn't it?'

'Yes. So all those women . . . ?'

'Mothers of children in the research wing of the hospital at the same time as Baby X. The children were anonymous, but not their parents. We just didn't know which mother's child was Baby X.'

'I wasn't searching for the women. I was searching for their children.'

'For one child. Baby X.'

'That's why all the other kids were sick.'

'Yes.'

'Why'd you give them money, those other women?'

'Because their children are sick.'

'And you knew the sick kids couldn't be Baby X?'

'Yes. We were looking for the one child who wasn't sick. You found her.'

'And when you're finished with her?'

'I'll give her mother ten million dollars. Or twenty. Or fifty. I don't care how much. If she'll save Zach. I'll set them up with new names, money, everything. Somewhere they'll be safe.'

'Safe from whom?'

'Andy, there'll always be someone looking for Baby X. Her secrets will never be safe.'

'I don't think she'll sell her child.'

'I don't want to buy her, Andy. I just want to buy her stem cells. Zach needs them.'

'And you'd kidnap her to get them? What was your plan, Russell?'

'Try to buy her stem cells. If that failed, then kidnap them, sedate them, extract her stem cells, and release them . . . with ten million in their bank account, wired from an offshore account untraceable to me.'

'The perfect crime.'

'A necessary crime.'

'Every crime has a victim.'

'What would you do, Andy, to save your son?'

'I wouldn't kidnap a kid.'

'Are you sure about that? If she meant life or death for your child? If you had the money – the power – to do that, to kidnap a child for a short time, just to extract her stem cells, would you just watch your son

422

die? Because her mother doesn't want to share the girl's gift?'

'It's wrong, Russell.'

'How can it be wrong to save your son?'

'When it hurts someone else.'

'I didn't hurt anyone, Andy. I tried to buy a longer life for my son. Why is that wrong? Zach will die without her stem cells. Do you want that?'

'No.'

'Then bring her in.'

'I can't make them, Russell.'

'Andy, talk to her, please. I'll pay whatever she wants.'

'You hired me for the SoCo projects so I'd already be your lawyer when you got her name and needed someone to find her.'

'Yes. We thought we were close to getting the name. Instead, we got seventeen names.'

'Why me?'

'C student, Andy. You wouldn't ask too many questions . . . or know the questions to ask. And you needed money. You wouldn't risk losing the fees. You were perfect.'

'I was stupid.'

'You were human. You needed money. I needed the girl. Will you talk to Frankie? For me?'

'Why should I?'

'Because you're my lawyer.'

'I *was* your lawyer.'

'Because I can help you.'

'I don't need your help.'

'Your father does.'

'How can you help him?'

'I can get him a new liver.'

'How?'

'A phone call.'

'You can do that?'

'Yes, Andy, I can do that. Fifteen billion dollars still means something in this world. I can make a call and move your father to the top of the waiting list. I can buy your father a longer life – if the girl will save Zach's life.'

Frankie said, 'What did Reeves say?'

Andy told her. When he finished, she said, 'So if he gets Jessie's stem cells, he'll get a liver for Paul?'

'That's what he said.'

'Do you believe him?'

Andy nodded. 'He's not a bad person, Frankie. He's just desperate. His son is going to die.'

'I'll talk to Jessie in the morning. It's her decision.'

Jessie rolled over and sat up.

'I'll do it. I'll do it to save the little boy. And Paul.'

'She'll do it, Russell,' Andy said into the cell phone. 'It's too late to come in tonight. Send Darrell and the limo out here in the morning. We're at the Blanco State Park. We'll meet him at the park store.'

'He'll be there at dawn. I'll have the doctors standing by. Thanks, Andy.'

'Russell, make the call. For my dad.'

They hung up.

'He'll save Paul?' Frankie said.

Andy nodded. He lay back in the warmth of the fire and stared at the stars above. Was it right to use Russell Reeves' money and power to save his father? To move him up the waiting list ahead of others who ranked higher? Was his father more deserving to live than the others? Was it cheating? Was it right? Or wrong? What would he do if he had Russell's money and could buy his father a longer life? What were the rules when it came to saving your father's life?

Or your son's life?

Chapter 24

Russell Reeves had changed Andy Prescott's life again.

He woke at dawn with a mane of hair across his face and an arm across his chest. But they didn't belong to Suzie or Bobbi or another Whole Foods girl. They belonged to Frankie. Of course, she was completely dressed, they had not gotten drunk at Qua the night before, and they had not had sex. She stirred and realized her position.

'Sorry. I must've gotten cold.'

But she didn't move. He looked at her; she looked for Jessie.

'She went down to the river.'

When she turned back, he kissed her. She started to kiss him back, then pulled away.

'Andy, I have to protect Jessie. I can't get involved. You're a good guy but—'

'But what?'

'But I've already got one child to raise. I can't take on another.'

'You mean me?'

'You're suffering deferred adolescence. Like Mickey did.'

'Is that a disease?'

'It was for me, living with Mickey. He refused to grow up. Like you, except you don't get drunk and beat up your wife.'

'I don't have a wife.'

'You wouldn't if you did.'

She removed her arm and sat up.

'I need coffee.'

Andy stood. 'I'll check up at the store. See if Darrell's here. You'll like him . . . about as much as a root canal.'

Andy took care of his restroom duties then rode the Slammer up to the store at the front of the park.

Frankie found Jessie down by a low dam on the river. The morning sun glistened on the smooth water that was almost white.

'Blanco means white in Spanish,' she said.

Jessie tossed a few rocks into the shallow river.

'Will it hurt?'

'Maybe a little.'

'But it might save the little boy?'

'Yes.'

'And his father will save Paul?'

'Yes.'

'I can do it.'

Frankie put an arm around her daughter.

'You've always been so brave.'

Andy arrived at the park store to find a black sedan parked outside. Not the limo. Not a Mercedes-Benz. And not Darrell.

Andy shifted the Slammer into gear.

A tall man got out of the passenger's seat. He raised his left hand. His right hand was tight to his leg. He was holding something. He called over to Andy.

'Andy Prescott?'

'Yeah.'

The man raised his right hand. He had a gun.

Andy gave the gas to the Slammer and spun it around. He ducked down and heard the gun discharge behind him. He sped down the dirt road.

Frankie turned at the sound of the motorcycle. She saw Andy driving fast toward the cabin and kicking up a cloud of dust. He was yelling.

'Come on.'

They ran back up to the cabin just as Andy skidded to a stop.

'Get on!'

'What's wrong?'

'Two men at the store. They're coming.'

'To pick us up?'

'I don't think so. They shot at me.'

'Darrell shot at you? Why?'

'It wasn't Darrell. And I didn't stop to ask.'

Frankie grabbed the sleeping bag and started rolling it up, but Andy shouted, 'Leave it!'

A black car barreled down the dirt road. Frankie wrapped her purse around her shoulders and jumped on the bike. Jessie squeezed on in between them.

'How'd they find us?'

'Russell must've told them.'

'But he needs her to save his son.'

Andy gunned the Slammer and drove around the cabin then sped away from the black car. They blew through the park exit and the town square, still vacant that early in the morning, then hit Highway 281 heading south to San Antonio. He opened the throttle; the speed limit was seventy, but he soon had the bike running ninety.

He checked the rearview. Nothing was in sight. He slowed, geared down, and turned east then doubled back north and headed to Henly. When they arrived in the tiny town, Andy pulled over at a gas station/convenience store. The Slammer needed gas, and he needed to call Russell Reeves. Andy hit the speed dial and waited for the call to ring through.

'Andy.'

The voice sounded small.

'Russell, why are your guys shooting at us? Call them off! She'll give you her stem cells! She'll save Zach!'

Russell said nothing, but Andy heard breathing on the line.

'Andy . . . Zach died last night.'

'Aw, Jesus.'

Little Zach. Gone.

'Russell, I'm sorry. Are you okay?'

'No, Andy, I'm not okay. My only son is dead and my wife had a nervous breakdown. She's in the psych ward.'

His son. His wife. His life. Andy couldn't save Zach or Kathryn or even Russell Reeves. But he had to save Jessie.

'Russell, this girl didn't kill Zach. Don't kill her. Call your people off.'

'I can't.'

'Why not?'

'They're not my people.'

'What do you mean?'

'I mean, I didn't send Darrell out there. I didn't send anyone out there. Those people shooting at you, they don't work for me.'

'Then who do they work for?'

'Drug companies, probably.'

'Why?'

'They don't want Baby X to ruin their business.'

'How would she ruin their business?'

'Andy, Baby X could be the greatest medical break-through in history. If her immune system could be cloned through her stem cells, suddenly there's no disease – no cancer, no AIDS, no common cold. And no drugs. No pharmaceuticals grossing hundreds of billions selling drugs for all those diseases. They're not going to allow a little girl to take that away.'

'How'd they find her?'

'Darrell.'

'Darrell?'

'They bribed him.'

'Darrell sold your secrets?'

'He's not a lawyer. Andy, no one knew if Baby X was real or just a myth. But just the idea scared the pharmaceuticals. They've been searching for her ever since word got out.'

'They wouldn't kill her just to keep their profits.'

'You said they shot at you. And Andy . . .'

'What?'

'I think they killed Larry Smith. And Mickey Doyle.'

'But she's just a kid!'

'Andy, the tobacco companies kill a thousand people a day and have for forty years. They knew their products were killing people, but they kept the real dangers secret all that time, to keep their profits. They killed millions of people for profit. What's one kid to the drug companies? These are people who will do anything to preserve their business model.'

'What business model?'

'Death and disease. Drug companies thrive on death and disease, Andy, not health and happiness.'

'Darrell's information was good,' Cecil said.

Harmon nodded. 'Prescott's pretty good on that bike,

but he can't lose us now. And he can't save the girl. Turn north.'

Harmon Payne had hired out to the pharmaceuticals after the Fed's Organized Crime Task Force put all the mob bosses in prison. He had gone corporate. Drug companies, now that's a racket. And it's all legal. Well, most of it. His work was definitely in the gray area, but it had put him in the green. With most of the contract assassins working for the US government in Iraq, he commanded a high price in the marketplace. He was good, he was professional, and he never stopped until the job was done.

'What are we going to do now?' Frankie asked.

Andy had pulled the Slammer around behind the convenience store next to a picnic table. He was sitting on the bike. Jessie was sitting on the table. Frankie was smoking.

'Are we going to save the little boy?' Jessie said.

'No, honey, the boy died last night.'

'Oh. What about Paul? Will he still get a liver?'

'I don't know.'

Andy pulled out his cell phone.

'I've got a friend who works for the federal government. Maybe he can help us.'

'People are shooting at you? With guns?'

'Yes, Tres, with guns. And bullets.'

'Jesus, Andy, what have you gotten into?'

'Trouble.'

'Dump 'em.'

'I can't, Tres. They're trying to kill her, the girl. I can't let that happen.'

'What do you want me to do?'

'Call the FDA or the FBI or the CIA – hell, call someone. Tell them I've got Baby X . . . or Patient X. Someone with the Feds knows about her. And tell them she's for real.'

'Okay, buddy, I'll see what I can find out.'

Andy hung up just as Frankie and Jessie came through the back door to the store.

'Andy, they're here.'

'Those guys?'

'Yeah, in the black car.'

'How'd they find us?'

'I don't know, but they're inside the store.'

'Both men?'

'Yeah. The car is parked out by the gas pumps.'

'If they're inside, they know we're around here, but they don't know we're right here.'

It was just like Russell's people knew he was in the loft building, but didn't know which loft.

'We've got to slow them down.'

Frankie pulled a pocketknife out of her purse.

'Will this help?'

'Get on.'

★   ★   ★

Inside the store, Harmon Payne said, 'A dozen donuts? Cecil, you'll have diabetes time you're fifty.'

'But they're good.'

Harmon held their coffees while Cecil paid.

'So your oldest girl's going to an Ivy League school?' Cecil said.

'Wellesley.'

'Isn't that expensive?'

'Yeah, but she's a smart girl, and I want her to have the opportunities I didn't.'

'You're a good father, Harmon.'

'I try. But it's hard raising kids in this world, all the bad influences in their lives – drugs, sex, cable . . .'

They turned to the door. Cecil pointed.

'Shit! Look!'

Outside, Prescott and the females had pulled up on the motorcycle on the far side of the Crown Vic. The woman jumped off and disappeared from sight. But Harmon knew.

'She's flattening the tires!'

He dropped the coffees, pulled his gun, and ran outside. But Prescott and the females sped off down the road. Harmon ran to the car and looked down at the flat tire. She only got one. He sighed.

'Why won't people just accept the fact that I'm gonna kill them? Why do we have to go through this every time?'

'Maybe they don't want to die.'

'Cecil, shut up and change the tire.'

★　★　★

Andy drove east on Highway 290 toward Austin. They had bought some time, so he kept the Slammer at the speed limit. If a state trooper pulled him over for riding three to the bike, just as well he not be speeding, too.

Other than a few big rigs blowing past them doing eighty and blasting their horns at the girls, it was a peaceful ride. Jessie pointed up at the vultures circling over dead deer lying on the side of the highway. The deer had come out of the brush to forage for food the prior evening and tried to cross 290; they didn't make it. Bad luck for them. Good luck for the vultures.

When they arrived in Dripping Springs, Andy pulled into a Dairy Queen next to the Cattleman's National Bank. Frankie and Jessie went inside for food and drinks. Andy sat on the Slammer and tried to figure things out: how had those guys found them at the park? And at the convenience store in Henly? And would they find them again? It was as if they were simply following them on a map, as if they had planted a tracking device—

A tracking device?

Andy pulled his cell phone out of his pocket. They were tracking his cell phone.

He hit the speed dial for Curtis Baxter. When he answered, Andy said, 'Dude, tell me about that cell phone tracking stuff.'

'Andy, Reeves' limo stopped coming for me.'

'Zach died last night.'

'Shit.'

After a moment of silence, Andy said, 'Tracking.'

'Yeah, okay. Every phone can be tracked with either GPS or triangulation. GPS uses three satellites to plot the phone's location using a trilateration process—'

'Curtis, bottom line, as long as I have my phone, they can find me?'

'They who?'

'Long story. But that's the deal?'

'That's the deal.'

'How can I stop it?'

'Turn it off.'

'That stops them for sure?'

'Pretty sure. Some people think they can track even if the phone is off.'

'What can I do to be sure?'

'Okay. Remove the back cover to your phone and pull out the SIM card then—'

'Dude. It's Andy.'

'Hide it.'

'The phone?'

'Yeah.'

'Where?'

'Where they can't ping it.'

'Curtis, there are cell towers everywhere.'

'Yeah, but they can't reach everywhere.'

'Like where?'

'Like in the canyons.'

'Like in the greenbelt.'

★   ★   ★

Thirty minutes later, Andy drove to the Camp Craft Road entrance to the Barton Creek Greenbelt. He parked the Slammer on the road. Frankie and Jessie climbed down first.

'Stay here,' Andy said. 'I've got to hide my phone down in the canyons.'

'Why don't you just smash it with a rock?'

'I'm gonna need it.'

'When?'

'When I want them to find us.'

Andy ran down the Hill of Life and then the creek trail until he arrived at Sculpture Falls. He waded into the shallow water to where the crevices in the limestone had formed. He stashed the phone deep inside a dry crevice. No way a cell signal could get through three feet of solid rock.

He ran back up to Frankie and Jessie.

'Andy,' Frankie said, 'it's going to be cold tonight and we left the sleeping bag and our blankets back at the park.'

'We can't camp out here – coyotes and bobcats roam the place at night. We can't stay at my place or with Tres and Natalie – she'd want to put Jessie on the news. We can't stay with Dave or Curtis and get them involved. We can't stay in a hotel, they can track a credit card.'

He saddled up on the Slammer.

'Let me borrow your calling card.'

She dug in her purse and pulled out the card. She handed it to him.

'I've got to find a phone. I'll be back.'

'Andy . . .'

'Yeah?'

'If you decide not to come back, I'll understand. This is our problem, not yours.'

'I'll be back.'

Andy rode the Slammer to a convenience store and called Dave. His buddy seemed distracted.

'Dude, quit combing your hair and listen. Don't you have a listing near the greenbelt? A foreclosed mansion?'

'Man, Russell Reeves must be paying you a fortune.'

'I'm not buying, Dave. We just need a place to stay tonight.'

'We who?'

'You don't want to know. But, Dave, it's an emergency.'

'She's hot, huh? Why don't you take her to a fancy hotel, you can afford it, Reeves' lawyer.'

'Not any more.'

'No kidding?'

'What about that place?'

'It's a mansion overlooking the greenbelt. Vacant, they just walked away, even left the furniture. Electricity's on. Here's the lockbox code.'

Dave gave Andy the code and the address. It was just a few blocks away.

'What if someone comes over to look at the place?'

'No one's looked at that place in two months. Credit crunch.'

'What about the neighbors? Will they call the cops if they see the lights on?'

'Nope. House has automatic timers. A few lights inside come on at dark, turn off at midnight. So criminals think someone's still there.'

'Thanks, Dave. I owe you, man.'

'Andy, if I can't let my good buddy trespass on one of my listings, what the hell good am I? But try not to stain the sheets, okay. They're satin.'

Andy hung up and dialed Tres.

'Andrew, how are you?'

Andrew? The only person who had ever called him Andrew was his mother back when he was a kid and she had been really mad at him.

'Man, Andrew, remember that time you took a header for those senior citizens?'

'Uh, yeah.'

'Have you been back out there since?'

'Well, as a matter of fact, I'm—'

'We need to do that again, Andrew.'

'Fly off the ravine?'

'No, sit right there and talk.'

'Well, okay, but first—'

'How about today, Andrew? At two.'

Tres hung up. It was one-thirty. Andy rode back to Frankie and Jessie at the greenbelt.

'I need to go down the trail, to meet someone.'

'Can we come?' Jessie said. 'I'm scared.'

Andy put his arm around her and led them down the trail.

Just before two, Tres rode up on his trail bike. Andy, Frankie, and Jessie were sitting on the same rock he had sat on after taking the header that day. Andy introduced everyone, then turned to Tres.

'*Andrew?* What's that about?'

'Didn't know if someone was listening in.'

'To your phone calls?'

'Hey, man, the Feds are spying on everyone these days.'

'But why you?'

'Because I asked the wrong question.'

'Which was?'

He glanced from Andy to Frankie and Jessie and back.

'It's okay.'

Tres gestured at Frankie.

'This is her? Patient X?'

'No.' Andy nodded at Jessie. 'That's her.'

'Thought Patient X was a woman?'

Andy shook his head. 'A girl. Baby X.'

'Well, you were right, the Feds know all about her.'

'You found something?'

He nodded. '"Patient X: A Cost–Benefit Analysis."'

'They studied her?'

'They studied the idea of her. No one knew if Patient

X was real or some kind of medical hoax, but they run analyses on all kinds of hypothetical scenarios. You know, what-ifs. Like war games. Would she be good or bad for the economy? They discovered Patient X could bankrupt the government, put the country into another Great Depression. At least that's the conclusion after they ran the numbers.'

'What numbers?'

'The decreased cost of Medicare and Medicaid if Patient X could cure even a few diseases – the numbers are staggering.'

'So that's good.'

'Yeah, but those numbers are nothing compared to the increased costs of social security. Right now, life expectancy is seventy-four. What if it were a hundred? People start living that long, it would bankrupt social security. They'd have to raise the tax to fifty, sixty percent on top of the income tax. People would be paying ninety percent of what they make to the federal government. Society would collapse, there'd be social chaos. Our social programs are predicated on people dying on time.'

'But I pay fifteen-point-nine percent of my income into the social security trust fund. The government's investing all that money to pay me when I retire.'

Tres laughed. 'Andy, there's no trust fund. Your taxes aren't invested. Social security is a Ponzi scheme: the money you pay in today is paid out to old folks tomorrow. Any money left over is spent just like regular tax money. Last year there was a $175 billion social security surplus. But it wasn't invested in the trust fund. It was spent for farm programs and the Iraq war and pet projects for members of Congress. The so-called "trust fund" is nothing more than a stack of IOUs from the government to the Social Security Administration. They're literally sitting in a file cabinet in DC. The trust fund is just a huge hoax on the American people.'

'So the government won't help her?'

Tres shrugged. 'I called a buddy over at the FBI. He said they'll take her into the witness protection program, give her a new identity, move her to a new place.'

'We don't need the FBI for that,' Frankie said. 'And if she goes into protective custody, she'll be a freak again.' She shook her head. 'We're on our own.'

'No, Frankie, you're not on your own. I'm here.'

'Mom, what are we gonna do?'

'What we've always done, honey. Run.'

Jessie started crying. 'Mom, I'm tired of running. I want to live with Jean and Paul and Max and the birds. I want to fish. And Paul's teaching me the guitar.'

Andy pulled Frankie aside and said, 'You can't run forever.'

'What choice do we have, Andy? They'll never stop coming for her, as long as she's alive.'

Andy looked over at Jessie sitting on the rock and crying with her face in her hands. He turned back to Frankie.

'Then we'll have to kill her.'

★   ★   ★

Three miles away, Cecil said, 'What do you want?'

Harmon put his hand over the phone. 'Caramel macchiato and a sugar-free brownie.'

Cecil got out of the car and went inside the Starbucks. Harmon said into the phone, 'Where the hell are they?'

'We don't know.'

The boss.

'Why don't you know?'

'We can't ping Prescott's phone.'

'Why not?'

'He either figured out we're tracking him with his cell phone and turned it off, or he's in a dead zone. When he comes out or turns it on, we'll have his location in minutes.'

Harmon hung up.

When Cecil returned, he said, 'Well?'

'We wait.'

Andy drove them to Dave's listing. He opened the lockbox, removed the front door key, and unlocked the door. They stepped inside and Jessie said, 'Wow.'

It was in fact a mansion.

'You guys check the place out, I'm going to run over to SoCo and pick up a few things. What kind of pizza do you like, Jessie?'

'Pepperoni and Italian sausage.'

'Frankie?'

'Same.'

'I'll be back in a few hours.'

★ ★ ★

By eleven that night, they had eaten pizza, drunk a few beers, and prepared everything for the next morning. Jessie had fallen asleep in a recliner. Frankie and Andy were on the couch, watching a movie on the TV: *The Way We Were* with Robert Redford. He was handsome. Frankie had rested her head against Andy's chest. He had his arm around her.

'Andy, what if we killed them instead?'

'I don't think we could. They're professionals. But even if we could, they'll just send someone else. You're right – they'll never stop coming for her. It's the only way.'

Chapter 25

Andy turned his cell phone on.

'Are you sure about this?' Frankie said.

'No. But we've got no choice.'

It was eight the next morning. They were in the vacant parking lot of the Barton Creek Square Mall on the Capital of Texas Highway, also known as Loop 360, on the southwest side of Austin. The greenbelt was just across the highway. But that Sunday morning Andy Prescott wasn't bombing the Hill of Life on a mountain bike. He had a different kind of adrenaline rush in mind today.

'Go.'

Frankie flicked her cigarette to the ground and hugged Jessie then jumped into the passenger's seat of Tres' Beemer.

'Good luck, Andy,' Tres said.

They drove off. Andy watched as they veered onto Loop 360 heading north, then he popped the top on a can of Red Bull.

'What's that?' Jessie asked.

'Rocket fuel.'

'Doesn't that have lots of caffeine?'

'It'd better.'

'That's bad for your health.'

'Two guys shooting at me is bad for my health.'

He downed the Red Bull then faced Jessie.

'You ready?'

'I'm scared, Andy.'

'Me, too.'

He gave her shoulder a little squeeze.

'Undo your hair.'

She removed the clip in the back and shook her hair loose. It hung to her shoulders and lay on the black jacket he had bought for her the day before.

'I wish my hair were still that long,' Andy said.

'Why?'

'The Samson theory.'

The black sedan entered the far end of the parking lot.

Harmon was riding shotgun. He spotted the big black motorcycle across the vacant parking lot. Prescott was kneeling beside it; the girl was standing next to the bike. He had engine problems. Harmon said into the cell phone, 'We got him, boss. I'll call you when it's done.'

He ended the call and released the safety on the Glock.

'Pull up next to them, Cecil. I'll pop her and we can be back on the highway before she hits the ground.'

Cecil accelerated the Crown Vic across the black asphalt. Harmon lowered his window, but Prescott spotted them and jumped up. He straddled the motorcycle; the girl jumped on behind him. They sped off.

'Damn, he got it going. Don't lose them, Cecil.'

The motorcycle exited the parking lot and accelerated onto Loop 360 heading north. The girl's red hair stood straight out behind her as they flew across Scottish Woods Drive. Cecil pointed to an undeveloped treed area on his left.

'That's the Barton Creek Greenbelt. Must've named it after the mall. Eight hundred acres. Got a creek and waterfalls. It's supposed to be really neat.'

'Maybe you should bring Harriet here for a vacation.'

'But then I couldn't get a hooker.'

'Life is full of dilemmas, Cecil.'

They were only a few car lengths back of the motorcycle, but Harmon had no chance of hitting the girl at that speed. Fortunately, traffic was light that early on a Sunday morning; there were more cyclists in the bike lane than cars on the highway. They crossed Lost Creek Boulevard; the valley to the east offered a big view of downtown Austin in the distance.

'Wow, look at that,' Cecil said.

'Look at the road.'

But Harmon had to admit it: Austin was a pretty place. Paradise compared to Jersey. Might be a nice place to retire to, although he kept a map with black dots at every city where he'd killed someone so he

447

knew if he were returning to the scene of an unsolved murder or murders. After today, it might be best to retire somewhere else.

'Stoplight up ahead,' Cecil said.

'On a highway?'

Traffic slowed to a stop at an intersection called Bee Caves Road. But the motorcycle didn't. Prescott swerved into the bike lane, drove around the stopped vehicles, and ran the red light.

'He's good.'

'Don't lose them, Cecil.'

The motorcycle was slowing down. Prescott was leaning over, driving with one hand and fiddling with the engine with the other.

'He's got engine problems.'

But when the light turned green, the motorcycle sped off again.

'Did.'

'We still got him.'

They followed the motorcycle past the Wild Basin Wilderness Preserve off to their right.

'Seven women founded that place thirty years ago,' Cecil said. 'They wanted to save a piece of the wilderness.'

As if Harmon gave a shit.

'Drive.'

The road turned up then down and left then right. Walls of white limestone rose on either side.

'All this land used to be a sea, millions of years ago,' Cecil said. 'Hence, the limestone.'

'*Hence?*' Harmon looked at his driver. 'Hence, Cecil?'

'I read it in that book about Austin last night.'

'I thought you were watching *Sex and the City* reruns?'

'I was reading and watching TV. I can do two things at the same time, Harmon.'

'Really? Well, do two things now: shut up and drive.'

The road began a long decline toward a suspension bridge over the river. Cecil drove in silence until they arrived at the bridge. Then he had to talk. He was like a kid in a car – he couldn't help himself.

'Pennybacker Bridge,' Cecil said. 'No part of the bridge touches Lake Austin.'

'Looks like a river.'

'It is. The Colorado River.'

'Then why do they call it Lake Austin?'

''Cause it's in Austin.'

'Cecil, shut up and drive.'

They drove over the bridge and through another limestone canyon, then the motorcycle abruptly exited the highway.

'He's getting off.'

'I got him.'

The motorcycle blew through the green light and turned left under the highway. The street sign read FM 2222. They caught the red light behind three other cars.

'Go around.'

Harmon gave him hell, but Cecil Durant was a skilled driver. He had never let Harmon down, and he wouldn't today. Cecil maneuvered the Crown Vic around the other cars to the right, drove onto the grass shoulder, then ran the red light and cut through the intersection and left under the highway.

'Nice work, Cecil. He's heading west.'

Cecil accelerated, but the motorcycle was nowhere in sight.

'Maybe he turned back.'

'Where are they?'

They passed several boat shops and shopping centers then stopped at a light at River Place Drive. A huge black Hummer pulled alongside; a cute blonde was driving. She smiled down at Harmon.

'You know,' Cecil said, 'with gas prices and global warming, driving one of those is just irresponsible.'

'Yep. But she's a real doll.'

'The Hummer?'

'The driver.'

When the light turned green and the Hummer accelerated off like it was the Indy 500, Harmon spotted the black motorcycle.

'There.'

Prescott had pulled over in the parking lot at the 3M plant. He was leaning over and fiddling with the engine again, but when they turned in, he sped across the lot and back onto the road heading west. The motorcycle flew through the intersection at FM 620, then the road reduced down to two tight lanes and became severely winding with steep descents. The girl hung on for dear life as they hit eighty and didn't slow for the curves.

'You know,' Cecil said, 'it's really not safe for her to be riding that motorcycle without a helmet. She's just a kid.'

'Cecil, we're trying to kill her.'

Cecil nodded. 'Good point.'

A few minutes later, they passed a sign for Hippie Hollow on the left.

'That's a famous beach,' Cecil said. 'Maybe we can stop in for a look on the way back.'

'No.'

'It's a nude beach.'

'Well, maybe for a minute.'

They stayed with the motorcycle until the blue water of a large lake came into view.

'Lake Travis,' Cecil said. 'Named after William Barret Travis. He died at the Alamo. Sixty-three miles long. Some places are two hundred feet deep. I read that, too.'

'Well, Cecil, that's very interesting. But right now—'

'Shut up and drive?'

'Exactly.'

The road turned into a gut-wrenching roller coaster. Another steep decline was followed by several hairpin turns on the narrow road. They had to slow down, but Prescott didn't. He seemed intent on doing their job for them. A sheer rock ledge rose on their right; a steep cliff dropped off on their left down to the lake.

Harmon breathed a sigh of relief when they came to a T-junction at Farm-to-Market Road 2769.

Prescott turned left and accelerated past a marina. They followed but lost sight of the motorcycle as the road made a series of S turns; the speed limit was only twenty miles an hour. The lake was to their left, thickly treed terrain to their right. Cecil negotiated the turns like the professional he was. They accelerated past Geronimo Street, Pocahontas Trail, and Navajo Pass and climbed to a high point above the lake. They came into a small town called Volente and drove past the Volente Beach and Water Park. The road turned winding again, but the motorcycle was just ahead.

Prescott had engine trouble.

The road tracked the lakeshore, cutting in and out around little coves down below, and was protected only by intermittent low guardrails. They were now high above the lake, and they were alone. No other cars were in sight.

'Now, Cecil.'

Cecil accelerated and got directly behind the motorcycle.

'He can't get enough power.'

Harmon rolled his window down and stuck the Glock out. He fired several times, but apparently missed.

'Damn, I thought for sure I hit her. Get on him.'

They made several hard curves, then caught up again on a short straightaway. Harmon fired three more rounds directly at the girl's black jacket. But she held on.

452

Another curve put them right on a ridgeline with the lake directly below them. Prescott kept glancing back.

'I can take her from here.'

Harmon leaned out the window, steadied his arm on the side mirror, and sighted the girl in. He emptied the clip. Prescott jerked as if he'd been hit.

'I got 'em.'

The motorcycle weaved back and forth across the road. Prescott had lost control of the bike. He was slumped down, and the girl with him. But they weren't slowing down. They were going even faster. The motorcycle veered hard inland and then hard back toward the lake – and didn't veer back. The motorcycle, Prescott, and the girl drove straight off the road; the massive black motorcycle hung in the blue sky a long moment and then disappeared from sight.

'Shit!' Cecil said. 'They went airborne!'

'Pull over!'

Cecil skidded to a stop. Harmon jumped out and ran to the other side of the road. Cecil followed. They stood on a steep cliff above the lake. The motorcycle lay crashed on the rocks a hundred feet below. Harmon didn't see Prescott or the girl.

Cecil pointed. 'There!'

Prescott and the girl were floating face down in the water.

'She's dead,' Cecil said.

'I'll make sure.'

Harmon ejected the spent clip then loaded another

into the Glock. He fired thirteen rounds at the girl. The bullets splashed into the water around her body, but several made direct impact into her black jacket.

'Now Baby X is dead.'

'What about Prescott?'

'Looks dead to me,' Harmon said. 'But I wasn't paid to kill Prescott. Only the girl.' Harmon spotted a car coming. 'Let's get out of here. We hurry, we can make the noon flight back to Jersey. I'm sick of Texas.'

'Are we going back to kill the Mexican that took your gun?'

'Cecil, we're professionals, just like lawyers and accountants. We don't kill out of revenge or passion or personal enjoyment. We kill because we're paid to kill. We're not being paid to kill that Mexican either, so we're not going to kill him. And as a professional, I have to consider the potential downside. What if the Mexican gets off a lucky shot, hits one of us? Then we're at a hospital answering questions from the police. That could end our careers. So killing the Mexican wouldn't be a smart move. Or professional.'

Cecil nodded. 'You're right. You're always right, Harmon. Still, I'd really like to shoot that Mexican son of a bitch, you know, on a purely personal, non-professional level.'

'Yeah, me, too.'

'Can we at least eat first? I'm starving.'

'Sure. But not Mexican again.'

'Barbecue?'

'Barbecue's good.'

Harmon Payne and Cecil Durant got into the Crown Vic, turned around, and headed back to Austin. But they stopped at Hippie Hollow for a quick look. As Harmon Payne always said, 'You only live once.'

Tres and Frankie jumped from rock to rock and splashed through the shallow water. They found Andy lying face down on the bank. They dropped to their knees next to him. Tres felt tears come into his eyes.

'Andy!'

They rolled him over. His eyes were closed; he was bleeding from his nose.

'Shit, Andy! Why'd you cut your hair?'

Frankie gave Tres an odd look, then slapped Andy's face.

'Andy!' Another hard slap. 'Andy!'

Andy opened his eyes.

'That hurt.'

'Oh, I didn't hit you that hard.'

'No. Falling into the lake hurt.'

'Oh.'

He was experiencing a full-body hurt. Water was harder than it looked. Andy pushed himself up on his elbows.

'Is she dead?'

Frankie nodded. 'Yes.'

She pointed at the body floating in the water. Tres

waded out and grabbed the girl's red hair; he pulled her onto the bank. Her hair came off in his hands, revealing a head as bald as a billiard ball. The mannequin's head.

'At least they think she's dead.'

'Are you okay, Andy?'

Andy turned to Jessie.

'I'm good.'

'Your plan worked, Andy,' Frankie said.

After losing the black sedan at the FM 2222 red light, Andy and Jessie had raced ahead and pulled into the 3M lot, where Tres and Frankie were waiting. Jessie had jumped off the Slammer, and Tres had secured the mannequin behind Andy with a belt under the black jacket. The day before, Andy had gone into SoCo and bought matching black jackets and pants and the mannequin with the red wig from the front display window at Lucy in Disguise with Diamonds. Frankie had dressed Jessie and the mannequin in identical clothes and secured the red wig to the mannequin's head. From behind, you wouldn't know the mannequin wasn't Jessie. Tres helped Andy to his feet.

'Dude, you flew right off the freaking cliff!'

Andy had picked that exact spot – a sheer fall to a deepwater cove below – to ride off the cliff.

'Did get the adrenaline pumping, I'll give it that. How's the Slammer?'

'It's toast.'

'Figured.'

They stared at each other a long moment, then Tres shook his head. He held an open hand up; they clasped hands and bumped shoulders, as close as two heterosexual males could comfortably come to a full-body hug.

'I'm glad you're not dead.'

'Me, too.'

Jessie hugged him. 'Thanks, Andy.'

Frankie stepped to Andy and embraced him tightly. When she released him, he said, 'Stay here. In Austin. With me.'

She cupped his face with both hands, then kissed him – on the cheek. A 'dear friend' kiss. Not an 'I love you' kiss.

'Andy, what you did, that was manly. I was wrong, you're not like Mickey. You're a grownup.'

'But?'

'But we can't be Karen and Jessie James anymore. We have to leave.'

Epilogue

At exactly seven-thirty on the first day of June, loud rock music woke Andy Prescott. He reached over and turned off the radio.

Another Monday morning.

He was back in the little house on Newton Street in SoCo. He was back riding a bike to the office and traffic court. He was back to his old life.

He felt like Cinderella after the ball.

But he wasn't hung over. He had not gotten drunk the night before at Güero's. In fact, he hadn't been drunk since the day Frankie and Jessie had left. He had gotten stupid drunk that night, but not since. He had lost interest.

They had been gone two hundred and three days now.

He let Max out the front door and waved to Liz walking her dog, then showered and dressed. He brushed his hair back; it was long again, almost to his shoulders. He went outside and saddled up on the Stumpjumper, the last remnant of that life, and rode down the porch steps and then the front sidewalk to the street. He didn't turn north to Nellie for a morning adrenaline rush. Instead, he turned south and glided down James Street to Jo's. He noticed a familiar Cadillac Escalade parked at the curb. Lorenzo Escobar was standing in line.

'Lorenzo.'

The PI gave him a big smile.

'Andy, my man.' They fist-punched. 'How you doing, brother?'

'I'm good. How's business?'

'Wives are still cheating, so business is good.'

Lorenzo filled his coffee with sugar then walked over to his Escalade. He turned back.

'Andy . . . you call me anytime you need someone to watch your back. No charge.'

'Thanks, Lorenzo.'

Andy watched the Escalade cruise south on Congress then grabbed a *Chronicle* off the rack and walked up to the window.

'Large.'

'Like I don't know.'

Guillermo Garza handed him the coffee and two banana nut muffins. Andy had told Guillermo only that he no longer worked for Russell Reeves and that he had wrecked the Slammer. Guillermo knew not to ask questions.

'Keep the faith, bro.'

Andy sat at a table and placed Max's muffin on a

napkin on the ground. He poured the dog some coffee then acknowledged the other regulars: Ray, still working on that novel; Darla, still dishing ice cream across the street; Oscar, still working at Güero's; George, still playing for tips; and Dwight, still blogging his life away.

Andy Prescott's life had changed and changed back again, but SoCo had remained unchanged – except for the new low-income housing. Russell Reeves had completed the three projects in SoCo: eight hundred town houses for low-income residents. But Russell had not come to SoCo for the grand openings; and they had never again spoken. Russell Reeves was seldom seen in public these days. Word was, Kathryn Reeves had been in and out of psychiatric hospitals around the country. It made Andy sad. He had never been able to work up any anger at Russell because he had never walked in Russell's shoes.

What would Andy have done to save his son?

Andy ate the muffin then bought Floyd T.'s breakfast. He saddled up and rode down Congress Avenue to his office. He found Floyd T. sitting on the stoop of the tattoo parlor with his grocery cart parked next to him. The parlor was closed, so Andy couldn't check his email. He had hoped every day for an email from Frankie, but none had ever come. He handed Floyd T. his breakfast and put a $5 bill in Floyd T.'s cigar box. Then he went upstairs to his office. He got that day's traffic tickets, his backpack, coat, and clip-on tie, folded the *Chronicle* lengthwise and stuck it in his back waistband for some courtroom reading, then rode the bike to traffic court.

Judge Judith now looked upon him as one would a tragic fallen figure, the same way people with homes viewed Floyd T.: 'He was once somebody – now look at him.' The municipal prosecutor, Ms Manning, ignored him. They had never banged out a plea bargain in her office. Andy could barely work up the interest to hand out his business cards on the way out.

He rode over to Whole Foods for lunch. Team Members Brad and Charlene still treated him the same, but a) Suzie was dating Rich Olson (he still drove a Porsche, the bastard), b) Bobbi no longer even acknowledged his existence, and c) Spandex did not seem like the most incredibly marvelous invention in history anymore. Okay, it was still in the top ten.

He still had $20,000 of the fees Russell had paid him, which could have kept him in the life and Suzie and Bobbi for a few more glorious months, but he had lost interest in all that, too. If he wasn't just thirty years old, he'd be worried that he might be suffering some kind of midlife crisis.

He stopped in at REI just to say hello to Wayne then rode south down Lamar Boulevard across the lake to Texas Custom Boots. His father's handmade black elk cowboy boots were ready. He paid the final installment then rode back over to Congress Avenue with the boot box under one arm. He called out to Ronda sweeping the front porch at Güero's; Andy and the guys still met there for their Sunday night beer bash. Dave and Curtis remained without female companionship, and Andy had rejoined them in their misery. Curtis was now Dr Baxter and would be teaching at MIT in the fall. Dave had gotten out of real estate and now sold women's lingerie at Victoria's Secret. He offered the employee discount to potential dates.

Tres and Natalie had married and their baby boy – Arthur Thorndike IV (apparently there was a naming rights stipulation in the trust fund) – was due any day now. They had already reserved personalized license plates for his sixteenth-birthday Beemer: CUATRO. Tres had quit the IRS and hired on with a big downtown law firm, Natalie was banking that her morning show series – *Baby Watch with Natalie* – would be her ticket to the networks, and their nanny-to-be was a sensuous nineteen-year-old Mexican girl.

Andy was a half-block down from his office when he noticed a crowd gathered in front of the tattoo parlor. And he knew: Floyd T. had suffered another heart attack. He rode fast then jumped off the bike and pushed his way through the crowd.

'Floyd T.!'

'What?'

Andy turned. Floyd T. was sitting there on the tattoo parlor's steps.

'You okay?'

Floyd T. shrugged. 'For a homeless person.'

'What's going on?'

'I like her.'

'Who?'

Ramon turned from the crowd.

'Andy.'

He was grinning. But he grinned often these days. He had a new love interest who had granted him free artistic expression with her flesh canvas. Ramon Cabrera was a happy man.

'What's going on, Ramon?'

Ramon stood aside to reveal a shiny black American IronHorse Slammer. A cute red-haired girl sat on the seat; her pretty red-haired mother stood next to it. Andy Prescott always had a thing for redheads.

Ramon slapped Andy on the back. 'Got some tickets for you, bro.' He went inside his shop where a customer was waiting. Andy turned to the red-haired woman.

'I'm Connie Cantrell,' she said. 'And this is my daughter, Cassie.'

'Connie and Cassie. Nice names.'

'We thought so.'

'So what brings you to my part of the world?'

'I need a lawyer.'

'Are you in trouble?'

The woman named Connie nodded. 'I got a traffic ticket. A big one. I heard you were the best traffic ticket lawyer in Austin.'

'Well, I don't like to brag, but . . .'

'Will you be my lawyer?'

'Are you guilty?'

463

'Completely.'

'Well, see, the thing is, I'll have to appeal it. And that'll take a year and a half, maybe two, before it comes to trial.'

Connie shrugged. 'I'm not going anywhere.'

'You sure about that?'

'I'm sure. Cassie is enrolled at St Ignatius in the fall—'

'Fourth grade,' Cassie said.

'—And I'm enrolled at UT. Art department.'

'Really?'

'Yep. I know people.'

'So you're an artist?'

'Yes, I am.'

'I'm a trail biker myself.'

'I'd like to try that.'

'I could teach you.'

'Okay, then. But one question: If you're my lawyer . . . *our* lawyer, anything you know about us, that's our secret, right? You can't tell anyone?'

Andy nodded. 'It's called the "privilege". Your secrets are safe with me.'

'Good.'

The girl named Cassie said, 'Can we go see Paul?'

'Yes, you can. And he can see you.' He turned to Connie. 'My dad—'

'Got his liver.'

His father would wear the black elk boots. But who had died so Paul Prescott could live? Who had not been saved so he could be? Had Russell Reeves pulled

464

some strings to move Paul Prescott to the top of the list? Had he bought a longer life for Andy's father? Andy didn't want to know the answers. All he knew was that he still had his father – and that Paul Prescott had finally gotten his big break.

'How'd you know?'

'Your mother.'

'You called her?'

Connie nodded. 'At her office.'

'She never told me.'

'She said she could keep a secret . . . and that you could, too.'

'How's *your* mother?'

She pointed inside Ramon's shop; Andy looked closely and saw that the customer was Colleen O'Hara. She was thumbing through Ramon's flash.

'She's living with us now. When we left here, Marty O'Connor sold her house, put her on a plane to Phoenix. I figured she couldn't wander off a seven-fifty-seven.'

'That's where you've been living, Phoenix?'

'Sedona.'

'Good art there.'

'I quit smoking there.'

Ramon poked his head out. 'Connie, your mother says she wants a heart on her butt – you okay with that?'

Connie shrugged. 'She's one of the tribe now.'

'Andy,' Cassie said, 'give me a ride.'

Her mother said, 'Put the helmet on,' then held the

key out to Andy. He removed the *Chronicle* from his back waistband and tossed it into the trash can then handed the boot box to Connie. He took the key. He threw a leg over the Slammer and started the engine. He stood the bike straight, kicked the stand back, and revved the engine. He felt the big S&S Sidewinder rumbling beneath him. He looked over at Connie; her lips moved, but he couldn't hear her words over the engine.

'What?'

She stepped closer. 'I said, I like your hair long.'

'The Samson theory.'

And she kissed him. On the lips.

Cassie wrapped her arms around him and held on tightly. He shifted into gear and drove down the side-walk and onto South Congress. He accelerated and felt the wind on his face, and he heard the girl scream with delight. And Andy Prescott thought, *I might not be much of a lawyer, but I'm her lawyer. And her secrets will always be safe with me.*

Other bestselling titles available by mail:

The Colour of Law	Mark Gimenez	£6.99
The Abduction	Mark Gimenez	£6.99
The Perk	Mark Gimenez	£6.99

The prices shown above are correct at time of going to press. However, the publishers reserve the right to increase prices on covers from those previously advertised, without further notice.

———————————— sphere ————————————

Please allow for postage and packing: **Free UK delivery.**
Europe; add 25% of retail price; Rest of World; 45% of retail price.

To order any of the above or any other Sphere titles, please call our credit card orderline or fill in this coupon and send/fax it to:

Sphere, P.O. Box 121, Kettering, Northants NN14 4ZQ
Fax: 01832 733076   Tel: 01832 737526
Email: aspenhouse@FSBDial.co.uk

☐ I enclose a UK bank cheque made payable to Sphere for £ . . . .
☐ Please charge £ . . . . . . to my Visa, Delta, Maestro.

Expiry Date ☐☐☐☐   Maestro Issue No. ☐☐

NAME (BLOCK LETTERS please) . . . .

ADDRESS . . . .

. . . .

. . . .

Postcode . . . . Telephone . . . .

Signature . . . .

Please allow 28 days for delivery within the UK. Offer subject to price and availability.